TEST DRIVE

D0019822

MARIE HARTE

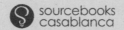
sourcebooks
casablanca

Published by Sourcebooks Casablanca, an imprint of Sourcebooks, Inc.
P.O. Box 4410, Naperville, Illinois 60567-4410
(630) 961-3900
Fax: (630) 961-2168
www.sourcebooks.com

Printed and bound in Canada.
MBP 10 9 8 7 6 5 4 3 2 1

*To D & R. Maybe someday, God willing,
my love of books will rub off on you.*

And to Dad and Anna. Love you guys!

Chapter 1

THE OPENING RIFF OF AN OLD-SCHOOL AC/DC SONG echoed through the garage. Johnny Devlin bit back a curse when he scraped his knuckles on the pump of the piece of crap Cadillac he was working on.

The smell of motor oil, sweat, and grease warmed the interior of Johnny's favorite place in the world. Webster's Garage boasted a double set of bay doors and a roomy interior complete with a cement floor and red-and-brown brick walls, a holdover from the original Tooley's Auto Shop.

"Hey, asshole," he heard Foley snarl. "We talked about this. Hands off my stuff."

Best buds Foley and Sam were squared off, staring holes through each other. When it came to order—and pretty much everything related to cleanliness—the two thugs sat on opposite ends of the spectrum. Foley—Mr. Tall, Dangerous, and Arrogant—was compulsively neat, while Sam might as well have had the word *chaos* tattooed on his forehead. Covered in tattoos, Sam was a walking billboard for badassery.

Lou stepped over to the radio near his work station, and soon loud classic rock drowned out the rest of the argument.

Just another day at the office.

A cool breeze made Johnny sigh. Seattle's unseasonably warm autumn temps continued to be a pleasant surprise this year, and they kept the garage doors open to let the air circulate through the sticky auto repair shop. Even at nine thirty in the morning, he had worked himself into a sweat.

Johnny cranked his wrench and stared at a stubborn pump assembly that refused to cooperate. He loosened it, got to the fan belt, then glared down at the problematic power steering pump.

After glancing over his shoulder to make sure he was in the clear, he softly muttered, "Shitty Cadillac."

The sound of someone shaking a familiar glass jar of coins made him tense. He heard it again, even over the blast of AC/DC. Ducking deeper under the Cadillac's hood, Johnny wondered who his sexy-scary boss was going to call out for cursing now. He was sure he hadn't been that loud.

"Seriously, guys?" Delilah Webster held the newly purposed amber glass growler out to Sam and Foley. The woman had a hard-on for swearwords lately.

Such a sad waste of a perfectly good beer container. Once the half-gallon jar had been home to a killer IPA flavored with hops and a hint of citrus. Now, it was nothing but a no-swearing jar filled with goddamn quarters.

As if the shop going clean would prevent Del from slipping up at her wedding.

He imagined her dolled up in a white gown, tats, piercings, and her hair all done up in some funky twist, looking like a million bucks. She'd be glowing at her behemoth of a fiancé before letting loose with an "I *fucking* do." With a snort, he buried himself back under the hood of the bastard of a car and did his best to calm his frustration. He never had anything pleasant to say before ten a.m. anyway. God knew he needed a jolt of caffeine, and soon, before he took a tire iron to the gray piece of crap he just *knew* was laughing at him.

Sam and Foley bitched about the new no-swear policy even as he heard them drop change into what Johnny had taken to calling the "Rattle of Oppression—ROP." A few clinks of change against glass and everyone seemed to sink into themselves, anxious that their fearsome boss would come storming back in, demanding a quarter for a "hell," "shit," or "damn."

Johnny knew better. Dubbed the smart one of the crew, he kept his nose out of trouble and everyone else on the straight and narrow. Mostly.

He heard Del step in his direction, grazed his already sore knuckle against the frame as he removed the assembly, and let it rip. "*Fudge.*"

"See?" Del yelled to be heard above a man on the radio screeching about shaking all night long. "At least *someone* can keep his friggin' mouth clean." She patted him on the shoulder, and he did his best not to flinch. Woman had hands like rocks. "Thanks, Johnny."

He kept his head down and continued to tinker, listening as her footsteps gradually faded. Then an office door closed, and he found it safe to look up.

"You are *such* a kiss ass." Sam frowned. Then again, Sam did nothing but frown.

Next to him, Foley crossed massive arms over a broad chest and made kissy noises. A glance across the garage showed Lou shaking his head, looking disappointed.

"What?" Johnny tossed up his hands. "Am I the *only* one smart enough to know you catch more bees with honey?" He smirked at the many middle fingers shot his way. "Thought so. Dumbasses."

Of the four of them currently in the shop, Sam was the one whose temper could turn on a dime. He'd gotten better over the years, but everyone knew to avoid the brute when he sank into a rage. Only Foley could talk him down, the pair closer than most brothers. Lou had a sense of humor like Johnny's, but without the quick wit—or so Johnny liked to constantly tell him.

Keeping on Sam's good side would be the smart thing to do.

So of course, Johnny had to prod him. "Hey, McSteroid, you and your boyfriend got plans for tonight?"

Foley sighed. Lou grinned.

Sam's frown darkened. "Why? You got a death wish, stick boy?"

Johnny flexed a greasy arm. "Seriously? Stick boy? Man, I'm ripped. And it's all natural." He raised a brow at Sam and pushed his bicep up from the back, trying to appear bigger.

Even Sam couldn't withstand the Devlin charm. A rare smiled appeared on his face. "Whatever. No, I don't have plans. And Foley—not my boyfriend, dickhead— has his own life."

"So." Lou looked Foley up and down. "No plans for you then?"

"Suck it."

Lou grinned. It took a lot to push the guy's buttons. "Back at you, hombre."

"I thought we'd hang at Ray's if you losers have nothing better to do. Darts rematch?" Johnny offered.

The others agreed.

"You're on." Lou looked eager. The only one of the group who gave Johnny a serious run for his money at the game. Intelligent, a real ladies' man, and he had a steady hand. A useful trait for a guy who painted with great attention to detail.

"Cool." Johnny gave them a thumbs-up. "Winner doesn't pay for drinks. So make sure you idiots bring your wallets."

"Dream on, motherfu—"

"*Foley*," Del snarled from the office door. "What the hell did I say about swearing?" The ROP had returned.

Johnny buried his head back under the hood of the car. He was pretty sure the others did the same. Survival of the fittest worked only if you let the weaker ones, like Foley, take one for the team.

A few hours later, he lounged outside on a picnic table, eating a sandwich Dale, their service writer, had picked up from their favorite shop two doors down. The rare sunshine, not marred by a single cloud, added to the perfection of the moment. A few birds chirped, cars buzzed down Rainier, and only Foley crunching on a huge bag of chips interrupted Johnny's peace.

Foley glanced at Johnny's third sandwich. "Where do you put all that food? You should be really fat."

"You should talk. And just because I don't spend my leisure time jerking off with weights doesn't mean I'm not in shape. I like running."

"From the law," Foley muttered and crunched some more, a sly grin on his face.

"Nah. That's in the past. The trick now is not to get caught." He wiggled his brows, and Foley laughed. "I run after work, if you're interested."

"Nope. I'd rather 'jerk off with weights,'" Foley sneered. "You know, with that smart mouth, it's a wonder no one's rearranged your face lately."

"It's been a few months," Johnny admitted. He had a hard time going without a fight, cursed with an inability to keep his mouth shut around less intelligent, ill-humored people. "I'm not a half-bad boxer. Hence my ability to still breathe on my own."

"I know. That's the only reason Sam and I tolerate you. That and if we're in a fight, we'll throw them the runt and mosey off."

Johnny laughed. Foley and Sam weren't known to *mosey* away from anything. The badass bros, as he and the others called them behind their backs, ended more shit than Johnny ever started. That weird moral code the pair insisted on keeping often had them interfering when a smarter man would steer clear.

"You still dating Alicia?" Foley asked out of the blue.

"Nah. She got a little clingy."

Foley sighed. "They all do."

"I take it you and Sue are quits then."

"Yep."

"Should make tonight at Ray's interesting." Johnny grinned. Sue waitressed at Ray's, and though he'd been curious, he'd been too intimidated by her rough edges to try her on for size. A sweetheart underneath the heavy kohl, many piercings, and fierce tats, Sue nevertheless didn't tolerate horny fools. Fuck with her and meet a bad end. Period.

Granted, Johnny wouldn't typically let a little thing like a woman kicking his ass stop him if he really wanted her. He'd charmed harder cases than Sue. But he didn't want to break her heart, then have to deal with her when he went back to the bar.

"It wasn't like we were serious."

"A little defensive, hoss?"

"Shut up. I am not."

"Uh-huh."

Foley groaned. "It was just supposed to be sex. Then she's texting me all the time. Can I help it if I'm damn good in bed? I mean, Jesus. A little oral foreplay, and the chick's hinting at wedding bells."

"Really?"

"Okay, so I'm exaggerating. But she wanted to go exclusive, so I backed out quick." Foley's ended relationship apparently hadn't dulled his appetite, because he finished the chips and started on a few cookies. Carrying around so much muscle obviously expended energy. "She said she's cool with it, but I haven't been face-to-face with her since Saturday night."

Johnny did the math. "That's nearly a week. Hey, with any luck, she'll be too slammed with orders tonight to notice you. You know how Fridays at Ray's can get." Johnny gave him a fake smile. "Good luck, friend."

Foley frowned at him. "You don't sound all that sincere."

"I'm not. I'll be placing bets on you leaving Ray's with at least one or two darts in your ass. You know Sue holds the bar record, right?"

"Hell."

Johnny snickered. Liam Webster, Del's old man and the other owner of the garage, approached alongside Sam. Before either could sit, Johnny announced the bet. "Okay, gentlemen—and I use that term loosely—ten bucks says Sue tries to attack Foley before we leave Ray's tonight."

Sam considered Foley. "I'll take that bet." To Foley he said, "I told you not to date the chicks at Ray's. You bonehead."

"We're going to Ray's, if you're interested," Johnny told Liam, the rational half of his employers.

Del's father had to be in his late fifties but looked years younger. He had height and muscle on him that Johnny, no matter how hard he worked, would never have. Liam also had an easygoing attitude and knowledge of mechanics that put most auto-thugs to shame. Del was his pride and joy, and J.T., his bruiser of a son, was always good for a laugh when he dropped by.

Liam had grown up poor, worked his tail off to make something of himself, and had raised two fine if aggressive kids. A terrific boss, he didn't judge, knew how difficult it could be to get a second chance, and always gave a guy the benefit of the doubt. Hell, he'd hired Johnny, and Johnny would never claim to be a saint. Not after that pesky felony. Friggin' cops refused to let a guy joyride without making it a huge deal.

Ah, but life at eighteen had seemed so simple back then.

"I'd love to join you boys at Ray's, but I have a date with a lady."

Johnny said kindly, "Blow-up dolls don't count, Liam."

Foley and Sam chuckled.

"Shut it, Son, before I shut it for you." Liam made a fist at Johnny, but his amusement was plain to see. They all knew he'd scored big time a few months ago, and ever since, he and Sophie, his lady friend, had been acting like a pair of lovebirds.

Sam shrugged and sat next to Foley, stealing the rest of his cookies.

"Hey."

Sam put an open hand on Foley's face and shoved while inhaling a cookie whole. He talked around his food, opening his mouth to Johnny, especially because the bastard knew it grossed Johnny out. "Still can't believe you got a classy lady like that to give you the time of day, Liam," he said around expelled cookie crumbs.

They all looked at Liam, who puffed up. "I know. Boggles the mind."

They shared a laugh, though Johnny knew they'd all been beyond pleased to see the boss finally get lucky. For thirty years the guy had mourned his true love, raised two hellions, and somehow run a successful garage. Johnny looked up to Liam. Hell, he wanted to *be* Liam, someday. Especially since Liam had scored a fine woman. A mystery to them all.

"So what are your plans? Going to take her ballroom dancing?" Johnny teased.

The whole garage had given Liam shit for the dancing date a month ago.

Liam frowned. "As a matter of fact, we're going fine dining."

Sam stuffed the last cookie in his mouth and mumbled "Good luck" while chewing.

"Sam, close your mouth." Johnny cringed, pushed past his limit. "Just…gross."

Foley snorted. "Hey, at least he's dressed and not scratching his ass, drinking straight from the milk carton, and busting into your room when you're trying to get lucky."

"With a girl?" Lou asked from behind them. "What happened to Sue?"

Foley growled, "Sue's a girl."

"Yeah, but you already got lucky, right?" Lou shrugged. "Once you're in, you're in. Unless you're doing it wrong." And Lou would know. The guy never hurt for women.

Liam sighed. "You guys are pitiful. Now get back to work."

"Yeah, yeah." Johnny stood with the others and filled Lou in on Foley's dilemma.

"Cool. I'm down for ten. I say she ignores him completely. Kind of the way Lara treats *you*, Johnny."

His face heated, but he pretended not to hear the other guys razzing him and hightailed it back into the garage.

Lara Valley—the lust of his life. He'd been going to Ray's forever, and the first time he'd seen her, four-plus years ago, he'd fallen hard. But his reputation had preceded him: a player and proud of it. He'd teased and flirted his way to learning her name and a few details about the stunning brunette, but little more.

Currently twenty-seven years old and still single, she had her mom, dad, and sister, two nieces she helped care for, and took classes at the community college. For nursing, if he wasn't mistaken. Man, she could help him heal up anytime.

He'd spent many a night at Ray's, discreetly watching her. Long brown hair, deep, chocolate-brown eyes, a slender body curved in all the right places. She worked hard, didn't take shit from anyone, and had a genuinely kind heart for the poor souls sobbing heartache into their beers.

He preferred when she tended bar, because it kept her fine ass away from grabby customers, unlike when she waitressed.

Just the thought of seeing her again made his heart leap, but he knew better. A smart guy didn't shit where he ate. Look at poor Foley and his breakup with Sue. Guaranteed the woman would make him pay in some way tonight. Johnny knew women. He knew what they liked and didn't like. And Sue would be gunning for the guy who'd dumped her, even if she claimed the breakup was no big deal.

He snorted, wondering how Foley could appear so together and be so clueless.

Now take Lara. Johnny wanted her, no question. For a night, a week, a month. Hell, he'd been obsessed with her for a while, and he knew it would take time to get her out of his system. First he had to get her to go out with him.

But Lara? She had a thing about not dating the guys who hung out at Ray's. A smart choice, actually. Johnny loved the joint, but Ray's catered to a rough crowd.

The perfect place for his kind of people, he thought with a grin.

Hours later and a dollar in quarters poorer, having been goaded into a few f-bombs though Sam had *sworn* Del was outside the garage, Johnny sat with his buddies near the darts at Ray's, drinking and preparing for his weekend.

"No plans, guys. For once, I'm a free man for two whole days." He kicked back and sighed with pleasure.

"So no work at your dad's club for you, huh?" Foley asked. "Too bad. I was going to offer to help."

"Me too," Sam added, his voice like the growl

of a wounded bear. "Damn. I was hoping to talk to
Candy again."

"Sorry, sport. Dear old Dad is Candy's new squeeze."

"Bummer." Sam shrugged. "But the guy's got good
taste."

He always had. Johnny had grown up without his
mother, but with a bevy of maternal support. His father
had a thing for strippers, so it made sense Jack Devlin
had finally ponied up and bought his own strip club a
few years back. Johnny had never faulted his father's
fascination with tits and ass. But it would have been
nice to have just *one* set around while growing up, and
getting to know more than the girl's stage name before
she squirreled.

"So have you seen Sue yet?" he asked Foley.

The others waited. Lou seemed especially amused.
Johnny knew that gleam in his friend's eyes.

"Ah, not yet."

Sam snorted. "He's been either hiding in the bathroom or ducking behind Earl."

Earl—a huge-ass bouncer Johnny had no intention of
annoying. Ever. And the same went for the other guy,
Big J, whom everyone said looked like Mr. Clean.

Foley flushed. "First off, I had to piss. Second, I
wasn't ducking behind Earl. I said hi to the guy, and he
asked me what I thought about Dodge trucks."

"Uh-huh. Sure you weren't asking him about Sue's
frame of mind?" Johnny teased. Over Foley's shoulder,
he saw Lara smiling at a woman over the bar. His heart
stuttered, and he did his best to act cool, collected. *She's
not interested. She's a nice girl. Leave her alone.*

Like clockwork, his perverse, inner loudmouth had

him offering to order the next round. "Be right back. And remember, don't hate the player, hate the game—when *I win*. Suckers."

Grinning, he left the guys at the table swearing, and nabbed a free place at the crowded bar. Lara, Sue, and a few others were hopping, grabbing drinks, and pouring like mad. Behind him he heard a scuffle break out, and he turned to see two guys who used to be friends hammering on each other.

"That's rough," a biker covered in tats next to him said. "But then, Jim should have known better than to hit up Sheila with her new guy right there."

"He really needs to lay off the tequila." Lara sounded exasperated. "I told Earl to keep an eye on him."

Johnny turned and locked gazes with her. She had her long brown hair pulled back in a familiar ponytail. The silky mass reached her lower back, and he was dying to see her hair down just once. She wore minimal makeup, a bit of liner and some thicker mascara. Growing up around women who glammed up for a living, he'd learned early on about a woman's trade secrets. But he doubted the red in her cheeks came from blush. More like from the heat in the place. And damn, it would have been nice if everyone around him cared about personal hygiene as much as he did.

He wrinkled his nose when a new guy replaced the one next to him and leaned toward Lara, wafting his less-than-pleasant scent. Lara wiped her hand over her nose and pretended a cough.

He and she shared a grin, and his pulse galloped like a racehorse. The sight of her smile, and that heart-stopping dimple, always made it hard for him to breathe. More than physical beauty, Lara possessed a warm inner core that got him hazy and drunk faster than a hometown IPA.

"So, you the bartender?" Smelly drunk guy wanted to know.

She glanced at her black T-shirt that read "Bartender" in bold white letters. "Um, yeah." Lara gave smelly guy a fake smile. "Another beer?"

"Yep. And keep the change." He slid a grimy twenty her way.

She poured his beer and handed him back a few bills. "You gave me a twenty. You sure about me keeping all that change?" She was so sweet, so honest.

Way too good for you, Devlin. Leave her alone.

The guy belched, then pulled back ten, giving her a few bucks. "Thanks, honey. I'll be back." He stumbled from the barstool, which was quickly occupied by a new customer. Thankfully, this one a woman who smelled like cheap perfume instead of BO.

"What can I get you, Johnny?"

He loved hearing his name on Lara's lips. She had a husky quality to her voice, and he could too easily imagine it whispering her pleasure while he showed her why she should take a chance on him. Foley thought he had oral foreplay down to a science, but Johnny could have written a book on how to please women, a virtual connoisseur by age sixteen.

He cleared his throat and tried to will away his lecherous thoughts. "A pitcher for the crew." He nodded to the guys across the bar then leaned closer to her, to be heard above the crowd. "So what's with Sue? I hear she and Foley split."

Lara rolled her eyes. Of all the staff at Ray's, she and
Rena seemed the most levelheaded. No drama for them.
"She's pining for the guy. I warned her about him, but
did she listen to me?"

"Foley's a good guy." He felt the need to defend
his friend.

"Sure, but he's not a *permanent* guy. None of you
are," she said with a direct gaze that aroused and
annoyed him at the same time.

"Maybe we just need to find the right woman." He
gave her the Devlin smile.

For a second it looked like he might have connected
with her, but then she laughed and shoved his pitcher at
him. "For you guys, there's a right woman, and a left
woman, and a woman on the side…"

The woman next to him laughed. "Seems like she's
got you pegged, sexy."

He gave her the Devlin smile and winked, and she
stared at him, her lips parted. So at least he hadn't lost
his magic. He took the pitcher from Lara, and their fingers brushed. He felt the tingle all the way to his cock
and swallowed a groan. Pasting on a sly grin, he said,
"But, Lara, if I had *you*, I wouldn't need any of those
others." He drew her hand to his mouth and kissed the
back of it. "See you later, gorgeous. And you know, you
ever change your mind about mixing pleasure with pleasure, you have my number."

"You mean business with pleasure," she corrected.

"Do I?" He grinned and left, doing his best not to
look over his shoulder at her, but it was damn hard.
Especially when she laughed. The sound carried like
wind chimes, and he felt a shiver start from his toes and

work its way up his body. That hollow in his gut hit him, because he had a crazy urge to go back to the bar just to stare at her. Take in her joy with life.

I am such an asswipe.

An *erect* asswipe. *Hell*. Time to cool off before he rejoined the crew.

"Jesus, what were you doing up there?" Foley bitched when he returned. "Waiting for the hops to grow?"

Lou snickered. "More like dying for a smile from sexy Lara." He moaned and patted his heart. "What I wouldn't give for some alone time with that gorgeous woman."

Sam had to add, "She can tend my bar anytime."

"Shut up, dickheads." Johnny glared. "Drink your beer, and let's throw a few darts."

He waited until Foley stepped to the line before he added, "Oh, and guess what Lara told me about Sue?" When Foley hit a lousy one *outside* the ring, Johnny smiled wide.

Foley rattled. Mission accomplished. Now to get in Lou's headspace and win the game. He shot a glance at the bar, saw his favorite brunette laugh, and thought about strategy. About his endgame.

Because Johnny always played to win.

Chapter 2

LARA DID HER BEST TO IGNORE HER REACTION TO Johnny Devlin, grateful for the Friday night crowd, and struggled to catch a breath as she poured glass after glass and pitcher after pitcher. Someone selected some techno from the digital jukebox, so for a while she could groove to some decent music, not all that alternative crap Ray had added to appeal to the new stoner crowd they'd picked up.

She poured a few house beers, grabbed two domestics, and wiped down the bar. But despite herself, she found her gaze drawn to Johnny and his hulking gang. All four men commanded attention just by breathing. She couldn't believe her friend Del had never tried to date any of the gorgeous guys who worked for her, but then Del was all about business. She'd never sex up an employee, because *she* had a head on her shoulders. Besides, she knew the guys.

Hell, Lara knew them too, but that didn't stop her from constantly fantasizing about Johnny. Not John or Jonathon. He was a funny, sly, too-handsome-for-his-own-good *Johnny*.

She sighed and served another beer. After four years of working at Ray's, she should have been past her infatuation. Talk about a bad boy with no promise of a tomorrow on the horizon. Still, the man had game.

Johnny could charm a snake out of its skin. He had

height and lean muscle, not puffed up like his muscular buddies, but the build of an athlete, maybe a runner. Broad shoulders, ropy biceps, rock-solid forearms, and long, graceful fingers never failed to tempt her into wondering *what if*.

She shivered, too easily remembering the feel of one of those fingers over her hand. Not to mention his warm lips. *God*. She had been dreaming about his wicked mouth for far too long.

"Yo, Lara. Help Josie on tables, would you?" Ray, her boss, asked. The ex-prizefighter looked like a human punching bag who'd doled out his fair share of whoop ass, but he had a marshmallow for a heart.

"Sure thing." She bustled to help Josie, giving herself an excuse to look at Johnny's table now and again.

He probably didn't style his hair, because it always looked like he'd just run his fingers through it. Sandy-brown, short on the sides and longer on the top, that silky hair framed a face almost too pretty to be masculine. He had longer lashes than she did, for cripes' sake. Full lips, a square jaw, and aquiline nose hinted at a man of control and strong passion. For all his flirting, his mossy green eyes seemed sharp, able to see through subterfuge.

"Hey, sweetie, gimme a pitcher of Everly."

She smiled as she worked, pleased to once more focus on her job. Two more rounds for the bikers in the corner, a food order for one of the regulars, and then she filled Sue's tray with tequila shots and two nasty cocktails that would do better as gas for her car. Lara tried to stretch out her time, but she couldn't help herself. She promised to get smelly guy a pitcher of the cheap crap Ray kept on tap for the fiscally impaired, then deliberately left her area to see if the guys needed anything. *From the bar*, she told herself. *Just the bar*.

Now Foley and Sam were a pair. They towered over her and had muscle to spare. Foley was all charm and grins, Sam all dark intensity that oddly, made her feel safe. She was fascinated by their tatted arms, wondering when she'd find the courage to go under the gun. They treated her with respect while always giving her that sly once-over that told her they liked what they saw. Flattering and pleasing, because she could flirt back, but she knew they'd never take what she didn't want to give.

Lou Cortez, on the other hand, made her a little uncomfortable. He seemed so domineering, so quiet and assessing all the time. He had a swarthy complexion and to-die-for brown eyes. Talk about handsome in a bottle. She wondered how hard someone would have to shake him to see him explode, because his powerful presence showed a distinct command of himself at all times.

Even now, while the others goaded Johnny, Lou sat back with a smirk on his face, as if laughing at a private joke.

"Look, Johnny, pretty Lara's come to watch you choke." Sam patted his knee and said to her, "Want a front-row seat?"

"I would but…" She nodded to the heavy tray on her arm. "This isn't even my section, but since I like you guys, I thought I'd see if you needed anything."

"Besides a brain for frick and frack?" Johnny said with a nod toward Foley and Sam. He stood at the line, holding a dart, sizing up the board.

Lou chuckled.

So did Lara. "Sorry, guys, that was funny."

"Don't encourage him." Foley tipped back a beer. "Honey, would you mind bringing us another round? It's sure to be on Devlin."

"Whatever, loser." Johnny launched the dart and hit the bull's-eye. He let out a whoop. "That's right, suckers. I am now too far ahead to catch. Though if you try hard, you guys might, and I mean *might*, reach Lou. You're really sucking tonight, Lou."

Lou sighed. "You know it's bad when Sam's close to tying me."

"Hey." Sam glared.

Lara grinned. "He's just jealous of your manliness, Sam."

"No shit." Sam flexed biceps anyone with ovaries could appreciate. *Down, girl.*

Yet her gaze sought Johnny again, as if drawn to him. Deliberately looking away, she asked Foley, "What are you having?" She accepted the pitcher from him and waited.

"Whatever's the least expensive on tap," Foley muttered.

"I'd suggest a step up from that one if you value your liver."

"Fine." Foley sighed. "He's never going to shut up about this."

"You are right about that." Johnny smirked for all he was worth. "I think you're lucky for me, Lara. Hurry back."

She did her best not to ogle him like one of his pathetic groupies. A glance at a few regulars nearby told her the sharks had sensed attractive, eligible bachelors and were circling. Despite the danger signs on all four men, even Lara knew a prime male specimen could be forgiven a few run-ins with the law when he looked like any one of these guys.

Superficial, stupid, yet true.

She turned and left, forcing herself not to run. *Breathe in. Breathe out.* So pathetic that she had to work to regulate her breathing whenever Johnny was around. *Relax. He's not looking at you.*

But a glance over her shoulder showed she'd been wrong. Johnny was staring at her ass, a lazy look of pleasure on his face. When he glanced up and saw her watching him, he put a hand over his heart and blew her a kiss, then made the phone sign with his fingers and mouthed "Call me."

She made her rounds and returned to the guys to drop off their drinks, just in time to catch Foley giving Johnny another ration of crap for not having the balls to ask her out. If only Foley knew… She pretended not to hear that last bit before turning to leave.

"Hey, Lara," Johnny said.

The others with him quieted. Inwardly, she tensed, but she gave no outward appearance of anything amiss. She turned back around. "Yeah?"

"Add a basket of fries to Foley's order, would you? A big one. We're hungry."

Both relieved yet oddly disappointed an offer for a date would not be coming her way tonight, she winked at Foley then left them to their taunting and one-upmanship.

Despite her fascination with Johnny, she knew without a doubt he would bring her nothing but trouble—the one thing she didn't need. If she ever wanted to get out of this part of town, she needed to focus on

her future, not on the potential for terrific sex with
a philandering hottie who might or might not have a
criminal record. The Websters did favor a particular
type at the garage.

Lara didn't discriminate. She knew better than most
that second chances could be fleeting, and she had no
problem making friends with those who'd gone through
rough patches in their own lives. Hell, her sister could
be the poster child for divorce; her parents had never
had more than two nickels to rub together; and most of
her cousins knew the inside of the county jail better than
they knew their own homes. How she'd never ended up
there, she still didn't know.

You're no better than any of these guys, she told herself. After a pause, she had to add, *But I could be*.

The arrogance of the thought shamed her. Then she
watched a few of Ray's regulars getting into yet another
fistfight while their barfly girlfriends egged them on.
Josie and Sue added to the commotion by placing bets,
and the entire bar laughed and jeered, heightening the
rowdy atmosphere.

Another Friday night in a long string of Friday nights
at Ray's. *If I don't get a move on with my classes, I'll
never get out of here. Hell, that'll be me betting on Judd,
or maybe I'll be the one dating Judd, just another girlfriend with a revolving door to anyone who can promise
a better life*.

Like Kristin. She sighed and started cleaning up
around the bar. Her sister had married four times, was
no doubt looking for a *fifth* Mr. Right, and could barely
handle her own kids. Lara loved her nieces, but Jesus,
they could be a handful. Four and eight going on thirty,

the pair of them. If Kristin would stop looking for validation from anything with a penis and get a damn job, maybe Lara wouldn't have to—

Her cell phone interrupted her thought before she lost herself down the rabbit hole of dysfunctional family. "Yeah?" she barked into it as she continued to wipe down the bar.

"Honey, it's Mom."

"Hi, Mom. I'm kind of busy, so—"

"I just wanted to let you know that Kristin got a new letter from Ron's attorney. Looks like he might be willing to settle."

Finally. The dickhead had money coming out his ass but refused to part with an extra five grand out of principle. What principle? That his cheating should somehow entitle him to a wife who shouldn't care what he did? Even though the creep had tried hitting on his wife's *own sister*? Ron gave her nothing but a bad vibe. "Good. The sooner he's out of her life, the better."

"He hasn't been bothering you, has he?"

Not lately. "No, why?"

"He said something to Kristin. Never mind. I'm sure it's nothing."

Terrific. As if working at the bar, dealing with family, and her nursing classes weren't draining enough, now she had to worry about Ron bugging her…*again*.

"Okay. Thanks. I've gotta get back to work. We're slammed."

"Right. Sorry for calling. Just wanted to make sure you're okay."

Lara heard noise in the background, the chatter of many people. "Are you at work?"

"I'm on break. Picked up some extra shifts this weekend." Her mother sounded excited.

Lara closed her eyes, tired for all of them. Then she forced herself to sound happy. "Awesome news. I'll see you tomorrow for lunch." And not a moment before.

"Bye, honey."

She tucked her phone back in her pocket and finished her shift. She told herself it was okay to appreciate the eye-candy playing darts but kept her distance. Lord knew she had a weakness when it came to Johnny. No sense showing him.

After closing, she walked out to her car with a few of the girls, then drove home to the ratty little apartment she could call her own. It might not be much, but it was all hers. The first thing in her life she could say that about. As usual, she couldn't help feeling relief to be independent, finally.

Living with a family who struggled and worked hard to make ends meet, she'd never taken anything she had for granted. But without a higher education, she hadn't been able to do much more than work just to pay the bills. Fortunately, she'd had a plan, even at the end of high school. One that had changed a few times, but still.

She just had to keep plugging away to make it happen.

Reaching her apartment complex in no time, she parked and darted into her building. After locking herself in and feeling safe despite the iffy nature of her neighbors, she took a quick shower to rid herself of the stale beer and hint of smoke she'd picked up from the "nonsmoking" restroom in Ray's. Though the city had locked down on tobacco use, Ray didn't always enforce the rules. To him, if he didn't see it, it didn't exist.

Her shower hit the spot. Now clean, she sank into her couch and put on some mind-numbing television. A sitcom she could laugh at would do the trick. Nothing that required too much thinking. She wrapped a blanket over herself and reclined on the couch. Like clockwork, her eyelids refused to stay open much past three a.m., and she let herself go.

Lara woke to a bright, chirpy Saturday morning. She took another shower just to wake up, then dressed in workout gear and brought along her books and a bag of casual clothes to change into later. She had plenty scheduled for the day. After lunch with the family, she had a study date with a few classmates, then dinner with Rena. And God, could she use the downtime.

Lately she felt frazzled. A weekend or a few nights off work would have helped, but she had too much coursework to do and work to manage so she could eventually pay off her tuition and books. Her student loans helped only so much. She knew it would be worth it in the long run, and she'd fully committed to nursing. But damn, a full course load and nights at Ray's were draining her.

She drove her clunker of a car to Seward Park, needing a short run to relax. The two-point-four-mile loop would be just the thing today to de-stress her. She could feel the tension building at thoughts of lunch with the family. Mention of Ron last night had put her on edge. She hated that prick.

After a light stretch and grateful for the overcast weather, hoping it might keep many of the overeager running enthusiasts at bay, she set out on a leisurely jog.

As if the devil on her shoulder last night hadn't been bad enough…

She greeted Johnny as they passed each other going in opposite directions. At least she'd seen him at the beginning of her run, so she didn't sound winded yet.

His wide grin before he'd passed warned her she'd be seeing him again soon, so she wasn't surprised when he suddenly joined her, jogging in step. "Hey, there. My favorite bartender. Fancy running into you here." He chuckled, not out of breath in the slightest.

"I happen to live around here. You?"

"There's some stupid race near my place, so I came here for a run." He snorted. "Bunch of yuppie types running for fun."

She glanced at him, trying not to appear is if she were ogling his muscular legs and broad chest. And those arms. She loved the muscle car that took up his entire left forearm, trailed by colorful work in some kind of tribal design that disappeared beneath his shirtsleeve. Yet another qualification for working in Del's garage. You had to have ink.

"It's okay, Lara. You can say it." Johnny pulled ahead of her.

She sped up to match his pace. "Say what?" Far be it from her to look slow. For all that she took after her mother in most things, she'd inherited her competitive streak from her father.

He turned around and ran backward, watching her with a shit-eating grin on his face. "How amazing I look in these shorts. Hugs me in all the right ways, eh?"

She laughed and shouldn't have, because it made it harder to breathe. "Whatever."

"Well, I have *no* problem saying you look amazing

in your shorts. And top. Yum." He turned around again, this time running next to her.

She pretended to ignore him and her horrifying reaction. Her nipples tightened, and she prayed he wouldn't notice, or at least he'd attribute the effect to the weather or the run. *Not, God forbid, from his presence.*

"So, um, if you scorn those who run for fun, why do *you* run?"

"Why? With my smart mouth, isn't it obvious I need the skills to run fast and far away? You've seen how big and ungainly the guys I work with are. Sam looks like he eats mountains for breakfast. And Foley and Lou are as bad. Not like me, all streamlined and buff."

"And pretty and amazing. Don't forget that," she teased, now panting because the bastard had started to speed up.

"I knew you'd noticed." He smirked.

"Ass."

"Ha. I knew you'd noticed my fine ass too." Before she could protest, he added, "So how about a date? You and me and a nice bottle of wine—somewhere that's not Ray's."

Her belly fluttered. "What's wrong with Ray's?"

"Nothing, if you don't mind a few fights and beer spatter. Or sticking to the floor. Plus it's noisy. You won't be able to appreciate, let alone hear, all my compliments if I have to shout them."

"Such a charmer." Oh man, he really was. A few drops of rain had become a downpour, and they plastered his shirt to his chest and his hair to his face, so he slicked it back, bringing more attention to his charming grin. Then he slowed his pace, and she wanted to kiss him.

"Come on. You know you want me."

She raised a brow.

"I mean, you want to *date* me."

"Uh-huh. Keep thinking that." *Fake it 'til you make it, dummy. Come on, Lara. No time for this. For him.* "I don't date guys from Ray's, no matter how appealing they think they are."

"Well, shit."

"See? That mouth might look pretty, but it's dirty, isn't it?"

He muttered something.

"What?"

"Nothing."

"'Cause I'm thinking you should put another quarter in the swear jar Del's keeping at work."

"Hell. You know about that?"

She grinned. "We have a bet going at the bar that she swears at some point during her wedding."

"You going?"

"Of course." Lara, Sue, and Rena had been invited from Ray's. And Ray, of course. Lara couldn't wait to see her friend walk down the aisle with handsome Mike McCauley.

That's what Lara wanted—Mr. Right. Not Mr. "Maybe I'll try a bazillion times until I get it right," which her sister continued to pick through. At thoughts of the last Mr. Horribly Wrong, she frowned.

"What's that look? You have a problem with Del marrying McCauley?"

"What? No. Just thinking about something else."

They ran in silence for a while, until she saw the end in sight. Then she put on a burst of speed and left him behind. When he caught up to her, he had a smug grin on his face.

"What are you smiling at? I won." She bent over to catch her breath.

"I'm thinking I'm the real winner here. I got to watch you from behind." He whistled. "You have the finest form."

"Shut up." Her face heated.

"So about this jealous thing you have going on with Del and her man…"

"Where do you get your ideas?" She straightened and poked him in the chest, now as wet as he was. What a typical Seattle day. "I'm *thrilled* Del found a good guy. Mike is perfect for her. As a matter of fact, I was thinking of all the losers my sister has dated and married and wondered if she'll ever find a good guy."

"Oh, sure."

Oddly, he looked…relieved?

"Were you invited to the wedding?" A pause as she twisted the knife. "Or is there a restraining order banning you from a church? You know, considering it's a holy place and all."

He laughed and tugged her wet ponytail. "Funny *and* sexy. The walls might shake, but I think I have heaven snowed. They'll let me in before they realize I don't belong there."

"Ha. You said it."

He leaned closer, and she froze. "But I'm thinking you don't belong there either. For someone so damn pretty and sweet, there's a part of you that wants what I can give you." His breath whispered over her lips, and man, oh man, her entire body felt like one giant exposed nerve. "A run for your money."

Then he slid a finger over her chin and up her cheek. "So damn pretty." He blew out a breath and moved back, turned on his heel, and took off in the rain.

Drenched, aroused, and annoyed she'd lost a grip on herself dealing with Johnny, she stalked to her car, not surprised when it failed to start.

The words she said would have filled Del's swear jar to the brim.

A knock on the window startled her, and she turned to see Johnny.

Rolling down the window, because of course she had nothing as fancy as automatic anything in her car, she barked, "What?"

"Need a jump?" he asked in the politest voice.

"Yeah, I do."

"You need a jump," he reiterated, trying to hold back a grin.

"Fuck. Just do it, okay?"

He walked away snickering, but he did help her with the car, then refused to accept any mention of payment.

"All in the line of duty, ma'am." He bowed, completely soaked.

She forced herself not to notice how impressive he looked in his clingy jogging shorts. "Still trying to get into heaven, eh?"

He winked. "You know it. See you next week at Ray's."

Not if I see you first. She drove off. *Oh, who am I kidding? That man is catnip, and I'm a scraggly mouser.* Time to talk to Kristin and be put off men again...forever.

Johnny sat in his car until his windows steamed. Talk about the perfect way to spend a Saturday morning. A wet Lara was a sight he'd take to his grave. Normally lean and mean in tight jeans and a black T-shirt proclaiming her job for the evening at Ray's, she made his heart race. But seeing those long, toned legs, that bitable ass and those generous breasts, giving her svelte build a perfect set of curves, he'd have a hard time sleeping without reliving his run.

Thank God for rain. Her nipples had been tight little knots, likely due to the weather, but a guy could dream they'd been hard for him. And dream he would. She'd already been his go-to fantasy when he wanted a quick one-off before sleeping. Now he'd take his time, remembering how she looked all wet.

"Hell." He glanced down at his tented running shorts. The reason he'd left her after caressing her cheek. A helluva move, and one that had almost backfired. He'd sworn he'd seen a reciprocal lust in her dark brown eyes. Problem was, he'd felt it as well, and it showed. Nothing like seducing a woman with a boner in a public park.

He glared down at himself. "Idiot." As he drove home, he wondered about the rush of relief that had filled him when he'd realized she didn't have a thing for McCauley. He didn't like the thought of Lara lusting after anyone but him, which made little sense.

Once again he'd tried asking her out, and once again she'd shot him down. He never took it personally though. He figured one of these times she had to say yes.

Pulling into the driveway of the house he rented, he parked, locked the car, and hurried past a flurry of raindrops into the house. Not a bad place, considering it was a lower-scale home in a decent neighborhood. Only took him twenty minutes to get to work, and most of the neighbors were like him, just trying to make a living.

As he stripped down on his way to the shower and stood under the hot water to warm up, he couldn't help wondering about Lara. She worked at Ray's and went to college. She seemed a step up from the hooligans at the bar, but not so high and mighty that she came from money. From what he knew, she'd grown up in Seattle. Her mom waitressed at a diner, and her dad managed a local hardware store in Skyway. Other than the recent news of a sister who hadn't married well, he didn't know a hell of a lot about her family.

She didn't seem to date much, if at all. He liked that she was selective, especially around Ray's. Not all the guys who drank at the bar were like him and his friends.

Amused he'd put himself and his buddies above the other knuckle-draggers at the bar, he hurried through his shower, ignored his erection, and decided to save playtime for later that night. If he didn't have a date by then, he'd take care of himself with memories of Lara in running shorts.

An entire day to do nothing but goof off. He smiled.

Hours later, he'd tuned up his ride, done some laundry that really needed washing, taken care of the squeaky back door and leaky faucet in the bathroom, and paid a few bills. Damn, but he'd worked up an appetite. Unfortunately, a glance in the fridge told him it was past time he did some shopping.

Johnny hit the closest market, determined to race through so he could get back and watch one of his favorite shows on TV. A boring evening by his usual standards, but damn if he could psych himself up for another night swilling beer and scoping out chicks.

Being around Lara was like that. It confused the shit out of him. Instead of wanting to sink into some willing and forgettable female, he wanted to go out on the town with the pretty brunette who never had time for him. A perverse sense that he was like his dad made him wary. Jack Devlin went through women like tissues, using them up and discarding them before they'd no doubt discard him. The few he'd actually liked had ditched his ass without a backward glance.

Johnny had plenty of women who wanted a ride on the Devlin motorway. But none of them had sparkling brown eyes that hid feminine secrets. Or long legs that could wrap around a man and still leave him wanting more. Or breasts that—

Enough, dipshit. He forced himself to think of Foley and Lou, of Sam mouthing off, anything to rid himself of his hard-on. After a few moments, it went away, and he hurried through the aisles, picking up only the essentials. Beer, cheese puffs, a loaf of bread, some deli meat. And of course, Twizzlers. Had he been able to cook, he might have added a few items from the produce section. Instead he grabbed a handful of microwave dinners and frozen pizzas to last him the week and headed for the cashier.

No one in line before him, because most people *with a life* did anything but grocery shop on the best night of the week. He sighed and put all his stuff on the conveyor belt. Cashier guy grabbed an item. Dragged it across the scanner. Took a moment to grab another item. An eternity later, he reached for another. Johnny thought maybe he'd landed in a *Twilight Zone* episode where time went backward.

"Hey, baby. How you been?"

He glanced up to see a sexy woman by the front of the store, dressed to kill and smiling at him from behind a bagged cart. *Shit.* "Cara, fancy meeting you here."

She laughed. "Grocery shopping, huh?" She looked over his cart. "No veggies?"

"Nah." He got those only when he begged his friends to cook for him. Lou, surprisingly, could do wonders in the kitchen. The badass bros, sadly, had about as much culinary skill as he did. Del had been a pleasant surprise with a cookbook. But now, with McCauley sucking up all her time...

"Haven't seen you in a while." Cara teased the spaghetti strap of her barely there red dress. The thing exposed her ample cleavage, teased at her creamy thighs, and molded to her rounded ass. The heels she wore gave her an extra three inches, and he wondered why anyone would try to look this good in SuperFoods on a Saturday night.

He glanced down at his T-shirt and jeans, spotting a few holes.

When he heard no beeping from the food scanner, he looked up to see the cashier staring at Cara's chest. Not that Johnny could blame him, but could the guy go any slower?

Johnny had fooled around with Cara months ago. One fun night—no, two—he recalled, because she'd shown up at his dad's bar the next night all dressed up and ready to blow. He was only human, and against his own self-imposed policy, he'd enjoyed her company and made sure she enjoyed his. Then he'd gently, kindly, called it quits.

She'd been nagging him for another go-round ever since. Apparently his *I'm not a steady guy* and *I'm not good enough for you* lines weren't sending her the message.

"Been busy at work," he said lamely.

Register guy slowed down even more to chew his gum, masticating like a fucking cow. Jesus. *It's not a show, kid. Hurry the hell up!* He cleared his throat, glared from the guy to his groceries, and wonder of wonders, the food started flying over the scanner.

Cara left her cart to walk to him, a sexy sway in her hips. "You busy tonight?" She still looked like a dream. Caramel-colored skin, thick, curly hair as black as sin, sexy red lips gleaming with lipstick, while her dark eyes begged him to take her home. A fiery lover who'd do anything he wanted, Cara Suarez should have been a no-brainer. His inner playboy screamed yes.

"Sorry, honey. I have plans tonight helping out a few friends." Left hand, meet right. He gave a real sigh. *I'm so pathetic.* "Car stuff. It never ends."

She pouted, but even the memory of those ripe lips around his cock did little to stir him. Instead he wondered if Lara had plans, and what she'd think about him and Cara going at it.

Would she even care?

"Too bad. Maybe another time?" Cara sounded hopeful.

He shrugged and smiled, keeping it light, casual. "Maybe. Have a great weekend, Cara."

She put an extra wiggle in her step as she walked away.

"Damn. You turned down *that*?" The cashier shook his head.

Johnny could almost hear the guy calling him a dumb
bastard. And he agreed. "How much?"

After he paid and left, he drove home, wondering
what the hell was wrong with him. Because on the drive,
he thought about Lara. And now he had an erection that
wouldn't quit—one Cara had been all too happy to take
care of.

Johnny wanted to blame his reticence on not wanting
Cara to cling. But it was more than that. Seeing Del, a
hard-as-nails woman he'd never thought would use the
l-word, find love and happiness with Mike McCauley,
had twisted something inside him. Then Liam had
secured himself a fine woman. It was like hell had
finally frozen over.

If the Websters could do it, and God knew they were
a fun but fucked-up bunch, why couldn't he? *Bah.
Happily ever after is for pussies*. Johnny could almost
hear his father laughing away his concerns while Jack
waited for his current squeeze of the month to come
down off her pole.

*So maybe I don't have to go the distance. Hell, mar-
riage is crazy. But why can't I at least date someone
halfway decent? Lara likes me. I think. Why not try to
get her to like me a little more?*

The plan had merit, and since he couldn't get himself
to even consider another woman lately, he might as well
try again. Three strikes and he'd be out, he told himself.
The same thing he'd told himself the time before, and
the time before that, and the time before… He sighed,
tallying up the many rejections she'd already sent his
way. A whopping twelve.

A sucker for punishment, Johnny figured he'd make

it thirteen just as soon as he saw her again. On the bright side, no matter what happened at the bar, he'd get a shot at seeing her at Del's wedding in a few more months. And if Lara looked that great in wet running gear, imagine what she'd do for a fancy dress?

The thought of peeling it off her got his motor revved again. Swearing—because he could without repercussions in his own home—he hurried into the bathroom and made short work of the tent in his jeans, an image of Lara in running shorts at the forefront of his thoughts.

Calmer, less stressed, and ready to enjoy the evening, he returned to the living room and sank into the couch. He popped open a beer and a bag of cheese puffs, two essential items in the food pyramid, he was sure, and settled down for a night on the town with *Mystery Science Theater*. Finally, some guys he could relate to.

Chapter 3

SOBS, RECRIMINATIONS, AND AN HOUR SPENT EITHER bitching about the lack of men in Kristin's life or her new love interests. That had been all Lara could handle from her sister before tuning the woman out. Her nieces, by comparison, hadn't been half-bad. They'd complained about tuna melts for lunch, begged for ice cream instead of yogurt as a healthy substitute, and argued with their mother about, well, everything.

Another Saturday spent with the family.

Lara sighed. Lately everything in her life seemed stale.

"I still don't understand why you never finished up your degree in accounting," Kristin said.

Lara swallowed the retort she'd made a dozen times since quitting the program *two years ago*. "We talked about this."

"It would have saved you money, though," her father said. "I mean, what else are you going to do with all those classes?" Mark Valley could spot a dime from across the street and always knew when he'd found a deal. He considered Lara's "wasted" accounting classes—all two of them—a crying shame.

"Dad, I can still use a lot of those other classes. My writing and math credits all transferred to nursing. In fact, they're higher courses than I need to get my degree."

"I still say you should have pursued being a CPA.

God knows we could use help getting some money back from the government at tax time."

"Yeah, and you could have helped me deal with the mess Ron's leaving me," Kristin whined.

Lara forced herself not to tell her family to take a flying leap. She said two plus two, they came up with five. Every time. She should know better by now than to try explaining herself. Still... "It would have cost way too much to continue my education for a four-year degree. Plus, I found out I didn't like it. Imagine going almost four years"—and thousands of dollars into debt—"only to realize I hated accounting."

"When you put it like that..." Her father shrugged.

Across the table, four-year-old Amelia pushed her glass of milk over with a sneer at her older sister.

Kay screeched, "It's coming closer! Hurry! It's at the edge of the table, Nana. Hurry! Ew. It's *ooooooozing*." *Oozing* turned into a four-syllable word, and more lunch drama, predictably, came to pass.

Like mother like daughter.

Lara watched the mayhem as Joy Valley, the family matriarch, scurried to clean up the table while her husband laughed at his grandkids' antics.

Kristin was not amused. "Haven't I told you two to be more careful at the table?"

Normally Lara would side with her nieces, but Amelia was a chronic spiller. Last Christmas she'd mistaken a gift of bath milk for the actual drinking kind. She continued to insist bath milk and cow milk had to be the same thing, and took any opportunity to bathe her sister in the white stuff to prove a point—that, like her mother, she was never in the wrong.

"I thought she had a sippy lid on it." Lara looked at the table, then peered under it and saw the lid on Amelia's seat. She bit her lip to keep from laughing when Amelia nudged it under her thigh.

"I don't know, Aunt Lara. It's gone." Amelia batted her big brown eyes. Like a miniature Kristin without all the baggage of bad relationships. A handful of cuteness and little-sister pranks that made Lara proud.

"You're a menace," Kay exclaimed. "My dress is now a disaster—like mom's hair. And you're precocious."

Lara's father raised a brow.

"That means intelligent, Kay." Lara tried not to laugh. "I think you meant obnoxious."

"Yeah." Kay stuck out her tongue at her sister. "Obnoxious."

"Well, at least she's got a vocabulary that's halfway decent." Kristin rested her chin in her hand. "Because Claude seriously messed up my last hairdo."

Lara silently agreed. "You should have seen Rena. You know she does it right."

"And at a discount," Joy added.

Just once, can we go without mentioning a great sale, deal, or way to save a buck? Lara knew her parents meant well, but they seemed fixated on money. Or rather, the family's lack thereof.

Having been raised to scrape by on every penny, Lara knew well the value of a dollar. But being constantly reminded of their lower middle-class status stung. Was it any wonder she had no time in her life for anything but school and work? Anything to get the hell out of this financial hole she seemed unable escape.

"Kristin, tell Lara about Ron," Joy prodded.

The girls didn't react to the mention of their step-father's name. He'd never been more than a token male in the house. Of their biological fathers, Kristin's first husband, Sean, had tried to be a good dad, but he hadn't measured up to Kristin's standards. Not enough money or flash to keep her interested.

Lara had liked him. He'd been cute and steady, and someone her sister could really lean on. Instead, Kristin moved on to sexy Josh—Amelia's dad—who'd then left *her* for someone better. A short marriage to Steve had come and gone, though she forgot why Kristin had ended that one. Something about Steve's performance in bed, maybe? A few more men had passed through her life without much fanfare.

Then Ron entered the picture. Ron had money, so Kristin had married him without seeming to consider more than financial security. Two years with him had been two too many, though. Lara had told her what a mistake she'd made after meeting him that first time. But Kristin knew best and had said she'd found her true "soul mate." *More like* fourth *soul mate, counting all the others*.

Ron was a complete dick.

Kristin had shiny blond hair, brown eyes, and a figure that rivaled that of an adult film star. She'd never hurt for male companionship and had a bubbly personality… as well as a tendency to jump from passion to passion without thinking things through. Yet for all her beauty and Ron's seeming interest, her jerk of an ex had hit on Lara during his and Kristin's first date.

Telling her sister had earned Ron a swift talking-to, then instant forgiveness on Kristin's part. Kristin wanted

an escape from the Valley family's social status as badly
as Lara did. To Kristin's credit, she wanted something
better for her children, not just herself. But Ron had
been a bad decision from the get-go.

"Yeah, Kristin. Tell me what Ron wants now."
Something other than in my pants, I can only hope.

"He said he'd settle with me if we cut out all the lawyers." Kristin nodded. "Believe it or not, I agree with
him. It's costing us a bundle." At Lara's look, Kristin
snapped, "Fine, it's costing *him* a bundle. Happy?"

"Not really."

"Point is, he wants the financial discussions to go
through you, since you're Miss I'm Capable while I'm
just a dumb blond."

Lara could well believe he'd said that, but then
Kristin had a tendency to overdramatize everything.
Lara wouldn't exactly call her dumb. That was cruel.
Flighty? Unable to see the big picture? Idiotic at times?
Yep to all of the above. "He really called you dumb?"

"Not in so many words, but that's what he meant."
Kristin sighed. "It would help a lot if you could deal
with him for me. Besides, he likes you. Maybe you can
get me more than my lawyer could."

Lara glanced at the girls. "Hey, guys. Go play upstairs
in the playroom, would you?"

"Sure, Aunt Lara." Amelia smiled.

"Okay." Kay agreed without much arm-twisting.
"Can we play Xbox?"

"Only a little," Kristin said.

They left, and with the zone now kid-free, Lara spoke
her mind. "Before, when I told you to get rid of your
lawyer, you told me I didn't know what I was talking

about. That Richard Parsons III was an amazing attorney and had your back." *Among other things.* "So I take it you and Slick Dick are on the skids?"

"Lara," her mother admonished.

"Mom, I told her not to get involved with her lawyer, but she's so desperate to latch on to a new man, she didn't listen. He's not working pro bono anymore, is he?" It took all her willpower not to change "pro bono" to "pro bon*er*," but heck, not in front of her parents.

Kristin's glum expression said it all.

"Kristin, seriously, you need to stay single for a while. Get strong on your own—*without* a man to help you."

Her father surprised her by agreeing. "Good advice. Kristin, you're smart and pretty, but your taste in men is terrible. Be on your own and figure out what works for you. Then find a man who fits your taste."

"And this time maybe put faithfulness and sincerity before wealth," Lara muttered.

"Screw you. I don't see a ring on your finger or kids in your crappy little apartment." Kristin flounced from the table.

"She's got me there. I'm single and childless. Oh, and happy. Did I mention that?"

"Lara." Her father tried to look stern but failed.

Then her mother laid into her for hurting her sister's feelings.

Kristin had been down but not out. She returned moments later, her cheeks a mess of running mascara, her eyes red and puffy, all crafted perfectly to portray the grieving almost-single mother of two. "For that crack, you owe me."

"What?"

"I need you to meet with Ron for me. He said he'd talk to *you* about the settlement, because he thinks you're good with numbers, and you won't 'freak out on him.' Apparently I'm too emotional about everything." Ron was an ass, but he had a point. "Besides, you know if he doesn't get what he wants, he'll drag this on forever. If that happens, the girls and I won't see a dime." A sincere look of fear entered Kristin's eyes.

Lara sighed. *Don't do it. Don't you do it.* But thoughts of the girls and Kristin living with her parents in this cramped house *again* made the decision for her. "Fine. I'll talk to the SOB, but I can't promise anything. Your best bet would be to get a new attorney—a woman this time—and make Ron do what the state of Washington says he should."

"Good girl, Lara." Her mother smiled.

"Thanks, sis. I owe you one." Kristin collapsed into her seat, her grief gone as if it had never been there.

Owe me one*? Try forty. Oh hell. I did it again.*

———

"You're a moron." Rena popped an olive in her mouth and washed it down with a sip of red wine as they sat in Rena's duplex on Sunday night, enjoying the rest of Lara's ruined weekend. "A repeat-offending idiot."

"Thanks so much for your observations." Lara could have done without the tough love tonight. Thoughts of Ron made her queasy enough.

"*And* you have split ends. Come on." Rena dragged her to the kitchen and sat her down in a chair. Then she found a spray bottle, comb, and a pair of scissors, and went to town snipping at Lara's hair.

"Call me an idiot if you want, but we can't all be workaholics with happy families."

Rena snorted. Del's cousin was such a sweetheart and a romantic under the exterior of a career woman with drive. Beneath her springy light brown curls, cocoa-brown skin, and laughing amber eyes lay a persuasive charmer who could talk her clients into anything. The woman also had a way of digging at the truth and letting nothing stand in her way when delivering said truth to friends and family.

"Honey, you and I have been friends for how long?"

Lara mentally counted. "Four—almost five—years. Since I started at Ray's." Where they both continued to work while striving to make their dreams a reality.

"And in those four—almost five—years, I've watched you put out fires and try to stop your sister from making stupid mistakes. Hasn't worked for you yet, but you keep on tryin'." Rena cut a few more strands, then moved to Lara's front. "Nah, I think we'll let your bangs continue to grow out."

"You sure?"

"You have the face for it. Trust me." Rena returned to the back of Lara's chair and cut some more. "Just evening this out." After a bit of silence, she added, "And since when is my family happy—or even normal? Del can't stop charging people for saying four-letter words. Mom's still as wacky as Kristin when it comes to finding a decent man. J.T. is a manwhore, and I'm hopeless."

Lara chuckled. "J.T. *is* a manwhore." A sexy, fine-ass hunk of daredevil appeal, but Lara had seen him in action. She knew better than to involve herself with Rena's cousin, Del's brother. "And you're not hopeless;

you're just dateless. Like me. But it's by choice. Not because no one wants you."

Like Lara, Rena had goals that prevented her from dating at present. Trying to earn enough to buy her own salon took time from a social life Rena wanted but couldn't yet afford. Lara eventually wanted a husband and kids too, but *after* she'd earned her nursing degree and had a solid financial framework. Not now, when she had more expenses than income. *Stupid student loans.*

"I could say the same about you." Rena finished and swept up the loose hair on the floor.

"I can do that," Lara offered. "You gave me a free haircut, after all."

"No. If I don't get every hair, Del will kill me. She hates a mess, though you couldn't tell from her room."

"She's barely here anyway. Always at Mike's."

Rena batted her eyelashes and gave a dreamy grin. "I know. He's sooo sexy. Mr. Romance."

"Mr. Romance? I didn't get the impression he was all that romantic. Good in bed, I get. But—"

"And then there's Colin," Rena interrupted. "I love his son. I'm Colin's aunt now. Not officially, but I count."

"Aunt Rena. I like it." Lara grinned.

"And Aunt Lara. You love your nieces."

"I do. It's their mother who drives me to drink." Lara sighed. "That sounds so mean. I love Kristin. I do. But she's…"

"Needy? Naive? Too pretty for her own good?" Rena dug into the refrigerator. Then she headed to the living room with a tray of goodies and a bottle of wine.

"Yes, yes, and yes." Lara followed her and grabbed a wineglass from the table. She held it out when Rena offered to pour. "I feel so sophisticated." She glanced at the tray. "Cheese, crackers, and…tapenade? What the hell is that?"

"Chopped-up olives." Rena held up her glass. "Cheers. Here's to me hosting book club next week. You're my test subject. What do you think of the wine and cheese?"

"Fancy." Lara liked it, but nothing beat a cold brew. "But I'd rather have a beer and nachos."

Rena's smile slipped. "Me too."

"Is this book club for your romance-reader pals and that author?"

"Yeah. Abby's so cool. I want to impress her."

"Why? I thought she and that gang were your friends."

"They are."

"So?"

"Lara, don't act clueless. I've seen you clean up your place when people are coming over."

Lara snorted. "What people? My apartment is barely bigger than a shoebox. I think you and Del are the most I've ever had over at one time. Not counting my nieces."

"Say what you want, but you clean up because you want to make a good impression. Same as me."

Rena seemed so earnest, so young. Despite being five years Lara's senior, Rena had an innocence about her, a vulnerability that made Lara feel protective. And old. "You always make a good impression. You're like Pollyanna on crack. A little too chipper sometimes, but that positivity is nice to be around."

"You'd think I'd have better karma." Rena sighed. "You should have seen my clients today."

"Tell me about it."

So Rena did. "…and then Cara walked in, talking about your favorite mechanic. Now, if I'd had Johnny in my chair, my day would have been awesome. He might have motor oil under his fingernails, but he's a good tipper. Plus, I just like to look at him."

Lara sipped a little more from her wineglass and did her best to appear as if she couldn't care less about one of Rena's clients talking about Johnny. "He is pretty," she said, and left it at that. After a moment of silence, Lara glanced into Rena's laughing eyes. "What?"

"You're dying to know exactly what Cara said. Admit it."

"I don't even know who Cara is."

"Sure you do. I call her Man-eater. She of the large breasts and loose thighs. Shee-oot, girl. I am *all* for a woman getting her happy on, but Cara lays more than the guys at the brickyard. I mean, come on. Johnny can do so much better than that."

It felt as if a brick had settled over her heart. Lara remembered hearing all about Man-eater's naughty adventures. The woman liked to share when getting her hair and nails done. And she loved Rena—who lived vicariously through her. "So Cara did Johnny? Big deal. They're both consenting adults. Who cares if they hook up?"

The thought of Man-eater getting a piece of Johnny hurt. Dumb, but she felt it all the same. She could still see him in her mind's eye, wet and seriously ripped in his running gear. That shirt had molded to him like loving hands. The rain had run down his face and body like she wanted to rain over him with hungry fingers and lips.

"No, see, that's where it gets interesting." Rena shifted on the couch to fully face Lara. She crossed her legs and leaned closer, meaning the gossip was getting good. "Cara saw Johnny at SuperFoods on Saturday night."

"So?"

"So Johnny 'I'm So Hot I Burn Myself' Devlin is grocery shopping on a Saturday night instead of going out with a woman? What is *that* about?"

"But Cara—"

"Threw herself at him—my words, not hers. According to her, she only hinted at going out, but I know her, and she's as obvious as they come. She no doubt propositioned him, and he gave her some BS excuse about helping the guys out with their cars." Rena huffed. "Please. I know for a fact J.T. was hanging with Lou last night."

"So maybe Johnny was helping Foley and Sam." Lara knew the guys were tight. In some ways she envied them their friendships. "Or he meant some other guys he's friends with."

"One, he was not helping Foley and Sam. Those two never work on the weekends. Lazy as they are fine. Yeah. And two, he has no other friends. Webster's is his everything. He's an amazing mechanic with no life. You two really are a lot alike."

"Thanks," Lara grumbled, trying to feel bad about being likened to Johnny Devlin. Except she loved the thought of having something in common with him. "So Cara didn't get a piece of Johnny Saturday night. This is front-page news because…?"

Rena smacked her in the head.

"Ow."

"Because when a man says no to a night with Cara, he's either in a committed relationship or thinking about getting into one. Now's your chance."

Lara drew a blank. "To what?"

"To grab on to him. We both know you want to."

"So maybe I do." Lara shrugged. No secret that she had a crush. "I also want to eat a dozen donuts every day. You'll notice I don't do that. Why? Because it's bad for me—and I'd get huge." Hell. Lara only had to look at a donut to gain five pounds and a cavity.

"While I grant you Johnny might not have a great track record with women"—Rena continued over Lara's snort—"he's a pretty thoughtful guy. He's great with Colin and respects women. You know Uncle Liam wouldn't have hired him if he didn't."

"I thought his dad owned a strip club."

"*Jack* does. *Johnny* doesn't. Oh, and he's always been nice to me. There's another plus in his column."

"Everyone's nice to you," Lara said, exasperated. "You are not the litmus test for *nice*. Now the fact he's been working for Del for seven years and hasn't murdered her yet, that speaks for his levels of tolerance and patience. But he could be a complete dick in private."

She loved Del Webster, but the woman could be a huge pain. Lara had overheard J.T. and the guys' occasional complaints over many a beer at Ray's.

"Uh-huh. So tell me again who fixed your car earlier this morning? You know, when you two were in private, not around the rest of us?"

She flushed. "I knew I should have kept that to myself."

"You really should have. Because every time you talk

about the guy, it's like you're trying harder and harder to tell yourself not to give him a shot. I say go for it."

Lara frowned. "I'm trying to focus on school."

"Take a break."

"*You* take a break."

"If I was as interested in Johnny as you are, I would have tried him on for size years ago. But I haven't found a man more exciting than my future salon yet. When I do, I'll go for it."

"Says the woman who's never met Mr. Really, *Really* Wrong." Lara chuckled and drank the rest of her wine. "Maybe you should come to my next lunch with the family. Talk to Kristin a little. I know! You can hang out with Ron and see what you're missing."

"Thanks, but no. And I've already had my 'milk bath' for the month." Rena frowned. "For the record, make sure Amelia knows I did not get any lighter." She held up her arm. "I'm always going to be café au lait. Not malted milk."

Lara laughed. "Too bad. Malted milk is Amelia's favorite flavor."

Rena rolled her eyes.

"But I still say men are nothing but trouble. My sister has been through the ringer. Donna and Josie are going through some stuff at work, and let's not even talk about Sue's mess with Foley."

"Done and dumped, huh?" Rena shook her head. "I told that girl not to do more than fool with him. Sure, sex him up. He's gotta be good in the sack. But much as I love Foley, he's not about settling down. And that's all Sue talks about lately. Girl is baby crazy."

"I know, right?" Lara munched on some cheese and

crackers. "You know, these aren't that bad. But you could maybe have some nachos or chips on the side, so you don't look like the major suck-up we know you are."

Rena gave her the finger, which made Lara laugh, because Rena looked so cute while trying to appear tough.

"What about you?" Rena asked. "Feeling the need to have kids yet?"

"Nope. I'm only twenty-seven. Maybe having nieces I can see every day has taken away the need. That or I'm just too tired trying to take care of myself, let alone tiny mouths to feed."

"I hear you."

Lara felt guilty, knowing how hard Rena worked, yet she'd given Lara a free cut. "I can pay you for the haircut, you know."

"Shut up." Rena scowled. "I'm just saying I know when money's tight. I'm doing okay now. In fact, if I wasn't saving every penny for my salon, I'd be flush." Rena's eyes lit with excitement. "I'm so close. I figure a little more to go in the bank, so I have money in case of an emergency. I'll nab a few more clients, and then I might finally be ready to break out."

"Here's to your big plans." Lara clinked her empty wineglass against Rena's. "I've been telling my classmates about you."

"I know. Michelle came to see me a few days ago. Your word-of-mouth is helping, girlfriend. So no paying for the haircut. We're even."

"If you say so."

"I do." They ate in silence for a moment, only the munching of crackers to be heard before Rena said, "So about coming to book club—"

"*No*." Lara had heard from Del that one had to be firm with the bookaholic staring at her with those puppy dog eyes. "I don't have time to read more than anatomy books. And I'm not a fan of romance."

"That's just sad."

"Oh, can it. The next time you see a happily ever after work out where the name McCauley isn't attached, let me know." She snorted. "That family is sappy, sweet, and unreal."

"Jealous much?"

"Are you kidding? Of course I am." Lara laughed with Rena, but at the mention of romance, her thoughts strayed to Johnny again.

He'd said no to Cara. She wondered if he'd been seeing some other woman instead. Perhaps he'd made up a story for Cara to spare her feelings. Lara could see Johnny doing that. He might get around when it came to the dating scene, but he'd never been anything but circumspect about his lady friends—or so rumor had it.

Then again, if she were to believe Rena, Johnny might be angling for a real relationship. Something more involved than just sex.

And I'm reaching here, I know it. She held out her glass for more wine, coming to like the tart drink, and decided to keep her eyes and ears open about Johnny. It couldn't hurt to do a bit of reconnaissance on the man, especially if she was *possibly* thinking about *maybe* considering a future in which she dated him.

Dating didn't mean she had to sleep with him. But all that might be moot. After having asked her and been rejected so many times, he might not ask her out again.

Didn't mean she couldn't ask him, though.

"Why are you so quiet, I wonder?" Rena asked with a smug grin. "Thinking about a certain someone with the last name of Devlin?"

Lara frowned. "If I am, it's your fault. Now quit talking him up, and let's discuss what's really on my mind lately."

"What?"

"Ron Howell and Kristin's plea that I handle him, since she dumped her lawyer—or Slick Dick dumped her. Either way, she and my parents want me to deal with him."

Rena stared, wide-eyed. "Are you going to?"

"What choice do I have?"

"Well, make sure you do it in public." Rena gave her a devilish grin. "And I know just the place."

Chapter 4

TUESDAY NIGHT, WITH HIS OLD MAN BACK IN TOWN, Johnny suddenly had plans for the following weekend. So much for another break from the grind. Admittedly he'd been spoiled by a few days with nothing to do but fantasize about Lara. Talk about some fevered dreams.

"So, who is she?" Jack Devlin asked.

"Who?"

"The woman who put that look on your face." Jack chuckled. "Got your dick twisted in a knot, eh?"

"Whatever." Johnny hoped he didn't look as pathetic as he felt and refused to outwardly look in Lara's direction. He'd come to Ray's tonight specifically to watch her, and what kind of loser hung around a bar just hoping to see someone who'd rejected him twelve times? Not a Devlin, that's for sure.

His father had been bagging women since he'd turned fourteen, to hear him tell it. Johnny knew his dad meant well, but the old man didn't understand women as well as he thought he did.

Fucking them and loving them had never gone hand in hand for Jack Devlin. Not since his wife had died. But Johnny had to wonder if his parents would have stayed together if his mom had lived.

So sad to be so jaded, but he'd understood the truth about his dad at a young age. Pretty women came and went out of Jack Devlin's life, and out of Johnny's. One had even lasted half a year before she'd split. His dad didn't normally do more than a few months at most, fidelity not in his makeup.

Despite his father's philandering, Jack Devlin was a genuinely good guy. Hell on relationships, yet a stand-up friend and father in many other ways.

"You see, boy, women are like flowers."

Johnny groaned. "Please. Not the flowers speech."

"Some are colorful, some are full, straight, or curvy. Others are fragrant or thorny. But they're all pretty in their own way."

"Please, Dad. Not now."

Lara nodded at some dickhead down at the bar, and the jerkoff smiled at her. What made it worse was that the guy didn't seem to be a regular, because he had on clothes that looked clean and pressed. A pricey watch too, unless it was a fake, but it seemed to match the designer jeans and expensive button-down. He couldn't be more than a few years older than Lara and didn't seem to be that bad looking either. Not good.

"Sometimes you have to take your time holding that flower, not too tight or too loose. Too tight and you'll get pricked. Too loose and she'll slip through your fingers. But when you get a good sniff of—"

"I'll get us more beers."

His father chuckled as he darted away. Before he could approach Lara, she stepped into the back, and Rena took her place.

When Rena saw him, she gave him a wide smile. "Hey there, sweetcheeks. What'll you have?"

He loved Del's cousin. She was always a bright spot with a ready smile, dimples, and a gorgeous face and body to match. If she wasn't related to Del, he might have taken a turn with her. But he knew better than to screw with the boss's family. Literally or otherwise.

He grinned at her. "Aren't you too pretty for words?"

"I am. I really am." Rena preened. "Need a refill?" She glanced at his empty bottle.

He nodded. "Two."

She grabbed them and angled her head in the direction of the preppy jerk who'd been smiling at Lara. "See that guy?"

"What guy?"

She frowned and turned directly to look for the loser. "He was just there."

"I saw him earlier."

She turned back to him, her smile one he could only describe as smug. "I'll bet you did."

"So the guy…?"

"Lara's almost ex-brother-in-law. A cheating, sniveling, rich worm who won't give her sister a dime unless Lara deals with him. The scum sucker has had the hots for Lara for years."

"Is that right?"

"Probably wouldn't be a bad idea to keep an eye on him, just in case he tries to give her a hard time." Rena leaned closer over the counter. "You could even mess him up a little. Just for fun. He's clearly out of his element in this place."

"But I'm not?"

She laughed. "Johnny, you live and breathe trouble. You're practically a Ray's staple."

"That's so sweet." He winked at her. "No wonder I like you best."

"Yeah, that's what they all say."

"But it's true." Well, pretty much. Most of the guys around the place had a real hard-on for Rena, but for Lara too, especially because it was well known she didn't date at all. A good thing, in his opinion. The woman could do so much better than the idiots around Ray's. Except for him, of course. "So, Rena, if I handle your boy, will this be considered a favor for her or you?"

"For me. You know Lara. She shies clear of the pretty ones." Rena gave him a pointed once-over.

"Fine. For you then. But you owe me."

"Okay. But only because it's you."

He chucked her chin, and she flirted with him some more. He paid for the beer, slipped her a generous tip, then returned to his dad.

"Now that is one good-looking girl. Think she'd like to dance for me?"

"No. Just no. Rena's a sweetheart. So hands off."

"Fine." His father raised his hands in surrender before chugging down his beer. "So you're good to help out this weekend? Bobby's off, and I need someone to fill in. And if you could rearrange some of the schedules for me, that'd be great too."

"I thought you wanted help behind the bar." Bobby was a bouncer at his dad's club.

"I do, but I need security more. You're good with your fists, even if you do try to talk everyone to death first."

Johnny sighed. "You really need to replace your general manager, Dad, because I can't keep popping in to help you when you're down a man. Get someone to replace George already. And trying to charm my way out of trouble has kept my record clean for years. I'd think you'd be happy about that."

"True enough." Jack shrugged. "Look, if you'd rather bartend, can you nab me some security help? What about your friends from work?"

Knowing Foley and Sam, Johnny had no problem pledging their services. The guys treated the dancers well and would easily walk away if told no.

Johnny half-listened to the club gossip, a rampant epidemic his father spread like the plague. He couldn't help noticing that the guy at the bar hadn't yet returned. And neither had Lara.

"Be right back. Gotta hit the bathroom."

"I'll be here." His dad ordered a plate of fries from a passing waitress.

Johnny casually strolled past the guy's still-empty seat at the bar and moved down the long stretch of hallway toward the restrooms. Not seeing Lara near, he darted into a side door marked "Employees Only." Inside, he nodded at two of the cooks and Sue.

"Seen Lara?" he asked.

Sue nodded. "Went outside for a break a few minutes ago. Not in the back, but the side lot. It's quieter there." She frowned. "Tell her she's due back inside. I need to make a phone call."

"Sure." He didn't like that she'd been away from her job so long. Lara took her work seriously. She was a heck of a waitress, and had a genuine smile for the customers. She also didn't take anyone's shit—a fact that had nearly gotten her in trouble more than once. With Big J still doing his bouncer duties by the front, Lara had no protection from any assholes wanting to bother her outside.

Johnny hurried his step and exited the side door, only to see Lara in the grip of the preppy jerk.

Anger clouded his vision, and he headed right for an altercation that was sure to end with one guy in a bloody heap—and Johnny had no intention of being that guy.

———

"I *said* take your hands off me." Lara's words dripped with icy reserve, but they finally broke through to Ron.

"Sorry." He let go of her shoulders but didn't move back. "But I don't think you understand what I'm saying."

"I understand just fine," she fumed. "I will *not* sleep with you to get my sister a bigger settlement. In fact, you and she are going to use your lawyers again." *What the hell was I thinking? That Ron might have developed a conscience since Kristin left? Right.*

"That's not a smart move. Not if you want to help Kristin and the kids."

Lara could understand what her sister had first seen in the guy. Ron's light hair and blue eyes framed a handsome face. He had the build of a tennis pro, as well as the wallet to hire one. He also gave to charities and encouraged his rich golf buddies to contribute. Looks, wealth, a giving heart—all outward appearances of being an all-around good guy.

And then, in private, the seemingly devoted husband took off his mask and opened his mouth.

Narcissistic with a capital *N*, Ron talked about himself and what *he* wanted constantly. As long as Kristin had been on board the Ron train, all had been well in the world. But when she'd stopped trying to please him, he'd acted like an immature, spoiled brat.

People rarely said no to him. As evidenced by his myriad flings throughout his marriage to Kristin, as they'd all come to find out. That Lara had not only rejected him but continued to do so must have made her special in his book, because he wouldn't leave her alone.

He'd called and texted her until she'd blocked his number. That had been a few months into his marriage with her sister. Since he hadn't tried to contact her since then, she'd thought they might be able to deal with each other in a civil way. She was wrong.

"Let me put it plainly," she enunciated. "I told Kristin I'd talk to you about her legal situation because she, like you, wants to cut out your lawyers."

"That's smart of her." He nodded, the patronizing SOB. Then he caressed her arm before she pulled it back.

"Look, Ron, you and I are *not* a couple and never will be. I wouldn't sleep with you when you were married to Kristin, and I sure as hell won't once you're divorced. Period." No misunderstanding that. At all.

He smiled, but the expression didn't reach his eyes. "That's only because you don't know what you're missing." Then he dragged her into his arms and *kissed* her.

Wet, disgusting, and dear Lord, something she didn't want to think about had grown in his pants as he ground against her. Even worse, he held her head still, making it difficult to sever the unwelcome connection.

She wrenched her mouth away and tried to push him back. "Get. Off." Before she could knee him in his unimpressive balls, he was ripped away from her.

Charming, laid-back Johnny Devlin stepped up to Ron, and he wasn't smiling. "You *motherfucking asshole*." He punched Ron in the face and busted his nose. Blood spurted.

She blinked, not sure what she was seeing. No stranger to violence—she did work at Ray's after all—she'd nevertheless never been in the center of it.

Ron swore and hit Johnny back. She knew he considered himself a decent boxer, since he'd often bragged about his private coaches at his overpriced gym. But he only managed to make contact with Johnny once out of the three or four swings he took.

Johnny's head snapped back when the punch landed on his cheek, but he didn't duck away. He punched back and made contact. Then he bobbed and weaved, looking like a pro, and she couldn't help but stare in shock and awe. Such aggression pouring out of a man she'd never seen do more than seduce a smile out of the women at the bar.

Johnny proceeded to punch Ron in the stomach then the chest. He finished with a kick right between Ron's legs. "Suck on that, you dick."

Ron fell to the ground, moaning, and curled into a ball, cupping his crotch while blood dripped down his face. He whimpered. "Going to…pay…for…this."

When Johnny moved to go after him again, she jumped between them. "Wait. Please."

He put his arms around her and turned them, holding her so tenderly while keeping himself between her and Ron. "Shit. You okay, Lara?"

She wanted to laugh and proclaim him her hero, but her eyes filled instead. She started shaking. While she hadn't really been afraid of Ron, not exactly, it had all happened so fast. Getting manhandled by him, then mauled with that sloppy kiss, to watching Johnny fight like a tornado of rage. So much brutality.

"Shh. It's okay. I have you." Johnny rocked her in his arms.

She should have been afraid of someone who could do that much damage to another person, but within his arms she felt safe. Cared for. And she snuggled closer and hugged him in thanks.

She heard Ron getting to his feet, and Johnny put her aside. "Why don't you go grab a bouncer for me? We'll let him take care of this piece of shit."

"Okay. Just don't hurt him anymore."

Johnny looked surprised. "Why not? You didn't want him kissing you, did you?"

"God no. But I don't want him trying to get you in trouble or anything." She glared at Ron. "If you try anything, I'll have ten witnesses from the bar letting a judge know you attacked me, so don't even think about it."

Johnny's lips curled. "What she said, dipshit." He stroked Lara's cheek. "Don't worry. We'll make nice while you go get Big J to throw his ass out of here."

She raced away and returned with the bouncer and her boss, Rena trailing behind. "They're here," she said, out of breath.

Johnny stood next to Ron, who now leaned up against the dirty brick wall. Ron had a few more bruises, and Johnny's knuckles looked battered, his cheek still rosy from where Ron had made contact. But Ron didn't make a peep as he stood in Johnny's shadow.

Johnny said something in a low voice.

Ron jerked away and spat, "Fuck you, asshole." To Lara, he said, "This isn't over, bitch."

She *so* didn't like the b-word.

Johnny would have launched himself at Ron again, except Ray intercepted him. Then Rena latched on to his arm.

"Hold off, son. We've got this." Ray nodded at the six-foot-five bouncer. "Toss his ass out. And, mister, you're not welcome here again."

"As if I'd come back to this shit hole voluntarily." Ron sneered at Ray and the others, but the malicious glare he turned on her made her want to run away and hide—very unlike her normal kick-ass self. "Tell Kristin she won't see a fucking dime, thanks to you."

"I'll be telling it to her lawyer," she said as Big J shoved him around the building toward the parking lot. She heard Ron swearing all the way.

"About par for the course on a Tuesday night." Ray sighed. "Lara, honey, you okay?"

"I'm good, thanks. I'll be right back in."

"No, she won't," Johnny said and pried his arm from Rena while Ray ducked back inside.

"Oh, sorry, Johnny." Rena shook her head. "No, Lara. Go home. We've got tonight covered."

"I'm fine. Really." Having some ape of a brother-in-law assault her should have pissed her off. She wanted to hold on to anger, to not feel like a victim. God, she knew better than to go out the side exit with the clientele that normally frequented the place. But most guys knew not to mess with Ray's staff. She just hadn't considered Ron would actually touch her.

He never had before.

Johnny's voice softened. "You're not fine."

Oh hell. She was shaking again.

"I can take her home," Rena offered.

"I've got her." Johnny put his arm around her shoulders. "That okay, Lara? I can see you home."

"I'm fine, I said." She tried to sound mad, but her voice came out shaky. "Fuck."

Johnny chuckled. "That's a quarter for the swear jar."

She smiled, and a tear escaped. "Damn it."

Rena came over and hugged her. "You take her home. I'll finish up. And, Lara, don't worry about tomorrow night either. Sue will cover."

"But I—"

"Thanks, Rena." Johnny steered Lara back inside, following Rena before she peeled away. "Hey, let my dad know I had to bail, okay?"

"No problem."

Ray reappeared and handed Johnny Lara's purse. "Sorry about this, Lara." Her boss clumsily patted her on the shoulder.

She felt stupid, so many people apologizing and walking on eggshells around her. "I'm okay, Ray. Maybe just a little tired. I'll be fine to work tomorrow though."

"Nah. Sue's got it. Rena's orders." He grinned. "You know she's really the boss around here."

"I thought I was," she tried to joke.

"You are when I say you are," Rena yelled from the kitchen.

Johnny tugged Lara with him back out the side exit, and she could have kissed him. She didn't want to show everyone what a wuss she was being. She subtly wiped her eyes and sniffed. They were halfway through the parking lot when he stopped and turned to face her.

"I am so sorry." He wiped her cheeks. "No one should mess with you like that."

"I'm really okay," she said, trying to convince herself. "It's just been a long day, and I'm tired. I wasn't expecting him to attack me is all. I'm fine."

Johnny just stared at her.

"What? Do I have snot coming out my nose?" She wiped her nose on the shoulder of her T-shirt. "Better?"

His slow grin made her heart race. Bruised and no doubt buzzing off the altercation, Johnny Devlin looked better than any man had a right to. "You're so pretty, even when you're crying. It's weird."

She managed a laugh. "Thanks. I think."

He took her by the hand and led her to his car, a loud, dark green muscle car. She had no idea what it was, an old Chevy, maybe. Something that said, "I'm a man."

"I drove here."

"One of the guys will drop it off later. Don't worry about it."

"I have to. I need it for class tomorrow."

He unlocked and opened the passenger door for her, helping her get in.

"I said I'm fine. Jeez, Johnny. You're the one who got hit. I just got lip-locked by a rich sissy in ugly clothing."

He laughed. "He hit like a girl, for sure. No offense."

She flipped him the finger, and he laughed some more. When he got in the car, the space seemed intimate, and way too small, despite his roomy bucket seats.

He drove her home, apparently not needing directions.

"How do you know where I live?" she asked suspiciously.

"I asked. Duh."

"Oh." A pause. "When?"

"A while ago. I believe my exact words were, 'Who is that bartender with the long brown hair, heavenly rack, and tight ass? Because that's the future Mrs. Devlin.'"

Her cheeks heated. "Shut up."

"You are so red right now." He snickered. "Actually, Rena told me where you lived a while ago, since she thought we'd make a nice couple."

Friggin' Rena considered herself a matchmaker. She still took credit for Del and Mike McCauley hooking up, despite the fact that Del had met Mike through his son.

They drove in silence for a while before Johnny spoke again. "You sure you're okay?"

"I really am. I think I was just freaked out because it all happened so fast."

In the passing shadows, she saw his expression darken. "Yeah, it can go down like that. I see that guy again, I'll turn him into a human pretzel." He glanced at her. "You let me know if he bothers you."

"I will." She most certainly would *not*. She refused to be responsible for Johnny landing in jail. Ron was just the type to goad Johnny into roughing him up where he'd have witnesses. Then he'd involve his many important connections to put her friend away.

Johnny Devlin—her friend.

They pulled into the parking lot of her building, and she directed him to her empty spot. Then he walked her upstairs to her unit. The halls were blissfully empty at ten o'clock on a Tuesday night. She could hear televisions, a few shouts, and laughter through the thin walls. She nodded at a familiar face, a cop who had a sister who lived in the place.

"It's not much, but it's home," she said as they stopped at her apartment. She fished the keys out of her purse and unlocked her door, then turned to him. He'd come to her rescue tonight in a big way. She owed him. That, and she wasn't ready for him to leave yet.

"Lara?"

"Come on in and let me take a look at that bruise."

"That's right. You're the nursing student." He watched her, looking for what, she didn't know.

"Please. It's the least I can do." She didn't want to beg him to stay, but she wanted to thank him, if at least in a small way.

"Okay." He stepped inside.

She closed and locked the door behind him, not sure what to do with him now that she had him. Fortunately, she'd gone grocery shopping yesterday.

"Can I get you something to eat or drink?"

He stood in her entryway, looking huge in her tiny apartment. Tucking his hands in his jeans pockets, he shrugged. "I'm good." His glance passed over her living room and kitchen and settled on the kitchen counter. On her plate of cookies.

She smiled. "How about a chocolate chip cookie? I baked some to take to class tomorrow." She had class work at the college instead of the hospital, so she'd baked some goodies to take her classmates' minds off their grueling schedule.

"I don't want to mess you up for school." Yet he took an awfully long time to look away from the plate.

"Come on. They're amazing. I'll even throw in a glass of milk…" she tempted. "Mmm. You know you want to."

He gave a mock sigh. "Peer pressure. Guess I'll have to say yes."

"Great. Go sit, and I'll be right back." She set the cookies and milk on the table and rushed down the hallway.

Now to change, force herself to relax, and figure out why it felt like everything between them had turned some weird but important corner.

Chapter 5

JOHNNY CALLED HIMSELF FIVE KINDS OF FOOL AS HE sat at the table in Lara's homey apartment. Too restless to remain seated, he snooped around, needing to know everything about her. The place was in a rough neighborhood but not so run-down he'd call it a slum or anything. She had a couch and table that had seen better days. A handcrafted quilt thrown over the back of the sofa made it cozy, and the stacked magazines and TV remote had been neatly placed on the coffee table.

A TV stand and potted plants in a windowsill sat across from the couch. In a small area near the tiny, open kitchen, a table and three chairs looked in decent enough condition. The kitchen had clean counters, a ceramic jug full of fresh-cut flowers, and an old-fashioned white refrigerator. The black-and-white tiles and antiquated white cupboards, which could use a coat of paint, gave the place a retro feel. Old and worn but functional. Like everything else he'd seen, the furniture might be hand-me-down but was kept clean and neat.

She'd disappeared down a hallway. He'd be surprised if she had more than one bedroom. They packed 'em tight in the Maryville Apartments. He knew, because he'd had a friend who used to live here. More like a one-night stand a few years ago who'd since moved back to Texas, but still…

He heard Lara moving around, as well as a few other

close-by tenants on either side of her place. It made him appreciate his rental all the more, because he never heard his neighbors.

His cheek throbbed and reminded him to watch out for Lara's asshole of a brother-in-law. Good for her sister for divorcing the schmuck. He'd met rich guys like Ron before. Dickheads who thought they could buy their way out of trouble. Ron might have financed his way through life, but he hadn't been able to buy Lara.

Satisfaction at her refusal almost made his aches go away. He sat back at the table and waited. His stomach rumbled, the sight of that plate of cookies so near causing him to salivate.

Lara returned in a pair of sweats and a worn, long-sleeve T-shirt. She had her hair still up in a ponytail, but she looked fresh, scrubbed clean. She came to the table, carrying a small box.

"Sorry. Had to get the stink of Ray's off me."

"You mean Ron."

She grinned. "Him too."

He couldn't stop thinking about what he'd felt when he'd seen her getting mauled. Pure, unadulterated rage. It had taken some serious control not to bash Ron's brains all over the concrete slab. He'd been distracted enough by the thought of her trauma to let the ass get a shot in. Sloppy of him, and he resolved to do better next time. With Ron, he had a feeling there'd be one.

"What's in the box?"

She set it down by him then slid a cookie his way.

An open invitation he couldn't refuse.

He took a bite and closed his eyes. "These are *sooo*

good," he moaned and blinked his eyes open. "I took a hit to the face. That means I get more than one, right?"

Her finger grazing his cheek stilled him, and he felt the contact all the way to his toes. He swallowed the cookie he'd been chewing and stared at her.

"I'm so sorry you got hurt because of me, Johnny."

Her hand felt like pure heaven, and he cupped it to him, loving her touch. "Not because of you, honey. Because some dickhead needed to be taught a lesson."

"If you say so." She tugged, and he let go. "At least let me patch you up."

Fascinated, because he hadn't had a woman take care of him in...*forever*...he sat still while she scooted her chair closer.

"Drink your milk." She nudged his glass to him.

"Yes, Mom."

"Smart-ass."

He chuckled and continued to watch her. She looked all professional as she withdrew some antiseptic, cotton balls, and a bandage from her plastic box. "So you're studying to become a nurse, huh?" He could totally envision her in one of those naughty nurse costumes from Halloween—which was coming up in another month. He wondered if he could talk her into wearing one.

"Yep. I've been piecing together classes for a few years now, but I finally decided to stop messing around and fully commit. I'm now full-time, and seriously, it's a bitch. We're starting clinicals again, where we actually follow a nurse around and do what they do—on real people." She smiled. "So you're not my first bandage. Fun stuff, let me tell you. Fall term just started, and I got a little lazy, having the summer off." She dabbed something onto a cotton ball and raised it to his cheek. "This might sting a little."

Hell. His cock was hurting worse, so he didn't much mind. Anytime around Lara, he ached with a fierce need to kiss her. Hug her. Slam her against a wall and fuck her until he passed out.

He'd never been so captivated by a woman before. He'd seen prettier women. But something about Lara Valley struck him in the heart, the brain, and yeah, right between his legs.

He hoped she kept her gaze on his face, because he couldn't do much about his erection with her so close.

She dabbed his cheek, and it stung. When she leaned in to get a closer look, he swallowed a moan. Dear Jesus, she was killing him. He smelled the flowery soap she'd used to wash her face. Fresh and clean, the way he always thought of her.

"Sorry."

"What?" He sounded hoarse and had to clear his throat.

"For hurting you. I saw you flinch."

From wanting you too much. "Don't tell the guys, okay? I have a rep."

She chuckled and continued to be gentle with him. "I promise. I owe you."

He stopped her from swabbing his cheek, his hand over hers. "No, you don't. You don't owe me a thing, Lara. I'm serious." He didn't want her gratitude. It made him uncomfortable, felt wrong, somehow. Taking care of her was no big thing. It just was.

Her slow smile warmed him all over again. "Okay. I don't owe you. Then can you do me another favor and be a willing patient while I practice my nursing skills on you?"

"Well, if you put it like that. And you did insist I eat your cookies."

"I did." She tried to look solemn, but her smile ruined her attempt.

He sat, staring at her, while she took care of him. Man, she was something else. So damn beautiful it hurt to look at her. She'd make eye contact before quickly glancing away, her eyes dark, a fathomless brown, rich and addicting and impossible to deny.

His heart raced anytime she was near. And damn if he didn't want to protect her from the world—himself included—while lusting after her all the same.

I am so totally gone on this chick.

He tried to act cool and collected but feared he looked like a love-struck ass. Not that love had anything to do with the way he was feeling—or so he'd been telling himself for years—but it probably described his expression better than anything he could come up with.

She put a bandage across his cheek. "There. You were bleeding a little, and you'll bruise, but you should be all better soon."

"Thanks, Nurse Feel-Good." He wiggled his brows, and she blushed.

Hell. If she looked down, she'd catch a real eyeful.

Fortunately, she put her tiny medical kit aside and moved back to her spot across the table from him. Then she took a cookie and eased into the bite. "Oh, these *are* good."

"I'm telling you. Whenever Ray puts your cookies on the menu, they sell like crazy. You sure you want to be a nurse? 'Cause I'm thinking you bake like an angel."

"An angel?" She raised a brow, the one she normally used with him to indicate she didn't believe a word of his crap. Another reason she'd captivated him. She saw through his bullshit. "That's the best you can do?"

He pleaded exhaustion. "I'm sorry. I took a blow to the head. It's all I've got." He put on his needy face. "Careful. I might swoon."

"Faker." She snickered. "I know you don't want my gratitude. So I'm thanking you with cookies." Her amusement faded, and she looked down, then up at him, then away again.

"Lara? What's wrong?"

She met his gaze and said in a rush, "How come you keep asking me out?"

Change of subject, but o-kay. "Because I wanted a date."

"Wanted?"

"Want, wanted. Whatever." He frowned. "Hold on. Don't all of a sudden agree to go out with me because you think you owe me something. We settled that. Cookies for bruises. It's a done deal." He stood and took a few steps back from the table, not wanting to loom over her. She'd been assaulted tonight, even if she insisted she was fine. "Say what you want, but you've had a rough night. I should probably go."

She just watched him with an expression he couldn't read.

But he couldn't leave just yet. "Lara, Ron's an asshole. No one should ever touch you when you don't want it." He scowled, annoyed and unable to hide it, and reiterated, "And I sure as shit don't want you going out with me out of some fucked-up sense that you *owe* me."

Damn. Talk about some money to add to the swear jar.

Her slow smile confused the hell out of him. "What?" he snapped, aware his legendary calm seemed to have deserted him. And talk about the wrong person and the wrong time to act like an ass. First Ron, now him.

She stood and crossed to him, then took his large hands in her smaller, softer ones. Christ, she was smooth. Her silky palms felt hot against his, and he wondered if his scars and calluses reminded her of their differences. Around her he felt like a big, uneducated grease monkey. Lara Valley, bartender, waitress, and college kid. Well, college *woman*. He'd never thought of her as a kid, not with those curves. Besides, he only had two years on her.

"Johnny?"

"Yeah?"

"Ask me again."

He stared down at her, at those eyes he could drown in. At that ripe mouth that looked so soft yet bore a bruise or two from fuckhead Ron. "Huh?"

"You know. Ask me." She tugged him closer, until they stood so close he could feel her breath over his chin.

Lust and tenderness swamped him, and it was all he could do not to grab her and shove her up against the nearest wall, right now. "Ask you…?"

"For a date," she whispered and pulled him forward.

To his shock, *she* kissed *him*. A soft taste of chocolate and Lara, homey goodness and sex appeal that had him hard and unable to think beyond getting more of her. She didn't use any tongue, but he was leery of ending the moment by taking charge, so he let her lead the way.

Soft presses of her lips moved from his mouth to his cheek. When she kissed him gently over the bandage, he felt trembly. Unsure and confused and totally not himself. All his sly one-liners escaped him, replaced with a crazy need to hold her close and never let go.

She pulled back and waited.

"Lara," he said, his voice husky. "Will you go out with me?"

"Yes. I think I will. How about dinner and a movie?"

How about I remember how to talk instead of staring at you? He swallowed audibly. "That would be nice."

She smiled. "Great. It's a date."

—⁂—

Two days later, Johnny was still kicking his own ass. *Nice?* He might as well have said *swell* or *nifty* and sounded even more like a loser. The woman had been jumped by a dirtbag, seen Johnny pound the snot out of the guy, then taken better care of him than anyone ever had. She didn't owe him jack shit, but she wanted to go out with him. And he'd lamely called the idea of a date with her *nice*?

"Hey, numbnuts, you still working on the VW?" Foley asked him.

"Yeah. Done the oil, now just a few more things to check off the list." Though he wished the VW's owner had taken his car to an oil-and-lube place. The simple stuff bored the crap out of him. He'd much rather rebuild an engine or fix a transmission. Something challenging. Johnny liked solving problems. Well, mechanical ones. Not personal bullshit.

He finished checking the car's fluids, topped off what was low, then checked under the chassis. The thing looked beat-up but in good shape, though the steering components could use a boost. After greasing up the front axle, he set the lift back down and drove the car outside.

His return walk turned into a run as he nearly froze to death. Jesus, a few days, and Seattle had turned from warm to Arctic-cold. In early September. Man, it was going to be a long-ass trip through winter.

After he closed the bay door to preserve a little heat, he walked back to his station and announced, "Colder than a witch's t—ah, hey there, Colin."

Sam smirked. "Nice save." He added a silent *dumbass* only Johnny would see.

The dick.

Colin McCauley stood just inside the side entrance, behind the low rope fence separating arriving clientele from the dangers of the garage. The little six-year-old waved like mad. Del's future stepson was a cute kid full of questions. He had a brain like a computer, too. Kid didn't miss much, and he never seemed to forget anything Johnny told him. Beside him, quivering on a leash, stood a lumbering puppy that seemed to have grown since the *last* time Del had brought Jekyll in. A few days ago.

"Hi, Johnny." Colin kept bobbing his head covered in a Chicago Bears beanie. "Me and Jekyll are here with Dad. We're visiting Mom."

Del bragged that the boy loved calling her Mom. She was such a trip. Tatted and pierced, bandying tough love to her gruff mechanics—some who'd done time— with no problem. He didn't think she'd ever been afraid of any of them. Like her father, Del didn't give a shit. She had the heart of a lion, and she'd do anything for those she cared for. She sure seemed to like mothering little Colin.

Seeing the kid again made Johnny wonder what it would be like to be a parent himself. For a long time he'd considered himself too young for parenthood. But he was almost thirty. Older than Del, come to think of it.

"That dog looks huge." Johnny wiped his hands and joined Colin and Jekyll. "Wasn't he two inches shorter on Tuesday?"

Colin stared at the dog, considering.

Mike McCauley entered and quickly shut the door behind him. "Damn, it's cold."

Across the garage, Foley rattled the jar.

"Shi—oot. She's got one here too?" Mike sighed.

The guys laughed.

Mike was built like a tank and did construction for a living but could have easily fit in with the gang at Webster's. Probably why Del had fallen for him. McCauley didn't put on airs, seemed like a solid worker, and had a thing about loyalty.

He wasn't intimidated by her, either. Del needed a guy stronger than her, physically and mentally. Johnny had realized that the moment he'd met her. He was good like that, able to sum up most people at first glance. Women especially.

Well, most women. Lara confused him.

Was that what Lara wanted? Some big, buff guy? One who could take care of her, the way he had the other day with Ron? He felt good every time he remembered how satisfying it had been to punch that guy in the face.

He felt even better remembering the smile Lara had given him for it.

"Yeah," Sam growled. "This pup is a keeper for sure." Sam had joined them while Johnny was wool-gathering. The big guy crouched, petting Jekyll, and induced doggie groans as Jekyll rolled over to show his belly.

"Total submission." Mike chuckled. "He knows you're dominant, Sam."

"Sam, dominant?" Johnny huffed. "Please. He's a pussycat." Johnny had the nerve to tease, especially with Colin close by.

Sam just stared at him. "Cats have claws, Johnny."

"That's true." Colin nodded. "But Jekyll likes cats. He was licking my friend Brian's cat yesterday."

Mike muttered, "More like tenderizing a meal." In a louder voice, he said, "Dogs and cats don't usually get along. We might want to keep Jekyll away from Furball."

"Who's Furball?" Colin looked puzzled.

"Isn't that Brian's cat?" Mike wore an identical expression.

It was weird and kind of cute, father and son looking so much alike.

If Johnny had a son, would the boy resemble him? Or would his daughter look more like her mother? An image of a mini-Lara sitting on his shoulders freaked him the hell out. Sure, she was hot. Sure, he wanted a date or three. But marriage and kids? Hell, he'd be lucky to call her a girlfriend.

Time to stop fixating on an impossible future and focus on the here and now. On his upcoming date. In just one more day. She had Friday night off, and he planned to take her out for dinner and a movie. He could do that. Be normal and low-key.

"Um, Johnny?" Mike frowned. "You okay?"

Johnny's cheeks heated. He'd been staring at McCauley and once again daydreaming about Lara.

"It's not you, Mike," Foley said kindly.

Hell.

"Johnny's got a girl on the brain," Sam added as he stood. "One girl in particular. Isn't that right, Romeo?"

Johnny glared. "Hey, girls are people too." Oh, what he wanted to say to Sam but couldn't…

"Johnny." Colin shook his head. He seemed disappointed. "Girls aren't really people." He looked around, then added in a low voice, "They wear perfume sometimes. And they have—boobs."

Mike blinked.

The guys laughed, Lou especially hard from his spot under a Camaro.

"Really? Is that what those are?" Johnny said.

"Devlin," Mike growled.

"Hey, he said it."

"And Mom and Aunt Vanessa and Maddie and Abby," Colin continued. "Oh, and Grandma. I think maybe Brian's mom has them too."

"Has what?" Del asked as she joined them.

Everyone stared at her in silence.

Johnny elbowed Sam in the gut. "Tell her."

"Shit, no. I mean, heck no."

Foley rattled the jar, and Del glanced from Sam to it and back.

Sam muttered something not meant for little ears and stormed away.

"Sorry about that," Johnny apologized for him. "His vocabulary is severely limited."

"Around here I'm not surprised." Mike sighed. "My fiancée can be a tough boss."

Johnny shook his head. "You think she's tough now, you should have seen her before you two started dating. Talk about mean."

Colin nodded, looking serious. "That's why she's so awesome. She's tough. Like a ninja!" He started doing karate moves and dancing around.

"See why I said no M&Ms?" Mike growled at her. "And that's our cue to get you and go." Mike stepped on Jekyll's leash before the dog could join Colin in a frenzy. Then he grabbed it off the floor and tossed it to Del. "Your turn with the puppy from hell. Come on, woman, or we'll be late for dinner."

"And you didn't invite us?" Johnny put on his sad face. "I'm wounded, Mike. I thought we were best friends."

"Ass."

"What did you say?" Johnny said loudly.

Foley shook the Rattle of Oppression jar just as Del swung Colin over her shoulder and turned back to scowl. "I heard that, McCauley. You know the rules. No cussing."

Mike made a face. "Here too?"

"Go give Foley a quarter."

"Hell."

"Make that two." Del narrowed her gray eyes.

"Fine. But we're going to talk about this later. I don't know why I have to watch my mouth when the things coming out of yours are turning my hair white."

Mike left and returned fifty cents poorer.

"We call it ROP—the Rattle of Oppression," Johnny said with sympathy. "You get used to it."

Mike started laughing. Before Del could blister Johnny for it, Mike kissed the fight out of her. She melted into him, and Johnny couldn't look away from his tough-as-nails boss in obvious love. A wave of envy hit him hard, surprising in its intensity.

So of course he had to make fun, anything to escape a yawning self-pity party growing near. In a singsong voice, he belted out, "Mike and Del, sitting in a tree…"

"K-I-S-S-I-N-G!" Colin laughed, then giggled some more when Del tickled him.

"Traitor," she said over her shoulder to the little boy dangling down her back. She set him down, then she turned to them once more. "Okay, slackers. I'm taking off early. Dad'll be here in another forty minutes. You can kick off at five if you want. We have a lot to get to tomorrow through next week."

Johnny nodded. "Sounds good."

"Oh, and to whoever came up with ROP? Bathroom duty."

A lot of moaning and groaning before Johnny found the obvious answer. "It was Dale."

The service writer Del had taken under her wing a few months ago, a nineteen-year-old bored with life who'd somehow become a vital part of the garage. He was taking some time visiting family in Oregon, so he'd missed a few days. Thus the perfect guy to throw under the bus.

"Yeah, Dale," Foley agreed.

"Yep," Sam and Lou chimed in.

Del rolled her eyes. "Like I'm believing that one." She poked Johnny in the chest. "I know it was you. But hey, you want me to pick on Dale? It's done."

She turned and walked toward the exit. "Foley, you have the shop," she called before she and her family, dancing dog included, left.

In the sudden quiet, Lou wheeled himself out from beneath the car and stood. He wiped his hands on the towel tucked into his back pocket. "So, Johnny. Now that we're alone, how about you tell us what went down Tuesday night at Ray's?"

The guys circled him.

"Not sure what you mean."

"So you what? Banged into a door for that shiner?" Lou asked.

Sam just stared at his bruised cheekbone.

"What shiner? It's a little purple," Johnny scoffed.

Foley laughed. "Yeah, right. So give us a play-by-play. Did you break the fucker's nose or what?"

Johnny sighed. "Rena told, didn't she?"

"Yep. Sang like a canary." Lou grinned. "I barely had to ask her. At least you won."

"So what exactly happened?" Sam asked.

"Some dickhead tried to force himself on Lara, so I broke his face."

"Huh." Foley looked at him.

"What?"

"You actually beat someone in a fight. I'm proud of you, little guy."

Sam snickered, and Lou laughed.

"Little guy? I'm six-two, Foley. Just because you guys bulk up to mask your"—*spot of genius here*—"*embarrassing* size doesn't mean we all need to."

Sam frowned. "Embarrassing size? What?"

"Sue told me about it," Johnny lied. "You know,

Foley, how you're small. Down there." He glanced at Foley's crotch.

Sam and Lou stared, wide-eyed.

Foley's brows shot sky-high. "She *said* that?"

"No, but you look scared. Did I hit a nerve or what?"

Foley took two steps toward him, and Johnny raced back toward his station. "Back to work, no-neck. You too, Sam. And Lou."

"Asshole," Foley growled, then turned on his heel and went back to work.

Lou gave him a thumbs-up, and even Sam gave a nod of approval.

Later, while Johnny was cleaning up, Lou joined him and sat to watch. "So. You and Lara."

Johnny shrugged. "I like her, and she didn't appreciate some jerk pawing her. Neither did I."

"Surprised you left his head on."

"Me too. But Lara and Ray insisted."

"Rena too." Lou gave him a toothy grin. "She told me."

"Rena." He huffed. Lou didn't move. "Go ahead and say whatever it is you want to say."

"You. And Lara."

Johnny noticed Foley and Sam watching him. Everyone had gone silent.

"There is no me and Lara." He didn't want the guys to know about his date, and he felt weird because he wanted to keep it a secret. "So I helped her. So what?"

Foley shook his head. "Brother, we know better than that."

"Not to change the subject, but my dad needs some help this weekend to—"

"Sure thing." Foley nodded.

"Count me in, too," Sam agreed.

Johnny shook his head. "Naked women, and you're all agreeable."

"And?" Sam just stared at him.

Predictable. "What about you, Lou? You want to hang out at the club?"

"Nah. Got some things to do this weekend. But if you want to grab a quick brew, call me."

"Will do."

"I mean, you'll want someone to talk to after you blow it with Lara. I have no doubt you'll manage to 'run into' her again. Just to check on her, I'll bet." Lou winked.

Johnny flipped him off, secretly counting down the hours until his date.

Chapter 6

LARA HAD WIPED HER PALMS ON HER JEANS FOUR times already. She checked her phone again. Another ten minutes and Johnny would be picking her up. God, she hadn't been so nervous for a date since tenth grade, when Mitch Hannah had asked her out. Her first date, and she'd been both thrilled and scared.

Kind of like how she felt now. She took a few deep breaths and tried not to think too hard. It was just Johnny. Her friend. The guy who'd pounded Ron for her. No big deal.

So why couldn't she settle down?

She wondered about her outfit and continued to stare at herself in the mirror. Though Seattle had officially started fall a week and a half ago, it sure felt as if winter had come early. The weather had shifted from freakishly, overly warm to freeze-your-butt cold in the span of a few days. So she'd decided on a pair of decent-enough jeans, boots, and an overlarge red sweater that hung off one shoulder. It made her feel sexy without revealing too much. A bare shoulder was no big deal. She'd vetoed several other shirts because the cleavage would give him the wrong impression, or at least an impression she knew better than to give.

She wanted him. *Bad*. But sex with Johnny might hurt her in the long run. She could see it now—they'd have sex, she'd confuse it for love, end up falling for him, then get dumped, gently—because Johnny was nothing if not a gentleman. Work at Ray's would be brutal, seeing him flirt with other women while he went back to being "just friends" with her.

So why bother going out with him? Because she couldn't help herself. She couldn't stop thinking about him. Especially how endearing he'd been, swearing up and down how she didn't owe him. Not exactly the actions of a man who just wanted in her pants. Most of the guys she knew would have used anything to their advantage to get with her.

She hadn't dated terrible people. A few had been questionable, but most of her exes just hadn't interested her enough. The past few years she'd aspired to make something of herself, and that meant putting a relationship on the back burner. The guys she'd dated hadn't been able to handle not being number one in her life. Truth to tell, if they'd been more remarkable, she might have put them first. Johnny, though, had that something that made her wonder. Could she lose herself in someone like him? He was certainly one of the best-looking dates she'd ever had—have. *He's not here yet. Maybe he'll back out.*

Disappointment, not relief, filled her at the thought. "Gah."

Yep, Johnny definitely intrigued her more than anyone else ever had.

A knock sounded at her door, and she nearly jumped out of her skin.

She deliberately took her time answering it. "Hi."

Johnny just stared at her.

Self-conscious and annoyed with herself for it, she raised a brow and pretended to be confident. "I'll try again. Hello there." She stepped back to let him inside, then shut the door behind him.

"You, ah, I've never seen you with your hair down before. It's nice." As he said it, he scowled.

"Then why do you look disgusted?"

He blew out a breath. "It's not you, it's me."

It sure was. He filled out a pair of black jeans amazingly well. He wore a beaten leather jacket over what looked like a button-down shirt. Not a T-shirt, but a dress shirt with an actual collar and buttons.

Her mouth dried. "Isn't it a little early for the 'it's not you, it's me' speech?"

He blinked, then grinned. "Yeah, that's supposed to be *your* line when you dump me after dinner. I figure if I can actually get you to the movie, I'll qualify the night as a success."

She smiled, feeling more at ease. "Unless you act like a complete idiot, I'm pretty sure I'll stick around for the movie."

He waited for her to grab her purse and don a jacket, then they left after she locked her door. He asked, "So what movie did you pick?"

He'd left the movie up to her, but he'd chosen the restaurant. She didn't know if she wanted him to pay, or even if he'd offer. It was always a toss-up to see how she felt about her date and his intentions, and she used the bill as a marker of his suitability. A nice guy with more than lint in his pockets would offer to pay.

And once again, growing up a hairsbreadth from poverty put money at the forefront of her thoughts. Although…she'd heard from a lot of friends that the true measure of a guy could often be found in the way he handled his money. Maybe she wasn't totally off the mark.

"I decided on something fun," she answered, thinking of the movie she wanted to see.

"Please no chick-flick. Please no chick-flick," he said under his breath, but loud enough to be heard.

She laughed. "I was thinking more along the lines of that new horror flick. The one about the possessed doll and the Ouija board?"

He lit up. "I was wanting to see that."

"Oh good. I passed the test. Your turn. What did you pick for dinner?"

He guided her to his car and opened the door for her. He stepped away for her to enter, but not far enough. She had to brush by him to get in, and the feel of him so close set those butterflies in her stomach to flying faster.

Once she'd buckled in, he crouched down and stared her in the eye. She saw his gaze pass over her face, her hair, and center on her mouth before he met her eyes again.

"Dinner?" she asked, wishing she didn't sound so breathy.

"You'll see." He winked, stood, then shut her door.

He whisked them off to their mystery restaurant in no time, and to her surprise, they listened to classic rock in companionable silence, enjoying the crisp evening.

"I know you like seafood, so I thought we'd go here," he said as they pulled into the parking lot.

"Oh, Ray's Café. I love this place." A very different Ray's from the bar where she worked. Rena and Del had treated her to Ray's Café last year on her birthday. It wasn't superexpensive and had amazing food, but it was a place she had to budget to frequent. "You like seafood?"

"Shrimp is my thing." He escorted her inside. "But I'm also a steak guy."

"You must have quite a grocery bill."

"Well now, I didn't say I cooked it. Just that I like to eat it." They came to the host. "Oh, hey, Lisa."

The older woman at the front smiled at them. "Johnny. Great to see you." She nodded to Lara. "Welcome to Ray's. I have your table. Follow me."

They sat and were soon given water, rolls, and menus. Their table by the window overlooked Puget Sound and the setting sun over the Olympic Mountains. Purple clouds dotted a pink-and-blue sky darkening as the sun set. Dappled sunlight glistened off the water, reflecting prisms of color that dazzled as she watched. A few birds wheeled overhead, adding to the natural splendor, while the mountains stood fast, anchoring the beauty all around.

"Gorgeous view." She couldn't take her eyes from it.

"Yeah, I know."

She turned back to him and saw him focused on her, not the window. "And, um, stellar service. Nice that we got such a great table without a wait." The restaurant looked crowded. Only a few unoccupied tables.

Johnny shrugged. "I worked on Lisa's car a few times. Her husband has a cherry 'Vette." He took a sip of water. "I also made reservations. Lisa and I aren't *that* tight." He grinned. "No need to be jealous."

She huffed her derision. "Please." She glanced at the menu and revised her idea of eating whatever she wanted. Between dinner and the movie, she'd have to pull some serious overtime at the bar.

She glanced up and saw him staring at her, so she buried her nose in the menu again.

"I'm buying, so eat up."

She looked over at him. "Lobster it is."

He chuckled. "Go for it. Might as well. I don't offer to buy all that often."

"No, you're too busy winning at darts and making the guys pay for you."

"Yeah. I'm damn good." He wiggled his brows. "Now figure out what you're gonna eat. We don't have all night, or we'll miss the movie."

And somehow, because he didn't seem to be trying too hard to impress her, she started to relax. She chose some crab cake sliders while he ordered the blackened rockfish and an appetizer for them to share. His dinner cost more, so she felt better about things.

"You don't want a drink?" he asked after ordering a beer.

"Water is fine for me." At his look, she said, "I'm a social drinker. But I like water with meals."

"So what? I'm not social enough for you?"

"I'm trying to keep my wits, Mr. Charm. Besides, water is free. You can thank me later when you're buying me a tub of popcorn at the movies."

"Is that right?"

"Yeah. I'll buy our tickets, but you're in charge of food." She gave him a big smile. "And I eat a lot."

He gave her an assessing once-over. "It's going to all the right places." He rubbed his heart. "Oh boy, is it."

"Stop. I'm wearing a sweater, for God's sake."

"Yeah, but ever since I found out you're going to be a nurse, I keep envisioning you in those naughty nurse outfits. How about it? Make my year and wear one in a few weeks for Halloween."

"Because a tiny white skirt, garters, and cleavage screams professional." She snorted. "Tell you what. I'll be a naughty nurse if you'll be a hunky mechanic. No shirt, just jeans and some manly sweat. Maybe even a dab of grease on your face to look authentic. Yeah, man-candy all the way."

"Done." He held out a hand across the table.

She stared at it. "What's this?"

"A deal. Shake on it."

She took his hand, her entire body flaming at his touch. He gripped her and pumped once, then let her go. Boy was she needing to get laid if a simple handshake turned her on.

He smiled at her. "I can't wait."

"I was joking."

"I wasn't."

The waiter returned with an appetizer of calamari, and they both ate while they asked each other questions. To her surprise, she and Johnny had quite a bit in common. They both lived alone, worked long hours, and enjoyed hanging with friends.

"Favorite color?" she asked.

"Black. You?"

"Red."

He nodded. "Figured."

"How's that?"

"I can just tell."

"Sure you can." She ate another bite of delicately battered squid. "Do you like all kinds of music or just classic rock?"

"Actually, I'm a fan of electronic dance music. Classic rock is manly. Trance and techno more fun."

"Hmm."

"What?"

She studied him, looking for signs of subterfuge. He kept liking the same things she did. "I like EDM too."

"Shows you have good taste in music." He pushed the last two pieces of their appetizer toward her. "Eat up. You need to save your energy for later."

She'd wondered if he'd try something at some point. Though disappointed, part of her felt relieved he was acting true to type. "Is that right?"

He managed to look wounded, his deep green eyes practically mournful, despite the glow of revelry in them. "Now, Lara, I have a feeling you're misreading me."

"Oh?"

"I just meant that after the movie you're going to be all pumped up. So when we hit that all-night batting cage, you'll need your strength."

"Yech. Baseball? I hate baseball."

"I knew you weren't perfect, but finding out like this, so early on our date, it's tough." He sighed.

She tried not to laugh but had to. "You're such a goof."

"A hot goof."

"Yeah. One who visits a lot of strip clubs, so I hear." He flushed. "My dad's place. I help out a lot."

"I bet you do."

The waiter brought their dinners and cleared off their empty plates.

"We'll get back to that comment later," he warned. "We have more important things to talk about."

"Like?"

"The rules. When you're out with me, you have to share." He glanced at her plate.

"What?" She tugged her amazing-looking crab cakes toward her. "No way. This dinner is mine."

"Sweetheart, you—"

"'Sweetheart'? What, this early in the date you're already forgetting my name?"

He glared at her. "You know, for a pretty woman everyone thinks is just a *sweetheart*, you're really a pain in the ass."

She beamed. "Why thank you, kind sir."

He chuckled. "What I was *going* to say was that the rules are pretty clear. We go to dinner. I pay. I get a taste of yours, and you get a taste of mine."

The way he said that was plain sinful.

"A taste of yours, eh? What if it's undercooked? Or just not to my taste?"

He held out a fork of his fish for her, his eyes intent. "Try it. You'll like it." She leaned forward and opened her mouth. His eyes darkened. "Wider. Don't want to miss a drop."

She closed her lips over the fork, disturbed to find her nipples rock hard. Damn, the man could make eating sexy. She seriously had to watch herself with him.

"Well? Is it 'to your taste'?" he mimicked.

She chewed and swallowed, then conceded, "It's amazing."

"Ha." He grinned at her. "Now my turn."

She cut him a piece and held it out to him. He had the nerve to watch *her*, not the food, while he opened his mouth. Then he took it in the sexiest way possible, giving her all kinds of improper thoughts. She wanted to fan herself but didn't want to give him the satisfaction.

"Don't make love to it, Johnny. Just eat it."

He blinked at her, swallowed, then started laughing. He laughed so hard he cried.

"What's so funny?"

"Baby, if that's what you think, you have a lot to learn."

She didn't get it until they'd left the restaurant and drove toward the theater.

Making love. Eating. Making love… Oh. "You are so immature."

"Just eat it," he mimicked and cracked up again. "Sorry. I am immature. But, Lara, don't worry. I have every intention of showing you how I 'eat my dinner' later, in private." He gave her a sly smile. "Don't worry. I'll catch you up in no time."

"Quit with all your wicked innuendo. I'm a simple girl."

"Simple my ass," he said as they found the theater.

When they left the car, the wind picked up, and she wished she'd brought a heavier jacket. So unnerved by his presence, she'd grabbed the first thing she'd found in the closet.

"Cold? Here. Let me help." Johnny hugged her to him, and the subtle scent of his cologne, which had driven her crazy all evening, hit her hard. "Stay close to me, and I'll keep you warm."

She felt his smile against her hair. "Is that a line?"

"Why? Is it working?"

"Not yet. But if it gets any colder out here, it might."

He laughed as they walked into the movie theater. After she purchased the horror film tickets, he grabbed her by the hand and squeezed. "Thank God. I thought for a minute there *Alfred's Three Loves* might have swayed you."

"No way. I'm not into period pieces." She made a face. "But I can do horror." She just had to say it. "I'm on a date with you, aren't I?"

"Ha-ha. Very funny." He swatted her on the ass, and she warmed all over. "After you." He motioned for her to precede him.

To her surprise, she enjoyed the frightfest. She jumped at all the right parts and laughed when he did the same. Unlike most guys, he didn't try to act macho. He had fun, made her laugh, and turned her on without trying. He was just so…Johnny.

They exited the theater amid chatter about the excessive gore in the movie. "Wasn't that *great*?" she gushed.

"A little over the top when the doll started bleeding from every orifice, don't you think?"

"I thought that made her seem more real."

He snorted. "Yeah. Dolls that bleed black and screech about demonic possession are so lifelike."

"Exactly."

He dragged her with him out of the way of a throng of theatergoers exiting from another movie. The multiplex had been packed, and she felt the crush as they moved toward the building's exit.

"Thanks," she said, breathless, as the wall of the corridor braced her back.

Then his mouth was on hers, a whisper of a kiss full of heat and desire. It was gone before she could blink, and she could only stare up at him, wanting more.

"I've been dying to do that all evening. And, well, a guy can only take so much temptation."

"Temptation?" she echoed weakly.

"Yeah." He sighed. "You loved a demonic doll. I

mean, you hate baseball, but you loved Suzy Oozy—she of the hellish diapers and acidic eats-through-anything vomit."

She nodded, still dazed. "I know, right? Great stuff."

He chuckled and moved closer, away from the crowd pushing through the complex.

"Problem is I really liked Suzy. Now I'm going to have to hide my niece's baby-cries-a-lot doll the next time I see it. Talk about super creepy." She rubbed her lips, staring at his, still reeling from that kiss.

"You say *creepy*, then you touch your mouth where I kissed you. I'm sensing a correlation."

"Big word for a self-proclaimed knuckle-dragger—wasn't that what you called your friends at Ray's the other night?"

"Well, them, sure. But I'm more advanced than that. I can even spell *correlation*." He paused. "With a dictionary."

She was enthralled with him, despite being on her guard not to be. "How are you so much fun? Is this part of your shtick?"

He frowned. "My what?"

"Your shtick. Your routine. Do you get your dates laughing so hard that they don't notice when you have them half-undressed?"

"Now, Lara. They *always* know when they're getting naked with me. How could you think otherwise? I have standards, you know."

He looked wounded, and she laughed and let him pull her along with the crowd. He kept his hand around hers, even when they left the theater, and she didn't pull away.

"So, batting cages?" he asked hopefully as they found the car.

She groaned. "No thank you."

He shrugged. "Your loss."

"Thanks, Kareem."

He looked pained. "That's basketball."

"Whatever. I'm not a fan of either sport."

"Obviously. *Kareem?*"

She laughed at him. "I was kidding. Kareem Abdul-Jabbar played for the Lakers from '79 to '85. Do you know what pro team he started with?"

"Do you?" He opened the car door for her, then circled to the driver's side.

"The Milwaukee Bucks in 1969."

"Okay, I'm impressed. That almost makes up for not liking baseball."

She got into the car with him and confessed, "I only know that because my dad used to force me to watch old games with him when I was a kid. The basketball I could tolerate, but show me a Mets game, and I want to throw up. I think my head might spin too, worse than Suzy's did for sure." She sat with him in the quiet of the moment, wondering if she'd gone too far. Vomit wasn't exactly sexy. "Um, not that sitting in absolute silence with you isn't awkward or anything—"

"Glad to hear it."

"—but if we're not going to do the baseball thing, what did you have in mind? And don't even think of suggesting we go back to your place." She liked that neither of them had yet mentioned just ending the date. It was only a little after ten on a Friday night. Early by anyone's standards.

"Well then. Take the wind out of my sails, why don't you?" He blew out a breath. "Fine. We'll go to yours."

"My place?"

He started the car and drove out of the lot. "Exactly. Great minds think alike."

Her heart pounded. "Exactly what *are* we thinking?"

"That we'll hang out at your place, where you'll practice more nursing on me. You can examine my pitiful bruised cheek. You know, the one I got rescuing a damsel in distress?"

"Going to milk that for all it's worth, aren't you?"

"Hell yeah. I figure if I remind you enough, you might take pity on me and let me kiss you again."

Chapter 7

HE HADN'T MEANT TO PUT IT OUT THERE, BUT NOW that he had, Johnny wanted another shot at holding her close.

"We— I— Well."

She hadn't flat-out said no. A victory, of sorts. He had to keep things light, to not scare her off. Because damn, he had to have her. That kiss had only whetted his already enormous appetite when it came to Lara Valley.

"So you and your dad watched basketball together?" Discussing her father should put her at ease, and he wanted to know everything he could about her anyway.

Out of the corner of his eye he saw her regard him with caution. Smart girl. "Yeah. We're close. The whole family is. Reason why I talked to Ron—the guy you beat up—even though I know he's an asshole. I was doing my sister a favor."

"I remember who Ron is," he said drily. "So how was getting attacked by him doing her a favor?"

"Ron said he'd give Kristin more in the divorce settlement if I mediated with him. He and my sister cut out the lawyers."

"A smart move, except for the part where he thought he was getting more than mediation."

"Yeah. Gross."

"So why didn't he meet with her instead of you? Do you have some kind of law background?"

"No. Ron's a sleaze. He couldn't get into my pants when he was married to my sister, so I guess he thought he'd try again now that they're almost divorced."

"What a dick."

"You said it."

He shook his head. "Your sister is fucked. No way is that guy going to play fair."

"I know." She sighed.

Great job. Why not be more of a downer? And watch the language! Maybe he should institute his own swear jar. "I should thank Ron," Johnny said to lighten the mood. "He gave me a workout."

"I can't believe you let him land a punch. I'm a little disappointed."

He glanced at her in surprise before turning back to the road. "Really?"

"No. I just wanted to screw with you."

"Honey, all you had to do was ask." He felt her staring at him, and predictably, he grew hard. Good thing he'd worn dark jeans to hide the fact.

"It's like everything I say has some sort of sexual innuendo with you."

"Yep."

She snorted. "Everything?"

"Uh-huh. Every*thing*—euphemism for penis. Next."

"Never mind. I don't think I want to know."

"You really don't." She sure the hell didn't want to know how badly he wanted to sink inside her, to feel her all around him.

They drove for a bit in silence before Lara spoke. "So I was thinking…"

"The four most dreaded words a woman can say."

"You're horrible."

He slanted a wink her way. "I try."

She laughed. "Stop it. Anyway, since I'm not into baseball, how about playing some cards? I'm pretty good at War."

He started. "I haven't played War since I was a kid."

"I have two nieces. When they're not warring on each other, they're warring with cards. I hate to admit it, but it's fun."

An excuse to hang with Lara. "Well, I guess…"

"Or we could call it a night and—"

"Fine. Stop begging. I'll play cards with you."

"I wasn't begging." She frowned. "But you—"

"We're here." He parked in a guest spot and turned off the car.

"Lucky for you I'm still feeling the pleasant aftereffects of that amazing dinner and tub of popcorn. Come on."

They walked to her floor. Unlike the last time he'd been by, the noise level had grown significantly. He heard shouting, laughter, loud music, and a couple going at it the way he wanted to with Lara.

She blushed. "Ignore Romeo and Juliet. Friday night is their date night."

"Must make it awkward, seeing them the next day or hitting the stairwell together."

"Oh, it is. Trust me. Especially when Jo-Jo's spent half the night riding Eric like a bucking bronco, complete with *wahoos* and *ride 'em cowboys*."

He grinned and waited while she opened her door. He noticed she locked it behind them, and he approved. A woman couldn't be too careful, especially after dealing with assholes like Ron. And speaking of which…

"So have you heard from Ron since?"

"Nope, and I like it that way just fine." She dropped her purse and hung up her jacket in the closet. Then she motioned for his, so he took it off and handed it to her. "You want something to drink?"

"What do you have?"

"Beer and water. I ran out of milk this morning."

Another thing they had in common. A tendency to put off grocery shopping. "How about a beer?"

"Good choice." He watched her putter in the kitchen, giving new testament to the term domestic *goddess*. That shoulder-baring sweater was driving him crazy with the need to pull the rest of it down. Anything to expose the creamy wealth of her breasts.

She handed him a beer and had one for herself, which he liked. She must trust him a little if she finally didn't mind drinking with him. "Wait here." She returned with a ratty deck of cards. "I deal."

"I'm a guest. Shouldn't I get to choose?" he asked as they settled at the kitchen table.

She shuffled the deck. "You're shifty. I've seen you at darts."

"That was sheer skill."

"According to Foley, you must have stepped over the line a few times to get closer."

He snorted. "Please. Foley's muscles get in the way of his aim. And his brain."

She snickered.

"I'm a precision kind of guy." He let her ponder that one while he studied her face and, a bit more subtly, her breasts.

She glanced up but only saw him gazing innocently

at her face. "Precision guy. Uh-huh. You're shifty. I'm dealing." She focused on the cards again.

Man, she was clever. Saw right through him. Brains always impressed the hell out of him, but wrapped in a package like hers, he had a hard time thinking about anything but making sweet love to Lara.

She kept her eyes on the cards. "And quit staring at me like I'm a lame bunny and you're a big bad wolf."

"I'm not—"

"Please. I can feel your pretty eyeballs all over me, Prince Charming. Drink your beer and be good, or your ass is out of here early."

She sounded as if she meant it. The fact she'd make him *work* to earn her, perversely made him want to try harder. *It's like she's playing me, and I'm letting her.*

He frowned. Was she? Was this all a game to her? Had she sensed the depth of his attraction and meant to use herself as bait? The way Amber had always been able to get what she wanted out of his father? Like dancing on a pole for money, she'd danced around Jack Devlin for affection. Then once she'd gotten it, she'd walked away without a backward glance, uncaring that she'd left more than one broken heart behind.

The sad thing was that his father continued to repeat the pattern. At least Johnny knew better.

Lara set down the cards. "I was kidding, Johnny. I mean, I don't think you're looking at me like that. It was a joke."

The vulnerability in her eyes touched him. No, Lara wasn't into games. Not like that. And man, did that make him want her more—and not just for sex.

Emotional asswipe. Grow a pair, Devlin. He could

almost hear Lou mocking him. He cleared his throat and felt his cheeks heat. "If you can't feel me looking at you like that, I must be doing it wrong."

She gave a relieved laugh and finished dealing the cards.

He spent the next forty-five minutes playing a kid's game, when he could have been maneuvering his way into her bedroom. That he hadn't tried to, that he'd enjoyed himself with her, trading barbs and just soaking up her company, told him more than anything that his interest in her meant something.

At first, all he'd wanted was to *do* her, to conquer the unattainable female. And sure, that was immature and beneath him, but he'd been a few years younger. Before he'd recognized that dimple she wore when she was happy. Or how her eyes turned a shade darker before she'd lay into a guy with a smart-ass remark, then laugh with rich enjoyment. Before he'd known she'd taste like heaven and addict him from one simple kiss. Now he wanted—he didn't know what he wanted, but it wasn't just sex. When was the last time he'd hung out with a woman for fun, no expectation of a fuck afterward?

Sure he wanted one. But tonight felt magical. He had no intention of ruining it. The only matter on his mind was how to get a second date with the sexy woman.

"War," he said, pleased when two jacks popped up.

"Oh man." She glanced from her pathetic card to his pile. "I have just enough. One card left…" She waited for him, and they turned their last cards over together.

His ace to her two of spades.

"That's just sad." He shook his head, flipped over her

cards, and saw he'd won a face card and a few number cards. "I won the queen." *If only*.

She frowned. "You must have cheated."

"For almost an hour? If I'd wanted to win that bad, I wouldn't have stretched this out for so long." He stood and stretched. "Ah, that feels good. Bathroom?"

She nodded to the hall and warned, "You'd better put the seat down when you're done, or I'll tell everyone you made a move on me and I laughed at your tiny pride and joy."

"Now we both know that's a lie. Tiny. Right." Johnny had no problem when it came to confidence in his body. He laughed his way into the bathroom and came back to see her sitting on the couch, nursing a second beer. He'd already had two and had stopped himself from having any more. He did have to drive tonight. Unfortunately.

He joined her on the couch and turned to face her instead of dragging her into his lap. "There's something we need to get clear."

"Oh?"

He fucking loved that challenging light in her eyes. Antagonizing yet playful. "Yeah, *oh*. That comment you made about me enjoying the stripper lifestyle."

"Do tell." She set her beer down.

"It's more a lifestyle proclivity than a fetish for strippers."

"You are just whipping out the big words right and left," she teased. "But color me intrigued. How is it a 'lifestyle proclivity'?"

"Simple. My dad has always had a thing for strippers. Don't get me wrong, I appreciate a good athlete."

"I'll bet you do."

"But I grew up around 'Daddy's friends' and saw

most of them as mother figures." Before they'd inevitably take off. "What can I say? My dad is fascinated with ti—ah, with breasts."

Her lips quirked.

"Trust me when I say the glamour of naked breasts lost its luster years ago. Strippers are just hardworking women who happen to take their clothes off for a living. Pretty, sure. But a naked woman is just a naked woman."

"Um, yeah, that's the point."

"No, it's not." He started to get annoyed. "I'm trying to tell you that I can look at a woman and see more than her body. I'm not all about tits and ass and nothing else," he growled, disappointed Lara didn't seem to understand him. "Knowing what they go through just to make a living has shown me they're more than—"

She cut him off by knocking him flat back against the couch.

"Lara?"

Her eyes narrowed, and she maneuvered him so he lay under her. Shocked, he let her move him around like a puppet, wondering what came next. A punch? A kiss? Praying for the latter, he lay still. Then she kissed the breath out of him.

And his entire world spun out of control.

Lara couldn't take it anymore. All night long she'd gotten new insights into Johnny Devlin, and they'd floored her. He acted like a playboy only interested in fixing cars or charming ladies. But Johnny was intelligent, had a vocabulary better than hers, and was downright *nice*.

Well, maybe nice wasn't the right word. But he had a good heart under that scheming soul.

She never would have guessed he'd be happy enough playing a juvenile card game, when he could no doubt have called Cara for a better time. And he hadn't made a move all night, well, not counting that sweet kiss at the theater.

He was driving her *crazy*.

Those subtle glances at her when he thought she wouldn't notice. Keeping her warm when she'd been cold. Going on and on defending women involved in a trade most men either jeered or leered at. A gentleman passionate about protecting others.

A girl could only take so much.

She had wanted to gobble him up when she'd pushed him onto the couch. This kiss… She loved the taste of beer on his breath, the feel of a strong man under her hands. God, his biceps were *huge*.

She learned the feel of his lips, the taut resistance of the broad chest under hers. Johnny had so much powerful muscle, yet he lay still, not dominating, but accepting her lead.

When she eased her tongue between his lips, he gave a loud groan and shuddered. She felt like a real queen with the power to command the tiger at her touch.

He broke the kiss, breathing hard, and stared up at her. "Fuck, Lara. You can't just… I was trying to be good, damn it." He drew her back down, wrapped his arms around her, and kissed the sense right out of her.

So much for taking charge. She could do nothing but follow as he stole her breath and turned her body into a pliant mass of need. Everywhere they connected felt hot, and her breasts ached as she imagined him touching her intimately.

"Yeah, that's so good," he murmured against her lips before angling her head for better access.

She stole a short breath of air before falling under his sorcery once more. When he dragged her closer to his body, letting her feel all the hard places under her, she shivered and gripped his arms hard enough to leave marks. But that only seemed to entice him. Johnny threaded his hands in her hair, holding her right where he wanted her.

The feeling of being controlled made her melt, because she'd imagined a real kiss with Johnny, and it had been hot, but not half as good as the real thing. Lara squirmed on top of him, lost to a primal need.

"More," he growled and hugged the small of her back, pulling her into a massive erection growing more solid beneath her by the second.

She moaned and ground against him, and he bucked up into her. She couldn't think, lost to a lust she hadn't felt in years, if ever. Never had she been so desperate for sex. She wrenched her mouth away and moved her hands to his face, cupping his cheeks. "Please," she begged, not sure what she was asking for.

Johnny to make love to her? To ease the burning ache between her legs?

He answered by staring into her eyes and dragging his hands up her sensitive ribs to her breasts. Watching her all the while, he stopped before fully cupping her, then trailed his fingers back down toward her jeans.

Excitement had her inching up to give him more

access. But Johnny gave a mean grin and changed the direction of his hands again.

"Uh-uh, baby. No rushing this."

She blew out a breath and watched his hair flutter. "Kiss me."

He accepted her hungry mouth, and as he did, his hands moved down to the bottom of her shirt again, but this time they slipped underneath.

When his palms met bare skin, she gasped into his mouth, and he penetrated with his tongue, mimicking what she hoped to hell he'd soon be doing with his cock. Once he eased back on the kiss, she moved her mouth to his ear and nipped his earlobe, gratified when he jerked up into her, his erection nearly poking a hole through her belly.

"Naughty girl." He tilted his head up to give her better access, while his large hands finally found her breasts. He cupped the mounds, and she soaked her panties, so aroused she couldn't breathe. His thumbs followed, riding over the crest of each nipple as he watched her lose all sense.

"So fucking sexy," he muttered and somehow fitted his hands inside her bra cups, so his callused palms rested against her hot flesh. "Christ, I'm close."

Close to heaven, was all she could think as she kept grinding over him, seeking a release that still wasn't near enough. She kissed him again, mashing against his lips, desperate to come. How had she never noticed how good he smelled? And the taste of him went straight to that hungry place between her legs.

She kept touching him, finding purchase in the firm breadth of his chest. As she moved her hands, so did he.

Pinching, teasing, caressing, his fingers were like magic, and she wondered if she might orgasm from just that. But then those clever fingers moved south, right where she needed them.

He delved down, unbuttoning her jeans and unzipping them in one smooth move before his fingers disappeared under her panties.

She cried out against his mouth and tried to take him inside her, but the stubborn man refused to finish with any haste. Instead, he slid his fingers along her folds, grazing but not giving her enough pressure.

"Lara, baby," he whispered. "You're so wet."

"In me," she begged. "Please." She wasn't sure what she meant, wanting his fingers, his cock, hell, anything to put out the fire burning her from the inside out.

He answered by shoving a finger deep inside her while another rubbed her clit.

Lara climaxed hard, gripping that finger for all she was worth as she yelled out and came.

He pumped a few more times against her while adding a second finger inside her.

Her orgasm seemed to last forever, and then her sensitivity became too much to bear. She reached between them to ease his hand away and rubbed against him in the process. Apparently that was the extra bit he needed to find satisfaction, because he groaned long and loud and stopped bucking against her.

"Yeah, oh yeah." He closed his eyes, his fingers hot and damp against her belly.

She collapsed against him, burying her head in his chest while her hormones vacated what used to be a rational single woman wanting no entanglements.

Oh my God. I just got off with Johnny Devlin.

Johnny's chest rose and fell, gradually easing into even breathing.

Lara had never hidden from confrontation, but she didn't know what to say. One friggin' date, and she'd let him do her? Could she be any easier?

Could she care any less?

She hadn't had a man-stimulated orgasm in *two years*. And that included her last few boring boyfriends. *Nothing at all boring about Johnny though.* She still wondered what he looked like naked, and having felt him large and thick underneath her, she kept imagining what he'd feel like inside her. Perfection, no doubt.

She inwardly berated herself for being such a chicken and raised her head. Johnny turned his gaze from the ceiling to her. His voice sounded like gravel when he said, "I totally need to clean up."

She flushed. "Oh, um, sure." She slowly got up, feeling dizzy and still so relaxed she might as well have been a wet noodle.

"I know where to go." He got to his feet and winced, then adjusted himself in his jeans before disappearing down the hall.

She fixed her own clothing, putting her bra back to rights and fastening her jeans. She'd have to clean up once he left, because no way was she going to drop her pants and wipe herself up in the kitchen.

What to do with him now was the question. Lara had no idea how Johnny would act. From what she knew, usually once he'd had his fun with a woman, he moved on. But he'd always been up front with his "girl-friends," at least, that's what Rena had told her. Rena knew everything about everyone, thus her career field in hairdressing—a natural fit.

She heard a toilet flush and the sink running. Johnny reappeared, looking calm and replete.

And why shouldn't he? He'd come in his jeans while she'd ground all over the poor guy. Should she apologize? Thank him? She'd never been in this kind of situation before. Lara didn't do one-night stands.

"So tonight." He stuck his hands in his pockets. "I hadn't prepared for this."

"Neither had I."

His somber expression unnerved her. "I feel a little…used."

She blinked. "Excuse me?"

"I mean, you took advantage of me."

"I—what?"

"You kissed me."

"You kissed me first. At the theater." Was he serious?

"Well, sure. You looked so cute, full of excitement over a demonic doll. But the sex… That's heavy stuff. I normally lay out the rules before I get with a girl."

She put her hands on her hips. "Is that right?"

"That way no one gets upset afterward. I'm an easy guy to understand."

"So I hear."

He nodded, earnest. And that look of sincerity on such a sexy, mischievous face had her wanting to do him all over again. This time without any clothes between them.

What the hell is happening to me? Where had her raging libido come from?

"You are totally shitting me," she said, blunt, direct, and daring him to disagree.

"I totally am." His slow smile melted her anger.

"You're a jerk."

"Right again." He chuckled. "You should have seen the look on your face. Lara, I'm not gonna lie. I was hoping for another good-night kiss. But that… all of it…was so beyond my expectations. So fucking hot." He blew out a breath, and she knew it would be all right. He'd tease, make her feel good while leaving, and they'd go their separate ways. No awkwardness at Ray's for them, not like it was for Sue and Foley.

She winked at him, telling herself not to feel let down. Dinner, a movie, and an orgasm. Not a bad way to spend a night. Plus, she'd never classify Johnny as casual. She'd known him for years. "You weren't so bad yourself, he of the magic fingers."

Johnny sighed. "Talk about a night to remember."

She smiled at him, at ease and not feeling as whorish as she should. Del or Rena would tell her to stop being so dramatic. Women could have sex *whenever* they wanted and with *whomever* they wanted. Being sexual did not equate to slutting around. She knew that. But it did make her feel a lot like her sister. And that she could have done without.

"So I guess I'll—"

"When are we going out again?" he asked, and leaned back against the wall, facing her. "I mean, we are going out again, right? You didn't just use me for a quickie, did you?"

"First of all, quickie?" Her heart raced. *He wants to go out again. Imaginary fist pump. Yes!* "I was begging for you to get me off, and you took forever."

"Someone needs to learn a little patience." That familiar smirk was back.

"For-ev-er," she reiterated. Sparring with Johnny was akin to foreplay. It seemed to lead to a deepening connection between them. Or else she'd let the sex go to her head. Just because the guy wanted to date her again didn't mean it wasn't about getting into her pants.

"Point being, you did get off," he said.

"So did you."

"I know. So embarrassing. I can last a lot longer than that."

"Ah. So another date to prove you can?"

He frowned. "I was kind of thinking we could hang out with sex off the table."

"Huh?" Did he not want her again? Had she turned him off? Could she stop being neurotic for *ten freakin' seconds*?

"You know. A date between friends."

"Friends." He didn't want her. Depressing, and just when she'd found a guy who could get her off like a rocket.

"Actually, friends *first*. I want to fuck you into tomorrow, but I'd feel better about it if we went out a few times to get to know each other better." He cleared his throat, looking almost…nervous?

She kept staring at him, befuddled.

"I mean, everyone knows how choosy you are." He scowled. "You don't date guys at Ray's."

"Ah. So this is about bragging rights."

"No." He blew out a frustrated breath. "Would you shut up for two seconds and let me finish?"

She found herself smiling, when any other guy telling her to shut up would have gotten the door.

"I didn't tell the guys we were going on a date. I don't kiss and tell." He shrugged and added, "Not all the time."

"Ah-ha."

"But I'd like to spend time with you. Like real people do in relationships."

Her heart threatened to leap from her chest. "So we're going out now?"

"Oh my God. You are so annoying." He stepped close, kissed her breathless, then strode for the door. "Before I forget myself and fuck you against the wall, I'm leaving. We're going out again. Just you and me. And it's no one's business but ours. Right?"

"Um. Right. Ours. Sure." She rubbed her tingling lips, staring at him.

Johnny looked furious, frustrated, and a little wild around the eyes. So unlike himself.

"Text me your schedule, and I'll text you mine. And before you ask, yeah, I'm going to a strip club tomorrow night to bartend while Foley and Sam act as bouncers. And no, I won't be doing any of the girls. They're like family, and I'm not into incest."

"O…kay."

"It's my dad's place, and he usually needs help because his guys are dicks. I told him to fire Micah, because the guy is clearly shooting up, but Dad feels this weird sense of loyalty. And he never replaced George, so I'm having to fill in for the manager too."

Johnny was rambling. She couldn't look away.

"Yeah, so, anyway. A date. Soon." He grabbed his jacket from her closet and put it on.

"A date. With you."

"One with no sex." He ran a hand through his hair. "Just you and me hanging out. No big deal. Just some fun." He turned and was halfway out the door when she stopped him.

"Another date. Okay. But no batting cages."

He glanced over his shoulder at her. "That I can do." He studied her for a moment. "Just so there's no confusion, don't think we won't get back to the sex. That's definitely on the agenda. We fit together." He seemed pleased at the idea.

She was too. "We do."

"You mean we *will*." He wiggled his brows and left.

Out of habit, she locked the door behind him, then turned and leaned against it, not sure what the hell had happened. Johnny had given her the most intense orgasm of her life. He'd come in his pants. Insisted they go out again—not for sex. And was refusing to tell his buddies he was banging her. It was like he had violated all the important guy codes in one fell swoop.

Which made her wonder, why? Why her?

And how the hell would she ever be able to look at her couch again without drenching her panties?

Chapter 8

"YO, JOHNNY. ANOTHER BEER." FOLEY NODDED TO the suit waiting impatiently for a drink.

Johnny blinked, stopped staring into space, and slid a cold brew into GQ's waiting hands. He took the guy's money and moved to the next order. The tiny bar just outside Strutt That Butt—Strutts for short—was always crowded. Since Washington had a no-booze policy in the clubs, customers had to purchase alcohol at a facility separate from the dancing girls. Hence the bar with a huge-ass HDTV showing what Bubbles was doing onstage next door.

"Dude, wake up." Foley leaned on the bar near him, his gaze on Johnny instead of the screen, where Bubbles was doing her best work to date. The woman could do aerial splits that made Johnny hurt for her. But *dayum*. Nice performance.

"Huh? I'm awake."

"And staring into la-la land, the way you've been doing all night." Foley snorted. "You need to get laid, my friend."

Been there, done that—well, kind of. Johnny shrugged. "Whatever. There's more to life than sex."

"No there ain't," said a nearby customer, his gaze glued to Bubbles's breasts onscreen.

"Yeah, not here. Not when there's so much pussy for the asking," his buddy said with a leer and looked around the bar, where a number of girls in bikinis roamed, asking if anyone wanted drinks. "No guy is gonna turn down *that*." He pointed to the large screen over Johnny's head.

A lingering sense of aggressive entitlement lined the guy's words, and it made Johnny cautious. Foley would need to keep an eye on this one. After so many years in the business of sizing people up, Johnny knew what to look for when trouble came calling.

"What? You don't agree?" Typical Strutts customer. Not a lot of liberated feminists hanging out around the place, despite the number of women in attendance. Just horny assholes who thought they could buy whatever they wanted. "Bitches just want to trade ass for cash. No biggie."

Johnny frowned. "Be careful with that attitude. A lot of the girls here are strictly into dancing. Period."

"Whatever." The macho head case flipped him off. "I want it, it's mine." He flashed a wad of cash right in Johnny's face.

Go time.

Johnny leaned over the bar, grabbed the guy by the collar, and jerked him close. "Look, shithead. If a girl says no, she means no. And this no-neck"—he cocked a thumb at Foley—"and his big brother over at the club are here to make sure you fuckheads understand what that means, got it?"

Next to them, his buddy opened his mouth.

Foley sent the guy's friend a warning look. Without a word, the friend took one glance at Foley, slunk off his stool, and went to sit at a far table.

"Well?" Johnny tightened his grip.

"Yeah, yeah. I get you. Ease up, man. I was just playin'."

"Good. Remember that."

The customer left with a few loudly uttered epithets.

Foley rapped his knuckles on the bar. "You know, that's no way to enhance customer relations."

Johnny told him where to shove it.

Foley laughed. "You're in a real mood, aren't you, sunshine?"

"I guess. I just get sick of the guys thinking the girls are for sale."

Foley nodded to the screen, and Johnny turned around to see Bubbles leave the stage to a round of applause. She sat in some yuppie guy's lap and whispered in his ear. Seconds later the pair walked away, headed in the direction of the VIP rooms.

Foley didn't say anything. But then, he didn't have to. They both knew what went on back there. Jack Devlin had always wanted to legalize prostitution and drugs, and he'd been doing his damnedest to create his own slice of tax-free, vice-full heaven with Strutts.

Johnny sighed.

Foley leaned over the bar to slap him on the shoulder. "Ow."

"Easy, princess. Look, no one's making Bubbles do anything she doesn't want to. Hell, she was bragging to me earlier that she makes more in a night than I do in a week."

"I know. It's just… I hate when the guys treat the girls like nothing more than fuck machines."

"You're a softie." Foley shook his head. "But I know what you mean." He glanced at the rude guys who stood to leave the bar, no doubt to head next door for a close-up show. "Want me to bounce 'em?"

"Have Sam keep an eye on them. I think Tricia's up next." A transgender stripper who kept the mystery afloat for newcomers and had her own fan club growing in leaps and bounds. She'd augmented a nice set of breasts she liked to show off. But Johnny could only imagine what those two throwbacks would think if they knew what lay beneath Tricia's packed G-string.

"I'll let him know." Foley left to pass the word to Sam.

Johnny appreciated the fact that though his friends could give him a hard time, they were a hell of a lot more open-minded than most of the guys in the place.

Despite the tawdry name, Strutts did stellar business. A mix of tacky fun, classy acts, and the right amount of sleaze. Jack Devlin had built a clientele of well-paying customers. No broke-ass degenerates for Jack. No, sir. Johnny's father had spent a lifetime hanging out in places like this, so who better than him to open a successful "clothing optional" venture?

Johnny glanced around, serving more customers and noting the time. After being with Lara last night, he wanted nothing more than to see her again. Serving drinks to these idiots and staring at naked women who weren't Lara did nothing but annoy him.

"What are you looking at?" asked one big dude at the end of the bar, where Johnny had unintentionally been staring without seeing. *Again.*

Johnny nodded to the guy's beer. "You look empty. Want another?"

"Oh. Sure."

Tension defused. *Damn, I am good. Time for Dad to gimme a raise.* He continued to serve as the hour wound down, and while he did, he sought the counsel of a few of his friends. Women who could be counted on for good advice about what he should do with Lara. Johnny hadn't become a charming ladies' man by accident. He had a brain, and who better to talk to about what women wanted than women? He'd been doing it for years, and he'd seen his social life more than full because of it.

Full, but not fulfilling. Now that he had a shot with Lara, he planned on doing his level best to keep her happily purring along at top speed. His friends Jenna and Dory were fonts of information and man-smart. Not that they always made the best decisions, but both girls knew when they were to blame, unlike some of the younger dancers in the place, who couldn't spot a decent relationship at any distance.

Johnny finished a nice discussion with both ladies about how to do right by his girl. They left just as Foley returned, and Johnny slid him a cold one.

"Thanks." Foley slugged it back. "Damn. I needed that. Tricia's good, but Kim… Shit. Do you know what she can do with her tongue? I think I popped a few blood vessels watching her and a banana." He glanced at his cell phone. "It's quarter after two. You wrapping up?"

The crowd seemed no smaller, despite the late hour. He saw Jenna, Dory, and Kyla wave as they clocked out. Another fifteen minutes 'til closing and only the employees seemed ready to leave.

"I'm shutting the doors at two thirty. Not a second later." His old man had stopped in earlier, long enough to see the traffic growing, the money flowing, and the girls beaming as they generated higher bar tabs and more interest in the goings-on next door.

Johnny reluctantly found it fascinating. For all

that the customers knew they were being played, they didn't care. Well, most of them didn't. He watched Foley insert himself between one grabby drunk and Shaya. When Foley had to lift and drag the guy outside, everyone watched him toss the drunk around like a football.

"Ten minutes," Foley bellowed.

Booing and hissing answered him. But Foley laughed it off. "Yeah? Try sticking around after we're closed, and you can join fucknut outside."

The negativity ceased.

Foley rejoined him at the bar, looked above his head, then swore. Johnny turned to see what had soured his friend, only to witness Sam beating the crap out of two customers. Without breaking a sweat, Sam knocked them together and dragged them to the door. Fortunately the club had mostly emptied out, the few stragglers being handled by the other bouncers. Foley hurried away, and Johnny continued closing up the bar, leaving the cleaning to the others in the back.

He'd grabbed a glass of water for himself and another for Foley and had just fetched his jacket when Foley returned.

"He's such a basket case," Foley muttered. "Asshole actually likes bloodying up his knuckles."

Johnny had recognized the scum Sam had dealt with. Both had been previously banned for harassing the girls. So much for a third chance at Strutts. Two strikes and you were out. "What? Not like either of them will bring charges. I'd be surprised if they're not dodging warrants." He snorted. "Just out of jail, and no doubt working to get back in."

Foley sighed. "It's not the fighting that bothers me so much. It's that Sam's getting pissy again. Stupid Louise Hamilton."

"Uh-oh."

Sam had a tendency to get even more aggressive after talking to his mom. For all that Johnny felt he'd lacked a maternal influence in his life, part of him thanked God his father had never married again. The moment a woman grew a little controlling, Jack shoved her out the door. Of course, the ones he wanted to stay ended up leaving him. Either way, Jack never had woman problems for long.

"Want to go talk him down? I'll hold the bar." Only four more customers remained, and it appeared Shaya and Nikki were cajoling their fan club out the door as he spoke.

"Nah." Foley took the glass of water Johnny had handed him. "Thanks." He drank it down. "I think the fight helped calm him down."

The girls waved at Johnny, and he shooed them away. Bart and Will were still in the back, tasked with closing down.

Foley pushed the glass back at Johnny. "So, what's your deal?"

"Me?"

"Yeah, you. I've been watching you, and you've done more staring at nothing tonight than you normally do. You know how when Liam likes to lecture us about something, and you kind of zone out while pretending to listen?"

"Oh." Johnny grinned. "I'm good at that."

"I know. But tonight you're not even trying to cover up the fact you're not all here. What gives?"

Johnny needed to talk to someone with a guy's point of view, and no way in hell would he expect his father to have any words of wisdom. Liam could get a little too fatherly, and his new romance skewed his perceptions, to Johnny's way of thinking. Of all his friends, Foley was the most levelheaded. And the guy loved his mom, so he had a pretty healthy relationship with women in general.

He took a chance on the big guy. "You ever feel something for a woman? I mean, besides a hard-on?" Foley smirked, and Johnny wished he'd kept his mouth shut. "Forget it."

"No, no." Foley crossed his huge forearms on the counter. "I'm here to help."

"I knew I shouldn't have opened my mouth."

"You really shouldn't have. But I'm gonna take pity on you, because I know where this is going."

"You do not."

Foley gave him a condescending look. "Uh-huh. Look, Johnny, I'm probably the best guy to talk to about this. Sam's antisocial. Lou's got too many chicks to keep track of. Your dad's a great guy, but…" He waved his hands around, indicating the bar and club.

"I know." Johnny sighed.

"And Del and Liam are too sappy in love to be of any help. God knows you don't have any other friends." He ignored Johnny's scowl. "So you've come to the right place." Foley cracked his knuckles. "The love doctor is in the building."

"Jesus. I must be hitting rock bottom to listen to this."

"Yep, you're talking to the one man who understands women," Foley talked over him. "Except for Sue, and that's a mistake I admit I made. What can I say? I was horny, she offered, end of story."

"Yeah, *your* end. Sue's a mean one."

Foley sighed. "I know." He shook his head, as if shaking her off, and cleared his throat. "So I've been in a couple long-term relationships over the years. Like, ones where I actually introduced the chick to my mother."

"Yeah?" For Foley, that was saying something.

"First girl was back in high school. Michelle Watts. She had a kickin' body and was the nicest girl you'd ever meet. Way too good for me. Then I ended up going away for a little bit, and when I got back, she was gone."

"Away as in the country club for criminals?"

Foley shrugged. "Hey, I served my time. It was what it was. I didn't expect her to wait on me, and she didn't. But it was still a bummer. So after I got back, I spread my wings. Got around, introduced some lucky ladies to fun with Foley." He wiggled his brows.

"Enough said. Go on."

"Then I met Desiree. I fixed her car, and she was eternally grateful." He leaned back, a smile on his face. "Girl could suck the paint off a fender, she was that good."

"And this is the girl you introduced to your mother."

"She was genuinely sweet. Had a smile that could just get to you, right here." Foley tapped the center of his chest.

"So what happened?"

"She wanted to get serious, and I was still playing around. Not cheating on her or anything." Foley had a thing about fidelity. "But I didn't want to marry her, and she obsessed about kids. It was only a few years ago. I couldn't imagine being a dad back then. Hell, I still can't." He paused. "Plus it used to bug her that Sam and I are tight."

"Glued-at-the-ass tight?" Johnny embellished, knowing it would set his friend on edge.

Predictably, Foley glared. "I'm trying to share, here."

"Kidding. I know you and Sam are"—Johnny put in air quotes—"*just friends*." He danced back when Foley tried to grab him.

"You're such a shit."

Johnny chuckled. "Sorry. I couldn't resist. So you cut it off with Desiree. You don't seem too broken up about it."

"I was at the time. I couldn't help ending things with Michelle, but Desiree and I really hit it off. It did bug me that she was so tiny and, well, nice. I always felt like I'd accidentally roll over on her in bed and squish her. And knowing her, she'd thank me for it."

Johnny tried not to laugh, but he couldn't help it.

"I know, sounds funny." He shrugged. "If she and I had gotten together back then, my life would be a lot different now."

"Good or bad?"

"Who knows?" Foley narrowed his gaze on Johnny. "But let's stop dancing around *your* issues. You're hot about a woman, and you don't know what to do about it. Not your fault, really. Growing up surrounded by beautiful, naked women couldn't have given you a reality check about relationships."

"I'm not stupid. I know the average woman doesn't grind on poles twenty-four seven." Johnny frowned. "I've had a few serious relationships. But lately… With Del and Liam hooking up, it got me thinking." *And I'm almost thirty. Christ.*

"That's the truth." Foley fiddled with his empty glass. "I'm thirty-three. You don't think I've had a few second guesses about where my life is going?"

Foley liked to give the impression of being no more than a bruiser who liked cars, but the guy had smarts. Not the kind from a book, but real-life common sense.

"Long as Del and her dad keep the place going, I'm good with sticking around the shop." Johnny knuckle-bumped Foley. "But my social life sucks. I'm bored with sex. Never thought I'd say that, but yeah, I am. You know Cara Suarez?"

"Who doesn't?"

"She came on to me last week. I lied to get away from her. What guy does that?"

"One who's not interested. Or gay." Foley gave him a look.

"I wish. Women are so complicated." He frowned, remembering Lara's shock when he'd said the word *relationship*. What? He couldn't be considered for something more than a quickie on the couch? "I'm not into dudes like that, but at least I understand them."

Foley nodded. "Guy gets hungry, he eats. Gets horny, he fucks. He doesn't have to talk crap to death." Foley poked him in the shoulder. "Take you and me. We can talk about women—like we are now—and go right back to work without oversharing shit. Tonight, we're just two guys telling it like it is."

"Right." Though Johnny could desperately use some advice. And truth be told, this was the deepest conversation he and Foley had ever had. Maybe he was growing up. *Damn. And now I'm a PSA for talking shit out.*

"Here's me telling it like it is: stop being such a pussy, and be straight with Lara."

Johnny paused. "I wasn't talking about her."

"Please. You get a boner anytime we go to Ray's, and I'm thinking that's not for the atmosphere."

"Shut up." He flushed. Had he been that transparent?

"I'm talking a metaphorical boner, but now I have to wonder." Foley laughed at him. "You are so red right now."

"You know no one likes you, right?"

"Lara's cool. You can't fuck around with her." Foley's smile faded. "She's straight, man. You helped her out with that asshole, and that's great. But we both know you've had a thing for her for years. I figure you can go about Lara a few different ways."

"Like…?"

"One—you fuck her and get her out of your system. You even have the talk with her. She'll tell you she's good with you splitting. Then she'll screw you over like Sue did with me, and Ray's will be an uncomfortable place to go for a while."

"What exactly did Sue do besides ignore you?"

Foley scowled. "After you losers left last week, she 'accidentally' spilled a pitcher of beer over my head."

"Sorry I missed that."

"Yeah, it was hilarious." Disgruntled, Foley continued, "Option two—you end up falling for the chick, and she breaks your heart and dumps you."

"You're just a ball of joy, aren't you?"

"I'm not done. Three—you turn into an annoying douche like McCauley, who does whatever his woman wants. You ever see how high he jumps when Del barks an order at him?"

Johnny frowned. "I'm thinking he's got her wrapped, not the other way around. She's taking on his kid. And a dog. And he's called her Delilah a few times without taking a shot to the head or kidneys for it."

"Hmm. She does seem pretty happy, true. But remember how it was touch and go for a while?"

Before their boss had gotten engaged to Mike McCauley, Del and he must have had some rough patches. After a near-fatal accident, she'd been an utter bee-yatch until she and McCauley had fixed things up. Thank God.

"And Liam," Foley continued. "Guy found his soul mate, then she died. Dude mourned for *decades*. Sure he's happy now, but thirty years of grief is brutal any way you look at it." Foley shook his head. "Then there's my mom. My dad died when I was four. She's *still* single."

"Yeah, but I doubt she's been miserable. Probably got herself some action when you, ah…" Johnny coughed when Foley glared at him. "I mean, she's probably single by choice." Foley's mom was a sweetheart. Rough around the edges, but sincere. She loved her boy more than anything, and she kept herself in great shape. She looked amazing, despite having given birth to and raising Foley, and looked years younger than her age.

Johnny kept his father *far* away from her.

"My point," Foley growled, "which you'd get if you'd shut the hell up and listen, is that doing nothing gets you nothing. Go big or go home, Devlin. You can't keep swirling around the drain, 'cause eventually you'll go down. Lara's hot. If you don't hurry up, she'll be taken before you know it. And with her hanging around a bunch of college dicks, you can bet your ass they're gonna grab her and wine and dine her. Then you'll be another loser mooning after her at Ray's."

Johnny knew he was right, but something about Foley's tone caught him off guard. "What about you? Why didn't you ever make a play for her?"

"I did. She turned me down. Flat-out said no." Foley looked incredulous. "I mean, who *does* that?"

They laughed.

"Nah. She's cool and hot. And I'd do her in a minute." Foley grinned at the glare Johnny shot him. "But she's a little too nice for me."

"She's a pain in the ass."

"To you. Not to me or the guys. Think about that." Foley watched him.

Sam came through the door and announced his readiness to leave. "Hey, ladies, get it in gear. I'm tired, and I need a ride."

"And a Valium," Johnny muttered. "Keep your shirt on, Mr. Fists. We're done." Johnny yelled to the guys in the back that he was leaving, then he and the badass bros all walked out together. "Where's your car?" he asked Sam.

"I'm reworking the engine. She's got a hitch in her purr." Sam waited for Foley to unlock his door, then slid in without saying good-bye.

Johnny didn't take it personally. He and Sam were good. If they weren't, he'd know, most likely alerted by his own intestines wrapped around his neck.

"Later, loser. Remember what I said." Foley gave him a two-finger salute, then got in the car and took off.

Johnny stood with his hands in his pockets, wondering what to do with Lara on their next date. Not having sex had seemed the thing to suggest—and the girls here had agreed. It showed he wanted her for more than a booty call—which was the truth. Though he'd sounded like a rambling loser, she'd agreed to go out with him. But what to do… The card game had been surprisingly fun. He liked her competitive streak and seeing how her mind worked.

Lara had a dry sense of humor. She never seemed to hold back with him.

"She's a pain in the ass."

"To you. Not to me or the guys," Foley had said. *"Think about that."*

So Johnny thought about it. Through the rest of his weekend into the beginning of the week, he'd done nothing *but* think about Lara. They had texted back and forth and decided on a light dinner at her place Tuesday night. No pressure, just a guy and a girl hanging out. Being friendly—until he drew her close for the kill. A relationship. Just him and Lara. And maybe this time he could make the big *R* work.

Tuesday evening rolled around in the blink of an eye. He swore to himself he would *not* look at her couch unless he absolutely had to. Just thinking about it brought to mind the feel of his finger inside her, of her lips on his, the smooth taste of beer only adding to the sexy spice that was Lara.

He shuddered, forced himself to stop thinking about sex, and glanced at his cell phone. Six o'clock on the dot. He knocked on her door and waited, praying for an option Foley hadn't mentioned. One where Johnny got the girl and lived happily ever after—or at least until her dumping him didn't hurt so much.

Chapter 9

THE DOOR OPENED. AN ADORABLE LITTLE GIRL WITH blond hair and big brown eyes stared up at him.

"Ah…" He checked the number on the door again. 307. Nope. Right place.

"Who are *you*?" The girl planted her hands on her hips and waited, watching with suspicion.

"I'm Johnny." In the background, he heard cartoons and…splashing?

She pursed her lips. Wearing a pair of pink tights under a jean skirt and a purple fuzzy sweatshirt, she looked like a miniature doll. Her blond hair lay in waves around her face, and he imagined the little boys in her class tugging at it to get her attention.

When the girl just stood there, staring, he tried again. "Is Lara here?"

"Maybe."

"Amelia, get back here!" Lara yelled from somewhere in her apartment. Youthful giggling followed, and he watched over the girl's head in front of him as a naked streaker covered in bubbles raced into the living room, circled the coffee table a few times, dodged Lara to round the dining table, then darted back down the hallway.

Lara froze when she saw him. "Oh, shit."

The door guard looked shocked. "*Aunt Lara*."

"I meant shoot." Lara scowled at the girl. "Kay, what did I tell you about opening the door to strangers?"

Kay said, all innocence, "But Aunt Lara, I know him. This is Johnny." She grabbed his hand and tugged him inside.

Her much-smaller palm felt warm in his, and he smiled down at her. "I'm no stranger. I'm standing here with Kay—your niece." Putting the pieces together quickly, he added, "And Amelia is slippery and wet and, I imagine, not wanting the bath she's supposed to be in."

"You got that right." Lara expelled a loud breath. She wore wet jeans with holes in them and a faded T-shirt. Water had molded the shirt to her breasts, and he did his best not to leer and pant like a dog. "I'm so sorry. I ended up covering for my sister's babysitter tonight—"

"She means Grandma," Kay said, still holding on to Johnny.

"Right." Amused, he watched as Lara flushed and continued her apology.

"My mom had to work the same shift as Kristin, because someone called in sick. And Dad was busy—"

"Playin' poker with his friends. But why he plays when he has no money, Grandma will never understand," Kay said.

Lara threw up her hands. "Stop interrupting."

"Yes, Aunt Lara," Kay agreed in a sickly sweet voice.

Johnny did his best to keep his mirth to himself.

"That really means 'go suck an egg,' I know." Lara didn't seem upset with Kay's tone. She looked like she was trying not to laugh herself. "If you can get your sister back in the bathtub, I'll give you fifty cents."

Kay narrowed her eyes. "A dollar."

"Seventy-five cents. Take it or leave it."

"It's a deal." Kay let go of Johnny and tore down the hallway, shouting for her sister.

Lara stood there, obviously frazzled. Even her trademark ponytail was half falling out of its band. "I should have called, and I meant to, but then I forgot. My demonic nieces sucked my brains clean out without even trying." She leaned her butt against the arm of the couch. "And don't even get me started on the papers I have due this term."

"Did you eat yet?" He didn't see anything cooking on the stove. Closing the door behind him, he walked to her tiny open kitchen and looked around. Nothing on the counters. Across from the low divider separating the small room from the rest of the apartment, he saw a few books, crayons, and a doll sitting in a neon purple backpack on a dining chair. From a pink backpack, an assortment of stuffed animals spilled onto the table. He also noted a few spiral notebooks and what looked like medical texts lying near a green bear with button eyes.

"I was planning dinner when Amelia spilled chocolate milk down her dress and somehow got it into her hair. So the plan was a quick cleanup then food." Laughter and splashing came from the hallway. "You can see how that turned out."

"Aunt Laaarrraaaa," Kay sang.

"I have to make sure Amelia doesn't drown herself, or worse, get drowned by her sister. I'm really sorry." She straightened. "Can we do dinner another night? I'll cook, I promise."

"Sure. No worries."

"Great. Thanks, Johnny. Call me." She gave him a quick kiss on the cheek that hit him right in the gut, then scurried toward the sounds of an escalating fight while he stood, wondering what to do next. He'd geared himself up for a night of learning about Lara. He had nothing better to do than hang out and stare at her. Hell, she didn't even have to talk if she didn't want to, though silence would not help him on his fact-finding mission.

And yet… A slow grin worked its way over his face. What better way to see what she was really like than to watch her with her nieces? If seventy-five cents would buy the older girl, imagine how easily the little one might narc for a quarter.

He'd figure out this thing with Lara. And now that he had a second date on the hook, it was time to put it to good use. Even better, he had no worries of sex to distract him with the girls underfoot. Pleased things were looking up, he pulled out his cell phone and started Googling pizza places. Time to get some food before his stomach ate itself.

<center>~~~</center>

Lara felt terrible, despite her amusement. How the hell had she forgotten to cancel her big date with Johnny? Oh, right. Kristin had needed her help, and Amelia had made them late to ballet class. Lara had been playing catch-up ever since when she should have cancelled her date.

Then again, this gave her an insight into his character. She might have expected a bit of attitude. God knew she wouldn't have been pleased to get all dressed and cleaned up only to be cancelled on at the last minute. Johnny had taken the news with good humor and patience. She sighed. *So much to like about this guy.*

"I like Johnny, Aunt Lara. He's pretty." Kay smiled. *And…another one bites the dust.*

"He's gross. He's a boy." Amelia pouted and cried again when Lara rubbed her wet hair.

"Um, Amelia?" Lara called on her patience. "You might want to save the tears until *after* I put the shampoo in your hair. It can't fall into your eyes if it's not on you, can it?"

"I'm practicing." Amelia glowered. Darker where Kay was light, she and her sister looked enough like each other to obviously be siblings. They were smart, beautiful, and loving…most of the time.

And devious as hell.

"I'm hungry." Kay rubbed her belly.

"Me too." Amelia squeezed her eyes shut when she saw the bottle of kid shampoo in Lara's hands. "And Johnny isn't pretty. Boys are ugly."

"Even Josh?" Kay taunted.

"Not Daddy. The others are though. *Sean* is." Amelia stuck out her tongue.

"Nuh-uh. He's the best dad there is. Better than stupid Josh," Kay fumed, and her eyes filled. "You take that back."

"No."

Sensitive about their paternity, the girls could always be counted on to engage each other in a knockdown fight if yapping about their fathers. Of Kristin's baby-daddies, Lara preferred Sean, who sent his monthly child support without issue and had begged to be involved in his daughter's life when he'd been living in the city. But after years of no possibility of reconnecting with Kristin and having to work around an impossible schedule to see his daughter, he'd eventually moved out of state to a better job.

Josh wanted nothing to do with either Kristin or his child. He sent his support payments and did nothing more than the law demanded of him. Poor Amelia had been only a baby when he'd left, so she didn't exactly miss him. Lara might have grown up without much in the way of material things, but she'd had a father who loved her and still did. "Girls, no more fighting. If you're good, popcorn for snack later. Okay?" Lara had no problem bribing them. She'd had her share of drama today, dealing with an unexpected snag with her registration at the college. Her financial aid had hit a hiccup, and dealing with the registrar had given her a headache. So jumping to Kristin's aid hadn't helped her frustration level any.

"*I* won't fight." Kay rocked on her heels and glared at her sister. "You should give me the popcorn. But not any for Amelia-Eelia. Eel-girl."

"I'm not an eel!"

"Slimy and fishy and smelly. Ew."

Dear Jesus. "Kay, enough." When Lara used the firm voice, the girls usually stopped. Kay shut her mouth and said no more. "I'm going to finish with Amelia's bath. Kay, you can watch TV, since you already finished your reading. Then we'll play a game together. But if you keep fighting, I'll make you baked beans for dinner"— which they hated—"and put you to bed early. Got it?"

"Okay. I'll be good. Promise." Kay skipped out of the room while Lara finished fighting Amelia in the tub. Of course the girl got soap in her eyes from squirming, despite Lara telling her to hold still. The water had run down her face, bringing the soap along with it. Cartoon laughter came from the living room, drowning out the girl's wails.

Ten minutes later, she'd dried Amelia and shoved her into pink fleece footed-pajamas decked out with dancing unicorns. She carried the cranky girl into the living room, grateful at least Kay had calmed down.

"Kay, how about a pizza for—You're still here?" She hugged Amelia tighter and stared at Kay and *Johnny* sitting on the floor, looking at Kay's books.

"Well, hello there. You must be the streaker," Johnny said to Amelia.

She picked her head off Lara's shoulder to study him. "He's not pretty," she mumbled and turned her head away.

Johnny smirked.

"I didn't say you were," Lara said. "That was Kay."

"You are. For a boy, you're pretty." Kay didn't seem to mind Johnny, which Lara found interesting. Since dealing with so many of Kristin's husbands and boyfriends, she pretty much either ignored or disdained anything male, with the exception of her grandfather. But she sat close to Johnny and had let him near her precious books.

"Thanks. I'm not only pretty, though. I'm super awesome. Did you know I beat your aunt at War?"

"No way." Kay's eyes widened. "That's pretty good. I beat her once, but Amelia never wins."

"I do too." Amelia struggled to be put down.

Lara dropped her mutinous niece to her feet and watched her stomp over to her sister and Johnny.

"Oh, wow. Are those unicorns?" He blinked. "And pink too? That's my favorite color."

"It—huh?" Amelia's tirade stopped before it had begun. "Really?"

"Yep. A lot of people think pink is only a girl's color, but I once saw a smokin' hot Mustang in a bright pink, and it was amazing. Great detail work on the car, but I mean, the color helped."

"Really? A pink car?" Amelia sidled closer to Johnny.

"Yep. And unicorns are legendary."

Lara would never have guessed he would be so natural with children. Johnny didn't use a fake voice or talk down to the girls. He simply talked to them on their level. She listened for a good two minutes while he and Amelia discussed the magic of a unicorn's horn, the animal's size, and favorite unicorn color before she had to cut in.

"I'm sorry to interrupt, but, Johnny, why are you still here?"

"I'm hungry."

"Me too." Amelia sat down next to him.

"We're having pizza," Kay announced from Johnny's other side. She picked up a book and held it out to him. "This one, okay?"

He glanced at it. "Well, I don't know. Are you sure that's age appropriate?"

Lara looked at the book, saw it had Kay's favorite characters on the cover, and then saw Kay blush.

"Yes. Skadi fights monsters. She's a half-giant. And she—"

"Johnny?" Lara cut in. When Kay got started on her favorite series, the girl could talk without cease.

"Hey, you said I *could* go home. Not that I should." He put on a wounded face. "Do you want me to go? And after I ordered pizza for us all?"

"No, Aunt Lara," Kay disagreed. "He should stay."

Amelia nodded. "He's kind of pretty now. And he likes unicorns. And he got pizza."

"Well, I mean, I'm fine with it. I just didn't think you'd, ah, want to." She felt foolish. But what grown man wanted to play with little girls unless he had sordid inclinations? Though she could be way wrong, Johnny didn't seem the type.

"I came over to play with *you*," he emphasized with a grin, as if reading her mind. "But I can share. How about we all eat pizza, and while we wait, Kay reads me this story about Sara—"

"Skadi," Kay corrected.

"Right. Skadi. When the pizza comes, we'll eat and talk about unicorns and whatever else little girls like. Then you and I can play War again."

"You really want to?" Baffling. Maybe he had meant all that bullshit about not having sex again and getting to know her.

"Yep. I have nothing else to do."

"You can play with us," Kay offered.

"Why not? Since Johnny obviously has nothing better to do." She felt jealous of his free time. *There. I admit it. I want to have nothing to do too.* But homework was a mainstay in her life, for the next three terms at least. *Just think, one more year.*

"Nope, not a thing," he said. "Not even some studying for…what is that? Abnormal psychology?"

"That's an older book I was looking through. I have lecture and clinicals now."

"Aunt Lara's going to be a nurse," Kay said with pride. "She's smart."

Johnny stared at her with such intensity she felt the burn of his attention all the way to her bones. "So I hear." Then he gave her that naughty grin that did bad things to her libido. "I can't wait to see her in her uniform."

The girls turned to him, and she gave him a subtle finger.

He chuckled and answered the girls' questions about what he thought nurses and doctors did, most of which he'd obviously gleaned from *Grey's Anatomy*.

The pizza was due to arrive twenty minutes later, and throughout their wait, Lara watched Johnny charm her nieces with little effort. He knew enough about mythology to entertain and ask the right questions of Kay, and his love of all things pink had already endeared him to Amelia. The girl sat in his lap, for goodness sake.

Yet through it all, he continued to glance from her to the girls. Seeking a resemblance, maybe? It was weird, and it made her feel funny. More maternal.

Hell no. No biological ticking time bomb. Just. No.

A knock at the door distracted her from her fixation on the devilish Johnny Devlin, and she moved to answer it. But Johnny nudged Amelia to the floor and vaulted to his feet to meet her at the door. "I'll get it."

"But—"

"Kay's reading. Cover for me." He nudged her back to Kay.

"Fine. But I'm paying." She tried to hand him a credit card, which he refused.

"Don't worry. We'll settle up after."

Mollified if not pleased at his taking charge—because damn it, she *liked* being taken care of by someone else— she sat and listened to Kay read through to the end of her chapter.

By the time Kay had finished, Johnny had the pizza on plates, and cups of water and juice at the table. Amelia rushed over to help him set the napkins. Kay joined them, and the three sat and waited for Lara.

She sat with the small group, watching him and waiting for his next move. Charming the girls? Nicely done. Arranging for dinner? Smooth. But setting the table and being polite, then getting her nieces to follow his lead? Priceless.

She swallowed a lump in her throat, knowing the girls might never have this with a man they could call Dad. "Thank you, Johnny." She gave the girls a look.

They both thanked him and dug into the pizza.

He'd ordered extra cheese pizza from her favorite place. She ate a slice and had to force herself not to inhale the rest of the pie. When Amelia needed another napkin, Lara left the table to fetch it. On her way back, she leaned close to whisper in his ear, "Don't think this is getting you bonus points, buddy. I'm on to you." Not really, but she felt at a disadvantage for some reason.

When she sat and saw his wide smile, she knew she'd been right about…something.

"You know, girls, your aunt is pretty smart. But she's too slow when it comes to pizza." He stole a slice when she would have put it on her plate.

"You'll pay for that." She tried to appear stern but couldn't stop smiling.

"Yeah, yeah."

"Be careful, Johnny," Kay said. "Aunt Lara always gets even. Mom said she's a real pain. Even grown-up."

"Your mother is such a flatterer." Lara wanted to shove a boot up Kristin's butt. At least the woman was working, but Kristin could have done a better job than taking for granted that her family would always watch her kids. Lara loved them, no question, but she didn't have free time out the ass. Hell, no one in her family did. Her dad's one concession to slowing down in his later years was to play poker once a month with "the guys." Whoop-dee-friggin'-doo.

Johnny wolfed down his slice and eyed another piece.

"Go ahead." She nodded to it. "They'll eat maybe one more piece between them. And I can only eat one more. You're a growing boy. You need it."

"You don't have to twist my arm." He grabbed the pizza and ate while they all watched.

"Wow. He eats more than Grandpa."

"Cause he's big." Amelia nodded. "Ron was big."

Johnny snorted. "Ron's a dick."

"*Johnny*," Lara sputtered.

"Well, he is."

Amelia and Kay giggled.

"Sorry." Johnny's cheeks flushed. "He's not a nice guy."

"No," Kay agreed, still grinning. "We don't like him at all. He used to leave his dirty socks around, and they were really gross."

"And he's bossy." Amelia's smile grew wider. "He's a dick."

Lara pinched the bridge of her nose. "Can we talk about something else, please?"

"He's a dickity dick dick," Amelia said with relish.

Kay kept giggling.

Johnny coughed to mask his laughter, but she heard it anyway. "Sorry about that."

"A great big—"

"*Amelia*," Lara cut in before the girl could repeat herself. "You're close to getting a mouthful of soap, missy. You know that's a bad word." To Johnny, she explained, "She's said it before."

"Amelia's a potty mouth," Kay shared.

Lara huffed. "She gets it honestly—from her mother."

"Right. So, let's change the subject." Johnny put his half-eaten pizza crust down. "What about Aunt Lara?" Johnny asked. "Does she date any mean, bossy guys?"

"Really?" She snorted. "Extorting information from my nieces?"

"Mom says Aunt Lara's like a nun," Kay offered, free of charge. "She never goes out."

"I do too. I just don't tell your mother everything."

"Yeah? Who was your last date, not including me?" Johnny asked.

"You went on a date with pretty Johnny?" Kay asked, wide-eyed. "Wow."

Johnny nodded. "I like the nickname. Pretty Johnny. It's catchy. Now answer the question, Aunt Lara." His unrepentant smile had her soon giving up the glare.

"I'm too busy to date. It's taking me way too long to get my nursing degree. Between working at Ray's, helping the family, and school, I'm—"

"Excuses. Everyone's got 'em." He pinned her with a green-eyed stare. "When was your last date besides me?"

"Fine. I don't know. Maybe…hmm. I think I went out with a friend of Sue's. Andy, maybe? We dated back in March. Or was it February? No, not Valentine's Day." She tried to remember. Sadly, it was far longer than V-Day since she'd had sex—not counting Johnny and his magic fingers.

She tingled just thinking about what they'd done and refused to meet his gaze. She took a bite of pizza and chewed slowly, getting her mind out of the gutter. When she met his gaze again, she saw confusion. "What?"

"I don't get you. You're gorgeous," he said bluntly. "Smart and hard working. How are you not hooked up with some guy by now?" He paused, studying her. "Nope. I don't see crazy eyes either."

"Thanks, so much," she said drily. "Like I said, I'm busy. And I'm selective. You really should count yourself lucky I lowered myself to go out with you."

He laughed. "Oh yeah. Totally lucky. I had fun the other night." His eyes darkened, and she knew he had to be remembering their time on the couch. Oh hell. He glanced over at it, and his smile grew wider.

"So, kids, how about we make Johnny play with us after dinner?"

"Yes!" Kay jumped from her seat, fetched a board game, and returned with it.

"No." Amelia pushed her pizza around. "I wanted to play Chutes and Ladders."

"That's for babies." Kay frowned.

"Why can't we play more than one game?" Johnny asked. "I like Chutes and Ladders, myself. But Kay's game looks like fun too."

The girls brightened up and chattered about anything Johnny wanted to talk about. Cars, lizards, Barbie. Lara watched it all, amazed at his skills, not to mention breadth of knowledge. He was like the pied piper of women, both young and old.

"I don't know how you do it," she said after the girls had excused themselves and put their plates away. The little hooligans sat on the living room floor, setting up the games.

"Do what?"

"You can charm anything with two X chromosomes. I've seen you at Ray's, and now I've witnessed it firsthand."

"I'm a talented guy." He stood and carried his plate to the sink.

She followed and dumped hers, then gasped when he turned quickly, right in her space.

"Oh, sorry." He didn't look sorry. He looked clever and wicked and smug. "I told you I grew up with a lot of women. My dad dated a lot."

"He sounds like my sister."

"Well, unless your sister likes guys who take their clothes off for a living, she's not like Jack Devlin."

"Oh. Right."

"I told you my dad has a type. He's had a lot of girlfriends throughout the years. None that stuck, unfortunately. But I've grown up around women. Single women, women with kids, around their kids. Trust me. I know a ton about girls."

"Not according to Foley," she taunted.

"Please. He's still afraid of Sue." Johnny snorted. "And he's not nearly as bright or sexy as I am." He stared into her eyes. "You're not hot for him, are you?"

She blinked. "For Foley?"

"The no-neck with all the tats. Yeah."

What a question. "He's good-looking. A girl would have to be blind not to notice that. And he's a nice guy."

"He's really not."

"He's got an amazing body." She started to like this annoy-Johnny game.

"So do I."

"I wasn't aware you were competing." She leaned closer, saw his gaze go straight to her mouth, and felt her heart race. She placed her hands on his chest, and he drew in a deep breath, letting it out slowly. "If it makes you feel any better, he's not my type."

"Yeah?"

"I like my men big, strong, and able to take a punch. Ones who know what unicorns are."

His frown turned into a sexy smile. "I like pink too. I'm in touch with my feminine side. Really." He ran a finger down her cheek. "In fact, I want to be in touch with *your* feminine side."

She laughed.

"If I beat you at Chutes and Ladders, will I win a kiss?"

"I suppose." She dropped her hands from his broad chest before she forgot herself and started groping him with her nieces just on the other side of the kitchen counter. "But I'm pretty good at games. Just ask the girls."

"I will."

And he did.

"She really likes when you pet her hair," Amelia told him.

"She hates dark chocolate, like me," Kay said. "We like milk chocolate best. The kind with stuff inside. Caramels, coconut, white cream. But especially strawberry."

"Aunt Lara loves strawberries," Amelia finished, though it came out like *stwawberries*.

The minutiae continued, until Lara lost at Sorry, Connect Four, and Chutes and Ladders. A tough night to lose, especially because Johnny kept a tally.

"That's three you owe me." He winked at her, glanced at her mouth, and started whistling.

"On that note, come on, girls. Time for bed."

"Aw, Aunt Lara." Amelia moped.

"But we have a guest," Kay tried.

"I am a guest," Johnny agreed. Then he stood and lifted the girls in both arms, making them squeal. "A guest who likes to tell bedtime stories."

Lara could have kissed him for that alone. She made them brush their teeth and go to the bathroom before hopping into her bed. Johnny ambled into the room, no doubt tired of waiting. It didn't escape her notice he took a good long look at her room. Invading her privacy under the guise of telling stories. Clever guy.

"Would you mind if I cleaned up the kitchen?"

"No problem. I offered a story." He nodded. "Trust me. I'll keep it clean."

"You'd better." She took her time doing the small amount of dishes and taking the pizza box down the hallway to the recycle chute. She returned in time to see him stroke their hair and smile down at something Kay was saying. A tender moment she wished she might have missed. How the hell could she pretend not to like him when he did things like that?

Especially because when Amelia reached out for Lara, he spun around with a flush on his cheeks. Johnny then ducked away with a muttered, "All yours."

She kissed the girls and tucked them into bed, then wandered into the living room, prepared to see the night through. All her assumptions and plans when it came to Johnny Devlin had turned sideways, and her ideas about her priorities in life felt murky.

And it was all his fault.

She had an idea of where she planned to end things this evening. And they weren't even close to getting there. Not yet.

Chapter 10

JOHNNY WAITED ON THE COUCH, WEIRDED OUT BY how much fun he'd had playing games with an eight- and four-year-old. Not to mention their hot aunt. *Fuck*. Lara was killing him. She looked so damn pretty, and so natural with her nieces. She'd been teasing and fun, full of laughter but not so giddy she'd let the girls push her over.

Unlike the women from his own childhood, Lara had a vested interest in the girls, and it showed. She was their aunt, yes, but she genuinely loved them. And they loved her.

So much so, Kay had decided to play matchmaker in lieu of a story.

Aunt Lara liked roses and violets. Purple was her favorite color. She didn't like cheese unless it topped a pizza or sandwich, and she liked boys who were nice to her parents. She fought with her sister, and sometimes she said bad words when she didn't think the girls were listening. She worked super hard to become a nurse, and she'd never had anyone's help but her own.

How Kay seemed to know so much was no accident. The girl considered herself a spy-in-the-making and eavesdropped on all kinds of conversations. He planned to get her alone again at some point in the future for more intel. As it was, she'd given him the info for free, but he'd donated a dollar for her thorough information anyway.

Now, sitting on the couch in the living room and nursing a beer, he wondered about what a grand time he'd had. Pizza and silly games with a woman and two kids, none of which belonged to him.

Yet.

Still pondering how to get to the endgame he wanted with Lara, he nearly jumped when she appeared out of the dim hallway to join him by the couch. With only the TV to illuminate the darkened space, he saw her in the flicker of cartoon sea life.

His pulse racing, he swore. "Shit. You scared me."

"I walk softly. Always have." She smirked at him and grabbed the TV remote. "No more cartoons, please." She changed the channel to a police procedural, then sat next to him.

"So. The girls good? Should I turn down the TV?"

"It's okay. I closed the door to the bedroom. The girls are fine. I swear Amelia's eyes closed before I hit the light, and Kay was yawning so hard I'm surprised she didn't crack her jaw. They're pretty tuckered out. It's not every day they get the amazing Johnny Devlin as an esteemed guest."

He smiled. "You're not mad I stuck around?"

"Are you kidding?" She grabbed his hand and squeezed. "You were so good with them tonight. Thanks." She held him tight, and he loved the feeling of her hand in his. Just touching her made his entire world right. "It's good for them to see that not all men—who aren't Grandpa—are assholes."

"Language."

She sighed. "I know. But it's true. So many of my sister's bad choices have fallen on the girls. Oh, nothing terrible. Nothing abusive," she said to forestall his next question. "It's just, they've never seen a man and woman in love. My parents are an example, I guess, but they're so busy all the time. And well, they're older. It's not the same as seeing your own mom and dad together, loving and laughing. Not that that's us or anything," she added quickly, "but you get what I'm saying."

"I do." He pulled her into his side and tucked an arm around her shoulders. Not smart, because a wave of her subtle, floral perfume went straight to his head…and his dick. He prayed she wouldn't notice. "You're a great example for the girls."

"Of a single woman working her ass off. Just like my parents, except I'm not married." She sighed. "At least I can help my sister out. She's a moron most days—and I mean that in a loving way."

He snorted.

"But she's trying to do right. She's working with my mom at the diner. Typically, for Kristin, working means finding a man to support her, so doing for herself this time is a step up."

"Hard to believe you're related. Between school and Ray's, you're pretty busy. And you've been working there for four or five years, right?" He could still remember the first time he'd seen her. He'd sucked in a breath and felt everything just stop.

"Almost five, yeah." She snuggled into him, and he had to suppress a groan. "Before Ray's, I was working just to pay the bills. I didn't want to dive into a career or anything right out of high school. I waitressed for a bit, worked retail. But minimum wage gets real old real fast."

"Tell me about it."

"You're a mechanic. You get more than that an hour, don't you?"

"Actually, I get twenty percent of labor costs. So you figure with what Liam and Del are undercharging the folks of greater Seattle, I'm *way* underpaid for my skills."

They shared a laugh. He felt warm all over, content in a way that was both foreign and more than welcome.

"You do have talent, I'll admit." She moved even closer to him, so her breasts pushed into the side of his chest.

He had a hard time not moving to cup her soft flesh. Instead, he clutched her shoulder and ordered himself to be good. "Um, Lara?"

"You beat me at all the games we played. I owe you three kisses."

"You do." He sounded hoarse, so he cleared his throat. "But keep it clean, woman. Remember, this is a no-sex date."

"Why no sex? Not that I'm offering, just curious."

Bummer. "Because we're getting to know each other without complications." And did he feel like a first-class jackass suggesting they abstain. But it felt right.

"Sex is a complication?"

She slid an arm around his belly, hugging him, and he tensed under her, unable to help it.

"Yeah. It gets people thinking, wanting. Clouding judgment."

"Kind of like drinking, hmm?" She moved her hand from his upper belly down his abdomen, and his body hardened into solid rock.

"What are you doing?" His brain fogged over as her hand inched nearer his cock.

"I'm petting Pretty Johnny," she teased. "The girls really liked you."

"I liked them too," came out as a growl.

"You're so sweet. But the best part is that it isn't an act, is it?"

"I'm a dickhead. Ask anyone." *Shouldn't have said dick, because now she's noticing. Fuck.*

"I have," she murmured. "They agree. You can be a first-class jerk."

"See?"

"But you're also a terrific guy with commitment issues. Thing is, I'm not trying to scare you. I just want to pay back my debt."

"Huh? What? I don't... Oh, damn. What are you doing?"

Her clever fingers had found bare skin under his shirt, and she was scratching her nails up his belly, lightly enough to not hurt, but hard enough to be felt. She might as well have gripped him around the shaft and stroked. He loved his belly touched. A happy zone she'd not-so-innocently wandered into.

"Lara, what—"

"Shh. You'll wake the girls. Let's just watch TV together and enjoy."

He couldn't think with her rubbing his stomach. Especially because she seemed to get a perverse enjoyment out of scratching down to the hem of his jeans, toying with the button of his fly before dragging toward his navel again. Back and forth. Slower each time.

His erection pushed against his restrictive clothing, and he ached.

"So can I ask you a question?"

"You can have my car if you keep touching me like that," he rasped.

He didn't have to see her smile to know it was there.

"Do you practice safe sex?"

His cock fucking jumped. "What kind of question is *that*?"

"One I want answered."

Those damn nails of hers veered to the waist of his jeans and lingered. He fought the urge to buck toward her with a cock needing attention. "Of course I use protection. I'm not stupid."

"So does that mean you always use condoms? Or that you're just good at pulling out before you come?"

Shit, shit, shit. She'd said *come. Condom.* She was asking about sex. Why did he think fucking her would not be in his best interests again? Something about rules and being memorable and wanting her to view him as more than a—

"*Lara*," he garbled on a strangled whisper.

The vixen had unsnapped his jeans and parted his fly. She ran her hand over his obvious hard-on through his boxer-briefs, no doubt noticing the huge and growing wet spot.

"Let's see what's under here."

"But, but I…" He helped despite not meaning to. When she tugged at his underwear, he lifted off his ass to help her pull it down.

Then his cock was bare, stiff, and standing tall.

"You *are* a big boy," she said and grinned up at him.

"Jesus. What are you doing?" He suddenly recalled the girls and froze.

"Easy, Johnny." Lara put her hand over him and squeezed, and he feared coming then and there. "I'll hear the bedroom door before anyone's even close." She paused and tilted her head up. "Now about those kisses I owe you…" She puckered up and kept her hot hand around his dick.

He couldn't stop himself from leaning down to kiss her.

More like ravage her. The moment his lips met hers, she started pumping him in slow drags of her palm. He licked and nibbled her lips, then pushed his tongue into her mouth and palmed her head, increasing the pressure.

The witch kept priming him, and he feared going off. So fucking hot having her seduce him like this. He hadn't thought she had it in her. He continued to kiss her, thrusting with his tongue and his cock in time.

Then she dragged her mouth away and trailed kisses down his throat to his neck.

He moaned and leaned his head back, lost to everything but her touch. She stopped kissing in one spot and then sucked like a damn vacuum. The bite of pain made him jerk, and he felt a burst of fluid leave him. She used it to lube her hand.

"Lara, baby." He thrust with her, in and out of her grip. So when she stopped jerking him off, he wanted to cry. "What—Oh, fuck, *yes*."

Lara's hair tickled his exposed thigh. Her breath washed over the head of his dick, and then she engulfed him. Her slick lips took the head of his shaft, then eased down the base of him, stopping midway. His balls felt like stones, rock hard and so ready to release it embarrassed him.

"Gonna come. So hard…" he groaned. "Wait, I…"

She moved over him, taking him deeper before pulling back. Up and down, she bobbed, and he finally found the energy to pull his head forward and open his eyes, watching that glorious ponytail wash back and forth over his leg while she blew him but good.

He couldn't hold back, not after seeing her do him.

From the hallway outside the apartment, footsteps sounded. She sucked harder, and her lips looked so red around his cock. He swore he saw her doorknob turn but couldn't bring himself to stop her. Then Lara was taking him deeper and rubbing his balls.

"I'm there," he warned when she shoved down and took him to the back of her throat. "Yes, yes," Johnny hissed and gripped her bound hair, holding her steady while he jetted down her throat. "Oh God. Fuck yeah."

Lara moaned as she swallowed him, and he continued to come, enraptured and out of his mind with lust. He swore he heard a roar inside himself, a rush of light and color and emotion as he finally spent inside the mouth of the woman he'd been fantasizing about for years.

When he'd given her everything, she pulled back, wiped her lips, and winked at him.

"So our three kisses are over. Too bad. It was just getting good."

He stared at her, out of breath and out of mind, thinking he'd never seen a woman more beautiful in his fucked-up life.

Lara continued to grin as she tucked his semi-hard cock back into his briefs and jeans. She took care zipping and buttoning him back up while he could only watch her in wonder. For the life of him, he hadn't seen this coming.

No pun intended.

He wanted to say something but had no idea what.

A knock at the door had her on her feet and him finally waking up. She checked the peephole before letting a gorgeous blond into the apartment. Had to be the sister, because little Kay was her spitting image.

"Thanks, sis. And I'm sorry I—" She blinked at Johnny, still sitting, stunned, on the couch. "And who is this?"

Behind her, Lara rolled her eyes. "This is my friend Johnny. Johnny, meet my sister Kristin—Amelia and Kay's mom."

Johnny stood up, relieved his legs would hold him. Lara acted as if nothing had happened between them while greeting her sister. It almost made him wonder if he'd imagined her taking him to heaven with her hands and mouth. "Hi. Nice to meet you."

"Nice to meet *you*." Even in a well-used waitress uniform of dull mustard and muddied white, Kristin had a mesmerizing beauty no exhaustion could hide. It was easy to see how Lara's sister had accumulated so many male friends in what had to be no more than thirty years. Kristin could have starred in her own showcase at Strutts. She had large breasts, a tight, round ass, and long legs. She stood an inch or two shorter than Lara, but whereas Lara had an athletic figure and all the right curves, Kristin put a man in mind of nothing but sex. She was all handfuls and a wavy blond mane. Normally his type.

But looking at her, he only appreciated her physical beauty. He took a step closer to Lara, still captivated by his tricky little nurse.

A thoughtful look crossed her face. "Johnny charmed the pants off the girls. Oh, and he bought us pizza." She turned to him. "I guess I still owe you."

"Yeah, you do." He saw the gleam of merriment in her eyes and knew she thought she'd bested him. She had—no question—but no way he'd concede she'd won anything in their unspoken battle of wills. He pulled her close for a kiss, right in front of her sister. "I'll collect, don't think I won't. You owe me a dinner. My place next time. I'll text you." So saying, he pulled back, nodded to her sister, and left.

He made it inside his car before he collapsed into the all-body shiver he'd been suppressing. *Good God. The woman sucked the life out of me.* Willingly, without being coerced. His sexy nurse had a naughty side to her he hadn't expected.

He smiled and broke out into laughter. Somehow he'd gotten sex while trying his best to remain celibate. *I really am The Man.* Too bad he couldn't share that with the guys. Lara was too important to waste on immature kiss-and-tell.

What need did he have to brag when he had the real deal? For as long as he had her, he intended to make the most of his relationship that wasn't exactly a relationship. What it was, he didn't know. But he refused to jinx his chances by making more of his feelings than he should…whatever those feelings might be.

Lara considered finally telling her sister about Ron's attack. She'd debated and decided not to tell her parents. More stress on top of financial worries would only burden them needlessly. After studying Kristin's chipped fingernails, sagging ponytail, and tired eyes, she realized she wouldn't be helping her sister with the truth either.

What would knowing about the attack do for anyone?

Ron would deny it, despite witnesses. After all, the "riffraff" at Ray's wouldn't stand up to bullying from his lawyers. And God knew Ray couldn't exactly afford legal people poking their noses into his business. Besides, if Lara kept quiet, Ron might believe she was playing nice. With any luck, he'd forget about the incident and give Kristin the settlement she deserved.

"Now that Johnny is one fine man." Kristin's eyes lit up. "A new *friend* of yours, you say? Just how friendly are you two?"

Lara refused to answer questions about Johnny, other than to say she knew him from Ray's. Her sister finally took the hint and stopped asking about him. She woke the girls and took the sleepy cuties home. Lara helped by carrying Kay—who seemed to weigh a ton, despite looking as light as a feather—to the car.

She hurried back into her apartment, suddenly more tired than she could stand. She sank into bed and didn't wake until seven the next morning. Her dreams had been filled with Johnny's smiling face, and no wonder.

"I really blew him. Right here in my apartment." She stood in her ratty robe in her living room, staring down at her magical couch.

She couldn't say why she'd gone down on Johnny last night. Like him, she agreed that no sex was best. It did complicate matters. But hearing him deny her, somehow sensing he meant it, not as some ploy to manipulate her but because he felt the truth of wanting to get to know her, had softened her. She'd already been a marshmallow after watching him with the girls.

Most guys thought "nice" was the kiss of death, but Lara wanted that dichotomy of nice in real life and a little mean in bed.

She clutched her robe tightly, remembering how thick and long he'd been, how much she'd swallowed when he'd come down her throat. She normally wasn't big on blowing a guy, and not one she wasn't even seeing steadily. But something about Johnny made her want to put her mark on him, to make it impossible for him to forget her. She might be a pretty brunette that worked at Ray's, the one girl he hadn't yet been able to get with. But she'd make sure once they *did* hit the sheets, naked all the way, she'd be more than memorable.

She had to admit it had been fun taking charge of such a stud. Lara normally let her dates handle the romantic aspect of things. Sure, she pulled the brakes when the intimacy rolled too fast or too far. But she let her dates lead the way.

Last night had been a complete shift from the norm. Lara didn't do casual flings. He hadn't used a condom, and she insisted on safe sex from her partners. She wanted to believe he'd been safe, but she couldn't be sure. Her pathology classes came to mind. Blowing him when others might have done the same thing with less than clean mouths—meh, something she didn't want to think about.

Sexual stupidity be thy name, girl.

Once again, done in by a pretty face. And a pretty personality, terrific sense of humor, gorgeous body, huge cock that—She fanned herself. She'd been close to getting off herself while doing him, but she'd been so focused on his pleasure she hadn't been able to wait. But thinking about him revved her engines all over again.

What had she expected from him afterward? Not a challenge, that was for sure. A thank-you, maybe. A sly wink and an "It's been fun. See you at Ray's." But another date?

She'd already been easy. Twice. He wanted a third time? Perhaps once they did the full deed, he'd lose interest. A perverse part of her wanted to push him, to see how far he'd string her along for affection. Another part didn't care about his intentions, because for once she wanted just to have fun and not care so much about the repercussions. Besides, they were friends. She'd known him for years. Was he really such a casual two-night stand?

Her cell phone made a loud, obnoxious quacking sound, and she realized if she didn't get a move on, she'd be late for class. Her second clinical at the hospital, so no time for dilly-dallying.

Yet instead of the rush of pleasure she normally felt when getting a chance to act like a real nurse, helping patients, she lamented her time away from Johnny.

Damn it. She missed him already. Priorities had shifted, and she didn't like it. As expected, being with Johnny tempted her to put him at the forefront of her thoughts.

She showered, hoping to rinse off memories as easily as she soaped off her grime, but had little luck in forgetting his sexual release. By the time she'd dressed in her bright blue scrubs and arrived at the hospital, she still felt overheated.

Time to regroup and focus. Center yourself. Think work, not Johnny. And no more sex on the brain! Lara took a few deep breaths in the car, concentrated on the here and now, and crashed into someone on her way to the elevator.

"I'm so sorry." And late if she didn't hurry. She helped the cute guy to his feet then jumped into the elevator before it left, the doors closing on his own apologies.

She made it to changeover and learned she'd be accompanying Nurse Angi Clement for the day. Cha-ching. Though last week she'd done her shift with Nurse Vu, a succinct perfectionist who kept chitchat to a minimum, she'd heard from a classmate that Nurse Clement—who preferred just "Angi"—was amazing. She answered all types of questions, encouraged a more personal approach in her mentoring, and shared her own perceptions of what to look out for with patients on the floor.

"You look happy today," Angi said, a bright smile on her face. The woman appeared to be in her late to mid-fifties and possessed an air of competence and confidence Lara envied.

Lara smiled back. "I am. I'm back on the floor and wearing my favorite scrubs. This is what I've been look-ing forward to since I first started the program." Though she'd had a less hands-on time in clinicals and with labs during her prior term, she would get to be much more involved at this stage.

"Outstanding. Then let's get to it."

Lara spent the next few hours doing real work. She performed a full-body assessment on a new admission. Under Angi's guidance, she also checked a frequent flier's—a repeat patient's—blood sugar levels. Since Tom suffered from diabetic ketoacidosis and didn't like sticking to his dietary regimen, Lara was instructed to give him a shot of insulin. She had him state his name and date of birth, then verified it with his wristband and the care mobile unit. After Angi's approving nod, Lara carefully injected the needle into Tom's upper thigh, and trooper that he was, he didn't even flinch.

"Really, Tom. *Four-ten?* You need to get those levels down," Angi counseled while Lara finished inputting what she'd just done into a small digital reader, a care mobile device, then scanned Tom's wristband. Angi checked off on her work while Tom gave a few feeble excuses for lingering over cake and cookies instead of his strict protein and veggie diet.

"Have a heart, Angi." He turned to Lara and winked. "You're new. And cute."

"Your wife's just outside," Angi said drily.

"I know. Don't worry, she'd say the same thing." Tom patted his heart. "Between Angi and all the pretty nurses she brings with her to help, my blood sugar is probably going through the roof. A piece of cake isn't causing my problems. It's all the lovely women around the place."

"Nice try." Angi snorted.

Lara blushed and laughed. "You're good."

"That's what Anna tells me." Tom sighed. "But sadly for you gals, I'm taken."

"All the good ones are," Lara agreed. "So when they overdose on cupcakes at their granddaughter's birthday party, it saddens those of us who haven't yet found Mr. Right." She looked Tom in the eye. "My uncle's Type 2, and my aunt is always on him to eat right. Does your wife know what you did?"

"Well, sure."

"Really?" Angi cut in. "I bet she knew about that first piece of cake. What about the others?"

"Ha. Nailed it." Lara read his guilt all too easily. "Next time tell whoever made them to use a sugar substitute. I know agave and some of the non-sugar sweeteners out there are low on the glycemic index. Try those. My aunt makes a killer lemon cake using Truvia. It can be done."

"Fine, fine." Tom scowled, but his eyes were playful. "Stop nagging. Like I don't hear it from Anna enough."

"Did someone say my name?" Anna entered, a pretty woman with sparkling brown eyes and short black curls sprinkled with white. "What lies are you telling now, Tom?"

"And that's our cue to go." Angi chuckled. "Lara will be back to check on him in an hour. Anna, make sure he behaves."

"Will do."

Angi and Lara left, and Lara felt like a real nurse. She'd checked Tom's vitals, his blood sugar, and given him his medication. All while feeling supremely confident, enough to joke with her patient. With *Angi's* patient. She glanced at her advisor and saw Angi's grin.

"You're a natural. Great job, though Tom's an easy patient. I love seeing him and his wife, but I hate why we see them. What can I say? He's got a rampant sweet tooth."

"So does my uncle. Tom reminded me of him."

"You used just the right amount of humor and

instruction," Angi said as they walked down the hall. "Bedside manner is as important as medical knowledge. I know you've heard that time and time again, but it's true."

Nurse Kim Guyen passed by them with a harried student after her.

Angi glanced at Nurse Guyen, then looked back at Lara with a grim expression. "There's more to a hospital experience than dotting every *i*. Not that you don't still have to do that. One mistake with a patient can be his last."

Lara nodded. It had been drilled into her over and over again that patient identification remained priority number one. *Always know the patient before administering anything, even advice.*

"But after getting everything right on paper, you need to show compassion. No one ever wants to be here." Angi sighed as she led Lara to the nurse's station. "But while they're here, we want them to be as comfortable as they can be." She waved to patients passing by. "Now let's show you how to update the patient's charts in the system. I'm going to grab a coffee. Want anything?"

"No thanks." Lara was eager to work, to show Angi her capabilities.

"Fine. Be right back. Get the paperwork in order and be ready to input data when I get back. But wait for me before you do anything."

"I will." Her preceptor had to okay the data before Lara submitted patient information, and Lara could only do it while under her direct supervision.

As Lara looked over the information, seated among bustling hospital staff, patients, and their family and friends wanting them well, she felt as if she truly belonged. Ray's might be fun and pay the bills, but this fulfilled her on another level entirely. She wondered what Johnny would think if he could see her, then forced him to the back of her mind, *where he belonged.*

Unfortunately, it took a lot more concentration than she liked to tuck him away. But damn it, she'd do it, because her future career depended on keeping sharp.

When Angi finally returned, Lara smiled up at her, looking forward to the next few hours of their shift. "So, boss, what's next?"

Chapter 11

Friday night at Ray's, Lara once again poured her ass off. Beers, a few mixed drinks, and taking orders for the back kitchen kept her busy from seven through ten.

"What's going on with all the traffic?" she yelled over her shoulder to Rena and Sue as they bustled behind the bar. Between the loud acid rock, laughter, and shouting from a bunch of no-neck bikers, it was tough to be heard.

Rena moved next to her and handed a guy a bottle over the bar. "Some rally downtown, I think. A good one, not a gang thing. Bikers for autism awareness? Something like that." She grinned. "Men in leather. Yum."

Lara laughed. "Long as they remember jeans under the chaps."

"You're such a stick in the mud." Rena's grin turned evil. "It's a wonder Johnny wants *another* date."

Lara's cheeks felt hot. Stupid Johnny and his big mouth. Not that she didn't mind him mentioning it, but he'd been adamant he wouldn't. So much for keeping their new, weird "relationship" strictly between them. "He told you?"

"Ha. No, I read your phone. You had a few texts."

"Way to invade my privacy. Nice." She wasn't sure she liked her sense of relief that Johnny had remained quiet about them.

"Hey. I thought it might be important, and you know

you can't hear a thing in the bar. When I saw your phone light up, I thought your mom might need you or something." She handed Lara her cell. "Here you go."

"Liar." Lara tucked the thing into her back pocket and sighed. "So what did it say?"

"That Johnny hopes to see you later. And that since you get off at one tonight, you can either go home with him for a late dinner, or you guys can get together tomorrow. For date number three." Rena practically danced in place. "*Three?* What happened to one and two? When did you go out? What did you do?" Rena's eyes widened. "Did you do *him*?"

"Would you shut up." Lara's face was on fire. "I'll tell you about it all later. Hey, how did he know I get off at one?"

"You told him. Actually, your phone told him. I texted for you."

Lara groaned. "Don't let anyone else know about this, okay?"

"Fine. But you owe me details. You know my social life exists through you." Across from them at the bar, a big man belched. "Yeah, so not happening here."

Lara chuckled and continued to serve. It was like people were coming out of the woodwork. Ray had to be bursting at the seams. Not that the place didn't bring in customers, but a lot of them had tabs they'd keep open for days on end. Regulars kept the bar steady, but new clientele paid by the order.

By the far front of the bar, she saw Earl and Big J handling a few rowdy patrons. The motorcycle do-gooders, a group of rough-looking guys gathered for a decent cause, didn't seem involved. Yet. It was only a matter of time before some drunk banged into one of them and started a brawl.

She watched as a few of their regulars gave the group the evil eye. "Hey, Sue."

Sue sidled next to her and gave her a hip bump. "Yeah?"

"Five bucks says either Drew, Jim, or Red starts some stuff with the new guys."

"Oh, you're on. I'm thinking it'll be Henry." Sue had a point, because Henry found himself a fight every time he showed up to Ray's. "I hate to take your money. Sure you want to bet on Drew, Jim, and Red?"

Lara knew her favorite local hotheads would never make it past midnight without starting something. She nodded. "Five bucks." Foley and Sam walked into the bar, followed by Johnny. *I'm not excited by his presence; it's just the rush of anticipating a fight. Yeah right.* "One more thing. If I win, you have to be nice to Foley all night too."

"That's harsh." Sue frowned, and the piercings in her brows nearly touched. "Okay. I'm nice to Foley if I lose. I win, you're nice to Johnny."

"And you say *I'm* harsh? Fine, you're on." Was she really that bitchy to Johnny that Sue would make that part of the bet? Sure, Lara had been a little standoffish, maybe even taunting before, but mostly that was in fun—and to stop her from throwing herself at him. Of course, that was all before their "dating" status.

Rena knew. That made it official, in some weird way. Rena—the gossip queen—knew.

Someone moved off the stool in front of her, and a new customer took his place.

"Be right back. I swear, your order is next on my list." She hurried from the bar and grabbed Rena in the back.

"What?"

Lara tugged Rena's golden-brown hair, and in a low voice said, "Swear you'll say nothing about me and Johnny, or I'll straighten all your glorious curls one by one. The *hard* way."

Rena squealed when she pulled. "Swear! Now let go. And, girl, you owe me some serious deets."

"Whatever. Just keep it quiet, loudmouth."

"I'm hurt. I never—"

Lara walked out on the rampant gossiper and returned to the bar. She served the guy waiting then turned to see Foley and Sam muscling their way toward her, cutting a swath through the crowd like Moses parting the Red Sea. But with drunks.

Sam grunted when he saw her, but Foley had a charming grin on his face. "Hi, beautiful."

Johnny edged in next to him, irritating the man who'd been sitting near Foley, though the guy said nothing. "Hey, Lara." He glared at Foley. "She's busy. Quit flirting and order something."

Foley only smiled wider. "Sure, sure. A pitcher for me and Sam. And a virgin daiquiri for Johnny. Choir boy is trying to keep his head on straight, lately."

"Virgin, huh?" Sam didn't smile, but he did smirk a little.

"Ass. Gimme a bottle," Johnny said. "And one for the poor guy I'm half stepping on." He nodded at the guy next to him.

The guy, with a neck almost as thick as Foley's, tipped his beer at Johnny. "Thanks."

Sam rolled his eyes.

Foley snorted and said loudly enough to be heard by everyone in the general vicinity, "Always afraid of offending somebody. Jesus, Johnny. Grow a pair."

"Such a pussy," Sam growled.

Johnny ignored the guys and paid his bill. Lara slid one beer to the man beside him, then opened a bottle of Johnny's favorite and gave it to him. A roar in the crowd behind him turned their attention.

"Sue!" Lara pointed at the fracas, where Drew had an annoyed biker in a headlock while the biker's large friends tried to pry him free. Then the hitting started.

"Now that's a dude I'd hang with." Sam took the pitcher Lara gave him and strode away, for a table right near all the trouble. As soon as he sat, someone bumped into him. Sam shoved back. The biker straightened and said something to Sam that had Sam standing and glowering like a demon. He clenched his fists and ducked the first swing aimed at his face.

"Shit. This was supposed to be a fun Friday. Hey, Lara, run me a tab." Foley gave her a credit card she tucked into her pocket.

"Sure. Oh, and Foley, if Sue's not nice to you tonight, you tell me."

"Huh?"

"I won our bet."

Foley brightened up. "Aw, sweetheart, you bet on me?" He leaned over the bar and planted a quick kiss on her mouth. "I owe ya."

He darted next to Sam into the fight, which had turned into a free-for-all. At least she didn't need to worry about ducking behind the bar. The bikers had rallied around those throwing punches, keeping them from dragging anyone else into the scuffle. She turned to see Johnny scowling at her.

"What the hell was that?"

"What? *He* kissed *me*."

"Yeah, not happy about that either," he muttered. "But what do you care if Sue's nice to him or not? You're all into Foley now?"

Johnny acted…jealous. The man did not, as long as she'd known him, do jealousy. Even Rena had commented on his laid-back attitude toward women. While dating, he treated his partners with courtesy and fidelity, if not extended commitment. Flirting was no big deal.

Yet he seemed to continue to break all his own rules. He hadn't told anyone about them dating. And actually caring about Foley flirting with her?

Lara didn't like playing games, but she couldn't help herself. Not now, with Johnny looking so fierce. And friggin' hot. His green eyes burned, and his firm lips twisted. He had a hint of shadow on his jaw, his hair was tousled, and the T-shirt he wore, in flagrant defiance of the cold weather outside, showed off his thick biceps to perfection.

She swallowed a sigh at said muscles and teased, "Well, I put Foley in the bet with Sue, mostly to needle Sue. But that kiss… That was nice."

His scowl darkened. "*Nice?*"

"Sweet." She smiled and played with her ponytail. "Foley's a great guy."

"Sweet," he repeated. "Nice." His scowl faded, replaced by a slow smile. "I'll make sure to tell him you said that." He chuckled then leaned close. "So tonight? My place?"

She'd been thinking of nothing but his offer since Rena had blabbed. Was she ready for Johnny? Staring into his eyes, it took all her willpower not to close the distance between them and kiss him. "Okay. Tonight." She felt hot all over.

His satisfaction was impossible to miss. "I'll send you directions, but feel free to follow me real close. Hang on tight, like you *want it*—dinner at my place, I mean," he added with a wicked grin on his face.

"Oh stop. I'm busy, Devlin."

"You will be," he said as he moved away.

Then another customer grabbed her attention, and she lost Johnny in the crowd.

———

Johnny sat at the table next to Foley, who wiped blood from his mouth, and watched Sam duke it out with some seven-foot-tall freak who made Foley look small. An even match, until the pair just stopped fighting and stepped back from each other.

"Nice," Sam grunted.

"Not bad." The biker held out a bloody-knuckled hand and shook Sam's.

"Come to Strutts next week. I'll be bouncing there. Can get you in for a discount."

"Sounds good." The big guy and his friends cheered Sam then just walked away.

Sam skirted poor Drew on the floor and sat with them. But Drew had to be dragged out of the bar by Earl. The bastard didn't look so good.

"What the fuck, Sam?" Foley's tone didn't bode for a peaceful evening.

Johnny waited for the shit to hit the fan.

"I blew off a little steam. So what?" Sam downed a glass of beer and poured another.

"One of these days you're going to pick a fight with the wrong guy. Then you're on your own."

Sam stilled for a moment, met Foley's gaze, then looked away. "Yeah, whatever."

"I mean it."

Sam finished a second beer in record time. Johnny glanced at Foley, who hadn't taken his gaze from his friend.

"Sorry, okay?" Sam sounded defensive. "I just needed to relax a little."

Foley shook his head. "Dude, smoke some weed. I know, I know. You don't do drugs. Get laid or something. Chill the fuck out before you're locked up again."

"Again?" Johnny asked, concerned.

Foley explained, "This asshole got into a fight a few months back and got booked, but his accuser backed off, so no charges were filed."

"Seriously?" Johnny knew that like him, the pair had been imprisoned at a young age for something stupid. Nothing so cool as car theft, more like breaking into a house and getting caught, then carted off to prison for burglary.

Sam emptied the pitcher into his glass. "I thought we were just fooling around, but when the guy lost in front of his girlfriend, he turned me in."

"Until I talked to him and he changed his mind," Foley said.

"Does 'talked to him' mean you threatened with your fists or your mouth?" Johnny asked. "You do have a tendency to talk people to death."

Foley gave a grim smile. "I just told him what an asshole he'd look like to his girl and buddies if they knew he'd put my friend in jail for a friendly fight *he* started."

Johnny protested. "See? That's what I would have done. And you called me a pussy for it earlier."

"I didn't."

"I did," Sam admitted. Instead of downing his drink, he took measured sips. "And you are. But Foley did me a solid, so he's good."

"I'm so glad." Johnny snorted. "Nice double standard you have there, Hamilton."

Sam gave him a rare grin. Despite his fight, he had nothing more than bruised knuckles to show for it. And his hands normally appeared pretty worn. But hearing he'd been in a friendly fight a few months ago confirmed a suspicion Johnny had had about his friend.

"So, Sam...do the underground fights pay much?"

Foley swore under his breath. "One word, Devlin, I break you in half."

"Please. Who am I going to tell? Lou? Del?" Johnny snorted. "If Lou doesn't already know, he'll only want in on the action. Del might protest a little, but she'll never can Sam. She has a soft spot for him."

Sam flushed. "She does not."

"Yeah, she does," Foley said. "Count yourself lucky."

Johnny nodded. "And if Liam knew, he'd just go all fatherly on your ass and lecture you to behave. Kind of the way he's been giving advice to all of us forever. Hell, in the seven years I've been there, he's always telling me to stay on the straight and narrow. I get it after the first few years, but we're going on seven and a half.

Just the other day he reminded me not to joyride in our client's Camaro. Seriously?"

Foley grinned, seeming more at ease, as had been Johnny's intention. "Maybe because he overheard you and Lou fighting about it. Next time you boost a car, don't do Lou's project."

"I just wanted to make sure I still had it."

Sam added, "Gave him a heart attack that it was missing. Maybe you should do it again."

Johnny let out a breath of relief. Easy Sam was back. "He is a little too full of himself sometimes, isn't he?"

"Yeah, but God knows he's got skills." Foley used his finger to draw in the condensation on the table. "He'll be gone next week, working that paint job for Molarino's Corvette. I think he talked Mol into being a little more dynamic, though."

"Should turn out nice. Lou still putting together his work for that portfolio Liam told him to build?"

Sam nodded. Talk centered around the garage and some of their favorite rebuilds. Then, as usual, it degenerated into bitching about their favorite *worst* clients, namely the older women who came in to ogle the guys. Del had moved to put a stop to it, being all anti-sexual harassment, until Foley had told her it helped drum up business, and none of them cared. Liam had kindly told her to un-PC her head out of her ass, because he'd hired real men to work for him, not assholes.

Liam, Lord love him, had not quite jumped on the progressive bandwagon, and probably never would. He was fair, nonjudgmental, but truly old school.

"I love how we get ROP, and she's telling the lot of

us to 'fuck off' and 'hell if she's ever standing up for our male rights again.'" Foley grinned. "Classic Del."

"Yeah." Johnny loved his boss. "McCauley dicks her over, his ass is toast. Cute kid or not, he'll be going down."

Sam nodded and cracked his knuckles, looking fierce.

"Easy, big guy." Foley sighed. "You're supposed to be chilling, since you just worked out your aggression. You know what you need? Some woman to fuck the fight right out of you."

"Now who's not PC?" Johnny had to add. "Let me tell you about women, my friends."

Sam groaned and drank more.

Foley glanced at the bar then back at Johnny. "Really? Didn't we just have a talk about—"

"Women like romance," Johnny interrupted. "Now, I'm not talking about 'til death do us part. I'm talking about finding a nice girl to have some fun with. Like, say, the ladies at Strutts you two have been circling for weeks. Yeah, Sam. I saw you ogling Shaya. Now, you want a shot with her? Let me tell you all you need to know. Number one, respect more than her ass."

"Hey." Sam frowned. "I like her tits just as much."

Foley winced. "It's like he's not even trying to be a jackass. It's natural."

Sam told him to stick his head somewhere unpleasant. Foley responded in kind. And Johnny's words were lost beneath juvenile insults that had him laughing so hard he almost snorted beer through his nose.

Talk about a sweet night. He looked over at the crowd by the bar. A night about to get seriously sweeter, if he had his way. He glanced at his cell phone.

Just two more hours.

Just one hour and fifty-five minutes…and fifty-three minutes…fifty-two…

He groaned, realizing the clock would now move backward for him, and wondered if Lara looked forward to their date, or if she regretted agreeing to a late night with him. One that might or might not mean more than dinner.

As usual, he couldn't be sure of the look she'd shot him earlier. Did "dinner" mean sex or a real meal? Either way, his dick got hard anytime he remembered what she'd done with those lips.

He swallowed a sigh.

"I'll grab us another pitcher," Foley offered.

Johnny grabbed him by the arm, in no condition to get up just then. "Let Sam do it. And no kissing the bartender," he ordered.

Sam glanced from him to Foley, grinned again—the bastard—and left with an empty pitcher. He returned with a full one and a smirk. "I got cheek. Closer than Johnny's getting, huh?"

Foley laughed his ass off, but Johnny found nothing humorous about Sam or his cheek.

"Either one of you kisses her again, I'll wipe the floor with you." Before Sam could threaten, Johnny added, "I'm fast, and I'm smart. I'll outflank you in no time. And remember, I have an in with all the girls at Strutts. Think hard about your next comment."

Sam opened and closed his mouth. Then sat with a sigh. "You suck." He poured them all beers, having even brought Johnny a glass, then drank.

Johnny drank with him, pleased to have shut Sam up. Even Foley remained quiet. Now if only he could win over Lara as easily…

—⁓—

She followed him home without issue. He made sure to drive slowly enough so as not to lose her, after he'd texted her his address and directions. He really didn't want her bailing on his invitation.

The whole ride home he kept wondering how to handle tonight. Yeah, he wanted sex. He wanted it hard, slow, then fast and intense. Everything and anything with Lara. But more than that, he wanted her to enjoy it, to crave it—with him.

They parked in his driveway, and he walked her to the front door, glad for the darkness that shrouded his bare lawn and abysmal gardening skills. The evergreens by the garage had grown wild, and he'd never had more than dead weeds bordering the front. The paint job could use another coat, but at least the cold made mowing the lawn unnecessary. Dormant gray grass seemed kept enough.

"This is your place, huh? Not what I was expecting."

He didn't know whether to take that as an insult or compliment.

"I mean, I don't see any poles or dancers." She sneered at him before losing the expression to a building laugh.

He shook his head, more than amused. As much as she liked to bring up his association—through *his father*—with strip clubs, she didn't seem put off by it. "Such a smart-ass." He unlocked the door and ushered her inside, then locked it behind them. It was all he could do not to rub his hands together gleefully and chortle like a villain. *Lovely Lara Valley, all to myself…*

Instead, he cleared his throat. "I have dinner for you."

"Really?" She looked surprised. "Like, a cooked dinner, or Hot Pockets?"

He frowned. "Hey, I can order in like anybody else." He motioned to the stove, where the oven remained on a low setting, keeping his Homemade-By-Diatavio's main dish warm. "A lasagna, waiting just for you."

She stared from it to him. "You left the oven on when you weren't home? That's not safe." At his frown, she gave him a too-bright smile. "But, um, thanks." Her smile turned genuine. "A hot dinner will really hit the spot, actually. And I love lasagna."

A fact he knew. He'd gathered many from Rena, Amelia, Kay, and even Lara. And now that Rena owed him a favor, she sang like a canary whenever he asked about his favorite bartending nurse. It helped that she clearly wanted him and Lara to get together. "Cool. There's some salad in the fridge, some beer and wine too. Unless you want tea or water."

"Wow. I'm impressed." She opened the oven door, and a hearty aroma made his stomach grumble. "You sure you want to eat at one thirty in the morning? I skipped dinner, but I can't imagine you did."

"Why's that?"

"You're huge. Guys as big as you always need to eat."

He wanted to preen, because she considered him big. Working at the garage surrounded by beefheads had a tendency to make him feel small, though he knew damn well he had muscle and breadth of shoulder to spare. Good thing he had a healthy confidence to fall back on.

"Well, sure, I had dinner. But I can always go for

something more. Second dinner sounds great." The idea
of a Hobbit "second breakfast" hit, but he didn't want to
geek out in front of her. Johnny had an image to main-
tain, after all.

"If you don't mind, can we eat now? I'm more hungry
than I'd thought."

He seated her at his table, wondering what she
thought of the place as she subtly glanced around.
While he put food on a plate and dished her a side of
salad, he took a look at his home and tried to see it
through her eyes.

His mismatched couches and chairs were clean but
tacky. Even he knew that. The gray walls had been that
color when he'd moved in a few years ago, but the big-
ass TV and stereo were all his. He had a few pictures of
his dad and the guys at work. One shot of him, Liam,
and Del he treasured, as well as a few pictures of muscle
cars on the walls. Johnny wasn't the neatest guy, but he
ran a clean place. He dusted regularly, and his stacks of
crap—mostly auto rags and the occasional literary mag-
azine he'd buried so as not to be revealed as a nerd—had
an orderliness to them. He didn't like dirt, and he didn't
own much, but what he did own provided comfort and
function over style.

Except when it came to cars or women, Johnny preferred cheap and easy living.

"Eat up," he said as he sat next to her. He watched
her like a hawk, hoping she liked the meal. So the salad
looked a little soggy. He probably should have waited
until he'd gotten home to put the dressing on. But whatever, he'd kept it cool in the refrigerator. And come on,
the lasagna from Diatavio's was killer good.

She made a face and tried to cover it with a smile. "This is great, thanks."

"You're a terrible liar." He frowned and took a bite of lasagna. Half of it was cold. Then he speared the soggy salad, took a bite, and nearly spat it out. "Well, shit."

Her lips quirked. "It, er, was really nice of you to put this together. Was the lasagna frozen, by any chance, when you got it?"

"Yeah," he growled, thoroughly embarrassed. *Smooth, Johnny. Real smooth.* "But I put it in at the temp the guy said. I think." Hell. He normally used the oven to dry out his winter gear when it got wet, because the fireplace had yet to be fully functional. Even after four years.

"How long were you supposed to cook it?"

"A few hours, I think." He felt like an idiot. "The salad is just gross."

"Well, uh, yeah, it is. You should really wait on dressing until right before you eat it. Unless it's a vinaigrette you want to marinate a little. Like a few minutes, maybe?" She shrugged. "Hey, I'm no chef. And this was very nice. I really appreciate the effort."

The cupboards were bare; he needed to go grocery shopping again, so he had nothing else to give her. "I can go out and—"

"It's no big deal. I'm not that hungry, actually."

At that moment her stomach grumbled, and he couldn't contain a pained laugh. "You really suck at lying."

Her cheeks flushed. Ms. Nice caught telling a lie. "Okay, I'm a little hungry."

"Yeah, me too. Even though I drank a few beers and had a few peanuts at Ray's, I can always eat more than one dinner."

"I don't know where you put it all." She patted her stomach. "I even look at a beer wrong, and I gain five pounds."

"Want to look at a beer wrong right now? *That* I know I have."

"Why not?"

He fetched her a bottle and popped one for himself. Then he remembered his stash. "Be right back."

He returned the victor and held out his spoils. "May I present...dinner."

Chapter 12

LARA GLANCED FROM THE PACKAGE OF STRAWBERRY licorice in Johnny's hand to his sparkling green eyes. Beer and licorice. The dinner of champions.

He was so cute actually trying to serve her a meal. He really hadn't been luring her back to his place for sex. Color her amazed. That he'd gone to so much trouble made her want to hug his embarrassment away. But really, beer and Twizzlers?

She took a piece of licorice and ate it, watching as he did the same. He guzzled his beer after, so she figured he combined the two often. When she drank after eating the candy, she wanted to undo the past ten seconds of her life.

"Ew. That is so—" At his eager expression, she amended *disgusting* to "unexpected." Not quite a lie.

He laughed. "It's an acquired taste. Trust me. You don't want to eat the black stuff then drink a beer. Totally nasty. But a whip of red, then a nice pilsner, and you'll start to see the light. Come on." He nodded to the living room. "How about a tour?"

"If you're offering…" She was dying to see his house.

What she'd seen so far fit him. The place had good bones but a rough veneer. Order and cleanliness under a poor sense of taste. Seriously, who had brown and green plaid couches anymore? But Johnny didn't seem to care about appearances. For all that he looked like a model, he saw beneath the surface on so many levels.

Before she followed him back into the living room, she turned off his oven, still drooling at the thought of a Diatavio lasagna. She joined him as he pointed out his amazing sound system and big-screen TV. Typical guy.

"And through there"—he nodded at the hallway—"are four bedrooms. I use one as a weight room, another as a study. The other two for actual sleeping."

"Oh, a study. I only have the one bedroom, but you saw that." She felt embarrassed at living in such a meager abode compared to this spacious one. "You rent, or did you buy this place?"

"Rent." He shrugged. "The landlady is a sweetheart. I do all the upkeep, and she makes sure the rent stays the same. It's a nice neighborhood, and with a little more care, this house would rock. I just don't want to pour a lot of effort and money into a house I'm renting. If I owned it, then yeah, I'd get it perfect. It's home, and it's comfy. Works for me."

He pointed out his weight room and spare bedroom—which had nothing in it. Johnny apparently didn't entertain much overnight. At least, not in a bed not his own.

"And this… The place where all the magic happens."

"Between you and rosy palm or what?" she couldn't help muttering.

He heard her and laughed. "You wound me." Still chuckling, he added, "But I deserve it after my pathetic attempt to feed you. No, Lara, this is my office."

She looked inside at rows of…*books*. "You're a reader?"

He no longer looked so pleased. "You don't have to sound so surprised."

"I can't help it. Okay, I get that you have a bazillion books on cars and manuals about how to fix them. But biographies? History books? Hey, is that Shakespeare? Edgar Allen Poe?" She goggled. "*Tolkien?* Holy crap. I think I even see a bible."

"Nah, that's not mine." He shrugged. "That I found on the street."

She saw a pile of books near it that seemed a little worse for wear. "You don't have to be embarrassed about being religious."

"I'm not." He didn't sound defensive. "I saw that literally lying in an alley near the garage. Nobody was near it, and no way I'd let a book just linger like that. Such a sad fate for words on a page."

Yet another quirky facet of Johnny Devlin. The man was a bookworm. It only added to his appeal. The sexy-as-hell muscle-bound mechanic slash book nerd. There were too many books with creased spines to think he had them in his study merely to impress others.

I am so getting a piece of this man tonight.

He nodded to her beer. "How's the combo treating you?"

She took another bite of licorice, then another tentative sip. "Shockingly, it's starting to taste okay. And I'm not drunk, so that's me admitting, *sober*, that I might like this."

"Told you."

"Smug is not your best look," she said drily and followed him out of his study.

"You sure about that?"

Damn him, he had a point. Johnny looked amazing no matter what. Angry, happy, mischievous. She couldn't say she'd ever seen him sad though. Frustrated or aggrieved, but not griev*ing*. "Okay,

Mr. Arrogant. What now?" She wiggled her brows, clearly mocking him. "Is this where we pause so you can show me your etchings?"

They'd stopped outside his bedroom door standing side by side. "Would it work?"

She decided to go big. She took another bite of candy and followed with a swig of beer. "Why don't you try it and find out?"

She couldn't read the look he shot her, but she followed him into his bedroom, intending to learn more.

This was most likely the room where the magic truly happened. He had a king-size bed. Go figure. A clean nightstand with a few books on it, an alarm clock, and a bedside light. A large closet with closed doors took up one wall. A tall dresser and hamper took up another. He had no mirror or other clutter in the bedroom. Nothing at all but a gorgeous, antique armoire that seemed out of place among the mission style furniture.

"No silk sheets?" she teased.

He didn't smile back.

She nibbled the candy and drank again, feeling his stare to her toes.

"Nah," he said slowly, still fixated on her. "You slide too much on silk. And I like to plant myself firmly at the start."

"The start?" she croaked.

He moved closer, took the beer from her hand and set it on the dresser, then drew the candy to her mouth. "Take another bite." She did. "Now give me some." She held it to his mouth, and he ate from her hand, taking the last piece.

Dear Jesus, the guy even made chewing look like

erotic art, and she couldn't look away as she swallowed the candy, a lump down her throat.

"I like when you swallow," he murmured. "You have no idea how many times I've replayed our last date in my mind." He kissed her, fast and barely there. "Those firm lips wrapped around me, swallowing me down." He kissed her again. "You really had me by the balls. Literally."

She wanted to laugh but couldn't draw in a breath. Instead, she stared into his eyes, trapped by the desire there.

"I was desperate for you. Would have done anything you wanted for you to finish." He stroked her cheek. "I want that for you. For you to feel that kind of need."

"Oh." Not the most intelligent response, but she couldn't think past her sexual glands.

"You like when I kiss you?"

"I-I do." She moaned into his lips when he sipped at her mouth. Good Lord, he'd put on the full-court press, and she hadn't been prepared. She'd figured to seduce *him* again, not be the one trapped by her libido.

"You taste so fucking good." The obscenity got lost under his groan. He kissed her with a hungry desperation. One she felt too.

She found herself clutching his shoulders and pulling him closer, shoving her breasts against his broad chest, and riding that long ridge of his desire against her belly.

His hands began moving, over her clothing everywhere, but not delving beneath.

Frustrated because, though he kissed her with fervor, he seemed way too slow in trying to get her naked, she tore herself from his hold, took the hem of her shirt, and whipped it over her head.

"Damn." His eyes appeared black, no longer green. "You're beautiful."

She felt beautiful. She'd never been looked at the way he stared at her, as if she was precious. Lara reached behind her, attempting to loosen the bra, when Johnny trapped her arms there.

"Don't move." He kissed her again, this time cupping her breasts in his hot hands.

"Oh yeah. Take it off," she encouraged when she could breathe. She thrust her chest forward, but Johnny would only caress her nipples, molding her breasts, not baring them. "Johnny…"

"Patience. That's our word of the day."

"Ass."

He gave a low laugh. "A three letter word for a place on you I'd like to know better."

"Johnny."

"No. This time I'm in charge, and I'm not rushing this. By the time I'm done with you, you're going to want to scream. You'll come so hard over my cock—the second time you come, I mean—that you'll squeeze an orgasm right out of me."

Before she could ask, he added, "I'll use condoms, I swear. And yeah, I said condom*s*, with an *S*. Because once won't cut it with you. No way in hell."

~~~

Johnny meant every word. Seeing Lara in nothing but a bra and jeans took his breath away. She had beautiful breasts, natural, high, firm, and with standout nipples he had to suck. Keeping his clothes on only made sense. He couldn't ruin everything by sliding inside her too soon. Not with his dick hampered by jeans and underwear.

But keeping *her* clad made little sense, except to prolong his own agony. Which he kind of liked. Self-denial made everything sweeter in the end.

He spread his hand over her belly and felt her tremble. Loving her responsiveness, he had to know. "You wet for me, baby?"

She moaned and tried to kiss him, but he kept her hands locked behind her, while with the other hand he stroked her smooth belly.

"I bet you are. Let's see." He slowly unbuttoned her pants, aware she offered no resistance. Sliding his fingers down, under her panties and between her legs, he found her wet, hot, and irresistible.

"I'm wet," she admitted, though he could all but drown in her warmth. "Ready for you. So come on. Get that condom on and get inside me."

"So romantic, Lara." He did his best to appear in control, when he really wanted to howl at the moon, rip those jeans and panties right off her, and bury his head between her legs for days. "I already told you I'm in charge. I'll fuck you when I'm good and ready. How about that?" He threw a bite of meanness in his voice.

She gasped and sought his mouth with a ravenous kiss.

She liked him not so nice after all. He kissed her, grinding against her as he finally unfastened her bra and let her lower her arms. "Hold on to my belt loops. Don't let go."

"I won't," she rasped and arched her neck to give him better access.

He sucked hard enough to leave a mark, then kissed his way to her breasts. The silky black bra still hanging on her shoulders hinted at her nipples but didn't show them. And he wanted to keep her waiting.

Johnny kissed past the upper slopes of her breasts and ended between them. He nuzzled there, gratified by her groan of pleasure. Then he settled his mouth over one taut peak through the material of her bra and sucked.

She cried out and gripped his hair, holding him tight. The bra impeded full sensation, at least for him, but it didn't stop his dick from threatening to burst from his jeans, so full and hard he ached to join her. Johnny sucked and licked over the lace, alternating between breasts.

"Such a tease," she breathed and arched toward him. Her hand wound between them, and she gripped his erection.

He sucked in a breath, then pushed her hand aside. "Thought I told you to hold on to my belt loops."

She complied, though with a grumble.

Needing to touch bare flesh, he pulled her straps over her shoulders and down her arms, then dropped the bra to the floor. "Oh yeah."

Her bare breasts looked better than any fantasy. Large mounds, definitely a handful, and pert pink nipples that begged for a wet kiss. Johnny took one peak in his mouth and sucked, teethed, and nibbled.

Lara went wild, bucking against him and holding on to his hips for dear life. A good thing, because had she sought his dick again, he probably would have come in his jeans. The woman turned him on without trying, but half-naked and impassioned, she was an erotic temptation more powerful than any force he'd ever known.

"*Johnny*." She let go of his pants to clutch his hair.

He turned his attention to her other breast while pushing down her jeans and underwear. Once he had her fully naked, he had to look his fill. He lowered her onto her back on his bed, staring into her eyes all the while. Then he eased back to stand, looming over her.

She had high breasts, a trim waist, and those long legs he couldn't wait to dive between. Her lips were parted, her cheeks flushed, and her eyes seemed impossibly dark. Lara made him ache.

"I'm gonna fuck you so hard," slipped out, though he'd meant to be a little more sophisticated.

"Yes." Her eyes darkened even more.

Johnny ripped off his shirt and toed off his shoes. His socks followed, but he kept his pants on. Anything to slow this down, to savor the experience. This was special; he felt it to his bones.

He climbed onto the bed and started kissing her. Everywhere.

Her sculpted calves, silky thighs, and up. To her soft hips, that sexy, taut belly, and her breasts… Christ, he could have stayed there all night. He continued up her neck to her lips, where he leaned over her, his weight on his elbows. His pelvis mashed against hers.

"You're so *hard*."

"Yeah, I am. And I want to last, so don't move," he ordered.

She moaned but obeyed, and his lust skyrocketed. Lara never took orders from him. But she apparently couldn't think to disobey at this point. He kissed her until they both needed air.

Then he slid back down her body. She smelled

amazing. Sultry, spicy and, as he drew closer to the thin strip of hair guarding her sex, like heaven.

"Fuck, Lara." Johnny buried his face between her legs and licked. And licked again. He closed his lips around her clit, sucking the plump bud while she writhed under him. Before he could add his fingers, she cried out and came.

He found himself humping the bed while she continued to gyrate against his mouth.

When he finally pulled himself up for air and glanced up at her, it was to find her staring at him in shock.

"I came." She panted. "Hard."

"You sound surprised." He tsked, wanting to see her climb once more. "That's just the first time, baby. Let's get you hot and bothered again."

"But I want you in me."

Damn right. "Me too. But not yet." He stroked her inner thighs, her cropped curls, her folds, sliding his rough fingers through flesh as fine as silk. Returning his mouth to her sex, he licked and sucked while he played with her, thrusting his finger in and out in a slow, building rhythm.

It didn't take her long to catch on, and then he had to free himself from the torture of his confining clothes.

"Yes," she said. "In me this time."

He stripped naked and fished in his pocket for a condom. After donning it with shaky hands, he slid back up her body and kissed her breasts. He teased himself by rubbing against her slick heat. Over and over, until he feared coming without ever penetrating.

She kept trying to tug him closer, and he finally let her.

Lara spread her legs wider and wrapped those strong thighs around his waist, opening herself to receive him. "In me, baby."

Shit. She'd called him baby. He kissed her and found her hot and welcoming. Then he slid, slowly, into the best place on earth. One slow inch at a time, he discovered the warmth that was Lara.

"Yes, Johnny. *Yes*." She locked her ankles behind the small of his back, and he sank inside her as deeply as he could go.

"You feel so good." *So fuckin' good*. He treasured the feeling, then had to move or he'd lose his mind. His balls were like rocks, his shaft thick to the point of pain. Johnny needed release.

Inside Lara.

He wished like hell he didn't have to use a condom, but he didn't want to freak her out. She trusted him. Besides, protected, they could go at it all night long without any worries. Like hell he'd ruin that.

He withdrew a bit, then slid back inside. His thrusts became faster, his ability to hold back a thing of the past.

"So close," he muttered as he fucked her. "So close." He could say nothing else as he hammered inside her. Not slow or patient, but fast, desperate, hungry for Lara.

He slammed inside her, grinding up against her clit with each pass. And like magic, she came again, her body like a vise, clamping down around his.

"*Fuck*," he shouted as he poured into her, unable to function past the bliss of her body.

She clenched and keened, her breathy satisfaction in pants and cries already committed to his memory.

Johnny couldn't do more than twitch as she milked

him of every ounce of pleasure. When he finally ceased coming, he wondered if he'd have enough energy to do this again. Because he *had* to. The need to tie himself to her was so overpowering it scared him.

"Oh, wow." Lara stroked his hair and finally loosened her grip around his waist. Her legs fell to either side of him, but Johnny didn't want to pull out yet. "That was incredible."

"Yeah." He tucked his head next to hers, breathing into the pillow, and tried to remember how to make coherent sentences. Nothing yet.

"You felt so big in me. So thick." She did something with her inner muscles that made him shudder and spurt again, though he'd thought himself done.

"Yeah."

She sighed, her hands on his hair totally relaxing. And a little…arousing? "It figures sex with you would be better than my fantasies."

He propped himself up on his elbows to see her. "Fantasies? Tell me more."

She laughed. "Okay, I admit I wondered a time or two what sleeping with you would be like."

"That's it?" He equated *sleeping with you* with actual sleeping, and found to his surprise that the idea had appeal. Holding Lara close, sleeping with her, waking up next to her, had him longing for so much more.

"I wouldn't call this sleeping." He withdrew a fraction, then surged deeper, still wearing the condom. He knew he needed to pull out and dispose of it, but she felt so damn good right now. "Come on. Tell me something real, in detail."

She sighed and clamped down on him, and he

fought a shiver. "Well, there's one fantasy where we're together…and your head is between my legs."

He moved faster, getting his second wind and growing.

Her voice lowered. "We're in a garage." She toyed with the hair at his nape. "You're working on some hot rod, a pretty red car. But when you see me, you have to put your tools aside, because you're so hungry for me." She moaned as he worked her harder. "Then you strip me, throw me down on the hood of that pretty car, and start eating me out." Lara clenched him inside her with a sharp contraction and gasped. "God, Johnny. Didn't you fill that thing already?"

"Yeah, and I'm gonna fill it again. Well, not this one." It killed him, but he withdrew and hurriedly pulled off the condom, tossing it discreetly next to the bed on the floor. "I need another one. *Now*."

He rolled off her and dug one out of his nightstand, aware of her gaze.

"Holy crap. You're huge. I mean, I felt you in me. But you're just… a grower, aren't you, Johnny Devlin?"

He flushed, and she laughed. "Stop," he growled.

"Oh, baby. A big package, and all for me."

He resheathed himself, amazed he could go again so soon. Then again, this was Lara. Half-hard, he tucked himself back in her hot pussy and closed his eyes, lost inside her.

He moved on instinct and kissed her, soon spurring new moans and pleas from her sweet lips. Then the world fell away as he reached ecstasy in Lara's arms again. He'd found the one woman who could tear his heart out and leave him a shell of a man—a fact he'd suspected four years and seven months ago. But now, having had her so close, he didn't know if he'd survive when she inevitably left.

A troubling dilemma, and one he'd try to figure out just as soon as he could get his brain to start working again.

They lay together, breathing heavily, Johnny so bone-deep content he had trouble thinking of anything but Lara.

"You're heavy," she whispered, sounding drowsy.

He reluctantly withdrew, scooping the used condom from the floor, and left for the bathroom, returning cleaned up. He slid into bed beside her and marveled that even spent and a little sweaty, Lara looked like an angel.

"I just need a tiny nap before I go."

He glanced at the clock and saw the hour had reached nearly three. She had to be beat, and truth was, Johnny didn't want her to leave. "Shh. Just close your eyes. I'm in no rush to boot your ass out the door."

She gave a low laugh, sighed, then curled into him. His heart did a weird flip in his chest and settled, her warmth making it impossible to keep any kind of safe distance, physically or emotionally. So he surrendered to the closeness and hugged her tight. He fell asleep spooning her, never wanting to let go.

Chapter 13

IF IT WAS A DREAM, IT WAS ONE OF THE BEST SHE'D ever had. Caught between sleep and wakefulness, Lara moaned into a man's mouth, his callused hands all over her breasts and belly. She was lying under him, spread-eagle, as he nuzzled his way from her mouth to her neck, kissing and caressing all the way.

She gripped him, loving the thick girth and steely evidence of his arousal. So big, so hungry for her.

He moaned and settled between her thighs. In one deep push he shoved inside her, until he could go no farther. She felt incredibly full, and so turned on she literally overheated. Then he was moving, faster and deeper, hitting all the right spots.

"Johnny," she sighed and hugged him tight.

"Yeah, baby. Lara…" The bed rocked, faster now, and she came fully awake to the glorious feel of Johnny inside her, reminding her that sometimes dreams do come true.

He inserted a hand between them as he leaned up, and those clever fingers found her happy spot without err. The added stimulation set her off, and she cried out as she came hard around him, holding him inside.

A swear word, then he pulled out and spent on her belly, his breath sawing in and out while he moaned his pleasure. It seemed forever as she clenched and spasmed around the emptiness where he'd just been.

"Damn, honey. I left a mess. Sorry about that." He reached beside him and found something to clean off her belly. Then he tossed it aside.

As she came down off her high, she realized what had almost happened. She froze.

Above her, Johnny tensed as well. "You okay?"

"You almost came inside me."

He swore under his breath then lay next to her on his side. "I know. I didn't mean to. Honest to God, I was half-dreaming you. I mean, I'm in bed, and there's this sexy woman with perfect curves grinding against me. Then your hand wrapped around my cock, and I lost it."

So, that had been real then. She blushed. Partly her fault, and except for almost having unprotected sex... "Wait. You were inside me. Without a condom."

"Yeah." He sounded a little too pleased about the fact.

She leaned up on her elbow, aware of his gaze straying to her mouth then her breasts. "So do I have anything to worry about?"

His lazy grin vanished, and his gaze snapped back to her face. "Huh? You mean... shit no. I'm not careless." His cheeks turned pink. "Not usually, at least. I always use a rubber."

"Even when your girlfriends sleep over?"

He turned even redder and lay back, slinging an arm over his face. He mumbled something.

"What?"

"I said they don't sleep over. I either sleep at their place, or we go our separate ways."

"So I'm christening a virgin bed?" Hard to believe.

"Not exactly. Damn, Lara. Do we have to talk about this? Now?"

"Um, let me think." She popped him in the chest.

"*Ow.*"

"*Yes,* we have to talk about this now," she said, feeling frantic. She did trust he took care of himself. But being with him felt *too* wonderful. She didn't want to leave. And it looked as though she'd spent the entire night with him. In his bed, waking to have more sex with the dynamo. Without being conscious of it, she'd grown addicted to Johnny Devlin, as she'd always feared she might. "We did the horizontal mambo without protection, and I don't know your sexual history. Well, except that you're a horndog."

"Now, baby, that's not exactly true."

She saw the grin he didn't hide. "Oh?"

"Sure, there've been women over the years. Not as many as you'd think, especially not recently." He sighed. "Look, I'm a stickler about keeping it clean. Had a problem back when I was a teenager that cleared up fast enough. Nothing serious, but it was enough to scare me straight. Trust me when I say you're the first woman I went into without protection."

"So your past blow jobs were with condoms too?"

He frowned. "Seriously? Hell no. I mean…"

"Exactly."

"Oh, come on. I'm done with one-night stands, have been for years." At her look, he amended, "Okay, months, but still. I'm different than I used to be. When I'm with a girl, I know if she's clean or not before I… before we… This is really awkward."

"You think?" Was it wrong for her to get a secret kick out of embarrassing the big bad stud?

He blew out a breath. "You want me to get tested or something? I'm due for a checkup anyway."

She blinked at him. "Tested?"

"You know. You're a nurse—almost. You know about this stuff. I can get a workup." He grew animated. "Hey, you can get one too, then go on the Pill, and we can ignore condoms all together. Sounds like a plan, huh?"

"Hold on."

He rolled over her and had her underneath him in seconds. "Well, why not? We both know this is the beginning with us, right? I mean, us hangin' out and having sex, having a good time. *That* us. Or are you telling me last night was enough and you want to call it quits already?"

"Is this your way of trying to get me to go steady with you?" she teased, half-serious. He'd been quick to amend "the beginning with us" to being casual buddies who hung out and fucked. Which was what she was in the market for, all said and done.

Sex with Johnny had truly relaxed her. Orgasmic sex apparently cured tension and headaches. Who knew? Before Johnny, she sure the hell hadn't.

Johnny stared at her. "I don't know if I'd call it steady, but I'm a one-woman guy. I don't do more than one woman at a time. I mean, there was that one night in Houston a while back, but…" He smirked at her.

"Shut up." Knowing Johnny, he might not be lying about more than one woman in his bed. "I get that you're selective. You have a lot of sex, but only with one woman at one time, and according to you, it's safe sex."

"I don't know I'd say I have *a lot* of sex, but—"

"I don't have casual sex." Sadly. "Never have." *Never* had—*until you*. Before he could contradict her, she admitted, "You're different. I've known you for years, so we're not exactly casual. Plus, you're really good in bed."

"Yeah?" He grinned.

"Please. Don't act surprised. You rocked my world, but I rocked yours right back."

"That's true. You're not half-bad when you're naked."

"So many compliments. I'm all aflutter," she dead-panned, and he laughed.

It hadn't been lost on her that he remained naked, his body all hard muscle and sexy lines. Not to mention that impressive part of him that seemed to stiffen when he shifted against her.

"So what do you say? I'll get myself checked out, you do the same. We can be together, the two of us. No one else." He shrugged, but his deliberate nonimposing tone alerted her to be wary.

"You're saying you want an exclusive relationship that's not serious?"

"We need to spell this whole thing out, huh?"

"Isn't that your MO?"

"Kind of." Johnny kissed her, then brushed her hair off her cheek with a tender touch. "Man, you're fuckin' gorgeous, you know that?"

"Stop changing the subject." *And stop messing with my head!*

"You're also a hard-ass. But I like that about you."

"So…?"

He sighed, loudly. "So…how about we keep this easy? We fool around, you and me. Like, we're dating."

"That does sound better than calling you my fuck buddy."

He flinched. "Ouch. Look, let's have fun together.

Just you and me. Until you get bored with me and take off."

He didn't sound like he was joking.

"Yeah. That's what'll happen." She snorted. "I'll get tired of you, the guy who has women throwing their panties at him."

"That is such crap. It happened just that one time at a concert."

"I was kidding." She stared up at him. "A woman really threw her panties at you?"

"Ah, so Foley never said anything about this?"

"No." But she planned on cornering the big guy for answers.

"Right. Well." He leaned into her, and his cock dragged over her belly, hard and ready to go. "Now that we have our status settled, how about I do you again?" He ground against her still-wet sex. "You get me hot and bothered by breathing. But naked… I can't resist." He kissed her until she forgot her own name.

But as he slid inside her on a groan, she put a hand on his chest. "Wait."

He froze. "You're killing me, you know that?"

"Not with the sex. I mean, just to clarify things—so we're now dating? Having fun and having sex?"

"Yeah." He started thrusting in and out of her, his eyes dark, cloudy with lust. "Just you and me. Fuck, you're amazing."

"So are you." She groaned. "But I meant it about condoms."

"I know, I know." He withdrew and rustled in his side table again. "But can we agree that if we both check out I can fuck you bareback? Please?" He sounded so hopeful.

"Well, I'll think about it."

"That's a yes." He put the condom on and slid back inside her on a moan. "That means I'm it for you for the foreseeable future."

"And I'm it for you, Romeo."

"Yeah, you are." He fucked her harder.

She couldn't talk anymore, and neither could he. Her morning passed by in a blur of sex, laughter, and more sex. By the time noon rolled around, she thought her stomach might cave in from lack of nutrients.

"I'm so hungry," she complained as she sat in her clothes from the day before. *I'm such a skank. An awesome, incredible skank. I rock!*

Johnny had finished his shower and now dried off in front of her. And yes, Johnny Devlin naked, wet, and in only a towel was as good a sight as she and Rena had once thought it might be.

"We're dating," he said. "You and me." A slow smile curled his lips. "How about that?"

"How about you keep this low-key, so when you move on to the next bimbo who can't say no to you, it's not such a jarring transition." *For me.*

"Now, Lara, you're the only bimbo who matters."

She tried to smack him, but he danced out of reach. Naked and laughing, he dressed in front of her. And all the while she kept asking herself what she thought she was doing with him, and why he made her so happy.

"I'm serious about my schoolwork," she blurted. "That's typically why I don't date anyone. With me, school comes first. Oh, and family."

"Gotcha."

"I mean it. In fact, today I'm supposed to watch the

girls for a few hours while Kristin and my mom work double shifts. Dad will get them this evening, when I'm working at Ray's."

Johnny sat down next to her on the bed and smoothed her hair behind her ear. When he used that gentle touch on her, watching her as if captivated, she wanted to melt. "I get you, Lara. You're busy. No problem. I'm busy during the week too, and sometimes on weekends. Ah, I might as well tell you that lately I've been helping my dad at his place. I mean, he's *supposed* to be replacing his general manager, but until he does, I'm helping to hold things together."

"At the strip club."

"Strutts." He nodded. "He should have hired a new manager months ago. Tell you what. How about I help you with your nieces, you come out to Strutts sometime and watch me behind the bar. Working there... I mean, it's not me trying to score, more like me protecting my little sisters. Who happen to get naked for a living. Yeah, it's fucked up, but I'm not trying to get it on with anyone. Business and pleasure don't mix."

"If I get an earlier shift one of these nights, I could always meet you at Strutts."

"*No.* I'll pick you up. I don't want you there without me." He frowned. "The customers might get the wrong idea."

"So you don't want me dancing on a pole for you?"

"Not at all." He stood and yanked her to her feet. "Now quit screwing with me, woman, and feed me."

"Do I look like a walking kitchen?"

He chuckled. "No. But I know a great diner that serves breakfast twenty-four seven. You drive me there, and I'll buy."

"You're on." She let him lead her by the hand through the house. Even kept her hand in his as they walked to her car. Once there, he pinned her for a kiss.

When he broke away, they were both breathing hard. "We'll be good together. You'll see." His smile, so sweet—and so intense. Johnny liked to keep things light, so she wondered if she ought to be concerned about the weight of his stare. Then he winked and gave her his trademark Devlin leer. "And when I say you'll see, I mean you'll see later tonight when I'm buried in you all over again." He wiggled his brows. "My own personal version of a lube job."

"Ew." She grinned, aware he always made her feel like laughing, brightening her mood. "So you're going to want to rotate my tires too, I guess?"

"Oh yeah. Let me get under that hood. I'll lick it right up." He smirked. "Told you I'd show you how I like to *eat* my dinner."

She recalled their first dinner out together, when she'd warned him to eat his dinner, not make love to it. Boy, had she been wrong. "You just had to bring that up, didn't you?"

"With you, Lara, everything's up, all the time." They both glanced down at his jeans, where she saw the hint of an erection. "Yep, hard and hurting. Guess you'll have to make it better later."

"If you're lucky."

"Baby, lucky is my middle name."

※

After driving back to her place so she could clean up, they ate a terrific breakfast at a hole of a diner, then ended up getting the girls early. The afternoon with her nieces had been a cakewalk. Her nieces loved Johnny—Mr. Pink Unicorn Guy, or as Kay called him, *Pretty Johnny*—and flirted with him unmercifully while the four of them watched the two-dollar movie at the Mormont Theater, a tiny treasure her sister had found last year. Both Kay and Amelia had insisted Johnny sit between them, leaving their poor aunt stuck carrying a tub of popcorn and drinks.

Johnny had admirably stuck it out through a Tinker Bell cartoon and follow-up group-led fairy talk. He wasn't the only guy in attendance, but Lara had a feeling he'd been the only nonparent there, excluding herself of course. But she was an official aunt, so she didn't count. Leave it to Johnny to fit in during a fairy movie and fairy talk with little girls.

She couldn't figure him out. He seemed to think she'd dump him before he tired of her. As if. The guy handled little kids in stride. He treated her to breakfast, had given her more orgasms in one night than she'd had from any guy in years, and continued to handle her as if she were special. Like they were really dating—which she guessed they were.

How had they ended up as a couple? Sex she understood. They had chemistry going for them, for damn sure. But she never would have guessed he'd want to take a sexual relationship to the next level. It was what she wanted…and it wasn't. The time she would have spent doing her homework she'd spent with him. Tonight she had to work, and afterward she'd be too tired to concentrate on medical jargon and practice writing patient forms.

How would a fuzzy brain get her nursing-care plan done in time for Monday's class?

"You okay?" he asked after they'd dropped the girls off with her dad. She'd made Johnny stay in the car while she ran the girls in, bribing both of them to stay quiet about Johnny, at least until she felt ready to tell her parents about him. But what the heck would she call him? Her new boyfriend?

He didn't mind her driving. What kind of a jerky womanizer who buried his hands in cars all day felt comfortable letting a woman drive? He was *so* not living up to any of her preconceived notions. Not a womanizer, but a charmer. Not a jerk, but a funny guy with a sense of humor she appreciated. Not a superficial, unfeeling lout. He loved books and enjoyed spending time with her. He talked *to* her, not *at* her. And when he kissed and touched her, he wasn't making love to *any*body, but to Lara. His immense good-guy persona made falling for him a dangerous possibility.

She cleared her throat. "Um, just thinking about a paper due on Monday I'm behind on."

"You probably should have worked on it this morning, huh? I don't want to distract you from school."

You're already distracting me, damn it. "I have no one to blame but myself. I'd rather spend time with you than my laptop." She groaned—because she meant it.

"So I guess coming back to my place after work is out? What if I promise not to molest you while you sleep?"

"What a great offer." They both laughed. "I should probably get a good night's rest—at my home—by myself. I'm off tomorrow night though. We could hang out if you want."

"Oh, I want." His green eyes lit with joy. "But only if you finish your work. I am not an excuse for lagging on assignments, Nurse Valley." He gave her his stern voice. Then his expression evened, and he changed the subject. "You know, I hadn't realized how often you help out with the girls. Kay was telling me they spend a lot of time with their favorite Aunt Lara."

"Their only Aunt Lara." She shrugged. "I know they're not my kids, but I feel responsible for them. I love Kristin, but she's a mess. While she gets herself together, my folks and I help with the girls." She'd always felt the need to give back, knowing how much her parents had sacrificed for her.

"You're a good person."

She blinked at him. He sounded so sincere.

"I mean it. A lot of people put on a good show, but you're genuinely kind."

She tried not to wince. "'Kind' is boring. Like saying you're a nice guy with a great personality, *but…*"

"Nah. It's underrated, you want my opinion. Anyone can look beautiful with the right clothes and makeup. Or lighting."

"So you're saying I'm hot as long as I'm in the dark?"

"Well…"

She scowled, trying not to grin.

He chuckled. "You're fucking sexy as hell. My point is, being pretty ain't what life's about. It's being good to other people."

"Says the guy who's so pretty he can get most any woman just by winking at them."

"Not true. I first winked at you over four years ago. You rolled your eyes and served Lou without a word to me."

She remembered the moment but was surprised he did. Instead of making a big deal out of it, she tried to change the subject. "Well, to continue our earlier discussion, I have to work 'til closing. I'll sleep in until nine, then bust my butt finishing up my paper. I should be done by dinnertime, and I do owe you for pizza the other night, when I forgot to cancel on you."

"That's true. You do owe me."

"So, do you want to come over, or what?"

"You have to ask me nicely. Remember, women everywhere want me. You're the lucky one at this moment. Make it last."

"Oh my God. You make me want to hit you just about every time we're together."

"I seem to have that effect on people. You wouldn't believe how many times I'm in danger at work."

"Knowing Sam and Lou, I can just imagine."

"Foley too. He's a real bastard."

He said nothing more, so she chanced a look at him before turning her attention back to the road. "What?"

"I just noticed you didn't include Foley. What's with you and him? He kissed you at the bar, and you're all thinking he's nice and safe. But maybe nice and safe are good things." He scowled.

"You have issues."

"He seems like he's this big teddy bear. Women love him before they realize he's not a commitment type of guy." A pregnant pause. "I mean, I'm not saying I'm out to marry you or anything, like *I'm* a big commitment guy. I'm just… I would never hurt you. Your heart, I mean. I don't hit women. Not that Foley does either. But—"

"I'll just stop you right there and say I get it." Inside, she was crowing with glee. Johnny was jealous of Foley, of all people. "For the record, I like Foley. He's a nice guy who's a friend. Like Rena is a friend. That's it."

"Yeah, okay. Good."

"So if you're done being green with jealousy for the sexy, amazing Foley Sanders"—she ignored his growl—"how about we get to Ray's before I'm late? I'm sorry. I wanted to drop you off so you'd have your car, but with the extra time we spent at the fairy Q&A, I don't have time to go back."

"What about your uniform?"

"I have an extra shirt in the trunk." She couldn't remember what her shirt said. Ray was all about keeping it simple. So if her shirt said "Bartender," she'd be tending bar.

"I hope it doesn't say Waitress. I don't like those assholes groping you."

"They don't. You're the only asshole groping me lately."

"Exactly."

She snickered at him, and he laughed as well. They made it to Ray's with ten minutes to spare, and after she grabbed her backpack from the trunk, he hustled her inside after sharing a fist bump with the bouncer.

"Big John and Johnny. You guys don't look alike. Maybe fraternal twins?" she teased and made a beeline for the back, threading through the already growing crowd—at barely seven in the evening? Oh right, dollar shots until nine. *Hell.*

Johnny followed, right on her heels. "Very funny. I suppose I should be glad you didn't say identical twins." Big J, the bouncer, had no neck. His eyes were very close together, and he shaved his head because he thought he looked meaner. It actually made him look like a mountain of a cue ball, but Lara hadn't wanted to hurt his feelings. Along with every other sane person in the place.

When they arrived in the back, near a storage closet Lara and the girls used as a place to store their belongings and occasionally as a changing room, Lara turned and bumped into Johnny. "Oh, sorry. Well, I guess I'll say good-bye, then."

"Not quite yet." He reached past her, turned the doorknob, and guided her inside. Then he shut the door behind them. "Now. That little matter of me being lucky…"

"What?" She couldn't see him in the dark.

He found the pull switch and bathed them in dim overhead lighting. In the shadows, he looked dark and mysterious, and of course, like a sexy temptation bent on her undoing.

"You know. You said you'd make me all better if I was lucky." He pulled her hand to his fly, and she felt him thick and hard beneath it. "I'm with you, so I consider myself lucky. *How lucky* is the question."

He smiled and leaned close to kiss her. Nothing sweet about the ravishment going on in here. She hadn't realized she'd dropped her bag until she heard it fall. Then he turned her to face the wall. She heard his zipper, the tear of a foil packet, and knew he'd donned a condom.

Already aroused from that kiss and the suggestion of something so…dirty…she felt ready for whatever came next. She'd never had sex at work before. It seemed fun, naughty, and something that fit right in with Ray's.

She had to stifle a giggle at the thought, feeling drunk on her own lust.

"I'm in love with this ass, Lara." Johnny palmed her through her jeans. "It's just bitable. But we'll have to save that for when we have more time." He pulled her hair out of the way and kissed her neck, then turned her head to kiss her lips.

While kissing her, those clever hands of his unbuttoned her jeans. He slid them and her panties down her legs to her ankles. "You ready for me?"

"I don't know... At work, Johnny?" she whispered, hearing her own excitement in the high pitch of her voice.

"Never done it at work before, huh? You're such a *good* girl." He nudged her feet as far apart as her jeans would let her and slid his fingers between her slick folds. Then he tilted her hips and spread her wide. "But not too good," he rasped and entered her in one swift push.

The intrusion, in her present position, made him feel *huge.* "*God.*"

"Yeah. I like this."

Outside she heard the bustle of the bar. Rena barked orders at Josie, while Ray and Brian cooked up a storm as they bitched about the work. And Johnny breathed hard while he pounded into her. He reached around to finger her clit, and the excitement became too much to bear. She'd never been quick on a climax, but damned if she wasn't going to come after a few thrusts.

"I'm coming," she whispered—and shattered.

"Me too." He hammered into her, no finesse, just good, hard fucking. And then he moaned and stilled, gripping her hips hard enough to leave bruises. He just stood there, emptying into her—into the condom— while she trembled, braced against the wall.

The doorknob rattled, and they both froze. "Who's in there?"

Lara blew out a breath while Johnny slowly withdrew from her body. "I'm getting changed, Sue. Out in a minute."

"Oh, hey, Lara. Sorry. Didn't see you come in." Footsteps signaled her leaving.

Lara remained bent over, toward the wall, trying to catch her breath.

She heard Johnny fiddling with his clothes. Then he eased her panties and jeans back up. He turned her around, holding the shirt she'd stashed in her bag. She stripped out of her sweatshirt and put on her work shirt. She'd packed a black bartender tee, which seemed to please him, because he nodded and handed her a hair band.

"Found it in the bag." He waited while she put her hair into her trademark ponytail. "Good. I don't want them seeing you with your hair down."

She said nothing, unsure of what to say after that *wham bam, thank you, Johnny,* session. He watched her, waiting, and she blurted, "You're not going to be all possessive now, are you?"

"Who me?" He kissed her, hard. "Nah. I know we're just having fun. But it's just *us* having fun. Not me and some other woman, and not you and some other dude."

"Right. Just us. Casually having fun dating." She smiled. "And doing wicked things in the closet."

"Yeah." He sighed. "I'll sleep like a baby tonight thanks to that. You're dreamy."

"Cheesy, but I'll take it."

His crooked grin melted more of her marshmallowy

heart. "Have a good shift. I'll swing by tomorrow for dinner, say six?"

"Okay."

"Want me to bring anything?" He kissed her again and stroked her cheek.

What was *with* that affectionate gesture? It made her want to hug him and keep on hugging him. She cleared her throat. "Just bring your sexy self and an appetite."

"That I can do. I'd stick around tonight, but the guys and I told Dad we'd help at Strutts. Even Lou's swinging by for a beer, and he considers himself above the T&A crowd."

"Don't you?"

"It's different with me. They're family." He shrugged.

"Well, go be with your family. Just keep your clothes on and your fly zipped," she warned.

His slow grin embarrassed her. "Yes, dear. Don't worry about me."

"And I'm not jealous."

"Uh-huh. Just like I'm not jealous of Foley. That ass." He chuckled then left before she could caution him to take care not to be seen as he departed out the back.

She needn't have bothered. After she tucked her shirt into her bag and left the closet, praying Johnny had at least taken his used condom with him, she ran into Rena, who stared at her with wide eyes.

Chapter 14

TUESDAY AFTERNOON, JOHNNY HADN'T NOTICED THE others around him until it dawned on him only his whistling could be heard in the confines of the garage. He looked out from under the hood of his favorite jalopy, which its owner had affectionately named Gizmo, since it was a green '75 AMC Gremlin, and saw the guys staring at him.

"What?" He wiped his hands on the towel hanging out the back pocket of his coveralls.

"We heard you on your way out yesterday," Lou said, brawny arms crossed over his chest in a surprisingly clean white T-shirt.

"About you and *Lara* having plans," Foley explained.

He'd known this was coming. "And?" *Play it cool, man. No more whistling. And stop smiling all the time.*

"*And* we want to know how long this has been going on," Lou said. "This is big news. I mean, she barely used to talk to you. Now you're dating?"

"She's seen the light. What can I say?"

"What the hell are you guys doing?" Del growled from her office doorway and marched toward them. "This isn't *a coffee klatch*. It's called work." Well, that answered that question. Apparently she *had* heard Foley the other day making fun of her for joining a book club. It wasn't that Del couldn't enjoy a good book, but that she'd joined a *romance* book club when she didn't seem to have a romantic bone in her tough-as-nails body.

Today she'd styled her ash-blond hair in some funky twisted braid. Her jeans had seen better days, but her steel-toed boots gleamed with black polish, and her Scooby-Doo T-shirt looked new. No doubt a gift from McCauley—the little one. She wore a new loop in her brow, and the overhead light caught the gleam of the ruby stud in her nose. Feminine but with an edge, their Del. "Scatter and chitchat on your own time."

"Technically, I'm on a break," Sam tried.

She glared at him, and he quickly took his big ass back to the Chevy he'd been working on earlier. Foley took one look at Del and joined him.

"You got something to say, Casanova?" She watched Lou like a hungry tiger.

Lou sighed and slunk back to the Camaro he'd nearly finished. With the paintwork all done, he had nothing to do but make a last check on the car. "Later," he warned Johnny.

"Whatever." Johnny turned back to the Gremlin, realized Del hadn't left, and faced her once more. "Yes, Your Majesty?"

"That's better." She smiled, and he knew what McCauley saw in her. Despite her mean, sexy vibe—and God knew his boss had a rack that didn't quit—under the hard outer shell, Del had a heart as big as the moon. Hell, she tolerated him and the guys, and he still had no idea why she'd kept them after her dad had taken them on.

She continued to stare at him, one hand on her hip. "So. You and Lara."

He pinched the bridge of his nose. "Jesus. I only mentioned it in passing last night when I told Foley I was too busy for a beer."

"I heard it from Rena on Sunday. So? What's the scoop?"

"There is no scoop. We're dating. I like her, she likes me. It's a mutual, ah…"

"Fuckfest?"

"*Del*."

Behind them, the ROP rattled.

"I know that's you, Foley." It shook again. "Fuck, I'll pay a dollar later. *O-kay?*" she barked, and it stopped. Her voice softened. "Come on, Johnny. Tell me the truth. Are you using Lara or what? I love you like a brother, but she's a friend of mine. Just like she's a friend of Rena and J.T. If you fuck her over, J.T. will skin you alive. After I'm done roasting you over."

"More like handing him his balls one by one. That, or roasting his balls, but skinning would probably work as well," Sam offered.

She looked over her shoulder at him.

"What? Am I lying? Fine, fine. I'll shut up."

Del turned back. "Well?"

Johnny blew out a breath, uncomfortable talking about Lara with anyone. "You know, my dating Lara is no one's business but my own." She just stared at him in silence. "I mean, I could claim harassment, you trying to get into my social life and all, making me talk about personal stuff."

Some grunting, muffled laughter, and a "What social life?" joined his disquiet.

Del raised her pierced brow.

"Fine." Johnny gave in. "There's nothing to worry

about, okay? I like her, and I'd like to date her for a while. It's no big deal. I date women all the time."

"Not like Lara." Del studied him, and he felt small under her gaze. "She's a hard worker and a genuine friend of mine. She's the real deal, Johnny. A nice girl with heart."

"I know." In the few days they'd been officially "dating," he'd witnessed her helping her nieces and family by running errands or babysitting. All her neighbors they'd run into had a nice word for her, and he damn well knew everyone at Ray's loved her. She'd made him one hell of a tuna casserole Sunday for dinner, and she'd repeated their version of "happy time in the closet" just last night. The woman could do no wrong in his book. "She's busting her ass to get through school while working full-time. I get it. She's cool. I'm not out to screw her over. If anything, you should be warning her not to dump me. I'll be the wounded party at the end. Believe me."

"How's that?"

"Because the jackass is in love with her," Lou added, not so helpfully.

Del's eyes widened. "Yeah?"

"I am not." His heart hammered in his chest. "Look, I have Gizmo to finish and three friggin' diagnostics to get to." His turn to take the jobs nobody wanted this week. Diagnostics could be a real bitch and take forever. "Can I get back to work?"

Del nodded. "Sure." Then she closed the distance between them and murmured, "Things get messy, you can always talk to me. In private, okay?" She patted him on the shoulder and walked back to her office.

"Quit burning daylight, you guys. Get to work! Dale's back next week, and Lou, you're fu—screwing up the ordering."

"Yeah, yeah." He said nothing more until she closed her office door. "Not *my* fucking job. Who the hell likes computers anyway? Give me paint, or give me death."

"I'd like to give you and your sorry ass death," Sam muttered. "Bitching day in and day out. Damn, Son. Cry me a river. Better yet, go drown yourself in one."

"Hey, not my fault Shaya liked my sparkling personality. Maybe if you opened your mouth to do more than grunt, the *chicas* would love on you better. A big dick can only get you so far, my friend."

Sam must have done something that caused Lou to mouth off in Spanish. Then Foley intervened, at which point Liam arrived.

"What the fuck is this?" the nicer of the two Websters yelled. "It's a garage, not a cage match, you assholes."

Before Johnny got sucked into the drama, he buried his head under Gizmo's hood, trying to think if he'd somehow given Del the impression he loved Lara. The l-word scared the hell out of him, and he did his level best never to feel so deeply if he could help it. He loved his father, the guys, and Del like family. But an abiding affection for a woman? That he could do without.

Because he wanted it so damn badly.

He had a bad feeling Lara was the one. The l-word. L *for Lara*. L *for love*. He tried to laugh off his worries but couldn't. A few days of committed dating, and he was seeing hearts and flowers and forever. It would have been embarrassing if anyone had known about it. Del had guessed, but then, she was good at reading people.

He had to make sure Lara had no idea. It would be beyond terrible for her to pity-date him. Or worse, feel sorry for him when she broke things off, the way some of his dad's past girlfriends had pitied Jack. Johnny could handle rejection—he hoped—as long as she thought it a mutual thing. So he needed to play it cool. To stop jumping on her texts or inviting himself into her life every time she had a second to spare.

He sighed, already tired of this repeat conversation with himself. He wondered what Lara thought when she remembered them together. How serious did she think they were? Did he rate a thought or mention when not in her presence? *And, Jesus, I'm a basket case.* They'd only been going out for a few days, even if it felt like forever.

Calling himself all kinds of stupid while he finished with Gizmo, he resolved to give Lara some space. *I won't see her again 'til Friday*, he told himself. Now he just had to have a little discipline and stop obsessing about her all the damn time.

He dragged his thumb across a stubborn bolt and drew blood.

And it didn't hurt nearly as much as the thought of not seeing her for another seventy-two hours and thirteen minutes. And counting.

Wednesday evening, Lara sighed and accepted her fate. She'd known she wouldn't be able to reach the weekend without being badgered. With Rena taking some time off from work, Lara had hoped to avoid this discussion. But Rena had finally tracked her down, demanded Lara order them a pizza, and cornered her in her own house.

"I cannot believe you didn't tell me any of this! I had to find out for myself, seeing Johnny exit the storage closet—*the storage closet*—ahead of disheveled Nurse Lara. You're such a ho. And then to avoid me for days!"

"You weren't at work."

"You have my number! You know where I live! *Oh*... On the outside you're pretty and nice, but on the inside, you're cruel and easy." Rena jumped next to her on the couch and bounced, munching on Skittles by the handful. "Tell me, tell me, tell me!"

"Oh my God. You're worse than my nieces. Give me that." She tore the candy bag away, wondering if Johnny was at this moment munching on Twizzlers and chasing them down with beer. "So you know Johnny and I are...dating."

"Is that a euphemism for doing the dirty all over the city?"

"It was just a spontaneous thing at Ray's," Lara snapped. "Get over it."

"So you're saying you've only done it once?"

And she'd silently accused Johnny of being a kiss-and-tell kind of guy. It turned out *she* was the one with the blabbermouth. "Look, you can't repeat this to anyone. You have to promise. It's important."

Rena seemed to calm down. "I swear. But come on. I'm your best friend. You *have* to tell me."

"Okay, okay." Lara took a deep breath and let it out. Let *all of it* out—her meet up with Johnny, her buried feelings, even dancing around the intimacies they'd shared, though she knew Rena would read between the lines. "So my real question is, since he and I are dating and monogamous, apparently, does this mean he's my boyfriend? Just some guy I'm fooling around with or what?"

"To be clear, is he planning to see other women while he's dating you?"

Lara frowned. "He was pretty adamant that it's just him and me bumping uglies."

"Ain't that a picture," Rena murmured, then cleared her throat. "So then, you're... If it were anyone else but Johnny, I'd say you're reaching toward a boyfriend. But Johnny's always nice but not too nice. So, probably, just dating? A little more than casual, but a little less than committed."

"That's what I thought." She sighed. "It's so stupid, and I know this will end badly for me, but I really like him."

"You always have." Rena nodded. "You guys spark each other up. I've seen it anytime he's in the bar near you. Even if he's sitting across the way, he looks for you. The guy is into you, but with Johnny, I'm not sure how far that goes. Either way, I think it's totally romantic he made you a half-frozen dinner after work last week."

"I know. It was so sweet. That's the problem. The Johnny I thought I knew was a player with little more on his mind than the girls at his dad's strip club. But he's been so nice to my nieces. Like, sincere-nice, not trying to get into my pants."

"Where he's already been several times around town."

"Rena."

"Sorry. Continue."

"He was so scary-tough when he beat Ron up. I didn't think he had it in him, and well, that hint of meanness is kind of a turn-on."

"Of course it is. What woman wants a guy who's a total pushover? You live in our neighborhood, you respect strength. And guess what? Women living it up on Mercer Island want it too. You really do need to come to our next book club. Abby's got this killer new romance with—"

"Rena, I can barely keep up with my class reading. Between it, work, and my family, I'm even having to squeeze Johnny in. Friday night I have off, and he and I are going out."

"Doing what?"

"I don't know. He told me he's setting it all up."

"See? That's romantic. Honestly, a guy who's already had you is going to the trouble of trying to impress you. That's a good sign."

Lara scowled. "Why do you keep acting like I gave away the cow for free? We only slept together a few times."

"You must have been good, because he's coming back for more." Rena wiggled her brows. "And we know he's a stud, because you still care about him."

"Shallow, but true. Man, he's amazing—and not just between the sheets." Lara sighed. "I just… It's too soon to think about tomorrows, but I *really* like him. Except I know they all look good at the beginning. It's seeing if they can stick around for the long haul that's the issue. Problem is, I want Johnny to stay. With my exes, I was past ready for them to go."

"So don't waste time. Bring your worlds together and see how Johnny handles it."

"My worlds?"

"Have him meet the folks. Have lunch with him at the hospital one day. Let him see the other parts of your life before you get in too deep with him. If he passes the test-drive portion of the relationship, then you think about leasing or buying, always with an option to trade him in at a later date."

"You do realize we're talking about a man and not a car, right?"

"Sorry. I just thought it tied in nicely with him being a mechanic and all." Rena smiled, her golden eyes glowing with mischief. "And you did like riding him, if I recall."

"Okay, no more bad puns for you."

"How big was his stick shift? Or was he all manual and smooth and—" Rena shrieked when Lara hit her in the face with a pillow. Then the girl hit back, and they laughed and mock fought until the pizza arrived.

The next day at the hospital during her lunch break, Lara wondered where her luck had gone. After an amazing day yesterday getting her work done, prepping for her next practical exam, and hanging with Rena—which always made life better—she'd nearly slept through her alarm this morning. Johnny hadn't texted. And she'd gotten Nurse Guyen, the ballbuster, as preceptor for the day.

She'd been either ignored, chastised, or forced to watch Nurse Guyen do everything at breakneck speed. Basically, Lara watched how *not* to treat one's patients, staff, or students. So in a way she was learning, she guessed.

"Is this spot taken?"

She glanced up from her lukewarm coffee to see a handsome man wearing a button-down shirt and tie. He looked to be about her age, if a little older, and he seemed somehow familiar.

"Um, sure." A glance around showed several other unoccupied tables. How did she know this man?

"We've never met, in case you're wondering." He smiled, showing even white teeth as he sat across from her. His sandy brown hair was shorter than Johnny's, and styled by a pro. The clothes he wore and his comfort in them hinted at a man of confidence and power.

"Oh, okay."

"That's if you don't count last week at the elevator."

She suddenly remembered nearly running him down. "I'm so sorry. I was running late and didn't even see you. Hope I didn't ruin your day."

"No, no." He opened the salad he'd bought, along with an iced tea, and grabbed his fork. "Trust me, getting run into by a beautiful nurse was a perk all in itself."

She blushed. "Well, you can't mean me. I'm not a nurse yet."

"A beautiful student then." His smile looked sincere, as did the appreciation in his bright blue eyes.

Attractive and forthright, two qualities she liked in a man. "Are you a doctor?" Best to nip his flirtation in the bud before it could begin. The students had been warned not to fool around with hospital staff, not that Lara ever planned on doing that. The *professional* doctors and nurses, unlike their fictional counterparts on television, didn't screw around at work. Too busy saving lives and caring for patients, they barely had time to finish a shift and eat before leaving so they could start fresh the next day.

"I'm no doctor. I don't even work at the hospital. Well, I guess technically I do." He took a drink of tea before holding out his hand. "Peter Fordham. I'm with Drey Consulting. We're instructing the staff on the new computer software you—they'll—soon start transitioning to."

"Hi." She shook his hand, surprised to feel it larger and firmer than she might have thought. Peter was more than a computer geek. He had a rangy frame and looked in decent shape. Not as muscular as Johnny, but handsome and wholesome all the same.

"And you are?" he prodded, still gripping her hand.

"Oh, sorry. It's been a long day." She eased her hand from his. "I'm Lara Valley, nurse in training. I'm here every Wednesday for morning shifts, I think. And some Thursdays, though that's been rotating with a nearby clinic." Where she learned more about working with behavioral-health clients.

"A long day, and it's only noon. Bummer for you."

"No kidding." She guzzled more caffeine.

"You think you have it bad, try dealing with Dr. Doyle. Excuse my French, but he's a real dick."

She smiled. She'd heard about Doyle, and most of the nurses said the same. "You don't say."

They chatted. Mostly he talked, and she listened, about funny things he'd seen in his week working at the hospital. By the time her break came to a close, she didn't want to leave.

"Well, shoot, Peter. I have to go."

"It's Pete, and I'm with you. Back to work." They

disposed of their trash—and he recycled. Another plus. They left the cafeteria together. "So I'll see you next week, same time?"

"I'll look forward to it," she said, sincere. "You made me laugh so hard I nearly choked on that bad coffee."

He grinned. "You think today was funny, wait until I see you again. I'll tell you about my brother, a chief surgeon who thinks he's God's gift to women and life in general." He made a face. "Trust me, you'll need to hear what I have to say if you end up working here. Brad will take one look at you and go in for the kill."

Her cheeks heated. "Yeah, right. Anyway, see you later."

He waved and left, heading in the opposite direction. As she made her way back to Nurse Guyen at the nurse's station, she wondered if having lunch with an attractive man was a bad thing. Even though she and Johnny were "dating," surely that didn't mean she couldn't talk to other guys, did it? Imagining him chatting with an attractive woman didn't make her feel good, but she couldn't say it put her on edge either. Not if Johnny had no intention of anything more than conversation with the woman.

"You're late, Ms. Valley." Nurse Guyen looked pointedly at her watch.

Over Guyen's shoulder, Lara saw Angi giving her a sympathetic look. "Sorry, Nurse Guyen. It won't happen again."

"It had better not."

One minute past the hour and she was late? This woman had a definite bug up her ass. "So, Nurse Guyen, when do we get to—"

"No time for questions. Follow me."

No time for questions? Wasn't that what this clinical was all about? Learning?

A fellow student joined them. Kelly something. "Nurse Guyen, I'm Kelly—"

"And *you're* late. Honestly, I have eleven patients today, and two students to take by the hand." She gave a loud sigh. "Try to keep up, ladies."

The shift seemed to last forever, and Lara didn't get to administer the medications or do the intakes she'd been told she'd do today. Instead, she'd been tasked with a lot of clean-up and busywork Nurse Guyen didn't have time for.

"Honestly, it's like she's running a race and losing," Kelly muttered as they emptied a patient's bedpan and cleared the sheets. Though housekeeping would be coming up to clean the room, Nurse Guyen had thought the experience of mopping up after a patient would do them good.

Lara didn't feel like she was too good to do anything, so it wasn't the idea of cleaning that bothered her. She'd washed her share of fluids and vomit from overstimulated little girls and the drunks at Ray's more than a time or two. She just wished she could have spent her time learning more medical procedure, not how to best scrub a floor.

"Yeah, she's not my favorite preceptor," Lara admitted. "You done your paper yet?"

"I'm presenting my ICU paper in two weeks. The paper is half the battle. It's the presentation part I hate."

"Ugh. Me too. And just think, we're only into our third week of the term."

"Kill me now." Kelly made a face.

Nurse Guyen arrived in the doorway and hurried them up. "Come on, ladies. We have a new admission, and I'd like for you to learn something about the process. I'll be at the desk. Chop-chop."

Kelly and Lara shared a pained groan. Time with Nurse Guyen would no doubt feel like an eternity.

When Lara arrived home that night, she was tired, hungry, and pissed off. Johnny hadn't texted her all day. Granted, they'd just started hooking up, but he hadn't responded to her message about Friday night. For once she had two nights off from work, and she had nothing to do for one of them.

Silly to feel let down just because a guy hadn't answered a simple text. Yet she had a feeling her disappointment was her own fault. Dating had rules a smart girl followed. *Rule number one: stop reading into every damn thing he does. Rule number two: stop caring so much, or your heart will be broken in tiny pieces when he eventually acts like a dumbass, as they all do.*

Groaning at her inability to reason like a mature woman, she deliberately avoided thinking about him. Instead, Lara dressed in her favorite grubby sweats, ate a PB&J for dinner, and washed it down with a glass of milk. She vegged out for an hour, but by eight she was dragging. Just as she'd started to fall asleep on the couch, watching her favorite sitcom, someone knocked on the door.

She debated ignoring it. Had it been important, someone would have called.

More door banging. "Hey, it's Johnny."

She woke in the blink of an eye and forced herself to calmly get up and walk, not run, to the door. After checking through the peephole and verifying it was, in fact, the-man-who-didn't-text, she again took her time answering.

She opened the door and waited. "Yeah?"

He held out a bouquet of flowers. "For you."

Nonplused, she took them and moved back when he stepped forward. He'd maneuvered himself into her apartment with ease.

"Smooth, Devlin."

"Thanks." He looked harried, which was unlike him. "You okay?"

"No." Before she could ask what was wrong, he dragged her into his arms and kissed the breath out of her. "There," he rasped. "Now I'm better. I've been dying to do that for days."

She clutched the flowers in one hand, his jacket in another. "Uh, hi."

His green eyes deepened as he smiled. "Hi." Then he did that thing where he caressed her cheek. He cupped her chin and kissed her again, so tenderly and with so much feeling she didn't know what to think. "I missed you."

"You did?" She frowned. "You didn't answer my text."

"Good."

"Excuse me?"

"I had Foley's phone, and he had mine. I'd be more worried if I'd texted you back, because it would have been Foley being a smart-ass. Don't worry, I'll get my phone back tomorrow. As it is, I've already spent a lot of time talking with Mrs. Sanders today. Foley's mom is such a trip."

Relieved he hadn't deliberately ignored her, she

perked up. "So what brought you by? You just happened to have a bouquet of flowers on hand with no one to give them to?"

"Something like that."

She left him to put them in water and thought they cheered her dented and dinged dining room table.

"So did you miss me?" he asked, his hands in his pockets. He'd thrown his jacket over the arm of the couch and wore a plain black T-shirt and jeans. It should have been illegal what the man could do to denim and cotton. The tattoos on his forearm stood out against his golden skin, and she wanted to trace them with her tongue.

Swallowing hard at the thought, she considered how to answer him. "Did I miss you? Hmm…"

"A simple yes-or-no question, Ms. Valley."

"Well, I missed some parts of you."

"Oh?" He grinned.

"Your charming wit. Your pretty face."

"And?"

"And that awesome tattoo I still haven't seen all of."

"I can remedy that." He pulled her with him to the couch and sat, then pushed up his sleeve, letting her look him over. "So what else did you miss?" He raised his brows up and down.

"That's about it. I'm good." She held his thick forearm, running her fingers over his ink. A muscle car, snakes, some tribal work, and hearts, of all things. The color pattern had been very well done, the art a thing of beauty. "Did J.T. do this?"

"Yeah. It's amazing, right? But don't tell him. He has a big head already." Del's brother could work wonders with ink. And he was a charmer to boot.

"Well then, I probably shouldn't tell you how amazing you are either. Your head is melon-sized as it is."

"Yeah, and other parts of me are just as big." He grinned but didn't pull her into contact with said parts.

A good thing, because her libido revved way hot way fast around Pretty Johnny.

She tried to subtly scoot away, but he held her fast. Instead of making a move, he cuddled her close in a hug. His body heat bled through quickly, and she snuggled back with a sigh. "You are *so* warm."

"I think you mean I'm hot. I hear that a lot."

She pinched him. "Braggart."

"Ow. Why are you always abusing me?"

She felt him kiss the top of her head and eased even deeper into him. "Because I can." She moaned when he started rubbing her free shoulder. "I had such a bad day." Well, except for her lunch, but she doubted Johnny wanted to know about Peter—Pete. She smiled. Her one bright spot had been a male version of Rena. A gossip who'd made her smile and laugh, and he hadn't been bad to look at either.

"Tell me all about it, baby. But hurry before the commercial's done. I love this show."

"Wouldn't want to interrupt prime-time programming," she said drily.

"I was kidding. You take your time."

She told him about Nurse Guyen around yawns. Then she closed her eyes, just for a minute, and enjoyed the warmth of his body and the joy in his laugh. *I could really grow to love this guy... Wonder if that's covered in the dating rules*, was her last thought before sleep overtook her.

Chapter 15

JOHNNY STARED DOWN AT LARA AND SIGHED. "YOU are so fucking beautiful it hurts." She gave a soft little moan and tried to move closer to him. Figuring she'd start to grow cold, he lifted her in his arms, noting how perfect she looked there, then took her into her bedroom. He laid her in bed, amused to see she hadn't made it that morning, and tucked her in.

Man, he was falling, *hard*. Hell. Who was he kidding? He'd already fall*en*. Just three short days until he'd been supposed to see her again, and he'd had to come a day early, unable to wait. She didn't seem upset that he'd arrived unannounced, but he knew he couldn't show up whenever he wanted, not without appearing like some desperate loser.

He hadn't been lying about having Foley's stupid phone. Not having heard from her had bothered him, and that he'd been bothered at all had annoyed and worried him. He was acting just like his father. When Jack Devlin went all in for a woman, he grew clingy, needy.

The good ones, the ones Johnny had loved and Jack had wanted to share his life with, had vanished when they finally learned all there was to know about Jack Devlin. Handsome and charming on the outside, apparently empty within. The ironic twist to Jack's sorry love life was that he dumped women who acted just like he did. Thus Johnny had grown up not knowing up from down when it came to relationships.

Sure, he could do sex. He'd refined the art at a young age, in fact. But he'd never been able to stick with a woman, never had one he wanted to stick with, to be honest.

He winced when he thought about his history. It was no secret he liked women. He helped out at a strip club and had dated his share of locals. But he'd never been a dick. Never cheated on any of them or had them cheat on him. In that he did not take after his father. Thank God.

But with Lara, a woman who meant the world to him, he worried he'd start acting idiotic. Like coming to her a day early and admitting he'd missed her. Like worrying about how to make their date super special so she'd want more. Talk about putting too much pressure on himself. *Damn, stop obsessing. Just roll with it. Enjoy spending time with her. Quit thinking so much about the future and enjoy the now.*

Easy to say, but hard for him to do. After giving her a quick kiss and leaving her a note, he locked up as he left and drove home.

Thursday he did oil jobs all morning and two more diagnostics during the afternoon. The mundane work and his annoying coworkers helped keep his mind off Lara. Foley and Lou could be *so* irritating when giving him woman advice. At least Sam had the sense to keep quiet, and with Liam on vacation and Del busy yelling at parts suppliers, he'd been spared Webster wisdom.

The majority of Friday had been spent finishing up

one diagnostic that took *forever*, which wouldn't have been so bad, but he'd also had to squeeze in two more crap jobs. Man, he was so sick of oil changes, lube jobs, and the other tedious shit any monkey with a wrench could do. Webster's Garage made its real money on the big stuff—emissions, engine rehauls, transmission work. Fixing difficult problems satisfied something in Johnny. Like he'd completed something important.

The clients always gave him a ready smile when he'd solved a vexing issue. Well, they gave *him* the smile. Del and Dale did the billing.

And speaking of…their service writer had returned from vacation in a much better frame of mind, even if Del did have him on bathroom duty. Today Dale wore blue-tipped blond hair that dragged past his eyes. He'd added larger gages to his ears but fortunately had decided against one in his nose. Jesus, Johnny didn't understand the next generation. Who the hell wanted weights in their ears and noses to make larger holes?

Ripped jeans, a long-sleeved skater tee, and a pair of boots completed the outfit, giving Dale a grunge-skater-motorhead look that the kid wore well. Went with the sneer too.

"Hey, Johnny." Somehow Dale turned his name into three syllables. "You done with Mrs. Rivera's car?"

"Yeah. It's just—" His phone buzzed. "Hold on. Hello?"

"Johnny." His father sounded…off.

Johnny tossed Mrs. Rivera's keys to Dale. "Hold on a sec, Dad. Yeah, Dale. All set and cleaned up too." He'd vacuumed the sucker as well as spruced up the inner windshields.

"Great. So *I* gotta move it?" Dale gave a pained sigh

but looked eager enough to get out from behind his service desk up front.

"Just do it, sunshine, and quit your bitching." Johnny took the call into the small lunchroom, where an old refrigerator that had seen better days hummed, on the throes of death. The Formica table and chairs were sturdy enough if not stylish. They went well with the scarred wooden cabinets, ancient microwave, sink, and overused coffeepot.

He kicked back in a chair. "Yo, Dad. What's up?"

"It's…well…"

Johnny knew that tone. With a heavy heart, he listened to his father's downtrodden explanation of his recent breakup from Kathy. Finally, a woman with a halfway normal name and decent personality, in addition to her silicone double-Fs and tiny waist. He'd thought his dad might have struck gold, especially because Johnny liked her.

"What did you do, Dad?"

"Hell if I know. Kathy just got to be too much. Said I wasn't sharing, kept it all to myself. Kept *what* all to myself? Shit, Son. You know me. Ain't got but a few thoughts rattling around in here as it is." His dad gave a half laugh.

"Are you okay? Want some company tonight?" They'd made a tradition of sharing a six-pack of Bad Breakup Beer each time Jack lost another one, followed by a rousing night of whatever sports game happened to be on TV.

"Nah. You go ahead. If I know you, you have plans with your new girlfriend."

"I do, but we can always reschedule." Johnny loved

his dad, maybe more because he knew he'd been the only constant in the old man's life since he could walk.

"I'm good. I, well, I broke it off with her. It was just too damn hard to get through a day without another lecture on how I'm closed off. Woman nagged too much, and life is about living and having fun. Not about wallowing in shitty feelings, right?"

"True enough." But Johnny knew his dad had been lectured on the same subject a number of times throughout the years. Johnny had no problems with his father. Life with Jack Devlin was about scoring a good time and enjoying the moment. Laughter, a good beer, and a nice-looking lady, and a guy's life would be complete.

But Jack's lady friends seemed to want more from the man. It made Johnny wonder if that's why he never seemed to gel with his own girlfriends. Was he the not-sharing type too? Would Lara eventually throw him over because he couldn't figure out how to communicate well? A sick feeling balled in the pit of his belly.

"Just thought you ought to know." His dad paused. "I'm holding interviews for a general manager position this week. So if you can stand by me for another couple of days, that would help a lot." And the pattern continued. When Jack went solo, he devoted himself to work. So much so he'd built a profitable business out of his club and bar in less time than it had taken many of his competitors.

"No problem. I'm good helping out, just not all the time." Johnny liked to keep up with the girls at Strutts, especially to make sure the dancers were taken care of. It helped that Jack made sure his people were nicely compensated, that the club was clean, and that no one was allowed to abuse his dancers.

"Yeah, well." His dad sighed. "I'll talk to you soon. I'll need you at the club during the evenings next week, but hopefully I'll have the new guy or gal in place by next Friday. Fingers crossed."

"Okay. Talk to you later." Johnny disconnected, knowing his father felt worse than he'd let on.

He was torn, wanting to be with Lara but also needing to support his dumbass of a father. Lord love him, but Jack hadn't had a lasting relationship in years. Even Kathy had only been a three-month fling. Hell, the one woman Johnny thought might have gone the distance had left fifteen years ago. To this day, he still thought about Amber and her generous heart. He wondered if his dad did too.

Now depressed when he should have been pumped about finally getting with Lara again, he finished work. He left for the day and cleaned up. Plans for a wine-and-dine date night seemed too superficial, something he'd do with just any girl. So he did what he'd decided earlier—to live in the now and appreciate what he had.

He picked up Lara at her apartment at six. She opened the door on the first knock. As usual, she turned girl-next-door pretty into casual-chic glamorous without trying. She wore her hair down, and it framed her face in a dark curtain of silk. A faint glitter of gold above her eyes, thick lashes, and a dusting of rose over her cheeks subtly blended to accentuate a beautiful face and slick, red lips he wanted to kiss and keep on kissing.

And there goes my cock. Hel-lo, Lara. "You look downright hot."

"Not too creative, but I'll take it." She smiled at him. "You don't look half-bad yourself. Anytime I see you out of a T-shirt, I think you're dressing up."

"I am. Impressed?" He tugged at the collar of his black button-down shirt, which he'd tucked into dark jeans capped with his favorite biker boots. He fingered his hair, wondering if he ought to see Rena about getting it cut.

Lara read his mind, stepping closer to run a hand through his long bangs. "I like it a little long up top." She kissed him, and his worries melted as he returned her embrace.

"Without a doubt, you're the best part of my day." A truth he really should start keeping to himself, but holding her, looking down at her, he had a hard time hiding his feelings. "So how did your Friday go?"

"About the same, and better than my Thursday. The bursar's office is still giving me trouble with my financial aid."

"Anything I can help with?" came out before he could think the better of it.

Fortunately, Lara just brushed him off. "Nah, I'll get it handled. Besides, this is my worry-free Friday. My one day with no classes, when I normally get most of my schoolwork done. But Ray needed some help with inventory earlier, so I scored an extra shift. Not a bad way to spend my afternoon, especially because I knew I had a hot date tonight."

"Really? With who?"

She chuckled, and they left her place and headed to his car. The air had a crisp, clean bite that refreshed him, and the cloudless evening let them watch the indigo sky blend into black.

"So, Mr. Hot Date, where are we headed?"

He sat with her in the car, unsure how to say what he wanted to express.

"This shouldn't be a hard question. What's going on? You look serious all of a sudden." She took his hand and held it in hers.

The warm comfort he felt made him want to tear his hair out, because he felt a schmaltzy feel-good moment and couldn't avoid it.

"I was totally pumped about tonight. I thought we'd hit dinner, maybe a show, add a little flowers and candlelight."

"Sounds good to me. But then, I'm happy just hanging out with you. I'm easy."

He paused, then had to say it. "Really? 'I'm easy'? You're just putting that out there for me to run with?"

"Please, Amelia could have run with that line."

"At her age, I'd hope not."

Lara rolled her eyes. "I *meant* I'm easy to get along with. Anyway, my point is we can just spend time together to have fun. I don't need a parade."

"Good. Because all that other stuff felt kind of fake. I'd rather spend time with you, focused on you and not some wackjob with a bad toupee serenading you with a violin while I try to act all romantic and shit."

"You know, you can fool the guys with your tough anti-romance talk, but I know you read literary magazines and *poetry*." She nodded. "Yeah, I saw those froufrou magazines you tried to hide behind your big books on literature and Hobbits in your study. You're a sensitive guy who likes to read. Own up to it, geek."

"Geek?" He sputtered, not sure he liked her knowing his books were for more than mechanical reference or decoration.

"Nerd? Dork? Does compassionate metrosexual work for you?"

"I am so gonna have to tie you up and act all caveman later to redeem myself."

"Sure thing, brain trust." She laughed when he cringed and covered his face in shame.

And then, somehow, his bad mood, depressing thoughts about breakups and lost love, dissipated as Lara's bright laughter lit him up from the inside out.

Lara didn't know what had put Johnny in a funk, but he seemed to break out of it easily enough. And if she could get past possibly having no funding for this term, meaning more loans that would cut into next term and delay—again—her degree, then he should be able to overcome a bad mood.

They spent an amazing evening walking downtown, hand in hand. They ate at her favorite soup-and-salad place, at his insisted expense, and simply shared the clear evening together. Later, they drove up to Queen Anne and enjoyed cocoa and a walk under the stars through a homey neighborhood she liked to pretend she'd soon move into.

"Yeah, see? That would be my style. An old Victorian with that gingerbread molding. Then I'd paint it blue, green, and purple."

"Seriously?" Johnny eyed her with dismay. "I thought only guys could be colorblind."

"Look. Tell me that's not beautiful." The moon shone over the house she pointed toward, illuminating its intricate detail. Looming oaks and sculpted shrubbery, in addition to the grand size of the place, had to put it worth close to a million, if not more.

"It's okay, I guess." He shrugged, one hand in hers, the other on his cup of hot chocolate. "You really like it, huh?"

"Yes." She sighed, in love with her life right now. A beautiful man by her side, in the most ideal neighborhood under a cloudless, moonlit sky. If she closed her eyes, she could almost dream of her perfect future and pretend it was real.

"So, what? You plan to move out here in a few years?" he joked.

"I wish." She kicked at a few yellow leaves on the sidewalk.

"You don't feel like it's a little too ritzy out here? I mean, half of these places have gotta go for at least six figures. Look, a BMW." He glanced across the street. "And a Mercedes. Now we're talkin'." He laughed and shook his head. "I don't know. This seems kind of unreal to me. Like, *real* people are living down the hill in *real* jobs. Upper Queen Anne is for a different sort."

"It looks just fine to me." She glanced at him but couldn't read the look on his face. "I'm not saying you have to move out here. But I'd sure like to."

"Why?"

"Why? Seriously?"

"I understand this looks nice on the outside, but everyone's got the same problems on the inside. Kids who don't listen, spouses who cheat, family who're out to rob you blind." He shrugged. "I don't know. I kind of like it more authentic. In my neighborhood, people aren't putting on airs. We are who we are. You come to my place, you know me. I work hard, I play hard, but I'm a real guy. Not some idiot wishing he had a bigger dick and compensating with a Porsche." He glanced at the shiny car in the driveway of the house they passed, this one twice as big as the last.

"My perspective is a little different." Funny that he seemed defensive about the neighborhood. Then again, a lot of her friends acted the same way. Better to make fun of the more affluent than to admit you wanted to be one and couldn't hope to aspire to that kind of money.

"How's that? Are you telling me you need a million-dollar house to make you happy? 'Cause I won't believe it."

"That's not what I'm saying."

"Of course not. You work hard to make a living. Or am I wrong? Do you work at Ray's just because it's fun? Amused by us peons, and screw the paycheck?"

"No, smart-ass. I grew up with parents always scraping by. I've watched them work just to make ends meet for too long. Don't get me wrong. We're a loving family, and I know I'm lucky to have parents who love me and are still married in this day and age. There's nothing I wouldn't do for my mom or dad." Because she owed them. Lara lived up to her responsibilities. She always had, always would.

"Yeah, I get that." He nodded and squeezed her hand. "But being rich isn't the answer. Being happy is."

"True, but I can guarantee money would make my folks smile a lot more. It's better now for them that I'm out of the house. If I can help get Kristin out too, then maybe they can take a vacation that's not one where they watch the grass grow in the front yard."

"Ouch." His smile looked brittle, but she had to make him understand.

"I'm not some money-grubber. I'd never be with a guy for money or what he could get me. I want my own money. I don't need to be rich, but I need to be comfortable. You've seen my apartment."

"Unfortunately, yeah."

She frowned at him, and he hurriedly corrected, "Your place is nice. But the building's sketchy, you have to admit."

"What? Our neighborhood meth heads aren't cutting it for you?"

He shuddered.

"It's not great, but it's the best I can afford while I'm taking classes. I'm not complaining," she said to forestall his comments. She didn't want him pitying her, or God forbid offering her money to help her out. "I'm proud of my own place. Of my schooling. I'm paying for all of it, and one day my education is going to pay for a nice house and a nice car."

"And if you're lucky, it'll pay for a quickie divorce from the boring bastard living in suburbia with your two-point-five kids. Ech. Come on, Lara. You're smart. You're pretty and determined. You don't need to live in Queen Anne to make something of your life. You'll be a terrific nurse, even though I think you're the best bartender I know."

She beamed. "Yeah? Even better than Sue and Rena?"

"Hell, yeah. I love Sue, but she's a little scary. And Rena spends too much time trying to pump me for questions about my love life."

"She's amazingly good at interrogation," Lara agreed. "Rena knows everything about everyone." She took a sip of her cocoa, pleased to find it still hot. "So you think I'll be a great nurse?"

"Nah, I *know* you will."

She smiled. "You're just trying to get lucky later."

"Honey, I'm lucky right now." He stared at her with an expression that shook her to her core, and she didn't know how to handle what she thought he might be feeling.

So she ignored it. "Oh, you're good. Not sure you're getting lucky later, but you're good."

The spell broken, he gave a half-hearted groan. "You're so mean. Must be why I keep coming back for more."

"Must be." She walked with him a ways before stopping in front of her favorite house. She still wanted him to agree with her, just once. "See that? It's got a porch swing, curb appeal, and it's not as big as all the others. It's like a cottage plus. That's my idea of a house. It's got potential for a happy family."

"And it's in Queen Anne." He snorted.

"It doesn't have to be here, but if I lived on this street, I wouldn't worry so much about my neighbors. I don't see any crackheads lying around, and everyone seems to throw their trash away in their—wait for it—trash cans."

"Ha-ha." He stared at the house.

"Come on. This house is nice. Admit it."

"Queen Anne is full of the same problems as everywhere else in Seattle."

"Yeah, but with grander houses."

He groaned. "Fine. The house is nice. I admit it. But it feels weird looking at other people's places and wanting in. I like my place just fine." He paused. "What do you think of it?"

"The neighborhood is nice. The house, um, well, I'd say it could use a woman's touch. I mean, there's no color or decoration besides your TV."

"What's your point?"

She blinked at him and would have responded, when she noted the twinkle in his eye. He sipped his cocoa while smirking, a man of many talents.

"Obviously you're not a fan of the home-and-garden network."

"I'd rather paint my fingernails neon green and tell Foley how handsome he is. So, um, no."

"Johnny." She tucked her hand in the crook of his elbow and started walking again. "I like decorating. It's that nesting thing women do. When I moved into my apartment, I had so much fun going to garage sales and thrift shops."

"Good with a buck, huh? That's a skill. My old man was pretty good at it when I was growing up. We never lived in a shack or anything." He smirked. "Or in a zoo, though you and I both know I'm an animal in bed."

"Bad pun… Though now that you mention it, I can totally see you behind bars." She raised a brow, wondering if he'd cop to the conviction he'd served, the one Rena had found out and told her about.

He coughed. "Well, uh, I was young when it happened."

"How young?"

"Not even twenty. And it was just that one car I borrowed."

"One car?"

"One I got caught riding in," he muttered. "I was going to give it back."

She groaned. "See? Bars. A zoo. It all fits."

"Speaking of zoos…" He paused, a glint in his eye. "I know how much you love my anaconda."

She stopped in her tracks. "Please, just stop. I don't think that even qualifies as a joke, it's that bad."

He laughed and kept on laughing until she tugged him to move again. "Sorry." He had to wipe his eyes, and the sight of his amusement did something to her insides, made the butterflies fly together and sigh with delight just looking at him. "Your cheeks are red, and not from the cold. You're fun to tease, baby."

He did his cheek-caressing thing again, and she felt her breath come faster, so she deliberately took a long sip of hot chocolate, finishing it off. "You're terrible. Funny, but terrible."

"And pretty, don't forget that." He drained his drink as well. "My dad provided a decent life for us. He built it on alcohol—he bartended forever before buying into Strutts. And he took business classes once I was old enough to be on my own. Dad's not good at relationships, but he's a pretty smart guy when it comes to money."

"Good for you. My dad's a big believer in working hard. Period. So he and my mom work hard all the time."

"No investments or anything?"

"When it's between getting through today or planning for tomorrow, you get through today."

"Yeah, point taken." He said nothing for a moment, then asked, "So let's say you had the opportunity to buy my place from my landlady. Would you?"

She had to think about it. "Well, the location is great. Your house is in a developing neighborhood, and I'd think the schools are probably decent."

"Schools?"

"You know, for people who have kids?"

He gave her a strange look.

"What?"

"I don't have kids."

"That you know of. Sorry, had to say it." She chuckled at his dark look. "I meant that homes near schools can have added property value because of their proximity to schools. So let's say you want to move someday. You might be able to sell easier because of the school district."

"Huh."

"Sorry. Kristin's second husband was a real estate guru. She picked up a few things she passed on to me, and I'm almost positive she told me that. With my obsession for the home network, I think about buying a house a lot. But not for a while, 'til I'm Nurse Valley in all my glory." She gave an evil, booming laugh, and Johnny just stared at her. "Sorry. I imagine myself wielding a hypodermic and get a little crazy off the power trip."

He laughed with her, and they continued walking. They passed house after house, domestic coziness dressed in wealth. But next to Johnny, laughing in the cold air, sharing stories and holding hands, she felt anything but lacking. She felt rich, cared for...whole.

Chapter 16

Tuesday evening, Lara pulled up outside Johnny's house and glanced at her phone. She had a few minutes to spare. He'd been emphatic about her arriving not one minute late *or* early.

He'd been awfully coy about what they would be doing tonight. He knew she had clinicals in the morning, but he insisted they needed the together time. Though they'd just seen each other on Sunday, she hadn't disagreed with him. A day without Johnny felt empty.

She'd been trying to figure out what he had in store for her, since he gave her weird taunts in his texts every time she tried guessing what they'd get up to. Knowing Johnny, the evening would end with her naked, but she had no intention of complaining.

Lara sighed. Talk about falling hard for a guy she never would have guessed would be so sweet.

Ten minutes later, as she stood in his living room and stared at him in dismay, she revised her earlier opinion. "Hold on. You're going to teach me how to work with different tools in your garage, on your car. For fun?" *Seriously?*

He wore a pair of jeans and a grease-stained T-shirt, and he held a wrench in one large hand. "Well, yeah. I figure it's a good thing to know, so no one can take advantage of you if you have car trouble. We'll just do some basic stuff. Nothing too complicated." He paused, gave her the kiss she'd been waiting for since she'd arrived, then added, "You're giving me a look. Damn. This is stupid, isn't it?"

"What?" She didn't understand.

"It's just... Working with cars is a big part of my life, and I wanted to share it with you." He shrugged, looking a little...hurt? "I was trying to be more creative with our time together, so you could see I like being around you for more than just sex."

Seeing him let down, knowing he'd put thought into this idea, she felt awful for doubting him. That he wanted to bring her into his world meant so much, deepening the intimacy between them. So even though she'd been anticipating a few orgasms, followed by mini marshmallows and hot cocoa, she put on her game face. "Okay. I'm in."

He blinked, then gave her the warmest smile. "You are such a sweetheart. Trust me. You're going to love this."

She doubted it, but for him, okay.

He took her jacket from her. "I have a space heater in the garage, so we'll be nice and toasty while we work. And don't worry. I cleaned up in there. Go on in." He prodded her toward the door leading to the garage.

Here goes nothing.

She followed him into the roomy two-car garage, adjusting to the bright work light hanging overhead. As expected, his garage reflected his personality. He had nothing but his car and tools in the place. No boxes or gardening gear anywhere to be seen. A neat workbench sat against the wall, buffered on one side by a large storage locker and on the other by what looked like a large air compressor. He'd rolled his giant toolbox next to a stool by his car.

His *red* car?

"Is this new?" She walked around it, curious, since she could have sworn his car was green and another make altogether. This one had a white stripe around the base. Thick tires and shiny silver hubcaps grounded the vehicle. To her surprise, she saw he now had a convertible.

"Nah. It belongs to a friend. Nice, huh?"

She nodded, peering into the windows, noting the deep black vinyl, the fuzzy dice. A pack of cigarettes? Definitely not his then.

She turned to see him taking off his shirt, and her mouth watered. Dear God, he also had a smudge of grease on one cheek. Her dream hunk of a mechanic come to life. She just stared at the sleeve of tattoos covering his left arm, at the play of muscle on his taut frame. She wanted to lick him from head to toe.

Totally not the effect he'd been going for, trying to share his life with her *without* sexing her up, for once. She totally respected him for that, even if she was having a hell of a time getting her body to agree.

Seeing where her gaze lingered, he gave a self-deprecating grin. "Sorry. I get really hot when I work. Do you want me to put my shirt back on?"

"*No*. Um, no. Be comfortable." Feeling like a dog in heat, she swallowed and turned back to the car. "So, ah…" She coughed to clear her throat. "Should we pop the hood?"

"Yeah." He moved to the car, took two pins out of the hood, then pulled a lever in the bumper and raised it. The thing stayed up on its own. "Would you look at that?"

She was doing her best to focus on the car and not the hot man next to her. "It's nice."

"Nice?" He snorted. "Honey, that's a work of art." He nodded for her to lean closer to the engine, which she had to admit looked clean enough to eat off of. "This beauty is four hundred fifty horsepower of cowl-inducted perfection." His low voice sounded like a purr—the same voice he used when he made love to her.

He shifted so she could get a better look. Then somehow he was behind her, leaning into her, his body hard and hot against the thin shirt and jeans she wore. She felt enveloped, overheated, and totally turned on.

"This," he whispered, "is a 1970 Chevelle. Dreamy, isn't she?" His breath grazed her ear, and she shivered. "Lean lines, power under the hood, and the noises she makes get me fuckin' hard."

Lara tried not to swallow her tongue. "Y-you really like this car, huh?"

"We're going to have some fun with her." He nibbled on her earlobe, and she felt faint. Good God, how could a half-naked man going on about a car be so damn erotic?

"Fun is good." She sounded breathless, but sue her.

"Yeah. Scoot back." He tugged her away from the engine and closed the hood. Then he set the hood pins back in place. "Grab that blanket, would you?"

She glanced around and saw a thick blanket on top of the counter against the wall. It felt soft and smelled as if it had been freshly laundered. "You're not going to get this dirty, are you?" The blue fabric looked too nice to mess up with grease and car parts.

"Nah. We're gonna protect the car with it. Can you fold it over, so it has some padding, and set it on the hood? Like in a four-by-four square?"

She did her best, making sure the thick material covered the car's shiny paint job. "Okay, now wh—"

He spun her around and kissed her. His mouth and hands were everywhere, the subtle scents of cologne and man infused with sex tantalizing her until she didn't know up from down. Clutching his arms while he eased her back, she started when she felt the car behind her.

"Johnny?"

His wicked grin warned her to be wary. "Oh yeah. Now let me show you how to work."

Still breathing hard, she watched as he lifted her shirt over her head and tossed it onto the stool, then unfastened her bra and added it to the growing pile. Her shoes hit the floor, then her socks. She couldn't speak, her mind and body in a knot as she realized he had staged a seduction…in his garage.

With slow tugs, he eased her jeans off her until she stood clad in a pair of skimpy red panties.

"Christ. You had to wear red, didn't you?" He sighed, then kissed his way up her legs, keeping his attention on her inner thighs. The drag of his stubbled chin and hot, firm lips made her shiver as he took her panties off.

"Cold?"

"No." She hadn't noticed the temperature since he'd taken off his shirt. But now that he mentioned it, the space heater gave the room ample warmth.

He smiled at her, the Devlin charm working overtime, and eased her back onto the blanket on the hood. Then he spread her thighs wide.

And it hit her.

Her fantasy—Johnny's head between her legs, in a garage, on top of a red car.

"Oh my God."

"Oh yeah," he agreed, and put his mouth over that taut, wet part of her screaming for his touch.

She arched into him, so ready she feared coming in seconds. His firm grip on her thighs hampered any escape, and he licked and teased with impassioned groans of his own.

Lara tried to hold out, but she'd never been consumed with such fervor. The relentless build of passion was overtaken by an explosion of pleasure. She cried out as she came, and Johnny continued to suck that hard nub while adding his fingers, stroking inside her.

"Too much," she moaned, overcome with sensation.

He raised his head. "Not enough," he growled back. His eyes seemed impossibly green, his lips shiny with her arousal. "Again."

He couldn't mean…

She said his name—a prayer, a curse, a plea—and gave herself up to the sensual caress of callused fingers and smooth lips. He didn't give her time to come down before ramping her up again.

"In me this time." She tugged at his silky hair.

He left her clit and nipped his way to her thighs. "Touch your breasts." He bit her gently, and she trembled. "Pinch your nipples. You've got me so hard, so ready to come."

"*Yes*." She pinched herself, aroused even more.

"That's it. You're so wet. I can slide right up into you, can't I?"

"Do it."

"Not yet." Then he shocked her by giving her a light slap, right *there*—between her legs.

She seized, incoherent while her world blew apart, only to feel his mouth over her again. And the ecstasy kept coming…

An hour later, while Lara lay on her bed and stared at her ceiling, she marveled at how she'd gotten from his garage, naked, to dressed and back in her bed in pajamas. The trip home had been a blur, her mind and body still reeling from a fantasy made real.

And through all of it, Johnny had refrained from taking his pleasure. Instead, he'd given her multiple orgasms, then tenderly dressed her and put her back into her car with words of advice: *"Good luck tomorrow, baby. Don't let that Nurse Guyen screw with you. Remember, don't get mad. Get even."*

Nope. The only person Lara planned on letting screw with her was a shifty mechanic with an oral fixation. That tricky, tricky Johnny. Teach her how to fix a car. Ha. He'd fixed her instead.

She smiled as she fell into sleep, the last thoughts on her mind…*I can't wait to get even with* you, *Johnny Devlin. And God bless that mouth of yours.*

Thursday afternoon, Lara discreetly frowned down at her phone. Four hang-ups in the past week. At first she'd thought it was a wrong number. Then a prank. But since Kristin had mentioned seeing Ron again and talking with him about their divorce, Lara had a bad feeling Ron hadn't taken their last altercation in stride. Of course, getting one's face bashed in and being rejected by the woman you wanted to grope couldn't be considered a character builder by the rich and elite.

Knowing that Ron could afford to live in any of the houses she and Johnny had looked at last week burned her. That huge jerk would have no problem shelling out a few grand for nursing classes, but she couldn't afford this term, let alone the next one. Financial aid wasn't aiding her at all, and she knew she'd have to make some decisions soon when it came time to register for next term.

Her instructor snapped her book closed. "Okay. We'll see you all next week. Enjoy your weekend."

Lara stood with her peers and left the classroom, determined to put her stupid cell phone and her lack of finances out of her mind. She'd finished her paper and given her presentation today. So she could check that major to-do off her list. Now she needed to work at Ray's throughout the weekend, finally pay off the cost of her textbooks with this week's check, and think about what she and Johnny might do together. It was her turn to plan their big date night.

After ducking into a restroom to change out of her scrubs, pleased she wouldn't have to wash the hell out of them, since they'd used a clinical day to present papers, she dressed once again in jeans and a sweater and left, feeling refreshed and recharged for the rest of the week.

With a smile, she walked into surprising sunshine. The past week with Johnny had been perfect. *Too* perfect. They spent time together—and though her fantasy continued to haunt her in only the best way—they'd made more than love. They'd made memories. She'd learned more about him, including the fact that he couldn't do more in the kitchen than point her to the microwave. They'd spent four of the past five days eating dinner together before going their separate ways, and the domesticity and intimacy of their time spent with each other meant more to her than the sex had.

Not exactly true, her girlie parts protested. Having had Johnny, she wanted him again. Not counting her fantasy on Tuesday night, they hadn't had sex since last Saturday, when they'd spent the afternoon in bed. Good Lord, that man knew how to use his tongue... Knowing he'd honed his skills on other women bothered her in some ways, but overjoyed her in too many others to count.

It wasn't as if she'd been virginal before sleeping with him either. But she'd never been so in tune with a partner like she was with him. Dating Johnny showed her a whole new way to interact with men. She found him genuinely funny and enjoyed spending time with him. Even better, she trusted him. Despite knowing he helped out at Strutts, she believed him when he said he viewed the girls as family.

She'd overheard Foley and Sam teasing him about it at the bar a time or two when they couldn't have known she'd been near. Her relief had been enormous. Trusting Johnny's word should have been enough, but for his friends to confirm it made all the difference.

"Not my fault, really. I don't know him all that well," she mumbled to herself on her way to her car. She'd want him to believe what *she* said without proof. But Lara wasn't a dating fiend, and the sex she had with Johnny meant something to her.

The question remained—what did it mean to him?

She reached her car and saw a folded note between the windshield and a wiper. Curious, she opened it and read, then stood there dumbfounded. She debated with herself and tucked it into her purse. A quick text to her sister told her Kristin was home—at their *parents'* home. So she drove there, ready for a showdown. At least the girls wouldn't be around for this conversation with her sister, occupied with dance practice after school.

Lara pulled into the driveway and took a deep breath before letting it out. It was past time she had a come-to-Jesus talk with Kristin. And past time her sister put on her big-girl panties and stopped using Lara to clean up her messes.

With that thought in mind, Lara entered the house and found Kristin sitting at the dining room table, her head in her hands, her hair a mess, as she stared at papers scattered over the tabletop.

"Um, am I interrupting anything?"

Kristin glanced up, annoyance in her light-brown eyes. "Actually, you are. This mess is what I now have to go through since you convinced me to ditch my lawyer."

"The same lawyer you were sleeping with? The one you got bored with and dumped? That lawyer?"

Kristin glared. "Yes, Ms. Perfect. Now I'm dealing with some woman legal eagle who wants me to organize all…this." She waved at the table in disgust.

You brought this on yourself by marrying a rich dickhead, Lara wanted to say but didn't. "Have you talked to Ron lately?"

"My two-timing scum of a husband?" Kristin said with a sneer. "The same one who hit on my prettier, smarter, all-around *better* younger sister, even though we're not divorced yet? That Ron?"

"You know, I don't appreciate your tone." Lara took

the paper from her purse and tossed it to her sister. "Your husband left me a note. Read it."

Kristin glanced down at the paper and began, "Dear Lara, I'm sorry for the other night. I don't know what came over me. You won't believe it, but my breakup with Kristin is hitting me hard." Kristin stopped reading and speared Lara with a frown.

Lara shook her head. "Yeah, I don't believe it either."

"What's he talking about? The other night?"

Lara gave her a vague explanation about Ron trying to steal a kiss and left it at that.

Kristin scowled. "What an ass." She turned back to the note and continued reading. "I messed up, and I'm sorry. My intention was not to hurt you. Quite the contrary. I was hoping we could be friends. I always liked you. Not like I love my wife, but we were family."

Lara watched Kristin tear up, wondering if her sister was starting to believe Ron's bullshit.

"I have only myself to blame, for my weakness for other…pleasures. I want only to part ways with Kristin as amicably as possible. So please let her know I've reconsidered my percentage for her in hopes for an uncontested divorce."

Then Kristin read a number that frankly made Lara weep to hear. Granted, they weren't talking millions, but with that amount, Kristin could care for herself and the girls, enough to get herself on her feet without stressing about bills for a few years.

"I hope that we can put the issue of child support to bed," Kristin kept reading. "I never adopted the girls, and I'm sorry to say we never bonded. With this amount and the small cottage in Ballard, Kristin should be set for a very long time, and she can give Kay and Amelia the love and support they need. Tell Kristin not to hesitate to talk to me, because the sooner we get this done, the sooner we can both move on." Kristin wiped her eyes. "Wow. I can't believe that."

"Neither can I." Ron wasn't the type to be sorry about anything, except getting caught.

"That figure was pretty generous, I guess."

"It's fair." Something Lara hadn't thought Ron would ever suggest. "Kristin, take it, sign the papers, and don't look back. Put this behind you and—"

"And what?" Kristin snapped, her sudden anger surprising.

"Kristin?"

"Go ahead, Lara. Tell me exactly how to make my life better, so I can be perfect like you."

"Excuse me?"

"I bet you were thrilled when Ron tried to kiss you."

"*What?*"

"So you could show me what a scum he is. What *another* terrible decision I'd made." Kristin started crying again, ugly, angry tears that were all the more shocking because they were real. This wasn't a pity-me moment, but a rare showing of her sister's deep feelings. "I'm sorry he did that, but if he felt anything like I've been feeling, I get it."

"What are you talking about? You're siding with Ron against me? What have I ever done but support you? Taking care of the girls, lending you a buck or two when I barely have any for myself?"

"That's right." Kristin stood and shoved her hair back from her flawless, tear-stained face. "The good daughter, the one who's never accepted a handout and made her own way in the world. What the fuck do you know about struggle? You, who's always made up your own rules as you go. You, who everyone looks at as if she's so smart. Intelligent and pretty, unlike her dopey older sister. 'Kristin's dumb as a brick, but at least she's beautiful. It won't last, but it's good enough for now.'"

"What are you talking about?" Lara lost her anger under a well of concern.

"You know *exactly* what I'm talking about. I have nothing more than *this* to work with." She gestured at her own body. "Yeah, I know you think I'm a slag who has nothing else going for her than sexing up the next potential husband."

Ashamed, because she had thought that a time or two when upset with her sister, Lara flushed. "No, that's not—"

"I don't blame you for it. That's all I'm good for. I don't like school. I don't know what else to do with myself. I can cook and clean, I'm good at being a mom." Her face crumpled. "Or maybe I'm not. I sure haven't shown Kay or Amelia how to stand on their own."

"Oh, Kristin." Lara took her sister in her arms and held her while she sobbed. "It'll be okay. I swear. We're here for you."

"But you shouldn't always have to be." Kristin gently disengaged and stepped back. "I love you, Lara. And I'm sorry I'm being such a bitch. It's just, it's so hard being your sister."

"What?"

"I always seem to keep failing, while you always seem to succeed. Lara, I'm ending my fourth marriage, and I just turned thirty. I keep finding guys that seem so great and turn out to be so wrong."

"Sean wasn't wrong," Lara pointed out. "He loved you. But you wanted more."

"We were too young, and my marriage was too hard. I thought it would be like the movies. The right house, the right yard, the right career man." She sighed. "I'm like you in some ways, little sister. I want out of this fucking life, like, yesterday."

"Huh?"

"Oh, come on. We all know you think you're better than all this. And like I said, I don't blame you. Mom and Dad might be happy working twenty-four seven, three hundred sixty-five days a year. No vacations, no breaks. Just work, work, work. But I want to enjoy life. And so do you—that's why you moved out of here as soon as you were able. We all know it. Independence is great, but you really wanted to be more than a minimum-wage flunkie."

"That's not true…" Not true, exactly…

"Why do you think I jumped at Sean's proposal? I wanted more. Except I got more of the same. And then I had to deal with the financial aspect of being a couple. Joint bills, accounts, his investments… You know money talk gives me a headache."

"So you married rich Josh."

"Another mistake." Kristin grabbed a tissue and wiped her nose. Despite her red-rimmed eyes, she still radiated beauty, and Lara hurt for her, seeing Kristin's pain in a new light. Knowing her sister acknowledged her own insecurities and failings made Lara feel terrible for her high-and-mighty attitude.

"Well, but you tried—"

"To fix a poor problem with money. Josh seemed so right on the outside, but he wanted someone more than me. You don't think I know why he married me, but I do. He wanted a pretty blond with an hourglass figure and an empty head. But he didn't know what to do with me when he got me."

"Kristin, you're not an empty head."

"Bullshit. I don't want a career. I don't want to work all the time and make my own way. I just want a family." Tears trailed down her cheeks. "I want someone to love me for me, to accept me as I am. And I keep finding the wrong guys. I have two beautiful children, and Josh wants nothing to do with Amelia." She hiccupped. "She's an angel, and because of me, he won't know her."

"What?"

"He says she reminds him of me, his stupid mistake that thankfully didn't cost him millions. Smart guy had a prenup I didn't mind signing. Like Ron." She sighed, looking sadder than Lara had ever seen her. "I wish I was like you, Lara. You don't care what anyone else thinks. You'd work your ass off in Mom's diner if you had to, and it wouldn't bother you at all to work for lousy tips and come-ons from guys who view you as nothing but a piece of ass."

"Oh, Kristin." She hugged her sister, and this time Kristin let her hold on.

"I'm sorry. I'm so sorry. I take you for granted with the girls because I know you love them. And it's easier for me to live here than being on my own. I'm so hopeless. I don't know how to get an apartment or manage my

bills. And after all Dad taught us about saving a penny."
She choked on a pitiful laugh. "Maybe I was adopted."

"Nah. You look too much like Mom. Good try,
though."

They both laughed, and Kristin pulled back. "I'm the
big sister. I'm supposed to be the one everyone leans on.
But in our family, it's you."

"Not true. When I was having a hard time after high
school, you helped me see there was more to life than
just this." She sighed. "I love Mom and Dad, but I'm
not like them. I can't stand that they still live here." In a
house forty years old with rundown furniture and appli-
ances breaking every other day. Her parents seemed so
content, never wanting to strive for more, for a challenge. Just the humdrum of an average life. Lara loved
them like crazy, but she just couldn't understand their
mentality. And they still weren't quite sure what to do
with a daughter who wanted a higher education and who
never seemed satisfied with what they had.

But Kristin understood, far too well, apparently.

"I can't stand that they live here either," Kristin
agreed. "But for them it's home. It's not home for us.
The difference is you're working for what you want, and
I'm failing to take a step beyond the door."

"You're working at the diner."

"It's all I'm qualified to do."

Lara teased, "Johnny's dad owns a strip club. You
could always work there."

Kristin's eyes narrowed, as if in consideration, and
Lara hastily said, "Kidding. *Totally* kidding. Look,
Kristin. You act like you want out of your circum-
stances. Do you really?"

"Yes. I don't want to live here anymore. I want to be independent, like you." Kristin shook her head. "Not *exactly* like you, but on my own like you."

"What does that mean?"

Kristin paused.

"No, tell me."

"I think you can help me. Teach me how to stand on my own two feet. With the money from the divorce and a house that's paid for, I'll be in a great spot to start over." She wiped her tears. "It's time for me to stop my pity party—and yeah, I've heard you and Mom talking about me."

"Sorry."

"No, you're not." Kristin gave her a watery smile. "In return for all the help you've given me and the girls, I'll help you."

"With what?"

"With learning how to take chances. Granted, I'm not a great example, but I put myself out there hoping for love. You're so closed off, it's like you've given up on having a social life."

"Hey, I'm busy with classes."

"And watching the girls and helping the family. Let me stop you before you get started. Honey, none of us asked you to step in. You volunteer yourself all the time. I'm thankful for you, Lord am I, but there's no one demanding you waste all your time on the family."

Lara was hurt. "You're saying you don't want my help? That you don't want me watching the girls? Mom doesn't like me helping out with dinners or groceries or giving Dad a hand when the heater conks out?"

"We all love you, and we're all happy for your help.

But it gives you an excuse to be so busy you don't have time for yourself."

"That's not true. I date."

"Not in the last few years."

"What about Johnny? You met him the other day."

"Oh, that's right. The sexy mechanic." Kristin folded her arms over her chest. "How long has it been? A week?"

"A few weeks. I've known him for years. Only recently it's been getting more serious." How serious, she still wondered. Because she was starting to fall for her "sexy mechanic," but she had no idea what he felt for her.

"Yeah? Bring him to lunch on Saturday. If he's so special, he should meet the family, shouldn't he?"

Just what Rena had suggested a few days ago. "I guess." Nervous at the thought of what he might think of the invitation, she hemmed and hawed about inviting him.

"No." Kristin shook her head. "If you like this guy, make a move."

"You don't think it's kind of soon to bring him to 'meet the family'?"

"He's already met Amelia and Kay. And he hasn't bolted yet. What's the harm in inviting him into your life? It's not like you have to marry the guy."

"I guess."

"I just think you should invite him if you're serious about him."

"It's only been a few weeks," Lara protested.

"You just told me you've known him for years. The way the girls talked about him, he sounds really into you."

She started. "They said that?"

"Kay did. And she's pretty perceptive. Amelia just likes him because he's into pink and unicorns." Kristin raised a brow. "You're sure he's into girls?"

"Ha-ha." Lara blew out a breath. "Fine. I'll invite him to family lunch. But you'd all better be on your best behavior."

"Hmm."

"Now what?"

"You're actually going to do it. You've never brought a guy to lunch. Must be love."

"Oh, shut up." Lara's face felt hot. "Now what are you going to do about Ron?"

Kristin sighed. "I'm going to talk to him like a rational adult. Then I'm going to get my head on straight and figure out what to do with my life. Away from Mom and Dad and little sister Lara. I can stand on my own two feet. At least, I'm pretty sure I can."

"Well, there's no law saying I can't help you with the math part of all this, is there?"

"God no. Help all you like."

Lara gave her another hug, and then they took a good hard look at Kristin's paperwork, pushing Ron's note aside.

<center>~~~</center>

Lara showed up to work at six, only to be turned away by Rena. "Hey. I'm working tonight."

"Sorry, honey. I'm on tonight with *Sue*. You're working Sue's shift on Monday, so you haven't lost any hours."

Lara frowned. "No one told me about this."

"It's a surprise," came a deep voice from behind her.

She spun around to see Johnny holding one long-stemmed rose out to her. "Huh?"

Rena chuckled. "Yeah, my girl needs help in the romance department. Good luck with that, *Pretty Johnny*."

He grimaced. "I have got to get rid of that nickname before the guys hear it." He bowed to Lara. "My lady? Your chariot awaits."

"My chariot? That's funny, because I don't think I've ever referred to my car as anything so regal."

He tugged her back outside with him amid a bunch of catcalls and hoots from the locals already parked and ready for wing night.

Lara went with him, bemused. "I thought I was choosing our date for this weekend."

"You work too hard. Thought I'd show you a good time instead." He put the thornless rose in her hand, and she clenched it tight, bemused at how the gesture touched her. They reached his car, and he pressed her against it and smiled down at her.

"This is sweet." She kissed him on the cheek. Or at least, she meant to. He turned his head before her mouth landed, and she met his lips instead.

When she finally came up for air, she felt him thick and hard against her, his body telling her in no uncertain terms what they'd get up to tonight.

She couldn't wait.

"So where to first, Pretty Johnny?"

He gave a pained laugh and ground against her. "I want to say my bed, but we have a few stops to make before that."

"Oh?"

"Yeah. Unfortunately, first on the list is Strutts."

She blinked. "You want to take me to your strip club?"

"Want? No. And it's not *my* club, it's my dad's. He hired a new GM, finally, and I have to drop off some paperwork. But right after that, we're on our way to funville."

"Is that a euphemism for your penis?"

He chuckled and ushered her into his car. "It should be, shouldn't it?"

"Hey, my car."

He circled to the driver's side and got in. "Rena will get it back to your place tonight. Hers is in the shop."

"She'll need my keys."

"She told me she has an extra set."

"You really did plan this out, didn't you?" Mystified, she sat next to him, excited and ready for some fun. Because if he could top that fantasy in his garage, walking bowlegged for the rest of her life might be worth it.

"I did." He leaned close to kiss her again. "Man, I love kissing you."

She sat back and stared at him. His amazing body, that sexy tattoo, and his deep green eyes. His full lips she wanted to taste all over again. Lethal, desirable, and so damn sweet. She felt like a woman teetering on the edge of discovery, and it scared her to death that she might be falling in love with the man.

She blurted, "You're invited to family lunch tomorrow."

He froze in the act of turning the key and glanced over at her. "Family lunch?"

"Yeah, that thing I do every weekend? I'm inviting you to it." She shrugged, trying to project a casual tone into her voice. "It's no big deal if you're busy. But I spend most Saturday afternoons with my family, and my sister said I should bring you."

"Wants to look me over, eh? Make sure I'm not messing with her sister, is that it?"

"No." Lara shook her head. "I mean, I don't think so. It's not a big deal, really. I'm sure you have better things to—"

"I'd love to come. I can drive us, since you're sleeping over tonight."

She blinked. "I am?"

"Hell yeah. You don't think I'm going to lure you into my bed then let you go, not after being without you for so long?"

Which for him had been four days. "Oh, well, in that case, I guess I should pack a bag."

"You won't need any clothes." He gave her a thorough once-over, then started the car.

She flushed, feeling hot and turned on and shy, all at the same time. "Oh."

He grinned. "Buckle up, baby. You're in for a wild ride tonight."

Chapter 17

STRUTTS WASN'T AT ALL WHAT LARA THOUGHT IT
would be. Yeah, it had neon lights and women wearing little to no clothing. She'd never seen so many full,
perky breasts in her life. The clientele surprised her too.
She'd expected creepy, leering jerkwads. A lot like the
guys at Ray's, only without the charm of familiarity.
And yeah, she saw some of that. But mostly she saw
corporate types, college guys, and halfway decently
dressed men trying to wind down, as well as women
in the crowds. *Dressed* women, who didn't appear to
work there.

"Not as scummy as you'd thought it would be, huh?"
Johnny handed her a fruit juice and sat down with her
at a table. He refused to go next door to the bar where
he worked, not wanting to leave her alone for a second.

"I admit I'm pleasantly surprised."

One of the topless girls walking by holding a tray
spotted Johnny and lit up like a Christmas tree. "Hey,
Johnny." She came by and leaned down to give him a
hug. "We've missed you."

She was cute, dark-haired, and bosomy. The short-
shorts she wore showed off her tight ass, abs, and thighs.
Not a jiggly ounce on the girl except for her flawlessly
sculpted breasts.

Johnny had the grace to flush and gently pull away.
"Hi, Dory. Dory, this is Lara. Lara, Dory." He stood.

"Hey, I need to go find my dad. Can you sit with Lara while I'm gone and keep the sharks at bay?"

Dory winked. "Sure thing. Go on."

Johnny flashed an apologetic smile at Lara and left before she could ask him not to go. It was one thing to visit a strip club with her date by her side, but another to sit with a topless woman who liked to give him hugs.

The woman's smile faded after Johnny left, and her cool appraisal settled over Lara. "So you're Lara."

"Um, yeah."

"I've heard all about you." She turned to another woman and waved her over. A pretty blond wearing pasties and a G-string sauntered to the table.

"Yeah?"

"Jenna, this is Lara. She's here with Johnny."

"So. You're Lara." Jenna's eyes narrowed. "You'd better be good to our boy."

"What?" Their boy? Johnny looked older than both of these women.

"Johnny's a good guy. He looks out for us, treats us like family," Jenna explained.

Dory nodded. "When my Bobby turned three, Johnny gave me some extra bucks to get my kid a present."

"He's always doing stuff like that." Jenna sat with them, ignoring the wolf whistles around them. "He acts all tough, and he's a god with that smile. But he's golden deep down, a gentleman to his core." Jenna pointed a red manicured nail Lara's way. "When he announced he had a girlfriend, you could see the stars in his eyes. And that ain't like Johnny."

"If he's so great, why isn't he dating one of you?"

Dory snorted. "Johnny isn't a guy to mess around at

work. And he views us as family. Always taking care of the girls."

"Got Bubbles some time off so she could go to her old man's release." Jenna nodded. "Makes sure Jack knows what we need before we need it. He's a great guy. So don't mess with his head, you hear me?"

"What makes you think he won't be messing with mine?" Fascinated didn't begin to describe this conversation. She might have imagined the girls being angry with her for taking away their man. Not being so protective of him.

"Because you're Lara," Jenna said, a bit cryptically.

"But I—"

Johnny returned, out of breath. "Sorry, didn't mean to take so long." He gave Jenna and Dory a smile. "Ladies."

"Be good, Johnny." Dory grinned. "But not too good. Nice meeting you, Lara."

"Yeah. Have fun, you two." Jenna stood and sauntered back into the crowd.

"You okay?" Johnny pulled her with him toward the exit.

"I'm fine." And confused.

Foley entered, followed by Sam. "Yo, J." They saw Lara, and their eyes widened. "Lara?"

"You gonna dance?" Sam asked with a straight face and held out a wad of bills. "I'm *so* glad I brought extra."

"Asshole," Johnny muttered and kept himself between Lara and his friends as they passed through to the outside.

She waved at them, and the guys waved back and smiled.

"Sorry about that," he apologized. "I dropped Dad

the files he needed. God forbid he accept a download-
able spreadsheet."

"Not a fan of computers?"

"No, and it's biting *me* in the ass. I have to make sure
his new GM is computer literate. Save him and the girls
a major headache in the long run."

They left the parking lot, headed only Johnny knew
where. "You're a big help to your dad, aren't you?"
She'd met Jack Devlin at Ray's, of course. A dissipated,
older version of Johnny, no doubt from a hard life. From
all accounts, Jack Devlin had buried his wife young and
raised a troublemaker all by himself.

"I love the guy. He hasn't always made the best
choices in life, but then again, I haven't either."

"How long has he owned the place?"

"Ten years. Before that he worked at clubs like it. I
grew up around women who take their clothes off for a
living. At first I was intrigued. But like I told you, nudity
wears thin after a while."

"No pun intended," she said, and they both laughed.

"Did it freak you out in there? I saw Jenna and Dory
looking kind of intense."

"Just warning me to be gentle with you."

He turned bright red. "They did not."

"They did." She put her hand on his leg, bemused by
his tension. "Hey, I think it's nice they worry about you.
You said you're all a big family, right?"

"I guess I did. But don't worry. We're not super
close. You don't need to worry about Jenna and Bubbles
coming to Thanksgiving dinner with their double-Gs."

Lara gaped. "G? Really?"

He nodded. "Personally, I think more than a handful

is overdoing it. But tits—I mean, breasts—sell out the club."

"So how come you don't want to work with your dad? You've been helping out. I bet he'd love it if you guys worked together, to hand over the reins of the business to his son."

Johnny shook his head. "No way. For one thing, there's constant drama over there. Too much estrogen."

"Nice."

"I'm serious. And two, I love fixing cars. I'm good at it, and it's fun even though it's work." He shrugged. "I'm happy where I am."

She watched him. "But do you ever think about owning your own garage? About being the boss?"

He glanced at her then settled his gaze on the road. "Nah. Not now, at least. The guys I work with, we're all tight. I love Del and Liam, but don't tell them I said that. Del's a pain in the ass as it is."

She grinned.

"What about you? I know you want to be a nurse. You work your ass off all the time. So once you're a nurse, then what?"

"Then I save up for a better apartment. I quit Ray's."

"No, you can't. You're why I go into that place."

"Not for the beer?"

"No offense, but no. Not even for cheap wing night."

"Man, Ray will hate to hear that." She squeezed his thigh, aware of the bunch of muscle beneath her palm.

"So what else? You going to move away or something? Become a nurse to some grizzled millionaire rancher out in Montana and make a fortune?"

She chuckled. "Where do you get your ideas? No, of

course not. I want to be near my family. I may get nutty with them, but I love them." She paused. "And to hear my sister tell it, I invite more busyness than I need."

"Yeah?"

"Kristin and I had a heart-to-heart today. Ron left a note on my car."

"The hell he did."

"No, it's okay." That didn't explain the hang-ups on her phone, but maybe he'd been trying to figure out how to ask for forgiveness. And maybe he hadn't been the one making the calls. "He basically apologized for being grabby, then offered Kristin a better sum than she was getting before. He wants it all over, and she does too."

"That's good, I guess. But if that douche bag tries anything again, you let me know."

"I will, I promise."

"Good." His grip around the steering wheel was telling. "So about tonight. What do you have planned, exactly?"

"You'll see." He relaxed, so she slid her hand higher on his thigh. Then, because she could, she reached between his legs and squeezed.

The car swerved before he righted it.

"*Jesus.* Don't *do* that." He looked pained.

She grinned. "I thought we were going to funville."

He groaned then laughed. "Oh, we are. We're just taking our time getting there. Now quit feeling me up before I come in my pants, woman. And get ready for some fun I know you're gonna like."

Lara didn't seem as amused as he'd hoped. "Seriously? A nurse's uniform?"

"Not just any uniform. A *sexy* nurse's uniform." He'd had to guess on the size, but the tighter the fit the better, in his opinion. "And you don't have to wear it until next week's party."

"As a matter of fact, people I know, from work, will be at next week's party. No way I can go as a sexy nurse."

They sat in the living room he'd cleaned from top to bottom, discussing the Halloween party he and the guys were invited to, courtesy of Del and McCauley. Some gathering in Queen Anne that everyone who was anyone went to.

"So what then?" He frowned. "This costume was meant for you, baby."

"Oh, please." She tried to glare but ruined it with a pained groan. "You're so bad."

"I try." Amused and charmed because she kept eyeing the costume despite denying she wanted to wear it, he changed the subject. "So, tonight, a hot, catered dinner that will knock your socks off. Then a scary movie, complete with popcorn and Junior Mints."

"My favorite." She smiled. She'd worn her hair down, and every time she moved, it flowed over her shoulders and swept her cheeks. Her brown eyes seemed impossibly deep, filled with joy. But he wanted to see them even darker, lost in pleasure while he filled her up.

"Oh, and something else." He left her and returned with the results of his physical. "I'm clean." He'd implored the clinic he'd visited to rush him the results. Fortunately, his doc had understood, being a guy with woman problems himself.

"I, um, I see." Her cheeks turned a pretty pink.

"You?"

"I'm clean too. Well, I mean, if I'm not, it's your fault." She shrugged. "I haven't been sexual with anyone in a year but you."

"Sure."

"I mean it." Man, she was so red. "I've been too busy for sex."

"That's just sad."

"I know." She sighed. "But I'm back on the Pill, so I'm covered, I guess."

His heartbeat raced. "You're safe now?"

"Yep. I'm all synced and ready to rock the old two percent chance of pregnancy. Go, team."

He blinked.

"You know, I think Angi's influence has rubbed off on me." At his confusion, she said, "She's one of my nursing instructors at the hospital. She's a trip, and she's kind of snarky. I learn a lot from her."

He remembered her talking about her work at the hospital, learning about administering meds, admitting patients, and going about a daily routine. He had to admit he was impressed. She was so smart, his Lara.

"All I know is if I was admitted, I'd want you giving me sponge baths. Just sayin'."

She rolled her eyes.

"And with that said, let's get some dinner."

They ate a delicious meal from Bill's Kitchen of seafood linguini, Caesar salad, decadent cheese bread rolls, and some froufrou wine the place had paired with it. To be honest, Johnny didn't care much for the wine, but Lara seemed to like it, so he nodded and smiled with her.

They talked about everything and nothing. With Lara, the simplest conversation felt intimate. Like finding the cause for engine cutout in an '89 Bronco. He hadn't meant to go on and on about it, but he had her laughing at his attempts to try to find the problem.

"Yeah, so Lou is harping on me to get that piece of crap out of *his* bay, as if he owns that spot in the garage. Sam's arguing with Foley, and the swearing is crazy. Then we all hear that damn jar shaking, and everyone's diving for cover."

She continued to laugh, and he was grinning wide.

"Liam comes out from under the car he's working on and starts with f-this and f-that, and you guys are f-ing assholes and can't a man find a moment of f-ing peace. And Del's standing right over him with that jar while the others hightailed it out for a break. I'm doing my best not to laugh, especially because right behind her is six-year-old Colin, staring from Liam to Del. Then the kid lets out an f-bomb, and I can't take it anymore."

She wiped her eyes. "My God. I bet her head was about to explode."

He grinned. "Especially because she had a new client, this little old lady standing behind Colin, waiting to hand over her keys. I swear, I was dying laughing, because Liam went beet-red, Colin was repeating everything he said, and Del looked shell-shocked. You had to be there."

"Actually, I'm getting a pretty good picture right here." She stood and helped him clear the table, despite his demand she sit tight and let him do the work. "You're funny, Johnny."

"Funny-looking? Come on, drop the hammer. You know you want to."

She bit her lower lip, trying to stifle more laughter,

and all the feeling in him went straight south, filling up his jeans. If sex would have been the whole of it, he wouldn't have been so unsure about how to handle her. But being with her like this, feeling such happiness, it caused that bubble inside him to burst, spreading warmth in all his cold places. He fucking loved being around her, just looking into her eyes, holding her hand. Hearing her laugh. He could stare into her eyes and never stop, addicted to such soul-deep beauty.

"What's that look?" she said, still grinning. "You're awfully intense."

"I'm trying to figure out the most romantic way to get you into bed. Because jumping you right now isn't going to send a good message."

"How's that?"

"That the Rattle of Oppression is somehow erotically charged."

She laughed again.

"Get your ass in the living room. I have a special treat for you tonight."

She wiggled her brows and stared at the noticeable erection straining his jeans. "Oh?"

"Just go sit down and get ready for something amazing."

"Brag much?" she asked as she sauntered out of the kitchen.

He had to take a moment to breathe, to get a handle on the emotional time bomb inside him. From all he'd heard, read, and tried to piece together, the best way to make a relationship stick involved a solid foundation between partners. And that meant more than just sex, unfortunately. Johnny excelled at being charming. But to woo and keep Lara, he needed more.

After a moment, he carried a tray of popcorn and candy into the living room, where he had the movie all set to go.

"More food? Are you trying to kill me?"

"Nah. This is to lull you into a food coma, so I can do whatever I want with you later."

"Good call." She eyed the Junior Mints. "I love these."

"I know."

"You seem to know a lot for a guy who can barely work an oven."

"I learn fast though. Note I had the meal catered, so no heating up necessary."

"You're spending too much money on me." Her smiled turned into a frown.

"You think? I hate to break it to you, but if you hadn't come over, I could have eaten our entire meal and had lunch with leftovers tomorrow. You ain't breaking the bank, sweetheart. Far from it. I might just be a mechanic, but I do all right." He did better than all right, actually. He might have started out making pennies, but he'd learned how to manage a buck from his dad.

Johnny had savings and a few investments. He lived in a cheap-enough house, had a car already paid for, and had few if any bills. A glance around his place showed he hadn't poured the money into furnishings. For all that though, he wasn't rich, and he'd probably never be able to afford an upscale place in Queen Anne for Lara, not unless he won the lottery.

Bummed at the thought, he filled the silence between them with a smile and light-hearted banter. When he pressed play on the streaming video, her unmistakable enthusiasm eased him once more.

"Oh wow. *Creature from the Black Lagoon?*"

"I thought we'd go classic tonight. And there's a follow-on if you're still in the mood. *The Wolf Man*, starring not just one, but *two* film legends of the dark screen."

"Lon Chaney Jr. and Bela Lugosi. Nice."

"A creature double feature for you."

She gushed, "With my own man-creature next to me. I am so blessed."

"Or damned, depending on your perspective." He gave an evil laugh. "Man, I love Halloween."

"Me too. It's my favorite holiday." She snuggled next to him.

They spent the next two hours giving a critique of all they loved about old Hollywood horror movies, and Johnny enjoyed verbally sparring with her. He'd been aroused all night, and from more than just being near her. Just talking to her, seeing her smile, turned him on. Even her scent, the unmistakable floral sexiness that was Lara, kept him on edge, yet the happiest he'd been in years. Hell, in forever.

As the movie came to a close, they both lamented the fact the creature had been killed.

Lara rolled her neck and sighed. "I love it, and I hate it. Why does the monster always have to die?"

"I know, right?" Johnny stopped the movie and stood to stretch. "Ah. Bathroom break." He took his time, doing his best to get his lust back under control, and returned to find her…not in the living room. "Lara?"

He walked through the house, finally stopping at the closed door to his bedroom. He tried to ignore the pounding of his pulse, but there was no getting around how much he'd hoped their date would end this way.

Except when he entered the room and looked around, he didn't see her. "Lar—ah!"

She'd jumped out at him from the shadows and scared the living shit out of him. Thankfully the little witch was laughing so hard she didn't seem to realize how high his voice had risen when he'd shrieked like a little girl.

"Funny, Lara. You—oh hell."

She was wearing the sexy nurse costume, and the erection he'd done his best to get rid of returned full force. If he didn't tone it down, he'd end up looking like a two-second wonder by the time he took himself out of his pants.

"Poor Johnny." She held a toy stethoscope in hand and twirled it around. She wore a white top that bared more than it covered. The white camisole piped in red hugged her breasts and tied around her neck. A slender strip of white material bisected her midsection and flared at her hips, exposing the toned, creamy lines of her slender belly. The woman had a body on her, for sure, and her nipples stood out, the areolas darker against the sheer white of the costume.

Yeah, she'd been right. No way in hell could she wear that in public.

He continued to stare at her, noting the tiny white skirt. If she bent over, it would show her ass and every-thing in between her glorious thighs.

She must have read his mind, because she dangled the stethoscope from her fingers as she watched him, then dropped it. "Uh-oh." She turned around and delib-erately took her time bending over to get it.

She wasn't wearing panties.

Johnny could only handle so much.

He pressed up against her backside and kept a hand on her lower back. "Stay down," he growled.

She chuckled, a sexy laugh from low in her throat, and he wanted to pant with pleasure. Instead, he did what he'd been wanting to from the very first. Time to show Lara how to handle one particular patient suffering from a bad case of unfulfilled desire.

Chapter 18

OKAY, SO SHE'D BEEN DYING TO TRY ON THAT naughty nurse outfit. She'd admit it—to herself. She'd always wanted to be sexy and bawdy instead of girl-next-door wholesome. Only with Johnny had she felt that she could let go of her inhibitions and be the sexual creature she was deep inside.

Only with Johnny did she feel the need to show him all of herself, even the scandalous parts she wasn't always comfortable with. Being with him tonight showed her so much more about him. He was a genuine person, a man she could—soon *would* if he kept being so damn charming—fall in love with.

He was so adorable, working hard to give her the perfect date night, which after her perfect fantasy, would have been tough to beat. Yet he'd produced all her favorites. Favorite meal, favorite candy, favorite movies. He had an inside source, no doubt Rena. But the fact that he took the trouble to learn what she liked and wanted to please her gave her warm fuzzies for the man all over again.

Seeing how his eyes glazed over, how he tensed and grew hard just looking at her in this getup, made her feel sexy and strong. Being with Johnny never degraded her. He empowered her.

And now, rubbing up against her while she remained bent over, he aroused her.

"Nurse Valley. I'm sick. Really, really sick."

She stifled the urge to laugh and groaned instead when he palmed her ass. His big, callused hands felt rough and erotic. "What seems to be the problem, Mr. Devlin?"

He nudged her ankles to widen her stance, but when she tried to rise, he put a hand on her back to keep her down. She heard his zipper slide down, and her arousal grew. She felt wet and achy, empty. Her breasts tingled, and knowing he'd gone to a doctor to get checked out—for her—gave her the excuse to invite him inside. She was on birth control, and the timing worked out.

They could have sex, no condoms or stopping the moment. Johnny inside her, skin to skin.

She panted, waiting, but he only stood behind her, stroking her ass with his hot hand while keeping her down.

The bite of control threw her lust into overdrive.

"Come on, Mr. Devlin. Tell me what's wrong."

"I've got a problem, nurse." He moved closer to her and she felt him, sliding against her ass. That cock big and slick at the tip. He was aroused, wanting *her*. "I'm aching and swollen. In fact, I'm having a hard time breathing, and I'm hot."

Was he. "Maybe you should take off your clothes and cool down."

"Or maybe I need some medicine to cool down my fever." He pulled back, and she straightened.

She turned around to see his pants down around his thighs, his erection thick and long. He pulled off his shirt as she watched, and the sight of his sexy upper body, those ropy muscles bunching as the light played over him was mesmerizing. The tattooed car on his arm seemed to beckon, inviting her to touch.

"You do look hot," she agreed, not surprised to find herself breathless.

"You look hot too." He stripped off his jeans and underwear, now totally naked. The light sprinkle of hair down his belly traveled to nest around his taut balls and cock. As he moved closer, she marveled at the sheer size of him.

"I might have a remedy for you," she teased and started to untie her top.

Johnny stopped her and walked her backward, toward the bed. "Yeah, I think you do." He kissed her, devouring her with hungry lips and a tongue that took what it wanted. He stroked in and out of her mouth while grinding against her belly, his desire enhancing her own.

He inserted a hand between them, cupping her breast, stroking her ribs, her hip, then sliding into the hot, wet arousal she couldn't hide.

He groaned and deepened the kiss but didn't penetrate with his finger. Instead he continued to play with her, getting close but not close enough to where she needed him. Johnny kissed his way to her ear and whispered, "I need healing, Nurse Valley. A release for the pent-up tension in me. Can you help?" He nibbled her earlobe, and she sank into him on a breathy moan, so far gone she had trouble thinking.

"Now about that medicine…" He kissed her neck, her shoulder, then trailed his mouth lower, between her breasts. He nuzzled there, and mixed with the lust, she felt a loving so deep it brought tears to her eyes.

Oh hell. She couldn't stop herself. She loved him.

Johnny pulled aside the material cupping her breasts

and set his mouth over her nipple, drawing and teething the nub until she found herself begging for him.

"God. In me. Now, please." She writhed against him, but he wouldn't be rushed. Instead, he gently lowered her to the bed and followed her down.

"Not yet. I'm too feverish. I need to cool down."

"I'm burning up," she confessed and tried to draw him up to kiss him again. Johnny gave the best kisses, ones that took her to another plane of pleasure and reinforced the idea that with the right man, ecstasy would be waiting.

"So fuckin' hot," he agreed and kissed her other breast. He untied her top while he played with her, then bared her breasts fully and leaned back. "All mine," he growled. "I don't like to share."

"Neither do I." She yanked him down and kissed him, angry and frustrated and in love.

He refused to let her draw his cock into her and broke the kiss. "Naughty nurse."

It soothed some of her pique that he sounded as out of control as she felt. But she couldn't understand how he could wait. She was on fire to have him inside her. *Now*.

"Johnny—"

He answered by kissing his way down her belly and gripping her thighs. She tensed in anticipation. He delivered, moving until he lay between her legs. He shoved the miniscule skirt up and stared down at her. "Oh yeah. Burning up, all right." Then he kissed her there, right over her throbbing clit. He drew her into his mouth, moaning and gripping her thighs, spreading her wide for him.

Just when she thought she'd go insane and come with or without him inside her, he scooted up her body and thrust home. She cried out and came while he pumped, faster and harder, no finesse, no lingering. Johnny fucked her hard, kissing her while she clamped down on him. He felt so good she continued to seize, a rush of moisture urging him to slide deeper.

He broke from the kiss and watched her, his face a study of sexual agony as he finally thrust once more and stilled, jetting into her for the first time without anything between them.

Her orgasm had wrung her out, and she held him, feeling a tenderness, an affection, that wouldn't go away. He stopped shuddering and withdrew, only to shove himself forward again and sag against her.

"I am *so* done. So incredibly fucking done in by you." He kissed her ear, her shoulder, then her mouth with a lingering sense of possession. When he pulled back, they were both breathing hard. "God. I fucking love you."

They stared at each other, he with satisfaction, she with a sense of growing panic and wonder.

But before she could ask just what *exactly* he meant by that, he withdrew, pulled her to her feet, and prodded her with him to the bathroom.

"Not to cut the moment short, but no wet spots on the bed, Lara."

She narrowed her gaze on him. "Well, who made the mess, do you think?"

"Both of us, I'd say." He looked way too pleased with himself as he stripped her out of her costume. "Next time, wear heels and a garter with this, would you?"

"Next time?" *God, I fucking love you too. But I mean mine from the heart. Was yours just a vow of great sex or the real deal?*

"You know, for when I need healing from when I'm sick and swelling…down there."

She glanced down at him, aware he'd pulled back, all lighthearted and joking Johnny again. "A bit of edema, hmm?" At his look, she smirked. "That's *swelling* for you nonmedical types."

He started the shower and tested it for heat. "Oh yeah. Cock edema. Is that the technical term?"

She snickered, despite wanting to call him on his love comment. "Right."

He tugged her into the shower with him, hogging all the hot water. But when she would have protested, he switched positions with her and put her back to the rain of heat. Then he soaped her all over, his large, slick hands creating a new burn she was surprised to feel so soon after her explosive climax.

Finally clean, and now squirming under his touch, she let him maneuver her so they both felt some shower, with her back to the tiled wall, her side to the shower-head. He knelt between her legs, staring at the private center of her—enraptured, by the look of him.

"You are just pretty all over, aren't you?" He kissed her clit, and lingered.

She put her hands in his hair, unable to stop herself from touching him.

He moaned and continued to tease her. "I can't believe I'm still so hungry." He licked her again before glancing up and winking. "Nurse Valley, I'm due for my second dose of medicine, aren't I?"

"Yes," she rasped, lost in him again.

Johnny made sure to take the full dose. And then some.

———~~~———

They spent the night making love. Fucking. Having hot then tender sex, and turning her world upside-down so many times she couldn't think straight. Except for that one declaration of "fucking love," he hadn't mentioned it again. And she was too confused to call him on it.

Wrung out and trying to appear cool, calm, and collected, she sat with Johnny at her parents' dining room table and saw her mother and father looking at her. Not just a casual glance, but the one that said, "What the hell are you up to?"

Wish I knew, guys.

"So, John," her father said.

"No, Grandpa," Kay corrected. "It's John-ny. It's on his birth certificate."

Mark Valley raised a brow. "Is that right?"

"Yep. He told me." Kay sounded smug.

Kristin glanced at her daughter and laughed. "You're a lot more like your aunt than you realize."

"Yeah? Because I think she takes after you more," Lara said. "The bossy older sister."

"I am bossy." Kay nodded.

Johnny coughed to cover laughter, but she heard him all the same. "Sorry, Mr. Valley. But she's right. I'm Johnny Walker Devlin."

"Johnny Walker? Like the whiskey?"

"What can I say? Dad wanted me to have a bad-a—um, a tough-sounding name. And he likes bars."

Her father laughed. "I like that. It's catchy. And call me Mark."

"And me Joy." Her mother liked Johnny. So did her dad and the girls. Only Kristin continued to give him the stink eye, which he ignored. "I hear you like pink."

"And unicorns." Amelia nodded. "And righteous fangs."

Kristin frowned. "What is she talking about?"

"Righteous fangs?" Joy repeated, her eyes wide.

Johnny looked pained.

Lara grinned. "What are you teaching my niece?"

"Not fangs. 'Stangs, as in Mustangs. We were talking about that pink car, remember?"

Amelia defended him before Lara could. "And he took us to the fairy show. Pretty Johnny is nice, Aunt Lara. You shouldn't tease him."

"Pretty Johnny?" Her father blinked.

Johnny pushed his plate aside and lowered his head to the table on a groan.

Everyone laughed, and even Kristin cracked a smile.

Lara grinned. "I really need to tell the guys at the garage about that. I'm surprised Rena hasn't blabbed it yet."

"Aunt Rena!" Amelia clapped. "I want a haircut."

"Yes, when is Rena coming around again? I miss that girl." Joy put more hot dogs on Johnny's plate, and he didn't complain.

Her man had a huge appetite, one he'd more than earned after last night—which had totally worn her out. She yawned.

"Tired, sis? Had a long night, did we?" Kristin taunted.

"Oh yeah." Johnny grinned, and Lara swore if he said something inappropriate in front of her family, she'd brain him with a hot dog roll. "We had a double feature. *Creature from the Black Lagoon* and *The Wolf Man*."

"The originals, not the remakes?" her father asked. "I love those films."

"Must be where Lara gets it then." Johnny smiled. "Ever seen *The Man with the X-Ray Eyes*?"

Her father nodded. "A classic. You know, they have a theater that shows old horror movies on the cheap on Wednesday nights."

"When they're not showing fairy films," Kristin said drily. "Where do you think Johnny and Lara took the girls last week?"

"Oh, right." Mark chewed his food before asking Johnny, "So how long have you and my daughter been dating?"

The table grew silent, and Lara's nieces stared from her to Johnny with wide eyes.

"I told you so," Amelia said in a loud whisper.

"Well, I guess it's been a few weeks. But I've known Lara for years."

"Is that so?" Kristin had a militant look on her face. Shocking, but it seemed like she wanted to take her big-sister responsibility seriously.

Lara sighed. "Kristin, don't be a pain."

Johnny put his hand over hers on the table, in front of everyone. Silly to be infatuated with that action, considering she'd brought him to lunch and introduced him as her special friend.

"Yeah, that's so." Johnny smiled, and Lara saw the effect of his appeal on her family. Hell, even her dad leaned toward the man. "I had a crush on her forever, but Lara doesn't date guys from Ray's."

"Thank God." Joy snorted. "I know all about the type that go there. No offense, Johnny."

"None taken. I know my type too." He chuckled. "She was smart for not dating me. But then, well, I wore her down. Took me only four years and eight months, but I got her in the end."

Lara did the math in her head, shocked he was right. Johnny seriously knew when they'd first met. How endearing. Especially since she'd committed the same date to memory. *Pretty Johnny Devlin is so much more than a pretty face. Is it any wonder I'm in love?*

"What's with that smile?" Kristin asked.

Lara immediately coughed and drank some water to cover her happiness. "Nothing. Just thinking"— Johnny's foot slid against hers—"that I didn't just go out with him. I made him work for it." She turned to her dad. "He took me to see *Ouija Death and the Doll*, Dad. It was awesome."

"Now that's a date."

Her mother sighed. "I don't know where I went wrong with those two. All that scary nonsense. I'd much rather watch a love story."

"Me too, Mom." Kristin shrugged. "Lara and Dad are bent." She pointed at her daughters. "Just like you two. Don't think I don't know you're in love with Scooby-Doo for the monsters."

Kay shook her head. "Aw, Mom. I like Daphne's neat dresses."

"And I like Scooby!" Amelia shouted.

Joy scolded, "Don't yell, Amelia."

"Okay!"

Lara's father groaned. "And we were doing so well this lunch. Not one spill…"

"*Dad*," Kristin and Lara said together. It was like the kiss of death, because no sooner had he mentioned a spill than Amelia managed to knock Johnny's glass over, into his lap.

"No problem." Johnny righted the glass and mopped up the small spill. "It was nearly done, and I only had water."

"Amelia." Lara frowned at her niece, who promptly went from laughing about it to crying.

"That's my cue to go to work. Time to head off for the job." Her father stood in a hurry, held out a hand to Johnny, and shook it.

"You have two more hours," Joy said with a frown.

Amelia screamed her apology to Johnny.

"Yeah, I'd better get going." Her father bolted for the front door.

Johnny laughed through it all, then motioned for Amelia to come closer. She approached him with dread, but he only lifted her up and set her down on his wet lap. "It's okay, Amelia. We pink-unicorn lovers need to stay strong, even when we're wet."

She sniffled, grimaced at the wet seat of her pants, and threw arms around Johnny. "I'm saw-wy."

He rubbed her back and smiled. "It's okay, sweetie. But maybe you should be more careful with glasses, huh?"

She nodded and hugged him tighter.

Lara's mother laughed. "You'd better not have any girls, Johnny. You're a soft touch."

"And you're not?" Kristin asked her mom. To Johnny, she said, "I'm impressed. She apologized and stopped shouting. You're two for two."

He smiled at Lara. "I'd say three for three, but I'm not so conceited I don't know that number could change at any moment."

"Oh, he's a keeper for sure." Her mother beamed at him. "A man that smart deserves cheesecake. I made you one, since Lara said it's your favorite."

Lara blushed when he gave her a look.

"You know all my secrets, hmm? Well, you're halfway right. Cheesecake is a favorite, but second to Lara's chocolate chip cookies."

"She makes the best," Kay agreed and moved to stand near Johnny, giving her sister occasional glares for taking up Johnny's lap. Then Johnny moved Amelia so Kay could sit on his other leg. With a happy smile, Kay joined Amelia, taking Johnny's attention.

They continued to talk desserts while Lara and Kristin cleared the table. In the separate kitchen, Kristin said in a low voice, "Okay, Mom's right. He's a keeper. Any man who can handle my daughters without breaking a sweat or trying too hard has my vote. But if he hurts you, I'll make him wish he'd never been born."

Lara nodded and held out a pinkie. Her sister took it and shook. "Deal."

The ride back to her place happened in companionable silence as they listened to Oingo Boingo's "Dead Man's Party." She would never have pegged Johnny to like so much of what she did, and it made her wonder.

"Did Rena tell you I like this song?" she asked out of the blue.

He blinked and glanced at her. "No. Why?"

"No reason," she grumbled.

"I'm sensing tension."

Keep it inside, keep it inside… "Why did you say you loved me last night?"

He grew still. They pulled into her apartment lot, and he parked the car in silence.

She cleared her throat. "I believe the quote was, 'God, I fucking love you.' Explain." She crossed her arms over her chest, irritated and not sure why. Maybe because he'd said something so monumental, and she had a bad feeling she'd read into it all wrong.

"I, um, why don't we talk upstairs?" He left the car in a hurry and waited for her to join him. After locking up, they walked to her apartment in a weird tension that hadn't been between them since they'd started dating. Or was it hooking up?

Once in her apartment, she closed and locked the door behind them. Then she watched Johnny pace and run his hand through his hair.

"This is fascinating. You look completely freaked out." She tried to tease, but she felt too tense herself to sound truly amused.

He must have heard her insecurity, because he stopped in his tracks. "What's wrong?"

"I'm waiting for you to answer my question." She crossed her arms over her chest and tapped her arm, edgy.

"Well…what do you want me to say?" He looked so cautious, so ready to bolt at any moment.

Her annoyance faded as the love she felt for him mixed with compassion and, yes, amusement. "I want you to tell me the truth, not what you think I want to hear."

After a moment, he answered. "I know women," he said bluntly. "I know how to please them, to make them laugh, to make them feel good about themselves. But you, Lara Valley, frustrate the fuck out of me."

"Huh?" She hadn't expected *that*.

"I don't know what the hell you're thinking. I think I do, but then you do the opposite of what I expect. If I knew what answer you wanted, I'd give it to you. And yeah, I'm a complete pussy, because I'm afraid if I give you the wrong answer, you'll dump my ass for good."

She laughed, and his dark expression deepened. "I'm sorry. I'm not laughing at you. Okay, maybe I am. I'm just not used to the bar Romeo being so weirded out by a simple question. You're the one who mentioned the l-word, big guy. Not me."

"And that's part of the problem," he growled.

Fireworks went off inside her, until she realized what owning up to her own feelings would mean. A serious acceleration of their relationship, and she still had three more nursing terms to go. She'd worked so hard to get to her place in life, and she didn't want to ever grow to resent Johnny. Not when she loved him.

She stepped close to him and drew him down for a kiss. Gradually, his unyielding frame softened, and he shared a tight embrace.

She pulled back to cup his cheek, in love and scared and happy, all at the same time. "I'm sorry for pressuring you. We're at such a great place right now. I don't want anything to change."

He seemed to sag in her embrace. "Me neither."

"I love making love to you." She stroked his smooth

cheek, knowing that in only a few more hours, he'd have sexy, dark stubble there.

"No argument from me."

"And I love spending time with you. So much so I sometimes want my clinicals and classes to speed up so I can get back to you. That's not a great feeling to have when going through school, you know."

"I'm a distraction," he said with pride. "Good. Because you distract the fu—crap out of me." He cleared his throat. "I might have said something in the heat of the moment."

Disappointment swelled. "Hey, it happens."

"Something I meant to say when we weren't fucking like rabbits and my head wasn't about to explode, while I filled you up the way I did," he confessed. "But we can save that for another day, okay?"

Her heart pounded when she realized he'd in fact *meant* the l-word. And that realization made her hesitate.

A hurt look appeared on his face before it vanished as quickly, making her wonder what she'd seen. "Why complicate what we have? We're dating, we're happy, and next week is Halloween." His bright grin broke her unease. "So let's enjoy what we have and live in the moment. Life is about the now sometimes, you know. It's not always a five-year plan."

"Good advice." Then, because she couldn't let him think he was the only one battling feelings, her heart racing out of her chest, she confessed, "I agree we shouldn't complicate this. So I'm only going to say this once—I fucking love you too." She ignored the shocked look on his face and pretended she hadn't said such a monumental thing. "Now how about I bake some cookies for you, so you have something to eat besides me when I'm studying for next week's quiz tomorrow, and you're mopey because I have no time for you?"

He blinked. "I, ah, yeah, sure. Want some help?"

"With my secret recipe?" She liked the mingled pleasure and shock on his face. "Well, only because it's you. You can't tell anyone though."

"On pain of death."

"Wait." She left and returned, holding a genuine Suzy Oozy. "Swear on her."

He laughed out loud and swore his oath. Then he hugged her tight, no words spoken, and showed her a better way to make cookies. Naked and with Johnny.

Chapter 19

JOHNNY HAD A HARD TIME HOLDING A THOUGHT IN his head lately. All week he'd been bobbling orders and forgetting shit. He couldn't accept what Lara had told him, and he dwelled on it constantly. Had she meant that about loving him? Or was that her way of easing him down from admitting what a complete sap he'd been?

He'd only once said the l-word to a woman, back in the tenth grade when he'd had a major crush on Rachel Delaney. Well, not counting Amber, the woman he'd thought of as a mom before she'd left him and his dad for greener pastures. Granted, he'd been all of eight years old back then, but he'd become way too attached, despite knowing better. He'd seen his father screw up countless relationships by that age, but Amber had treated him like he mattered. Like they mattered as a family.

Depressed and not sure why, considering he had the hottest girlfriend on the planet, who seemed to be just as into him, he stared around at the Halloween party, thrumming to some amazing DJ fresh from a European tour. Somebody knew somebody, and they'd landed a hot ticket, which only increased the buzz about the party.

Without the invitation, he doubted he and Lara would have been able to get in.

"This is fuckin' awesome." Foley stood next to him, his arms crossed, watching the scene. He wore a cop

uniform, and Sam had laughed more tonight—sober—
than he had since Johnny had known him. Then again,
Foley masquerading as law enforcement was damn
amusing. "And quit laughing at my badge."

"The sexy police? Really?" Johnny grimaced. "Even
for you, that's cheesy."

"What do you mean, even for me?"

Sam had shown up in prison blues, looking every inch
a convict. Or serial killer. Either way, he fit in with the
party. "Here." He handed them beers. "Lou's coming."

"Always late, that guy." Johnny took a swift chug,
needing the alcohol for reinforcement.

"You and Lara look good." Foley nodded in her
direction.

Johnny glanced over to see her with Del, Rena, and a
bunch of McCauley fiancées, laughing about something.
The family Del was marrying into came with four brothers, her fiancé the oldest of the bunch. The other guys
seemed okay, and he'd admit he felt better that they all
seemed coupled up, at least. Because according to Rena
and Lara, they were a sexy, hot bunch of fantasy material. He could only be thankful Rena hadn't managed to
push Lara into reading her romance books. It was tough
enough trying to act all confident and dominant when
he felt like a scared boy wondering when she planned to
cut and run. He'd been so damn happy lately. He could
almost feel the tugging on the rug about to be pulled out
from beneath him.

"I like her costume," Sam said.

"Yeah, well, don't like it too much," Johnny warned.
Lara had dressed up as the girl from *The Exorcist*. He'd
accompanied her as the priest.

"Sure thing…Father."

Foley and Sam laughed long and loud.

He scowled. "What's with all the joy, Sam? I'm not comfortable with your happiness."

"He's finally getting laid," Foley explained.

Sam flushed. "Shut up, copper."

Johnny grinned. "Shaya warmed up to you, did she?"

"Maybe."

"She's a good girl."

"We have a mutual understanding," Sam said. "Besides, she's leaving in another month. We're just hanging out 'til she moves back with her sister down South."

"Oh. Okay then. But you better treat her like gold before she leaves."

Sam and Foley exchanged a glance, then exchanged bills.

"What's that about?"

Sam shrugged. "Foley thought I was shitting him about you being a mother hen. But it's true. Ease up, man. I'm not gonna fuck Shaya over. Seriously though, with this many hot chicks around, you're wasting opportunity with all the protective crap. There are some fine women at Strutts, you ask me."

"I didn't ask *you*. And I don't need opportunities when I have the real deal. Ah, here comes my demonic princess."

Foley groaned. "All this sweetness is killing me, priest. Come on, Sam. Let's go find Del in the crowd before Father Love Bunches makes me throw up."

"Amen."

Johnny gave them both the blessed finger, then put it away when Lara and Rena arrived.

"Nice gesture." Rena chuckled. "You make a hot but not believable priest."

"And just who are you, my child?" He tucked a possessive arm around his gorgeous girlfriend.

"Meet Selena Blackwood."

Rena looked amazing in a cropped top, short coveralls, and brown work boots. She had a fake tool belt around her waist and her hair done up in a clip that let stray curls dance around her face and neck. As usual, she had a joyous glow that only added to her beauty.

"Should I know you?"

Rena sighed. "It's a terrific costume if you read Abby's forthcoming book. I did, because I'm her number one fan."

Lara shuddered. "Wasn't there a Stephen King book about some stalker with a mallet who breaks the author's ankles?"

"*And so* I got to read the book before publication." Rena ignored her, appearing annoyed. Except annoyance on Rena only made her cuter. "I'm the heroine she based on Del."

Johnny paused in the act of taking another sip of beer. "Wait. On Del?" His enthusiasm for the evening increased. "Has she seen you yet?"

"Yeah." Rena frowned. "That's why she's way over there." She motioned to the opposite side of the room.

"No, we can't waste this. Let's go find Sam and Foley. And Lou, too, if he's here. Then we need to see Del and you together." His wicked grin lured Rena to his side, but Lara saw some people she wanted to talk to.

"I'll find you in a few." She gave him a kiss.

On the lips. Right in front of Rena and anyone else watching. Man, he *loved* that.

"Okay. But no vomiting on anyone but me."

Rena stared from him to Lara. "That's gross…and strangely romantic."

"Isn't he the best?" Lara smiled then waved to some friends and left.

"Come on, Selena." Johnny crooked his arm and waited for Rena to take it. She did, and they hunted down his boss. He couldn't resist the opportunity to bait her. His smile widened when he saw her and McCauley—the one she was planning to marry. "Please tell me I'm not dreaming this."

Rena laughed. "Nope. Mike convinced her to wear a Delilah costume. He's Samson, by the way."

"I figured, with the sandals and the toga. Oh man. I get to call her Delilah all night long. This is too perfect to be real." He tugged Rena with him. "Let's go."

Lara was glad to see Kelly and a few of her friends from school, determined to ignore the two rumor-mongers who'd also arrived. When she'd mentioned her party plans in class the other day, a few had mentioned they had invites as well. Some big tax firm and a few other companies got together every year to throw the Halloween party of the year. It had gained popularity in the past few years, and she'd been dying to go, ever since she'd heard from Rena and Del about it.

"Lara?"

She turned from her friends and got another surprise.

"Pete." She accepted his hug and returned it, then stepped back to see him. "Wow. You look good."

He wore some kind of zombie-hunter costume, baring a nice bit of arms and chest. Not on par with Johnny, but still handsome all the same. Her lunch buddy laughed. "You look good too...for being possessed."

"Nice. You recognize me." She'd taken pains with the growths on her face and the scraggly hair, though it pained her to mess with her straight, clean ponytail.

"Hey, *The Exorcist* is a classic."

"You like horror movies?"

"Yeah. I guess we hadn't gotten to that yet, had we?"

"No, just office gossip. Thanks for that, at least."

They chatted about his favorite movies and hers, then more about Nurse Guyen and the student she'd made cry the day after Lara had been with her.

"I swear, she's a nasty, mean woman." Lara shook her head. "I don't know why she volunteers to help us, when the only thing she's doing is teaching me how *not* to act."

"Yeah, well, I think she was told she had to mentor you guys. I overheard one of the nurses complaining about her during training."

"How's that going?"

"Pretty good, actually." He frowned.

"What's wrong?"

"Well, I don't mean to pry, and it's certainly none of my business..."

"Pete, what is it?" Was she in some kind of trouble at the hospital?

"I overheard you on your phone the other day at lunch. Something about a financial aid situation?"

She blushed. "It's nothing."

"Well, that's your business, and I totally don't mean to be intrusive. I was just going to say that if you're interested, my company has a few grants we give out every year, and the deadline for them is Sunday."

She narrowed her eyes, suspicious of the timing. She hadn't imagined Pete's interest, though she'd done her best to prove herself no more than a friend. Hell, she'd even mentioned Johnny a few times, so he knew she had a boyfriend—though at the time she hadn't been sure what Johnny was to her.

"I know that look." He laughed, and something in her eased. "You can check Drey Consulting's website. We give away five scholarships a year. It's a great tax write-off for the company, and our boss put herself through school a long time go. Julie's into giving back."

"You're serious."

"As a heartbeat." He paused. "Or in the case of those I hunt, no heartbeat." He held up his fake crossbow. "I swear."

She felt a sense of renewed hope. She'd been trying to deny it, but the thought of not following through on her schooling scared her. Working full-time while taking her course load was the hardest thing she'd ever had to do. And she'd done it all on her own. She refused to ask her parents for help, because their savings was all they had. Kristin had her own worries. And no way in hell would she ask Johnny for a dime. They were dating, not married. Besides, a girl had her pride.

Overjoyed, she yanked Pete to her and gave him a huge hug. When she pulled back, she felt her grin stretching from ear to ear. "Thank you so much."

"Anytime." He stared back at her, a little too seriously.

"I, ah, I mean—"

He blinked then smiled, easygoing Pete again. "No problem. Make sure to send in the online application ASAP. The grant is good to cover a full term, and you can reapply each year. The essay is key. And before you ask, I have absolutely nothing more to do with this than getting the word out. We sent out an email to the admissions staff, and they were supposed to have disseminated it to everyone a while ago." He frowned.

"I might have missed it," she admitted. Caught up in Johnny, work, and her family's troubles.

"In any case, now you know. I love being the bearer of good news. Money and zombies. You can't go wrong with that." He gave a wry grin. "And—"

"Lara."

The bite in Johnny's voice warned her to be wary. She turned an overly bright smile on her boyfriend and didn't shrug Johnny's heavy arm off her shoulder. "Hey, baby. Johnny, this is Pete, a friend from work. Pete, this is my boyfriend, Johnny."

Pete didn't flinch at Johnny's stone face. Nor did he make a big deal when Lou, Sam, and Foley surrounded him like a ring of thugs.

"And that's Lou, Sam, and Foley. They work with Johnny at Webster's Garage."

"Hi, Johnny," Pete said in a calm, friendly voice. *Go Pete*. Though she'd mentioned Johnny, seeing him in the flesh had a lot more…punch. "Lara's told me a lot about you."

Johnny seemed to relax. "Yeah?"

"Yeah. In fact, I'm glad you're here. You mind a little shop talk?"

Johnny kept his arm around her but eased his hand

from her shoulder, stroking now instead of gripping. "Sure thing. What's up?"

Behind Pete, the guys watched her and Johnny, and she glared at them.

"My brother has a '63 Dodge Polara he…"

She lost the rest of what Pete was saying, too busy giving Foley the evil eye. He shrugged and pointed at Johnny. Sam nodded and remained quiet. Lou smiled, but she didn't trust him to keep his big, handsome head out of her business.

Before Pete and Johnny stepped another second into the conversation, Lou interrupted, not fooling anyone in that stupid angel costume. "So what's with all the hugging, Pete? Made my boy nervous."

Pete, to his credit, didn't react except to tell the truth. "Just delivering some good news."

Let it go, Lou. She scowled at him, but he ignored her. "Oh?"

"My company has a few grants we give out to hard-working students, and I told Lara she should apply, what with her situation. And before anyone here asks," he said drily, "I have nothing to do with the awards. I'm just in charge of making sure the word gets out."

Johnny turned to her. "You still having problems with financial aid?"

"It's no big deal." She had no intention of sharing her financial worries with the entire garage and Pete.

She wormed her way out from Johnny's arm and clamped on to Pete by the wrist. "You have to do me a favor and meet Kelly. Don't let her know I told you, but she's been hounding me about my cute lunch buddy. And I'm not talking about Mrs. Norris."

He chuckled and held out a hand to Johnny. "I'll do that. Great meeting you, Johnny. Maybe I can bend your ear about the Dodge some other time?"

"Yeah, sure. Call the garage and ask for me."

They walked away, but Johnny kept his gaze on her. She felt him glaring a hole into her back, and she didn't like it.

"Thanks for the save," he said under his breath, though he needn't have bothered. The music swelled around them as they cut through the dance floor to see her friends by the other bar.

"No problem."

"Do they feed them muscle enhancer at that garage or what?"

She chuckled nervously, still on edge. Johnny had never acted outwardly jealous before. The one time he'd been so volatile with another man in her presence had been Ron. And that had not turned out well at all.

"Lara, if I can give you any advice after having been divorced once and engaged twice, it's that financial problems can impact a relationship." He sighed. "People are slow to forgive those who hold on to bad news."

"I'll take that into consideration."

"Do that." He stopped her before they reached Kelly and the others. "If things don't work out between you and the angry priest, you know where to find me." He squeezed her hand. "See you at lunch on Wednesday?"

She nodded. "You're a good friend, Pete."

He winked. "I could be an even better friend if you'd let me. But just to do you a favor, I'll talk to Kelly, okay?"

She snorted. "Doesn't hurt that she's pretty."

Pete laughed. "No, it doesn't."

She watched him go, saw her friends envelop him, and made her way to the bar. After the hellish week she'd had, she deserved a drink. Or two.

—⁓—

Johnny watched his pretty, possessed girlfriend downing a glass at the bar. He shook his head and started to head over when he heard her name mentioned. He slowed and listened in to the two women chatting and drinking, keeping a large Frankenstein and his ghoul posse between them.

"Can you believe Lara would rather have that guy than Pete?" a sexy blond in a bunny costume asked her friend. "Sure, the priest is sexy. But Pete in that zombie-hunter costume? Please let me be his mattress." The women giggled. "Lara's so stupid."

He tensed.

"I don't know about stupid, but I agree about Pete. Oh man." The witch who answered the sexy bunny wiggled her eyebrows.

The bunny laughed.

"But you know what I mean." She lowered her voice, and Johnny leaned closer to overhear. "Lara was talking about him in class last week. I think he's a mechanic."

"Seriously?" The bunny shook her head. "She'd rather have some minimum-wage schlub over Pete? A six-figure professional?" Bunny took a drink. "Hey, I've done the lowbrow thing before. A big cock and tough-guy attitude is only sexy for so long. I want a guy with substance."

"I think you mean a substantial bank account," her friend said drily.

"Well, sure." They both laughed. "But I mean, what do Lara and her sexy priest talk about? Nuts and bolts? Cars?" She snorted. "I doubt they're talking about investment strategies and career advancement. Or about his ex-wife and the Porsche she got out of him in the divorce."

The witch sighed. "This isn't about Lara, is it? It's about Brendan."

"He's such a shit." Bunny shrugged. "But at least he's got money and a brain under *his* looks. What do you suppose Lara's mechanic has under his coveralls, other than tattoos and greasy nails?"

They spotted another of their "friends" and started talking about the growing size of her ass and her ineptitude with needles, and Johnny moved away.

Bitchy, drunk women at a party. He'd seen his share over the years. But their words lingered, and he sought out Pete, standing with a few women, all smiles and polish, apparently with a big wallet.

Johnny frowned. He had more than a big dick going for him. He had a steady job, a good life with good friends. He had substance…

Didn't he?

When Johnny found her again, Lara had already downed two rum and Cokes and had ordered another. "Please," she said to forestall him. "I've had a hell of a week, and I was really looking forward to tonight. So no more talk about my personal finances, or I'll throw this amazing drink all over your saintly ass."

Next to her, Frankenstein chuckled. "I'd believe her,

man. If you're Johnny, she's been ranting about you for like ten minutes." He left, and Johnny took his place after ordering what she had.

"What?" She'd pounded back her drink, liking the burn, only to see him staring at her.

Two—no, three—drinks. Her minimum to a good time. Not that she needed to drink to have fun, but it had been so long since she'd had a nice buzz. She wasn't driving, and damn it, she deserved to forget about her problems just once.

"I agree," Johnny said, a hint of humor in his eyes.

"Huh?"

"You were talking out loud, said you deserved to forget your problems."

"Yeah, well, you try managing a full course load, mean precepts, working at Ray's, and a needy boyfriend who doesn't have the balls to tell you he loves you." *That* he didn't seem to find amusing. "Then again, maybe he doesn't love me."

"Maybe you don't love him."

"Maybe I don't." Maybe this, maybe that. "Maybe he's just using me until something better comes along."

He stood and pulled her close. "Or maybe he's afraid you'll dump him if he pours his heart out to you."

Feeling the burn of alcohol and the liberation of telling the truth, she responded with, "Well, maybe he's a pussy who can't open up. Maybe that's why he doesn't have a girlfriend."

And maybe she'd hit a little too hard. His eyes looked like jade shards.

"I like this maybe game." He slapped a few bills on the bar and pulled her with him toward the exit. "Maybe you've had a little too much to drink. Maybe you have a mean side to you after all."

"And maybe you'd better get me to a toilet before I'm sick."

She made it to the bathroom in time to expel the contents of her three drinks and some appetizers. "Oh. I was right. Those cheese balls were sitting out too long." She groaned and felt gentle hands holding back her hair.

"When I said not to vomit on anyone earlier, I meant you too."

"Hell." She pushed herself to stand, glad at least she'd held it until the restroom. Outside the stall, Johnny still helped hold her upright, and she saw sympathy and appreciation in the women around her. Sympathy for her illness, appreciation for Johnny. "Hey, he's with me." She yanked him with her outside the restroom and outside the party.

Then she stopped. "Sorry. I don't mean to ruin tonight for you. Call me a cab, and I'll go home."

"I don't think so. You're possessed all right." He helped her to his car, then drove her back to her place while she alternated between staring at the dark city outside and dozing, suddenly bone-deep exhausted. She hadn't been lying when she'd mentioned her long week. When they arrived at her apartment, instead of berating her for the maybe game, Johnny made sure she got inside, helped her change into her favorite ratty pajamas, and waited while she brushed her teeth, then tucked her in bed.

Suddenly she didn't want him to go. "Wait." She shot out a hand and gripped his larger one. A pitiful move, but enough to keep him there. Tears burned behind her eyes. "Why are you such a douche?"

"What?" He blinked down at her, and she wasn't so tired she couldn't tell she'd surprised him.

"You're distracting me from my work. I spend too much time and money on you. You're nice to my nieces, and even I find them scary." She paused, trying to get her thoughts together.

"Go on. I know you have more you need to say," he said, sounding stiff and a little angry and...so damn pretty.

She chuckled. "You're too good-looking for your own good. You snagged me with those green eyes and that amazing body. Too bad the rest of you isn't just pretty."

He froze, but she didn't make anything of his reaction, too caught up in her feelings. *I could handle just pretty. But mesmerizing, amazing, good at heart, that's too tough to deny.* She mumbled an "I love you" but thought she heard the door shut on her words. No matter. She'd tell him later. Her stomach rumbled. Right after she threw up a few more times. Damn cheeseballs.

Chapter 20

WELL, HE COULDN'T SAY HE HADN'T KNOWN IT would be coming. Johnny Devlin, fallen for a woman only to have her dump him right when he'd fallen in real, fucking love with her. Wait. *Johnny* Devlin? Sounded a lot like *Jack* Devlin.

"I am so like my father," he muttered Monday afternoon as he worked like an automaton. "Fuck, fuck, fuck." Standing over an engine and battering a stubborn bolt that refused to release, he felt someone tugging at his back pocket. "What?" he snarled.

"In my office," Del growled. "Now."

He added another "*Fuck*" for good measure. But no one reminded him of ROP. They'd taken one look at him this morning and said little. The guys had seen Pete on Saturday night. No doubt they thought Lara had thrown him over for some rich asshole in a killer zombie-hunter outfit. And by killer he meant good. Figured the guy she ditched him for would be someone into the movies they liked.

All along he'd known this relationship would end. Seeing Pete with Lara had reinforced just how much better she could do than him. *Too bad the rest of you isn't just pretty...* His heart broke all over again. He dropped his wrench with a clatter and stormed past concerned faces to Del's office. Once inside, he dropped into the chair across from her desk, determined to keep a civil tongue in his head. He was hurting like a bitch. Like a motherfucking, soul-sucking bitch, but insulting his boss was a sure-fire way to sever him from the only thing that mattered right now in his life.

"I need some time off," he said evenly, knowing he needed a break before he *broke*.

Del rounded her desk and leaned her butt against it. She crossed her tatted forearms over her chest and just stared at him. No concern, no affection, not even annoyance. The blank stare annoyed him.

"What?" he snapped. "I owe you money, right? I'll have to dig it out *fucking* later."

She just watched him with those icy gray eyes. How the hell did McCauley sleep at night next to such a predatory female? "Johnny." Just his name, and he felt burning behind his eyes.

"I need a break," he said again, worried his voice would catch and he'd dissolve in tears. Humiliating to be such a pussy after working so hard to show he wasn't one. He might like books, he might care about women's feelings, but he could be a macho head case like the best of them.

Del laid a hand on his knee, and he tensed. "Honey, you take as long as you need. Dad and I are right here anytime you need to talk." Then she fucked him over royally by kissing him on the top of the head.

Those tears he'd been fighting back swam in his eyes.

He rose and bolted through the other door, so the guys wouldn't see him. He wiped his cheeks once out of the garage. Then he drove home, swearing all the way.

Lara had no idea what to do. Johnny had avoided her yesterday, and she felt like a horse's ass for drinking too much and eating those nasty appetizers when she knew better. She remembered everything—of course— because far be it from God to be merciful to fools who couldn't hold their liquor or their cheeseballs.

Johnny might have mistaken her words. No *maybe* about it. She cringed at the thought of the words. Not a great game to play when feeling ill. Still, despite saying whatever she'd exactly said, he should have been around to talk to about it. Their first fight. In a way, it made her smile. Now they were a real couple. No one got along all the time. Better to fight now than to dig in deep with a relationship and realize later they had no idea how to patch things up.

She drove to the garage, determined to speak with him. She hadn't wanted to miss class, so she'd waited until after noon. Now, neat and pretty and dressed in her finest ass-hugging denims and a soft pink sweater, she left her car and headed for Del's office.

Walking through the garage was an eye-opener. She'd never seen where Johnny worked. She looked around for him but saw nothing but hostility. So she stopped.

"Don't even *think* about looking at me like that." She planted her hands on her hips, aggravated with men in general. She glanced around but still saw no sign of Johnny. "There wasn't, nor is there, anything going on between me and Pete. And my finances are my own business. Where's Del?"

Foley frowned at her. "What happened with you two?"

She sighed. "I need to talk to Mr. Blows Things Out of Proportion. Is he around?"

"Ah, no. You might want to talk to Del."

"Why?" She glanced at Del's door. "Is he in there?"

"He was," Lou said, looking stern. "Don't fuck with my boy."

"Don't fuck with *me*." She walked into Lou's personal space, ignoring the tools and greasy stuff around them. "Next time I'm with my boyfriend, you keep your nosey ass out of it." She poked him in his rock-hard chest for good measure, then turned on her heel to find Del. Behind her, she heard clapping.

"Sam, not now," Foley said.

"And fuck you too, Sam," Lou growled.

"We told you you were wrong. Asshole."

Lou and Sam started going at it, until Liam poked his head out from a spare room and sighed. "It's a Monday, for sure."

She hurried to Del's office, only to be met with a glare similar to the one Lou had shot her.

"Don't even." Lara shut the door behind her. "Where's Johnny?"

"He's taking the day off. Apparently you broke his heart."

Lara groaned and fell into a surprisingly comfortable office chair. "God. I was half-smashed and sick from a mild case of food poisoning. Mr. Sensitive refused to take my calls yesterday. I mean, Jesus. We can't have a simple fight, and he's ducking me? That's kind of pathetic."

"What did you say to him?"

"I'm not exactly sure. Something about him being pretty and not so pretty. But I must have pushed some buttons, because he's avoiding me."

"So you're not breaking it off with him." Del watched her.

"Not that I'm aware of." Lara stood. "But if we can't even have a fight and we're over, what did we really have to start with?"

A good question Del couldn't answer, and neither could Lara. On her way to Johnny's house, Lara kept asking herself how to make this right. An apology, sure. But then… They had to talk about this. If they had any chance of moving forward, they had to be able to fight and make up. Considering Johnny didn't seem to have much history in the way of long-term relationships, she figured maybe she'd teach him a thing or two.

When she arrived at his house, she didn't see his car. So she left. She tried calling him a few times that day. And the next. And the day after that.

A full week went by.

Still no word from Johnny. The jackass apparently meant they were over. This was no game, and it appeared she had no say-so in the matter.

Well fuck that.

She refused to go to the garage, looking for a confrontation. What needed to be said would happen between them and them alone. She didn't mention her problems to her family or friends, wanting to talk to her friggin' boyfriend about them first. Rena knew, by the sympathy in her gaze, but she didn't say anything about it, respecting Lara's need to handle it herself.

"Here if you need me," Rena had murmured once at Ray's, then said nothing more.

A good friend, unlike the dumbass destroying her heart.

A week later, Lara tried his house again and hit pay dirt. His car sat in the driveway.

Before she lost her anger in a fit of tears, she told herself to remain strong and knocked on his door.

Taking a page out of his book, she slipped inside past him the moment he opened it. "Well? Shut the door, and let's talk about this."

He closed it and turned to face her. He had his shirt off, his arms and chest gleaming with sweat. A mean look darkened his eyes.

She forced herself to swallow and think about anything but sex. Except he must have been thinking the same thing, because he met her midway, no words needed. They ate at each other, tearing at clothing. Then he bent her over the couch, ripped her pants and panties down, and unzipped enough to free his cock. He pushed inside her, and she knew nothing but raw need. Flesh slapped flesh, the scent of sex and desperation settled over them, and she wanted him more than anything.

In no time he was banging her into a roaring orgasm and following her with a groan of his own. Leaning over the couch, now replete and a bit giddy, she clenched her thighs, keeping him inside her. Tears sprouted, because she'd missed this—missed *him*.

She waited for him to withdraw, hoping he'd say something—anything—but wasn't surprised he kept silent. The stubborn SOB. Feeling vulnerable, she rushed to clean up in the bathroom, shoring her nerve for what she knew would be a major confrontation. Talk about hurt feelings.

Lara returned to find him drinking a beer and leaning against the kitchen counter.

He hadn't done more than button up his jeans half-way, and he could have modeled for a Bad Boys with 'Tude calendar, he was that much a combination of "angry meets sexy."

"Good to know I'm pretty enough for a fast fuck."

"*And* we're back to reality." She sighed. "What's going on, Johnny?"

He put the beer down and planted his hands on his hips, probably so he wouldn't be tempted to put them around her neck. "You have some serious balls to ask me that. Don't you remember what you said to me?"

"What is this really about? Look. We had a tiny fight. Are you saying we can't get past this?" Whatever *this* was.

"*Tiny fight?*" He huffed. "Baby, you basically called me worthless. You seemed to have more fun with your preppy dickhead *lunch buddy* at the party. The guy who knows all about your money problems. You don't share important shit with *me*, but you do with him? But that's right. I'm the guy you hate because I'm taking you away from your regularly scheduled life."

Angry again and glad of it, she forced herself to speak slowly, calmly, and with icy disdain. "First of all, I was sick and not in my right mind."

"You mean you finally had the stones to tell me the truth. Good for fucking you."

She ignored that. Barely. "Second, Pete is my friend. That's all."

"Then why didn't you ever mention him?"

"Because it wasn't a big deal to me. Do you mention all the women you're friends with to me? All the Dorys and Jennas and Bubbles? You know, the ones who prance around *half-naked*?"

Not even a flinch. "I introduced you to them."

"Not all of them. And Pete's never danced naked for me, so I have to say, I think I'm winning *that* argument."

Johnny looked like he wanted to yell right back—and when had she raised her voice?—before his expression just deadened. "This is stupid. You know what? I knew we wouldn't last. That you'd dump me eventually. I saved you the trouble. I'm good for a lay, for some fun, and hey, a laugh or two. We can still be friends. But we should dial back the dating thing before it gets too serious, huh?"

She just stared at him, seeing a lot she hadn't seen before. "You're scared."

"What?"

"You. You're scared. Of me."

He looked hunted then scowled. "Lara, I think you should leave. I've tolerated a lot from you, but you just keep insulting me. And I'm done with it." *With you* went unsaid.

Her heart seemed to rip in two, but then she started putting the pieces of the puzzle together. His father, a stream of women through his life, his friends warning her to treat him gently. All the years of them dancing around each other until *she'd* taken the initiative with him and seen him as more than a fun-filled fling.

"Yeah? Well I'm not done with *you*." She walked right up to him and would have poked him like she'd poked Lou, but to her shock, Johnny picked her up and physically carried her out of the house. He put her on her feet on his welcome mat then *locked her out*.

Stunned, she turned and faced the door. She knocked once, then again. "You coward! How dare you?" She waited a moment, got no response, then continued, "Fine. You want to have this conversation through a *door*? You got it." She raged at him, and an image of her sister's words popped into her head. "My sister told me to take a chance. *I did it and got screwed for it*. So up yours, Johnny. I'm not scared to try. I put myself out there for a guy everyone knows gets around. Mr. One-Night Stand, but I thought you were different. I get that you have issues. Everyone does. But you won't even fight for me? Not an argument or some tears? Just giving in?

"Well, fuck you. I deserve better than that." *Great. Now I'm crying.* "I hate that you'd rather throw us away than try. Really? So you can do it before I do? Guess what, genius? You just made your own fears come true. Except it's not me dumping us. It's *you*.

"I'm not going to wait around forever. If you don't have any interest in fighting for me—for *us*—then I don't have time for you."

She kicked his screen door and left a dent. She meant to leave before looking like an insane woman, but she couldn't help it. She screamed, needing to release a little of her own rage and pain. "You are such a dick! I can't believe you're so scared of being dumped that you'd ruin such a great thing. And over what? A throwaway comment about being pretty? *Oh*. You make me want to…" She kicked his door again, then realized the futility of it. "What the fuck am I angry over? This was all apparently just a nothing of a relationship to begin with, wasn't it? All in my head that we could be something special."

And then, before she did something really destructive—like driving her car through his friggin' house—she turned on her heel and left. She had better things to do than waste her precious time on a loser not willing to fight for her. She had enough crap to do with school, her family, work…

If Johnny was smart, he wouldn't dare show his face at the bar. Because she'd make Sue's treatment of Foley look like a walk in the park for that cowardly asshole she'd made the mistake of falling in love with.

Johnny felt like shit. He tried to lock her words out, but he heard them all the same. The temptation to take her at face value was almost unbearable. But then he'd remember his father acting the same way, trying to hold out for any tiny lick of hope that maybe, just maybe, he could patch things up with whatever flavor of the month he'd actually fallen for.

Such a silly thing, his barely there relationship with Lara. Hell, he'd known her for years. If things had been meant to happen between them, wouldn't they have occurred years ago? And really, after a few weeks of dating, he'd thought of commitment and forever. How stupid.

He was a pitiful excuse for a man to leap for crumbs of affection from a woman who clearly wanted nothing more than sex. *That* they did really fucking well. Too bad she couldn't tell him about shit that mattered, the way she had with that asshole Pete.

He sighed and forced himself to get back into a regular routine. At work, the guys rallied around him by not prying. Even Del and Liam acted like everything was all right, and he loved them for that.

He nodded, spoke, even smiled a time or two. But he didn't mention Lara, didn't go to Ray's, and no one suggested he do either.

Time passed. Without her near, it grew easier to remember his time with Lara as a fun fantasy. Something that would no longer hurt when he thought about it. She'd tried calling him once, a few days after yelling at him, but he didn't pick up, and she didn't try again.

As much as he tried telling himself he hadn't lost anything to begin with, his heart knew better. He couldn't eat. He couldn't sleep. He had no desire in sex, not even to jerk off. A few women had tried inviting him out, but he wanted nothing to do with anyone outside of work.

After a while, he wondered if Lara and her "lunch buddy" had hooked up in his absence.

Rage that she might had him destroying his office. And he didn't care.

Needing something to take the edge off, he spent the week casing cars when not at the garage. Just wondering, thinking about how amazing it would feel to slide behind the wheel of a cherry Mustang, maybe a Shelby, and joyride away from the city, just drive away from all his problems.

There was no rule he had to live in Seattle forever. That he couldn't at least take a break from life and get fucked up.

Saturday night, while he sat at home in front of the TV, he actually considered going to Ray's, just to feel again. He'd even welcome pain, because by now Lara would have hooked up with someone else, and seeing it or hearing about it might jumpstart his will to be more than the mopey asshole Lou had called him.

Before he could do anything, someone knocked at his door. The thought that it might be Lara shocked his heart into beating again. Racing, anticipating...

"Johnny, open the fuck up."

His loss settled deep, pulling him back under. Foley wasn't Lara. And Lara didn't matter, because they'd never had anything real anyway. And even if they *could* have, he'd ruined it by being too much of a chickenshit to matter. Hadn't she already told him what she really thought?

The door opened, and he frowned.

"I still have your spare," Foley told him.

Del entered behind him, and Johnny groaned and slumped onto his couch. "Go away, please. I'm tired."

"No, you're screwed up." Foley turned to Del. "Note I said 'screwed' instead of 'fucked' like I wanted to. Out of respect for you."

Del sighed. "Yeah, right after 'open the fuck up.' Thanks, Foley. You're all heart."

"You're welcome."

Del walked pretty as you please through Johnny's home and sat next to him. "Bottom line, you're an idiot."

"Christ. You're supposed to be the nice one," Foley muttered. "I knew I should have brought Liam."

"No. He needs to hear it. Tough talk and all. Look, Johnny, we all know you love Lara. It's as plain as the handsome nose on your handsome face."

"I don't know I'd be saying handsome so much."

"Shut it, Foley."

If Johnny hadn't been so depressed, he'd have laughed. *"You're too good-looking for your own good. You snagged me with those green eyes and that amazing body. Too bad the rest of you isn't just pretty."*

Her words had cut deep, because she'd said everything Johnny had known his whole life. No one stayed. They never did. As pretty as he and his father were, they were missing that vital ingredient that let women love them. Sad and worthless—and he'd never in a million years confess something so damn pitiable.

"You know, I talked to your dad," Del said.

Johnny leaned back and covered his face with his arm, feigning disinterest.

"We had quite a talk…after Lara was done with him."

He lowered his arm in a hurry and blinked at her. "What?"

"Yep. Seems a certain someone wanted to know why you considered yourself so…what did she call it, Foley?"

"Worthless."

"That's it. Worthless." Del gave him an insincere smile. "You are the biggest dumbass I know, and I'm marrying into the McCauley family."

"Del." Foley shook his head, a smirk on his face. "That's not nice. Accurate, but still."

"True, and you've both met my brother. He's completely clueless. Johnny, you've let yourself think you can't love anyone, because no one ever loved you."

"That's not true." He frowned. "I love my dad. I know he loves me."

"But that's family," Foley pointed out. "They don't count, because they have to love you."

"Yeah?" Johnny scowled. "Tell that to Sam's mom."

Foley shrugged. "You got me there."

"Besides, you want the truth? I loved Lara."

"In the past? Loved?" Foley asked.

"I still love her. She's smart and funny. Amazing, really. All of her is just so... Look, it's over. Can we just let this go?"

"Sorry. But you hurt my friend." Del looked mean. She slapped his arm.

"Hey."

The slap didn't hurt so much as surprise him. But following the slap, Foley's punch to his stomach had him sucking major wind. He planned to slug his friend back—just as soon as he could breathe again.

"You really are a dumbass. Sam and I agree. Tell him, Del."

"Lara's been crying over you, Johnny. She fell in love with you, took a chance on a major player, and instead of loving her back, you shit all over her feelings. What did I tell you about us ripping your balls off? Be glad Foley's with me. J.T. wanted to come over and rearrange your pretty face."

Hearing that Lara had cried over him, gone to see his father, started his heart pumping again. "She's really upset?"

"Did she or did she not come over here and yell outside your door at you? I heard all about it." Del looked him over, must have found him wanting, and looked away. "I love you like a brother, and if J.T. pulled this crap, I'd beat him over the head until he made it right. With a tire iron, I might add."

"Made it right with a tire iron?" Foley asked.

"No, Foley, I'd *beat him* with a tire iron. Would you just shut up?" Del blew out a breath and turned back to Johnny. "If you don't love her, if you changed your mind about her, at least tell her to her face. She's a good person, Johnny. Let her down easy, okay?"

"Let her down?" He rubbed his eyes, tired and alive at the same time.

Foley blew out a breath. "Dude, the girl is so damn in love with you it's pathetic. But to hear her tell it, you don't give a shit. I mean, you don't give a goddamn," he barked at Johnny. "You fucked up." He glanced at Del and swore again, then handed her a bill. "There, Del. That's a buck's worth. Just keep it."

Del grinned at him, tucked the dollar away, then slapped Johnny in the back of the head and stood. "Stop being a jackass. Go make up with Lara. You know, Rena is also not very happy with you. And between J.T. and Rena, my cousin scares me more than my brother does."

Johnny stood slowly, feeling like an old man. "Lara really misses me?" *She loves me?*

"If I had a woman like Lara, I'd never let her go," Foley said, his voice low, sincere. "You have baggage. I get it. Hell, we all have it. Don't even get me started on Sam. But if Liam and Del can get over their shit, what makes you so special you can't get past yours?"

Del raised a brow. "Thanks, Foley, I think. Johnny, make this right. And if I were you, I wouldn't meet Lara at Ray's. You have people gunning for you at the bar."

"Ah, okay."

"Yeah. Get yourself together, man." Foley knocked him in the arm, hard enough to leave a bruise. "Don't be such a pussy. You love her? You should take a chance on her. Woman like that comes along once in a lifetime for guys like us."

"That's for sure." Del nodded. "Come on, Foley. We have lives to get back to. Hint, hint, Johnny. *The Walking Dead* is a television show, not a lifestyle."

They left him feeling hope for the first time in weeks. Lara missed him? She might have meant all those things she'd said. And well, if she'd changed her mind, at least he could own up to his cowardice and put her mind at ease. Their breakup had been all him, not her.

Hell.

What if she believed *she* wasn't good enough? That he'd somehow found *her* lacking? For the first time since their breakup, he worried about Lara and her pain instead of his own. God, he had to make things right. Oh man, she loved him? What if she still did?

Hope kept him awake well into the night.

———

Out in Foley's truck, Del and Foley sat.

"You still think it was smart to lie to him like that?" Foley asked, unconvinced. It had killed him to see Johnny so hurt, but he wasn't sure this idea made any more sense than just shoving another beer into him.

"Yeah. Trust me. I'm sure Lara was in tears over his ass. It's the image he needs to get him moving in the right direction." She grinned. "And he's gonna lose his fucking mind seeing her with Lou."

Only Del could come up with some harebrained notion to get Johnny jealous and come to his senses. "I would have said to let him see her with Pete. That guy bugged the shit out of him."

"True, but Lou's just like Johnny. If Lou's good enough for her, so's Johnny." She shrugged. "Besides, I like Pete. His brother's car is bringing us some serious cash, as well as more contacts. Wouldn't seem right to let Johnny rip his arms off. At least with Lou, Lou will stand his own. Give Johnny a wake-up right upside his handsome, fucked-up head." She pulled the dollar out of her pocket and gave it back to him. "Here you go. Didn't feel right taking it from you in there. Especially because you hit him as hard as I've wanted to." She shook her head. "Poor dumb bastard. Wait until Lara gets a shot at him."

Foley started up the truck and drove them back to the garage, where they'd been working late on a pet project of Del's, something she wanted to give one of her future brothers-in-law. "Does McCauley know what he's getting into with you? Because I gotta tell you, you Websters in love scare the shit out of me."

She patted him on the shoulder.

And yeah, he flinched when she grinned and said, "Ain't love grand?"

Chapter 21

LARA ANSWERED HER PHONE, AND AGAIN, THE unidentified caller hung up. "Oh my God, you are so annoying!" she yelled at it and threw it at her softly cushioned couch. She might be angry, but she had no intention of paying for something *else* she couldn't afford, like a new cell phone.

Her tuition had officially fallen through last week, on her *birthday*, when she'd spent the night alone and lonely. "Nowhere to go, no one to blow," she'd said with ill humor. Her friends and family had wanted to take her out, but she'd told everyone she had plans with everyone else, while the truth remained she wanted nothing to do with life in general. Even on Thanksgiving, she'd only put in a token appearance at her family's, where she'd complained of feeling sick and neatly deflected questions about Johnny.

The past weeks, she'd sunk into class work and cleaned and babysat with an enthusiasm bordering on obsession, according to Kristin.

At least one good thing had come of her life lately. Kristin lashing out at her had opened her sister's festering wound about herself. In other good Kristin news, her sister and Ron had come to an agreement, and papers had been signed. Kristin still had no idea what she wanted to do with her life, but she'd scheduled some counseling.

Smart move for such a dumb blond, Lara had teased her sister, who had blushed and accepted the compliment.

Since Lara had the night off from work, she was at loose ends. She planned to meet Rena and Del at six for a special Sunday night dinner. Just the girls, because if J.T. asked her one more time if she wanted him to beat up on Johnny, she'd lose it.

So what if she'd gone to talk to Johnny's dad? All Jack Devlin's explanations had done were to put that final nail in the coffin of her relationship. Johnny had been damaged as a kid. Knowing Jack felt responsible for his son's inability to form lasting commitments hurt as well as helped. The poor guy had never been able to open up to the important women in his life, and he'd never recovered from the one who got away.

In leaving, that woman had damaged young Johnny's tender heart. The imbecile clearly thought he was inferior in some way, never allowing himself to get hurt by keeping himself distant from women.

But even Jack had commented on how different Johnny had been with Lara. Hell. Dory and Jenna were in tears, begging her to take Johnny back. And when she'd said he'd broken it off with her, they'd asked her to be patient with him.

With that great big jerk.

Anger consumed her, and tears pricked her eyes. Someone banged on the door. Probably Lou, following Del's stupid plan to make Johnny jealous. She checked her clock. Time to let him in and wait for Johnny to show. Did Lara really believe Johnny seeing them together would make him so enraged he'd realize how much he loved her?

She'd give Johnny's friends credit for thinking the best of him. Personally, she wanted to brain him with a frying pan, then kiss him all better. Then kick his ass all over again.

A nurse probably shouldn't want to cause harm, but he was being dense, so she felt entitled.

More banging. "Hold on," she yelled to Lou.

She looked through the peephole but saw no one there. Great. He'd probably walked away.

She opened the door and stepped out, and something slammed into her jaw.

Stunned, she was draped over someone's shoulder and forcibly carried back into her apartment, too dazed to function.

The door slammed shut. Then she heard it lock, and her heart raced a mile a minute.

"You little bitch." Ron Howell was a lot stronger than he looked. He dumped her on the floor, and she landed hard on her hip. "Did you really think I wouldn't get what I want?" He unbuckled his belt and removed it. "You and your friend aren't the only ones who can make up an alibi."

What the hell was he talking about?

"I reported your boyfriend to the police. But guess what? Apparently the assholes at Ray's didn't remember anyone bloodying up my face. Well you know, I'm pretty sure I'm at my country club right now, having a drink in a private room with friends."

He tossed his belt to the floor, apparently not planning on beating her with it. She knew she should be more scared than she was, but after all her emotional drama over Johnny, she felt nothing but a building rage for all Y-chromosome-related stupidity. Ron's hands went to the snap of his trousers, and he paused.

So he meant to rape her? *Oh, bring it on, little man.* Yeah, Kristin had shared. And none of it had been good.

Lara stared up at him, pretending confusion. "Ron?"

"I put an app on your phone to find your location, and a friend of mine with spy software disguised it as a ring tone." He scoffed and unzipped his pants, showing an erection beneath silk boxers. "You really are stupid. Get on your knees and blow me, and I won't hit you again. Or maybe I will…if you're not any good."

She cowed while feeling murderous. Best not to let him see her eyes. "P-please, Ron. Don't h-hurt me." She didn't have to force angry tears and crawled toward him.

Yes, Ron kept in shape. But like most men of his ilk, he didn't see women as a threat. Just as pawns he could use to do his bidding.

"That's right." His lust was impossible to miss, especially when he pushed his meager member through the slit in his boxers. "Suck me dry, bitch. You know you want to."

"I w-want to."

"Yeah, say it. You want to." He widened his stance and held himself out to her.

"I w-want to…" And then she did what she'd *so* wanted to do for such a long, long time.

———

Johnny took a deep breath and let it out. He'd finished climbing the steps to Lara's floor, and with each footfall closer, his heart threatened to leap out of his chest. Fuck, she loved him. He'd believed Del more each time he thought about how compassionate she'd looked sitting on his couch with Foley. Del knew what it was to almost throw something away. Or at least, her moron of a fiancé did. Johnny knew the story, of how McCauley had almost let fear of losing her cost him the woman he loved.

At the time, he'd wondered how McCauley could be so foolish.

"And now I know." He had to make this right with Lara. With his last breath, he'd be sure to—

"*And that's for my sister, you prick. And for Kay. And Amelia.*" He heard Lara yelling, and she didn't sound as if she were playing.

He rushed to her door and tried to open it but found it locked. "Lara?"

"And if you ever touch me again, *I will fucking kill you.*"

He'd heard enough. Johnny drilled his shoulder into the door and broke through her flimsy lock with ease. To his shock, he saw her kicking the shit out of her ex-brother-in-law. The guy was on the ground, moaning, his dick out, as Lara pummeled him everywhere she could reach. Kicking, punching, his girl was whaling on the guy making broken sounds as he curled into a ball.

Knowing what that exposed dick meant, Johnny saw nothing more than the guy's gravestone.

He marched forward and grabbed the hand she'd cocked back.

Lara started. "Johnny?"

"I love you, baby." He saw the bruise on her cheekbone, and kissed it tenderly. Then he pulled her to the kitchen and handed her his cell phone. "Call 9-1-1. And hurry, before I kill him."

She dialed, her eyes wide, and Johnny hauled Ron to his feet. He had to hold the guy away from him, because Ron started to piss himself. *Nicely done, Lara.*

"Wait, Johnny." She quickly reported the incident to the police, then hung up and stepped outside her door, yelling down the hallway for help.

Her apartment soon crowded with neighbors, and she told them what had happened. To Johnny's surprise, one of the guys in the apartment happened to be a cop visiting family in the building.

"Well, well. One of the upper class slumming so far away from his grand real estate on Mercer Island." Officer Brewer sounded way too pleased. "I know you, don't I? You sold my grandmother's property out from under her a few years ago." The cop took a step toward Ron.

"Hold on." Johnny pretended to drop Ron and slugged him in the same cheekbone Ron had bruised on Lara. "Oh, sorry about that. Nearly dropped him."

"Drop-kick him off the roof," Lara muttered. "He told me he has bigwig buddies who'll vouch for his whereabouts. Of course, that was right before he tried to rape me."

The cop's face flushed, and Johnny dropped Ron on his ass before he did kill him.

"So you prey on old ladies and young women too?" Brewer growled. Now more worried for the cop than Ron, Johnny planted himself in front of the moaning mound of shit on the floor, keeping Brewer from reaching him. "Hey, can we get some pics of this guy for proof?" He heard a dozen cameras going off, the cop's included. Then Brewer was on the phone. In less than ten minutes, two uniforms and some EMTs arrived to take Ron away.

Johnny introduced himself to Officer Brewer and described what he'd witnessed. "Lara won't be in any trouble, will she?"

"Oh, hell no. I have witnesses and pictures as proof. From what Lara mentioned, he did this before at the bar where she works too."

Next to him, Lara nodded.

"I was there," Johnny said. "I'll testify to it. So can Lara's boss and a few others."

Brewer smiled. "I can't stand types like Howell. They take what they want when they want it and step over everyone in the way. Lara, I'm glad you're okay."

"Thanks, Matt."

"I can't promise he'll do a lot of time, because he does have contacts in high places. But I can guarantee he gets in front of the right judge for attempted rape, assault, hmm, maybe robbery too? You were clearly here when he entered."

"He's a rich guy. Doubt that would stick," Johnny had to mention.

Lara added, "My door was op—"

"Stepping away now. Can't hear you. Gotta go book a dirtbag. You staying with her?" Brewer asked Johnny.

"Yeah."

"Good. Lara, Johnny." Brewer left her apartment with the others.

Then just Johnny and Lara remained.

She looked wild, her hair still in disarray, her poor

cheek a purple oval. She had bruises on her hands and probably her feet too. She'd beaten the hell out of Howell.

Johnny couldn't be prouder.

Lara, apparently, couldn't be angrier. "Why are you here?" she bit out.

"Let's get you cleaned up, hmm?"

"I don't need your help. You shut me out, remember?"

She walked stiffly to the couch and sat, no doubt trying to look tough, in control. But he saw her tremor, and he wanted to kill Ron for it.

He sat on her rickety coffee table, facing her. He frowned when she clasped her shaking hands together. "Let's take you in to see a doctor."

"No. I'm not leaving my apartment. I'm staying. 'Cause that's what I do. *I* have staying power. *I* don't walk away when life gets rough." Her eyes reflected unshed tears.

Johnny grew fiercer. "Fine. I'll stay with you."

"For how long?" she blurted. "Until you get scared again? Please. I can take care of myself. I don't need you to do it."

"Then why did you say you loved me?" he asked, confused. "You don't need me."

"No. I don't."

"So why then?"

"Because I love you, you idiot. I don't have to need you to love you. When I told you it was too bad all of you wasn't so pretty, I meant it. I could ignore just a pretty face. But you're so much more than that. You care for people. You're generous, kind, amazing in bed, and you make me laugh. And you're so smart." She scowled.

"So how are you *so stupid*? Do you really not know how much I love you? You big m-moron."

He sat and watched her spew anger and tears. She said something else, because he saw her lips form words, but he heard nothing more than that she still loved him.

She wiped her nose on her sleeve. "Well?"

"You're even pretty when you cry."

She blinked, her eyes swollen from tears, her nose red and stuffy, her cheek a purplish-blue. "Did you hear anything I said?"

"I don't need you to tell me I'm spineless when it comes to relationships." He sighed and rubbed her knees, being careful of her in such a frail state. "Lara, I'm good at sex. Well, and jokes. I'm a funny guy. I grew up watching my dad laugh off every bad thing that happened to him. He makes smart financial decisions, but when it comes to women, he's clueless."

"And so are you," she accused and wiped her eyes again.

"And so am I." He left his spot and returned with a box of tissues he handed to her.

"Thanks."

"You're welcome." He just stared at her, and it all came pouring out. "I love you so much it hurts. I think I loved you from the first moment I laid eyes on you, if you can believe it."

"Oh, Johnny."

"I was glad you turned me down so many times. You didn't want a hookup, which was all I was after at the time. I knew you were—and are—way too good for me. But I wanted you anyway. When that asshole assaulted you that first time, it let me be someone you could need. Someone who had something to give you. My help."

"Your fists."

He took her hand in his and kissed her bruises.

"Stop."

He heard the quiver in her voice and set her hand down, then picked up the other and gave it the same attention. "I hear you missed me." He looked into her eyes.

"Maybe I missed you a little. But I have no respect for someone who could—who could th-throw me away like that."

The tears came down in earnest, and Johnny swore. He moved to the couch, took her carefully into his arms, and held her until the storm passed.

"I love you," he said over and over until she subsided into tearful shudders. "Let me care for you, okay? I owe you."

"You do," came the quiet rejoinder.

He fixed her a bath, then helped her ease into it. With the exception of the bruise on her cheek and those from where she'd hit the bastard, she looked physically fine. But her sleepy eyes and little shakes hurt him deep inside. His poor woman had been through a lot tonight.

He finally took her from the bath and dried her off.

"Quit being nice to me," she whispered.

"Quit being bitchy," he whispered back and saw a smile she tried to hide.

Then he lifted her in his arms and took her to bed. He didn't bother with nightclothes, just slid her between the sheets and lay with her, holding her close.

When Lara woke, it was to a sunny day and the smell of bacon frying and coffee brewing. She sat up, feeling achy despite only getting punched in the face. As the events from the previous day unfolded, she got up, stretched a little, and found she felt fine—except for her throbbing cheekbone.

"Shit, I'm late." Hustling into sweats and a T-shirt she'd change out of at the hospital, she grabbed a set of scrubs and raced into the living room, then stopped short.

Lou Cortez held a bouquet of flowers in his hand and was gesturing to Johnny, who stood stonily and shook his head.

The pair must have sensed her, because they both turned.

She gasped. "What happened to you?" she asked Lou.

He sported a black eye and a displeased expression. "I ran into a door."

"Um, okay." She took the flowers he handed her.

He looked her over, then grunted and turned to Johnny. "We square?"

"Yeah."

Lou left her with more questions than answers.

"Really?" Johnny shook his head. "I might have believed you and Foley having a thing, but not you and Lou."

She flushed. "Not my idea. Del thought that if you saw me with another guy, you'd get jealous."

"No shit."

She didn't know what to say.

"Lara, I know you went through a lot yesterday, and you might not remember me saying this, but I fucking love you." The exact same words he'd said the first time they'd truly made love.

She blinked so as not to cry, but the jerk saw it. "I'm not crying because of you."

"Yeah, and I didn't run far away because I thought I had nothing to give you but a good time."

"You really thought that?"

"I'm really that much of a dumbass. So I've been told by everyone over and over and over again. So please, don't feel the need to hold back."

"You're a dumbass."

He groaned and pinched the bridge of his nose. "Can you forgive me for bailing? I mean, if you can't, I get it. But this time I'm not going away. I'll just keep annoying you until you finally give in and forgive me." He walked to her and stopped, then caressed her cheek with a finger. The Johnny move. The one she couldn't ignore.

"I don't know why I love you."

His smile turned him from handsome into earth-shatteringly beautiful. "Maybe it's because you're so smart you're scary. Because you know if anyone's obsessed with you it's me. Or maybe you like nursing so much you need a wounded soul in your life. Or maybe—"

"I just have great taste," she finished for him and did what she'd been wanting to do—she kissed him.

When they finally parted, he cupped her cheeks and kissed her once more. "I love you so damn much." The joy in his eyes made his love plain to see.

"That's a quarter for the swear jar."

"Fuck it. Let's make it a solid damn dollar for my shitty treatment of the most beautiful, smartest, funniest woman in the world."

"Well, if you put it like that..." She kissed him again, but before they turned hot and heavy, he stopped her.

"A few things."

"Really?" She gripped the solid evidence of his arousal, and he hissed. "You want to talk now?"

"Really." He sounded strangled. "First, you're not going to school today. I called Kelly from your class—she's on your cell phone—and explained. You're covered for the week."

"But—"

"*No.*" Forceful Johnny had returned, and she shivered in his arms. "Second, we need to get you to the police station so you can make a statement."

A good thing Ron had already settled with Kristin in one lump-sum payment. Being rich had its perks. Especially when it came to expediting the legal process.

"Okay."

"I'm not done," he said when she groped him again. His breathing grew faster. "Third, I want you to move in with me."

She froze.

"I know this is soon, but, honey, I love you. I don't want to smother you or anything, but your security sucks. I broke down your door in two seconds."

"Because you're a brute."

He smiled. "Gee, thanks."

"Well, maybe. After Ron, I admit the place is kind of tainted."

"Look at it this way. I need more help than you do. I can't cook worth a damn."

She studied him, seeing what she'd missed earlier. "Aw, Johnny. You lost weight. You were mourning me, weren't you?" Delighted at the thought of his misery, because, well, he'd earned it, she smiled, then laughed when he blushed. "And you're turning red. So cute."

"You can be so mean sometimes." He sighed. "That's another reason why I love you. Do you know Jenna called to see if I'd come to my senses and snapped you up? My father is on my ass to stop being stupid and hold on to you. Lou—even after I punched him in the face for pretending to act like you and he had a thing—actually said you're the best thing that ever happened to me."

"Lou said that? Wow. That's surprising. Del had to twist his arm to agree to this stupid stunt—according to Lou. I thought he hated me."

"Nah. He's just protective." Johnny's eyes blurred, and she couldn't tell if it was because of her tears or his. "He's family. My extended, loud-mouthed Webster-centered family thinks I'm a sucky human being without you." He wiped her eyes, then his. "Lara, I'm not perfect." Before she could say *no shit*, he muzzled her with his hand. "My head is messed up about stuff, but for you, I'll get help. And I won't run the next time I have a problem."

She kissed his hand, and when he removed it, she kissed those sweet lips, telling him everything would be all right. "I love you too, baby."

He moaned. "I love when you call me *baby*."

She smiled. "I know. I can feel how much you love it." She rubbed against him. "So if we could hurry up and get done all the mushy stuff, I'll move in with you."

"Great."

"But I'll pay rent."

"You cook and do laundry, we'll call it even."

She opened her mouth to argue, thought the better of it, then nodded. "Okay. That will help with my college fund. And don't even think about offering to help me pay for it," she threatened. She still didn't know if she'd gotten that scholarship or not, but not having to pay rent would be a huge load off her financial shoulders.

"Fine. But once we're engaged, you know, when you finally get that bug out of your ass about needing to be with some rich guy in Upper Queen Anne, can I help you pay for things then?"

She gaped like a fish, not sure if she'd received a marriage proposal or not. "But, I, um…"

"I know I'm hot, so looks and a big dick aren't the problem."

She closed her eyes, feeling flush, then opened them, unable to look away from his shining gaze for long.

"Sweetheart, I love you. I want to marry you, warts and all." He kissed her tenderly.

"Wait a minute. Who has warts?"

"I meant me. I'm a frog who's never going to turn into a prince."

"But you're my frog." She kissed him again and moaned when he cupped her breasts and flicked her nipples. "And you have a really big dick."

He smiled against her lips. "Don't forget the sexy tattoo and dominant personality in bed. You know, the stuff that gets you all wet for me."

"Oh God. Would you stop sweet-talking me? Okay, I'll marry you."

"You will?"

She snickered. "That's what you were asking, isn't it?"

"I, ah, yeah. But I thought you'd make me wait."

His surprised pleasure grounded her despite her sky-rocketing arousal. "Oh, we'll wait. I want a long engagement, and some therapy for you and me, together. And maybe, just maybe, I'll wear that nurse uniform for you for your birthday."

He gave her a smug grin. "That's in another week."

"Yeah, well you missed mine, baby. So I figure you owe me first."

He took off her shirt and stripped her down to her panties. "How about we let you feel my mighty hot rod between your legs and see how you feel?"

She moaned when he slid two fingers inside her and stroked. "Only if it's a one-way trip to funville."

"For you, baby, anything. Anything at all."

Chapter 22

TWO WEEKS UNTIL CHRISTMAS, AND FOLEY GLARED at Johnny, who'd taken to fucking singing Christmas carols during the day. Ass was all in love and grooving to his own tunes now that Lara had taken pity on him. A fine woman like that and Johnny Devlin. Maybe hell *had* frozen over.

"Hey, Foley, did you take my quarter-inch ratchet?" Sam yelled.

"Huh?"

"Dude, my quarter-inch air ratchet. I can't find it."

Foley glanced at Sam's toolbox and cringed at the abundant disorganization. "I'm surprised you can find your toolbox under that grime."

Sam studied his station. "What?"

"Nothing." Poor bastard had been living in clutter since he was a kid, and despite Foley and Foley's mom's best attempts to organize him, Sam refused to cooperate. "Check the counter over there." Where he'd last seen Sam messing around with a part.

"Oh, right."

Foley nodded, content with his place in the grand scheme of things. He watched over the garage when Liam or Del weren't around, like this afternoon. Lou often had painting assignments and hung out at Heller's Paint Shop lately, though they'd managed to snag him for the shit work this week. His turn, after all. Plus, the guy could always be counted on for a good time at Ray's.

Now that Sue had finally forgiven Foley for, gee, adhering to the rules *they'd both* set for themselves before fooling around, he figured Ray's was a safe enough place to hang out this weekend. Truth be told, he was tired of pulling security at Strutts. The strip club had been fun, but he didn't want an easy blow job with no strings attached anymore.

Watching Johnny find happiness had woken something inside him. It gave him hope that maybe, someday, he and Sam might find the same with their own women. But Foley wouldn't get it from some chick accepting dollar bills while she slid down a pole. And he sure the hell wouldn't get it in here, a garage filled with testosterone, bad singing—he glared at Johnny—and friggin' Bob Dylan on the radio. He loathed folk music.

He needed to find a nice woman, someone like Lara. A chick who wouldn't take his shit, but would look at him the way Lara looked at Johnny, like he hung the stars and the moon. A sincere, pretty woman with—

"Who the hell is in charge in here?"

He glanced up. The body accompanying the husky voice seething with rage belonged to a virtual Amazon. Tall, long-legged, curvy, and with a face men would die for. She had wine-red hair curling over amazing breasts—mounds that were high, firm, and, just the way he liked them—*big*.

He glanced at his hands. He glanced at her breasts, then back at his hands again, itching to cup her.

"You. Foley Sanders, right?" She took a step in his direction, and he had to check his mouth for drool.

"That's me." *She knows my name. Thank you, God, for whatever I did to deserve this.* "What can I do to you—for you?" he amended, but not quickly enough.

Sam appeared next to him, and out of the corner of his eye, Foley saw Sam's interest as his buddy didn't even try to disguise eye-fucking the woman.

"Dibs," Foley called under his breath.

"Well, shit." Sam turned and went back to looking for his air ratchet.

A storm brewed in the deep brown of the Amazon's eyes. "Hey, Sanders, my eyes are up here." She pointed to her face with long, fire-engine-red nails, her body clad in a close-fitting black dress that clung to her voluptuous frame.

Damn, Foley felt hot. To his chagrin, he started to get hard. Good thing he wore coveralls.

"Sorry. Got distracted." He'd rolled his coveralls down earlier and wore them around his waist, his T-shirt covering his overheating torso. He wiped his forehead with his forearm, since his hands were covered with grease, and saw her narrowed eyes follow the movement, lingering on his biceps. *Probably not used to seeing guys with guns this big covered in tats. Come on, baby, look all you want. Touch, even.*

But she stopped looking, and she didn't touch. Instead, she threatened to tow the overflow of cars from her lot. Cars that belonged to Webster's Garage—something Dale had supposedly worked out with the owners of the shop a few doors down.

"Liam and Del told me if I had problems to get with you." The Websters had both taken an early Christmas vacation—leaving Foley in charge. "But after four phone calls and now this useless face-to-face, I can see I'm going to have to contact a towing service instead."

Before Foley could promise to make things right, she tore out the door on black high heels that shaped her muscular calves.

"*Bruja*," Lou said from the far doorway, fanning himself. "Those legs make a man think of what they'd look like wrapped around him in the dark."

"Fuck the dark. I'd want the light on when I'm deep inside her," Foley said, blunt honesty always his policy. "And you're damn right she's a witch. *My* witch."

"He called dibs," Sam said.

Johnny agreed. "He did."

"Well, damn. She's a bit too forceful for my tastes anyway." Lou shrugged. "Good luck with that woman, Foley. You're going to need it just to get a smile out of her."

Johnny snickered. "She didn't seem to like you much."

"After your near fuckup with Lara, seems to me you shouldn't be talking much, Devlin."

Johnny just kept laughing.

Foley shouted for Dale, the one responsible for this parking mess, all the while wondering just who he'd have to kill to get that redheaded hellion's number. And how deep he'd have to bury the body.

ROADSIDE ASSISTANCE

FOLEY SANDERS STARED AT THE DOOR, WHERE MINUTES ago one sexy, pissed off woman had stalked out of the garage. She'd worked the hell out of those black heels. Talk about a fine pair of legs. God love him—*a redhead*. The woman had wine-red hair so dark it looked almost brown. And that body... She had curves, a lot of them. And height.

Man, talk about Santa coming to town early. Just breathing, the woman qualified as a statuesque knockout. But angry? A serious threat to his sanity. Now how to calm her down... Oh, right. Find and kill Dale, then get their cars out of her lot.

"Dale," he yelled, then remembered the young service writer of Webster's Garage had taken off early today.

"He's not here, genius." Johnny Devlin, one of the mouthier mechanics in the garage, lovingly stated the obvious. "Boy had plans to help his sister move, I think. He'll be in first thing Monday morning."

"Hell." Foley rubbed his eyes, irritated. He needed to get a bunch of cars moved out of the fiery siren's lot before she had them towed. Had Dale left the keys where Del normally kept them? Or had he taken to reorganizing again, so no one could find anything without the kid's help?

Johnny went back to cheerfully whistling a Christmas tune while Credence Clearwater Revival came on the radio to replace some seriously awful folk music. Thank God. Now if Foley could just get Johnny to shut up.

"*Must* you whistle?" he growled, a headache brewing as the temperature started to get to him. They kept the garage bay doors closed but the cold didn't seem to care, and the T-shirt and jeans he wore under his coveralls weren't doing him any favors.

The bastard grinned back at him. "I must." Johnny had recently fallen in love and now considered himself a dating guru. Well, technically the little bastard *was* pretty good with the ladies. He had a pretty face, a big brain, and had grown up around a bevy of strippers, so he had the female perspective down pat. Still, Foley would rather pull out his own teeth than admit Johnny knew more than he did about chicks.

Women, not chicks, you Neanderthal, he imagined his mother saying before slapping him on the back of the head. He rubbed the imagined smack and sighed.

"Ha! I found it." His best friend, Sam, victoriously raised his previously misplaced air ratchet and narrowed his gaze on Foley. "Quit fucking with my gear."

Foley frowned, still off-kilter from the angry beauty in heels. "I told you I didn't touch your tools. You need to clean up that mess." He nodded at Sam's tool bench, a clutter of disorganization that hurt to look at.

After nearly two decades spent around Sam and Sam's chaos in regards to living, Foley should have known better than to try. But he figured one of these days Sam might actually heed his advice.

"I'm not seeing the problem." Sam shrugged and tapped the ratchet into his huge palm. "You seeing a problem, big man? Want me to fix it? How about I fix *you*?"

He glanced at Sam's thick, tattooed biceps, then at his own, and raised a brow. "I know you don't think you can seriously take me down."

Sam's scowl lightened into what for Sam could be considered a grin. "You want to go, *boss man*?"

"Must chafe your ass that Del and Liam left me in charge." Foley crossed his arms over his chest, amused at the thought of Sam taking the lead. His buddy didn't want the responsibility. He just liked needling Foley for being a—quote—*kiss ass*. Foley continued his rant, "But then, what choice did they have?" He looked at Johnny, monkeying under the hood of a Honda. "The happy whistler who can't think beyond his new girlfriend?" A glance at Lou, who leaned against his workbench, smirking at them. "The resident Romeo who's better with a paint gun than a wrench?"

"Watch it, hombre, or I'll paint your face a new color." Lou didn't put any heat behind his words, but his mammoth frame would be a challenge if it came to a fight. He was as big as Foley, though not as badass. Then again, Foley had never actually battled the garage's resident know-it-all. He wondered, between them, who might actually win, and could see Lou thinking the same, his lips curling into a grin.

Thoughts of fighting brought Foley's attention back to Sam. "Or you." Foley scrutinized his buddy, teasing to conceal the worry he'd been feeling. "You're practically all skin and bones. Eat a sandwich, jackass. It won't kill you. Unless you're starving yourself to impress Shaya?"

Sam snorted. "Shaya likes me just fine."

"You mean she likes the wad of bills you stash down her G-string at Strutts," Lou said under his breath.

Sam turned a cold eye on him. "Anytime you want to throw down, Cortez. I'm game."

Johnny took a break from his work, straightened, and faced them. "Guys, it's almost Christmas. Tone down the testosterone, would you?"

Lou took a threatening step toward Sam, then stopped, grinned, and held out a hand. "Pay up, Hamilton. I told you he'd make sure none of us shake the peace around here. Getting laid has made our Johnny a lover, not a fighter."

Foley laughed. They placed bets on everything in the garage, and Johnny's maddening good mood was fair game. Good to know Foley wasn't the only one who could use less whistling, more classic rock.

Sam gave Johnny a sad look. "Johnny, Johnny. All that happiness is turning you into a pussy. Does Lara know what she's getting with you, man?"

"Turning into?" Foley repeated. "I thought he was born that way." He laughed at the finger Johnny shot him.

Then in a sly tone, Johnny said, "Calling me names and betting on me isn't getting you guys any closer to an invite to dinner next weekend."

Foley and Sam exchanged a glance. Free food changed things.

Sam coughed. "I don't suppose Lara would make anything special for us. Like, say, chocolate chip cookies?"

"I don't know." Johnny rubbed his greasy nails on his coveralls. "How sorry are you for being a dick?"

"*I'm* sorry Sam's a dick," Lou apologized, ignoring Sam's suggestion of where to stick his head. "And that you have to constantly deal with lowbrow humor from the badass bros."

Foley rolled his eyes. They'd been calling him and Sam that for years, and he hated to admit it, but he kind of liked the title.

"Lowbrow, my ass," Sam muttered.

Lou shrugged. "Just my opinion." He turned to Foley. "But then, I'm just a lowly peon working for the big man."

"Please." The guys always ribbed Foley whenever the Websters left him in charge. "Like you work for anyone but yourself." All of them contracted their work for a percentage. With the raw talent and experience Webster's had pooled the past few years with their current team of mechanics, it was no wonder the garage had overflowing lots and no time to spare anymore.

"That's true." Lou grinned. "But right now, I'm more than glad Del and Liam left you in charge. I wouldn't want to be you when you're standing in front of them, explaining why all our cars got towed away."

Foley had been trying to avoid the pressing need to fix the situation. "Shit."

"Good thing Del's not here to collect on all the swearing," Johnny just *had* to remind them.

As one, they glanced at the change-filled glass jar on a nearby counter. The ROP—Rattle of Oppression, as they'd taken to calling it—had been getting filled on a weekly basis. The boss had decided that in an effort to not swear at her upcoming wedding, she'd practice clean speech at work. Unfortunately, if she had to talk nice, she expected them all to do the same.

Foley grinned. "You have to admit it's a challenge. Even Liam has cut back on his 'fucks' and 'goddamns.'"

The guys chuckled.

Foley finished putting his tools away, then realized he'd only given himself a ten-minute reprieve. "Oh, hell. I'll be at the coffee shop, dealing with our angry neighbor. If you guys leave before I get back, have a good weekend. And, Johnny? I'm marking my calendar about dinner next weekend."

"With cookies, right?" Sam asked.

"Maybe." Johnny shrugged. "Lara seems to like you, though I have no idea why."

Foley removed his coveralls and hung them in his locker in the break room, leaving him in jeans, steel-toed boots, and a thin T-shirt. When working, he tended to run hot. But as soon as he stopped, the cold hit him. He washed his hands thoroughly and tried to finger-comb his hair, wanting to make a better impression on the sexy redhead. He grabbed his jacket and headed toward the exit.

Johnny hummed the funeral march, which earned a rare chuckle from Sam.

Lou called out, "Good luck, *jefe*."

"Quit calling me boss," he barked.

"Okay, walking dead man." Lou laughed. "Wonder if she'll puncture a lung with those heels. Might be worth it to see." Lou made as if to follow him, and Foley ordered him to stay the hell away.

He didn't need an audience when he worked his charms on that delectable redhead. And he especially didn't need any unasked for competition when it came to getting that first date. That was, if he could convince her not to stomp his head in with those four-inch heels.

He grinned. He loved them mean.

His grin faded and he turned around and headed for the service desk. First, he had to find those damn keys.

Cynthia Nichols had done some stupid things in her time, but not wearing a jacket in this weather ranked among her top five. Her earlier phone conversation had made her so blasted angry, she'd torn out of the shop without thinking. She shivered and glanced at the mass of vehicles taking up her customers' spots and swore at all things car related.

Hurrying through the café door, she inhaled the scent of coffee and freshly baked goods and let out a sigh. Nichols Caffè Bar—her most recent acquisition and newest workplace.

Warmth embraced her, internally and externally, as the heat sunk in. For years she'd been investing in businesses, getting them going, then leaving once they turned a profit. But this was the first one she'd decided to work and keep as her own. A family-run company, since she owned half of it and her brother and sister-in-law owned the other half. She finally felt at home.

"Where have you been?" said sister-in-law, Nina, asked before calling out a name for the cup on the counter.

Cyn joined her behind the counter. "I went over to Webster's Garage to talk to the idiot in charge."

Nina frowned. "I like Liam, and I wouldn't exactly call Del an idiot. Not to her face."

Cyn understood. The gang at Webster's was decidedly...rough. Liam Webster had to be in his late fifties, yet the man looked like he could bench-press *her*—and she hadn't been a lightweight since the fourth grade.

Del, his daughter, had ash-blond hair, a few piercings, tattoos, and the meanest glare on a woman Cyn had ever seen. She had been nice and polite the few times Cyn had run into her, but Cyn had sensed a predator behind those cold gray eyes from the first.

Eyes a lot like those of the testosterone-laden idiot she'd just lambasted with a bit of redheaded temper. Dear God, where did the Websters find their mechanics? San Quentin? Rikers? Baddies-R-Us?

Aware her sister-in-law waited for an answer, Cyn said, "The Websters are out of town, so they left Foley Sanders in charge."

Nina sighed. "Foley."

"Hey. You're married to my brother, remember?" Cyn frowned. "Do the names Vinnie and Alex ring a bell? You know, your *children*?"

Nina laughed. "Hard to forget a house full of boys and your manly brother. Hubba hubba."

"Ew. Forget I asked."

"But Foley Sanders." Nina wiggled her brows. "He's so big and strong and just...yum."

Nina wasn't exaggerating. Which made Cyn dislike him all the more. She knew all about guys like Foley. Men who had looks and muscle, the envy of other men, and the fantasies of heterosexual women. Men who acted like they didn't mind what a girl looked like, then dumped her for a skinnier, younger model.

"Yum or not, it's his job to be responsible for the

garage, and you'll notice that over half our lot is full of cars that don't belong to us." She knew for a fact that they had come from Webster's because she'd seen their blue-haired clerk parking them randomly in the lot earlier today.

"So who else was there?" Nina prodded.

"Three other brutes." Sexy, big, and handsome men wearing tattoos and attitude. The kind of men her mother had long ago taught her to beware.

"God, kill me now. It's a good thing I'm happily married to my own stud. I can't believe how close we are to all that man candy." Nina practically glowed. "Sam is so hunky but scary. He's got those tattoos all over. I wonder how far down they go?"

"*Nina.*"

"Then there's Lou. The brooding Latin lover. I swear, he gives me goose bumps when I see him."

"What?"

"Johnny Devlin's a real charmer. He's the one that looks like a cover model. He flirts a good game, but he's never been serious. Probably because I'm married." Nina fingered her ring.

"So glad you remembered," Cyn muttered, now trying not to laugh. Nina was a petite beauty with blond hair, green eyes, and a sunny personality. It had been a no-brainer as to what her brother saw in Nina. After twelve years, they still had a happy, healthy marriage and two handsome sons to prove it. "I don't think I've ever heard you go on about the Webster guys before."

"Matt has." Nina grinned. "But hey, I let my dear husband have that girlie calendar in his office at home, so we're even."

"You mean his Grannies for Nannies, calendar? The one my mom was in to promote her side babysitting business?"

"Hey, they're women. They count."

Cyn laughed. "That's just mean."

"And funny. But it's all good. Matt's friends with Liam and his guys. Del too. They're actually a nice bunch of people. And they buy a lot from us. Don't make enemies," Nina warned.

Too late. In the month she'd been working in the shop, Cyn had only ever encountered Del and Liam. A good thing, because she had issues with men she was still trying to get over. But a lifetime of disappointments made it a long process.

She now felt a little bad about her behavior in the garage. It was Sanders's misfortune that she'd talked with one of her chauvinistic ex-business partners prior to dealing with the car situation. Dan Fawkes was such a dick. The word *scruples* had never entered his pretty little head. The oily bastard. If he thought he could cheat her out of her entitled shareholder distributions, he could think again. She never let anyone screw her over when it came to business.

Now her personal life, on the other hand… That had taken a beating one too many times. But she'd learned. Or so she told herself.

She and Nina worked together to help a few more customers. Funny how the rushes came and went with no discernible pattern, not counting the morning craziness.

"Have I mentioned I'm thinking about becoming the neighborhood cat lady?" she said to Nina just as the bell over the front door chimed again. She finished cleaning up after the last order, not looking at Nina. But her friend's silence made her curious.

A glance at Nina's smirk had her groaning inside, because trouble was sure to follow.

"Hey, *Foley*," Nina said with way too much pleasure. "How are you?"

"Lookin' good, Nina. How's Matt?"

"He's great. And if he's smart, he's done all his Christmas shopping by now. Not like last year's fiasco."

The deep chuckle went straight through Cyn…and had her bristling at her reaction.

"I, ah, I'm here to apologize to your friend, actually."

Cyn took that as her cue to turn around. Hell. Foley Sanders looked even better under the bright lights of the shop. She tried to pretend she wasn't studying him as intently as he studied her.

But damn, where the hell had he come from? He topped her own grand six feet by a few inches, and even despite his layers of clothing, she couldn't detect any body fat on the man. He had broad shoulders and—as she vividly recalled from eyeballing him at the garage— huge, tattooed arms.

Short black hair framed a handsome face. Rough and manly. He had a five-o'clock shadow, and that rumpled hair look that on her would have appeared messy but on him shouted "sexy." Bright gray eyes watched her with caution, showing he had a measure of intelligence under all that muscle and ink.

She steeled herself not to get taken in by so much manliness. *Neighborhood cat lady, remember? Besides, his cars are littering the parking lot! Men suck. He's probably only into skinny chicks anyway.*

That made her feel better, imagining his intolerance for real women.

But real women can be any size. Plump or stick thin, fat or slender, tall or…Shut up, Cyn! This isn't time for a life lesson. Deal with Conan and love your gender later.

"Yes?" she said with an icy politeness that had Nina trying to bite back a grin.

"I'm sorry. I think we got off on the wrong foot." He smiled, but she wasn't buying the charm. "I'm Foley Sanders." He held out a hand.

Nina stepped on her foot, and she jerked toward Foley before realizing it. She glared at Nina before reminding herself to be a professional. She'd dealt with overwhelming men before and would no doubt again. So she held out her hand and pasted a smile on her face. "Cyn Nichols."

He blinked. "You're related to Matt?"

"Yes, is there a problem with that?" She didn't even have to pretend to be tired of that question. Matt was so handsome and in shape and popular. What tree had they shaken her out of?

"Not at all." His grin broadened. "I just hadn't realized Matt had such a hot sister."

She blinked. "What?"

"Before I somehow piss you off again, I'm here to get the cars," he said in a hurry. "Dale, our new guy, must have parked them in the wrong spot. Apparently our agreement was with the sewing place next door, not your parking lot. And I'm sorry I never answered your calls. I misplaced my phone again." He gave her a disarming smile that—damn it—worked.

She felt herself blushing. "Oh. Sorry if I came on a

little strong." A little? Even she knew she'd been over-the-top bitchy. "It's just that we had some complaints from customers, and I couldn't understand why no one had gotten back to me." She still didn't understand that. What professional these days ever parted with his or her cell phone? But he'd made amends, so she could forgive him the lapse. "So you'll move the cars?"

He held up a ring of tagged keys. "Right away, Ms. Nichols."

"How do you know I'm not a Mrs.?" she asked, annoyed with the assumption. Was she so unattractive and ungainly she couldn't land a man?

He had the gall to wink and nodded to her hand. "No ring. Trust me. First thing I checked…after that dress. That's a really, really nice dress you're wearing." He let out a small sigh and left before she could think of something to say.

Like *I'm sorry for being so damn defensive about my size. It's not you, it's me. But then, it's guys like you who made me this way. Well, you and my mother.*

"Ahem."

Knowing she had to face the inevitable, she looked at the smug woman standing next to her and groaned at Nina's wide smile.

"You and Foley Sanders. Oh my God, will you guys have the best-looking, tallest babies or what?"

COMING SEPTEMBER 2016

A Sure Thing

WORST DAY OF THE FRIGGIN' YEAR. SEATTLE HAD ITS doozies, but this one by far smacked of depression. In addition, it had been overcast and miserable all day, with rain continuing into the early evening. A glance around the surprisingly crowded gym full of men *and* women made Landon Donnigan wish for a return to the scorching heat of Afghanistan. Better that than the danger of desperate singles looking to hook up on Valentine's Day.

God save me.

Though life in the Marine Corps had been fraught with risk—and not the bullshit emotional kinds of risks he'd been told he didn't take—he'd enjoyed his time both overseas and in the States. During his service, he'd thought a civilian life behind a desk would be worse than anything he might imagine. Now he took his current job in stride, pleased to be useful once more.

But Valentine's Day surrounded by flirting singles, in *a gym*? Sacrilege. Landon did his best not to make eye contact with anyone, especially the small group of women who kept looking his way. With any luck, they hadn't noticed him, their attention on his supposedly charming younger brother Gavin standing next to him. He placed the hand weights he'd been using back on the rack, figuring he'd cut himself a break on his workout, just this once.

His brother glanced over his shoulder at the staring women. "Is it just me? Or do you feel almost hunted right now?" Gavin waved, and they waved back. "I mean, I *have* to be here. I'm a trainer. But shouldn't all these women be out with their significant others celebrating with flowers and chocolates? I thought lonely women on V-Day stayed at home, sobbing into their Earl Grey and fighting their twenty-plus cats for bonbons. Kind of like you on any night of the week—alone and lonely."

"You're an ass."

Gavin chuckled. "Yeah, I am. I'm kidding…about the women." He ignored the finger Landon shot him. "Seriously though, most of the women I know are either out with friends or pissed off at men in general and sitting at home."

"Like Hope, you mean?" Landon drawled. Their little sister had supposedly broken up with her latest dickhead boyfriend yesterday. God willing, the next guy she dated wouldn't be so toxic.

"Yeah. Like Hope." Gavin nodded. "No worries, bro. Hope's situation will work out." Gavin took after their father in looks and temperament. Dark haired, *too* laid-back, and for some reason, was well-liked by the ladies, who continued to watch him.

Landon followed his brother's gaze to the attractive group. "They seem interested. Why not go ask 'em out?"

"No way in hell." Gavin frowned. "We don't fraternize with clients. Mac's orders."

"Really? Because you've got a mess of opportunity right over there."

"That group is way too loaded for my blood. And by loaded, I mean richer than shit. They're looking for a boy toy to play with. And rumor has it they break their toys." Gavin glanced around him, then murmured, "Mac didn't actually say I couldn't date gym members. But when I tell them that, they leave me alone. I mean, they don't want me fired from my job."

With any luck, Gavin would hold onto this one for a while. The last two jobs hadn't gone well. Landon wasn't the only one adjusting to civilian life after the Corps. He subtly leaned closer to Gavin. Good. No scent of alcohol on little brother's breath tonight.

"Smart excuse," he said, trying to cover the sniff check.

"Smart. That's me." Gavin didn't do smug as well as he thought he did. Not like their youngest brother, who'd come out of the womb smirking at life in general. "But why are *you* here? I'd have thought you and Claudia would be getting romantic. Hell, bro, it's Saturday. You can't use work as an excuse."

Landon shrugged and retrieved his towel and water bottle from the floor. "I thought I told you we broke up. We were never more than friends anyway." *Intimate* friends. He'd been smart enough to end their casual relationship two months ago when Claudia had been hinting about changing their status to something much more serious. He'd been getting bored, and her constant neediness grated. As if Landon had time for more trouble when he had so much work to do fixing his dysfunctional family.

"Yeah? That's not what I heard." A pause. "From Claudia."

Crap. "She's been to the gym lately?" She'd quit when they'd broken up. Landon had only seen her once since then. Just last week. They'd exchanged a pleasant greeting, nothing more.

"Yep. Heard her talking to Marsha about you yesterday, as if you two were still an item. Then she told me to say hi from her." Gavin smiled wide. "So, hi."

"Shut up."

Gavin snickered.

Landon glanced around, praying the woman wasn't there tonight. He hated hurting anyone, and he'd been surprised she'd taken their "friend" breakup so hard. Which only reinforced the notion he'd been right to sever it in the first place. Dating should be fun, not a minefield. He'd had enough of *those* to last a lifetime.

He scowled, feeling hemmed in. Jameson's Gym was supposed to be his refuge in this chaotic civilian world. Landon appreciated the hell out of the owner giving his brother a job. Mac Jameson seemed to be a stand-up guy. He'd been a master sergeant in the Marine Corps before doing permanent damage to his knee, ending his time early. They shared that connection—common core values, an appreciation for discipline and order, and medical bullshit ending a guy's dream.

"Mac here?" he asked.

Gavin shook his head. "Seriously? You've seen his wife, right? She's hot as hell. No doubt they're hanging at home for some 'alone-time.'" Gavin sighed. "I miss uncomplicated sex."

At his words, a pretty blond in tights stopped behind him and gave a toothy grin. "Hey, Gavin. How's it going?"

His younger brother cringed, then turned around and gave her an insincere smile back. "Oh, ah, hi, Michelle. How are you?"

"Great. I just finished my workout." She eyed Gavin the way a lion would a helpless gazelle. The comparison made it hard not to laugh, especially with the hunted look on Gavin's face. "Shouldn't you be out with your girlfriend tonight?" Michelle asked, her voice breathy. "Hope, right?"

"Hope's my sister."

"Oh, so you *are* single then. Megan and I were talking."

"I'm single, yeah, but I don't mingle with—"

Michelle grabbed him by the arm, her sharp nails a bright pink. "Lucky for me you're here. I could really use a spotter."

"I thought you said you were done with your workout."

"I mean I'm *almost* done."

Gavin couldn't rightly refuse to help Michelle train. Landon ignored the beseeching look his brother shot him and subtly stepped away.

She tugged Gavin with her. "Then after, maybe you and I can do a casual dinner." She blinked back at Landon. "How about you, Landon?"

Gavin hemmed, "Well, I don't know. My brother and I were supposed to—"

"Go ahead, Gav." Landon almost felt sorry for him. Then he remembered what Gavin had said and smiled. "Sorry, Michelle. I have plans. I'll be at home drinking Earl Grey and playing with my cats."

Gavin scowled at him.

"It was worse. Way worse." Ava Rosenthal couldn't believe how badly the date had gone.

Elliot blinked. "Seriously? Chris was so sexy and smart. I thought for sure you two would hit it off." Her cousin, confidant, and workout partner, Elliot was a total player. He was the one who had set her up on last night's date, and he had a little explaining to do.

As they walked next to each other on their treadmills Saturday afternoon, Ava took a good look around the gym, making sure she didn't know anyone around her. Elliot loved to gossip, and she needed to get a few things off her chest. But as a therapist, she knew well the value of discretion. Elliot…not so much.

"You have to keep this quiet. I think he lives around here."

"So what? Tell me. You know I'm dying to know how the date went."

Ava felt the sweat pouring off her and started to relax. In retrospect, dating Chris "Handsy" Handsman was funny. Kind of. "Well, remember how I said I liked men closer to my size? Not huge or muscle-bound, but slender and scholarly?"

"Dorky Indiana Jones. I get it."

She frowned. "Not exactly. I just feel more comfortable with men closer to my height. It's easier to handle them if they get out of control."

"No. Way." Elliot paused his machine and leaned over the railing. "Chris Handsman, Mr. Zen, got grabby? Do you need me to beat his ass?"

She flushed. "Yes and no." Her cheeks rivaled the

surface of the sun for heat. "He acted like the perfect gentleman. He picked me up at the door. We had a lovely dinner. He actually asked me about myself and listened when I answered. It wasn't all about him." She still didn't know where Chris had gotten the wrong signals. "But after he drove me home, he turned off the car and went straight for second base." She lowered her voice. "And I hadn't once signaled him to steal."

"I know it's bad when you're using baseball analogies." He started up his machine again.

"Not funny."

"But true." Elliot shook his head. "Damn. Never would have pegged Chris for being the aggressive type. You sure you're okay?"

"I'm fine. I told him *no* in no uncertain terms, and he pulled away. Then I asked him what the hell he thought he was doing."

"Ouch."

She glared at her cousin. "It seems *someone* told him I was up for some 'fun.'" She made air quotes.

"Oh. Huh. Well." Elliot blinked, his green eyes a mirror for hers. "I might have said you were looking for a good man to break a dating dry spell. Someone impressive. Hung like a horse…"

"*Elliot.*"

"Kidding. About the hung part, I mean." Elliot paused. "So was he?"

"Was he what?"

"You know. Hung?"

"Like a toy poodle." When he goggled, she huffed. "How the heck would I know? The minute he tried going for my shirt, the date was O. V. E. R."

"You're so dramatic."

"Me?" She set her pace faster. "It's one thing if I'm getting hot and heavy with a guy and he gets a little handsy." At her cousin's grin, she glared. "Yes, I'm aware of the play on words. Chris Handsman was *handsy*. Ha-ha. Hilarious."

He chuckled, then coughed. "Sorry. Something stuck in my throat."

"Your foot, maybe," she muttered.

"Come on, Ava. You have to admit you need help."

"Not from him." She arched a brow and looked down her nose at him, because she knew how much he hated that expression. "Or you."

"Seriously? Of the two of us, who gets more dates?"

"Having sex and dating aren't the same thing."

She must have said that a little too loudly, because the blond giant walking past her stopped and stared.

"What?" she snapped, embarrassed and not needing extra male attention after her recent dating disaster.

"Not a thing," the giant said, his deep voice giving her shivers. He gave her a less than subtle once-over, then moved on.

She and Elliot watched him walk away. For some reason, she fixated on his tight, tight glutes, trying to be clinical about his physique instead of mesmerized. *Totally not my type. Too muscle-y.*

COMING NOVEMBER 2016

Acknowledgments

A huge thank-you to Jason from Townsend Auto Repair. I can't tell you how much it helped that you took valuable time out of your day to educate me on how a shop should run and what mechanics actually do. No wonder you're so busy all the time!

To Lisa S., for introducing me to the ins and outs of the legal system and the differences between felonies and misdemeanors, prison and jail. I truly appreciate it.

To Angi Clingan, for your help as a reader, friend, and for your expertise in nursing education. Thanks for all you do, and congrats on your LPN.

Kathleen V., I miss you as my neighbor, and I'll always treasure your breadth of knowledge in medicine. You're still my go-to for all things medical- and hospital-related.

Thanks to everyone who helped with my research. Any mistakes in this story are mine.

Cat C. and the amazing people at Sourcebooks, I'm so fortunate to be working with you. You make the process so easy.

About the Author

Caffeine addict, boy referee, and romance aficionado, *New York Times* and *USA Today* bestselling author Marie Harte is a confessed bibliophile and devotee of action movies. Whether hiking in Central Oregon, biking around town, or hanging at the local tea shop, she's constantly plotting to give everyone a happily ever after. Visit http://marieharte.com and fall in love.